The Jeweler's Wife

By Madeline Connelly

To my littlest dear, Madeline Elizabeth

Contents

"Art washes away from the soul the dust of everyday life." - Pablo Picasso

Chapter 1

Paris 1936

It was intoxicating, like falling in love for the first time. It was spring, a season of fresh beginnings, and elegance had returned to its rightful place—Paris. No one could have imagined that a necklace would create such a buzz. But you could feel it. An emerald-cut ruby, embellished with multi-colored sapphires and a dazzling array of diamonds, splashed across the cover of *Vogue France.* Years after a bitter war and a market crash, women everywhere had grown weary of plain cameos and dainty lockets. The French celebrated; glamour was back in style. And with it, the hope of prosperity.

The brilliant necklace also caught the discerning eye of Duke Federico Verdi. Called Freddie by the Americans, the designer rubbed elbows with Hollywood stars and European royalty. He knew a craze when he saw one. The Italian did not waste a minute to meet the up-and-coming jeweler.

Federico opened polished mahogany doors and stepped inside the intimate boutique, Maison Bijoux. A white floral centerpiece gave off a delicate scent of rose and jasmine.

Federico said, "Pierre Bessette! Please, come and join me for a drink."

It was one of those splendid sunny days teased by a light breeze. A little after four o'clock, the gentlemen strolled up leafy Avenue de l'Opera and meandered over to Harry's New

York Bar—a venerable retreat with fluted columns, a rich walnut bar and the perfect martini. They wandered past outdoor cafés where chattering Parisians savored carafes of red wine and the day's ambiance. Flowers bloomed everywhere; red geraniums tumbled lavishly from lacy wrought iron window boxes. Along the way, their stories unfolded with a quip and an easy laugh.

Coeds sipping espressos looked up from their books to steal a glimpse of the two men. The jeweler stood six-foot-tall with dark wavy hair and an olive complexion. Pierre's navy suit brought out his steel-blue eyes. A paisley scarf, casually draped around Federico's tan neck, enhanced what the French like to call *je ne sais quoi*—that certain something.

At times, the newly-acquainted friends, and the jeweler's wife, would linger over dinners at best-loved restaurants.

Ellie Bessette said, "Federico, join Pierre and me Saturday night at Chez Bossa!"

At the jazz club, Ellie turned heads in a shimmery ivory cocktail dress from the House of Lanvin. Champagne flutes sparkled, candlelight glowed, and laughter rippled across dinner tables draped in snow-white linens.

Jazz kings Django Reinhardt and Stephane Grappelli kept the club jumping all night long. At the closing hour, Pierre held Ellie in his arms as they swayed to the rhythm of Stardust.

From time to time, Pierre and "the Duke" would talk shop at the Bessette's spacious home—an inviting mix of Ellie's Scandinavian background and Pierre's sophisticated French taste. Dove gray walls created a soothing backdrop behind a Louis XIV armoire. A cozy sofa and a walnut coffee table were grouped together with a pair of rose-and-cream colored plaid Biedermeier armchairs.

A Swedish Grandfather clock chimed softly at the top of the hour when Ellie would place a simmering beef bourguignon on their dining table. Federico would lean in to savor caramelized onions soaked in herbs and wine. When the Italian smiled, a few laugh lines crinkled around the corners of his warm brown eyes. Federico would place his thumb and forefingers to his lips and playfully toss them into the air— "Bellissimo!" Never immune to the Duke's charms, Ellie would feel the tinge of a blush warm her cheeks.

Pierre would raise his wine glass in a toast to his wife, "I love you, chérie." Her radiant smile always lit up a room. For Ellie Lindstrom Bessette, these were the halcyon days...

Ellie's childhood had not been so rosy. Her starving-artist mother had been young and reckless; mother and daughter lived penniless during the Great War, and it hit Ellie hard. Years later, the 1929 crash made its way across the Atlantic and landed in France about 1931.

Today the jeweler's wife flourished as a wife and mother. Grateful for the stability in her life and her good fortune, Ellie set her heart on helping Parisians who had lost everything during the French Depression.

Chapter 2

Three Years Later

A dear friend, Antoine Segal, ventured into town. Antoine had arrived with an interesting proposal that he planned to divulge. But first, he dined with the Bessette family at Le Meurice, an historic hotel with a gilded restaurant overlooking the Tuileries Garden in the heart of Paris.

After Sunday lunch—consommé, roast beef en croute, green beans with hazelnuts and a mixed salad—they strolled through the colorful garden, Ellie and Pierre hand in hand. Nine-year old Michel, nicknamed Michi, and his younger sister Annika, skipped along the winding paths lined with age-old statues and royal fountains. Up ahead, a chorus of children giggled at their favorite puppet shows. Ellie called out, "Michi, stay with your sister, please."

It was then that Antoine sounded the alarm. He lowered his voice, "Whispers of war are growing louder. Come with us to Provence. Sophie and I have plenty of room for you and the children. It may be safer away from the city."

Ellie's smile faded. She reflected on the misery growing up during the Great War. A shiver ran down her spine.

Summer in the country would be a great adventure for the children and perhaps safer.

It was a tempting dilemma. Antoine's half-Italian wife,

Sophie, had inherited an eighteenth-century stone country house. She had updated the historic home with indoor plumbing and all the modern conveniences. The property included a sun-dappled terrace with a magnificent view of surrounding vineyards and swaying fields of lavender.

Pierre smiled, "Antoine, I can just imagine unhurried afternoons sipping aperitifs by the garden or on the terrace. Not to mention a creamy chèvre spread on a fresh baguette."

Antoine nudged Pierre along, "What do you say then? Let's wait it out together in Saint Rémy."

Pierre replied, "But I have my family to support, and my business is in Paris. I doubt that the Germans can break through the Maginot Line; our border is a concrete fortress. If the unthinkable were to happen, the mayor has promised us security." The popular jeweler was well-acquainted with government leaders.

Pierre clapped Antoine's back. "We'll all be fine my friend, you'll see."

Noting Antoine's disappointment, Ellie said, "Give my love to Sophie, and thank you both for your kind invitation."

Not long after, the Bessette's attended the annual Chambre de Commerce garden party. Clumps of blue forget-me-nots tangled with buttery primroses that bordered the elegant Pavilion Gabriel. In a show of military pride, Mediterranean fleet officers mingled with mademoiselles dressed in pretty spring dresses.

Despite the picture-perfect setting, Ellie felt ruffled by the military presence. A sense of unease was lurking, and she could not hold back her concern. She tried to bait the midshipmen in their crisp navy uniforms. "Gentlemen, more young men have been called up for military duty. I've watched anxious neighbors clear out to the south of France or to America."

The officers merely smiled and reassured Ellie along with her lady friends, Veronique and Chloe, that the French army was ready and formidable. Veronique wore a new dress, tiny in the waist with a skirt flowing in pink silk organza. She sighed, "Oh, Ellie. Please let's not ruin our lovely day with sad thoughts." Sipping champagne, Veronique had caught the eye of a handsome captain.

Ellie took Pierre's arm. She walked with him beneath a canopy of cherry blossoms.

While a string quartet played Vivaldi's *Le Printemps*, her voice wavered. "Pierre, trenches *are* being dug around the city and gas masks have been distributed. I'm worried. Let's reconsider Antoine and Sophie's invitation and go to their country home. Before it's too late, *d'accord?*"

Pierre turned to reassure his wife. "Chérie, France is well-fortified and Paris is just taking precautions. We have not declared war on Germany." Pierre took her hand. "Our government friends have assured me that we will be safe. It'll be alright."

In July, Federico sailed for the United States aboard the French luxury liner *Ile de France.* Concerned that gold and silver might be hoarded, he planned to hedge his bets and open a New York boutique. A lock of ebony hair fell across his forehead as the Duke waved goodbye from the ship's deck. "We'll meet up soon, my friends. Save me a seat at the Ritz!"

But Pierre would not cut and run. His mind was made up. "Ellie, my overseas clients are eager for the 'Paris mystique,' Boucheron, Chanel... and now Bijoux. It would be a mistake to disappoint my clientele now."

He turned toward his wife, "My love, it's always been our hope that we would be able to uplift Parisians who had lost so much when the economy crashed. Now we are making a real difference in our community."

With little recourse, Ellie focused on her volunteer work helping needy families and as a docent at the Louvre art museum. But in late August 1939, the museum closed for three days for "repairs." Ellie stood to one side and watched as workers removed priceless art collections out the back door en route to Chateau de Chambord for safekeeping. The staff hung replicas in place of the masterpieces that had been evacuated to hiding places around the countryside. Some walls remained vacant. Sandbags were placed around architectural landmarks.

"Is it just me, or do I see what my husband and others around me refuse to see?"

Ellie knew the answer; she felt an unwelcome feeling percolate—fear.

Chapter 3

June 14, 1940

T he starry night had been mild. But after nine months of relative calm, in a faint morning light Pierre awoke to a ruckus. Bleary eyed, he pushed open French doors and stepped onto a Juliette balcony. He maneuvered around flower pots and craned his neck toward the noise. Rows of drab olive-green helmets bobbed in the distance; loudspeakers announced an invasion.

Pierre ran his fingers through his thick hair and watched in disbelief as beefy German soldiers marched toward their sleepy street. *Where on God's earth is our national army?*

Half asleep, Ellie stumbled across the room to join her bewildered husband on the balcony. Ellie held her slender arms across her shaking body and whispered, "Oh, my God!" German troops appeared far from underfed and not sickly as their politicians had led them to believe.

Just days earlier, the Luftwaffe, Germany's air force, had bombed a Citroen car factory. Demoralized Parisians waited anxiously while the French government debated how to respond to the atrocity. Meanwhile terrified citizens, those without government friends, had crammed their worldly possessions into automobiles and carts and fled Paris in a panic.

Like thieves in the night, the Germans had avoided the Maginot Line by sneaking into France through the dense

Ardennes forest. At the border, the French army ran away to avoid any bombing of historic monuments.

Germany had accomplished the impossible. But Pierre never could have imagined that Paris would be declared an "open city" with no armed resistance! The Germans occupied not only his country but his beloved city as well.

Days later, the jeweler was forced to share more grim news: "Ellie, we have been betrayed." He rubbed his furrowed brow. "I just came from the Ministry. Our mayor and the national secretary have lost their power. I can't believe it. The cowards have fled to Tours and Bordeaux. *Merde!* We are on our own."

Ellie crossed her arms tightly to hold herself together. "I've never shaken my memories of the Great War—the shortage of food, those freezing nights without heat. Now misery lies on our doorstep."

Pierre wrapped Ellie in his arms. She inhaled the subtle woodsy fragrance of his aftershave. He whispered, "I am so sorry." The Bessettes harbored a troubling secret. As a boy, Pierre attended Temple in the Jewish section of Paris, the Marais. Ellie closed her eyes and held tightly to the father of her children and the man she loved with all her heart.

Ellie had grown up without a father. She whispered to her husband, "Without you, our children would endure the same hardships that stole my childhood."

He whispered back, "It won't be the same. I will take care of us."

Not long after, the Nazi governor requisitioned Hotel Le Meurice as his headquarters. The lobby that gleamed in marble, richly carved moldings, tapestries and oil paintings stood in contrast to the garish black and red swastika flags that now flew overhead. Though it had become their Sunday tradition, Ellie and Pierre could no longer stomach another meal at Le Meurice. Ellie insisted, "We will see our family through this together and look for small pleasures. By pure luck, I've discovered a family-owned bistro open for Sunday lunch. It's perfect."

Le Chat Noir, with its small vegetable garden, was tucked away on a narrow side street hidden away from the invaders' scrutiny.

The resident kitten, Minette, stretched on warm cobblestones and gave the children a soft, honeyed meow before skittering away. In the café's rustic dining room, on the main floor of the limestone house, Annika chased after the elusive black cat.

Ellie watched her playful daughter and smiled, "I prefer this sweet little café... out of the public eye."

Pierre put his arms around his wife. "Ellie, it is good to see you relax a little."

She leaned forward and lowered her voice. "Pierre, just promise me. Stay out of the limelight now. For our children's sake, you must be very, very careful."

Pierre nodded, and ruffled his son's hair. "Michi, please take your elbows off the table."

Thank God my children are fair like their mother.

Now that his political pals had been thrown out of office, Pierre had to consider Ellie's personal safety: German soldiers looked a little too long at his Swedish wife with her sunny blonde hair, full face and lovely cheekbones.

"Ellie, I promise. We'll avoid public places that could call attention to us."

Pierre hesitated... "But chérie, we have already accepted Coco's invitation. She is Federico's dear friend. We can't disappoint her after all she has done to help grow my business. We'll have one drink and that's all. It will be the usual fashion crowd. Artists will be among her guests as well as American celebrities. We'll just pop in for a short while, yes?"

Ellie said, "Pierre, you've heard the rumors about Coco

and a German lover. A Nazi or two might attend. Are you certain it's wise for us to mingle with them?"

Ellie wore a black cocktail dress with a V-neckline by Chanel. A necklace sparkled around her neck: a breathtaking marquise diamond dropped just above her cleavage.

Coco Chanel warmly greeted the stylish couple. "Ellie, you are an inspiration as always, so elegant!"

Ellie smiled and thanked her hostess. Coco looked chic in a grey jersey dress adorned with multiple strands of large, lustrous pearls.

Pierre greeted Coco with "*la bise*," an air kiss beside each cheek.

Coco said, "Darling, I love Ellie's necklace —a stunning work of art! Everyone will notice! Let's have champagne like old times. I am so happy you are here. Come my friends!"

They walked into the room. Ellie's hand shook when she reached for a flute of bubbly champagne causing the silver tray to tumble to the floor. The room was packed with upper-echelon Nazi officers, their wives or mistresses. Everyone turned toward the commotion. Surrounded by the enemy, the jeweler and his wife endured an uneasy hour of polite small talk and then slipped away.

Before long, an increasing horde of menacing occupiers roamed the streets while flaunting their rifles. Paris became subdued during the day, and curfew cloaked the evenings in darkness. The Bessettes kept closer to home. They played cards with friends, and puzzles and games with the children and Cousin Kristin.

Ellie's younger cousin, Kristin, had been orphaned at twelve years old. She had endured an uneasy life in Sweden with poor, distant relatives. Kristin joined Ellie for a brief visit and then stayed when Michi was born. Kristin was a beloved family member who was like a big sister to Michi and Annika. Kristin had been born with a slight limp but that did not keep her from rough-housing with her younger cousins.

One Friday afternoon, Kristin took the children to the park, and Ellie started dinner. She added wine, chicken stock and carrots to coq au vin simmering on the stove when someone knocked on her door. Ellie wiped her hands on her apron and slowly opened the door. She breathed a quiet sigh of relief and smiled. "Gil, it's good to see you. Please, come in."

A friend, Gilbert Dupont stood fidgeting with his beret in hand; he seemed a bit on edge. "Bonjour Ellie. I am sorry to interrupt but I am alone at the cheese shop. Pierre needs these drawings from me today. My assistant is ill; and I must return right away to what is left of my business. Please, can you give these to Pierre?"

Pierre had offered to design a necklace for Gilbert's daughter's wedding. Ellie looked at the papers in her hand and understood that Pierre would need them in a timely manner. Although many shops were forced to close, luckily Pierre's boutique had not been shut down.

She placed the pot of chicken in the oven. She would stop at the boulangerie for bread.

Perhaps I'll take a baguette over to old Monsieur Blum and check on him.

On her walk, Ellie realized that in her haste she had forgotten a scarf to hide her long wavy hair. Around the corner, three Nazis lingered by a lamp post smoking their cigarettes. They taunted her in German and grabbed at her. Ellie kept her eyes straight ahead and shifted out of their reach. By the time she got to Pierre's boutique, tears were streaming down her cheek.

Parisians distressed daily over increased shortages of milk, butter, cheese, beef and poultry. In a bitter predicament, toasted barley mixed with chicory was substituted for coffee. Soon, food exchange tickets were distributed and radios and bicycles were confiscated. Many restaurants boarded up and bread lines formed.

More than ever, Ellie worked around the clock to raise money for the increasing numbers of needy who pleaded for help She confided to her husband, "These miserable times make it almost impossible to solicit donations."

Time was running out for one family facing eviction from their humble home. Their father, Charles, a disabled stone mason, had pleaded, "Madame, our government is gone. The soup stations are closing and I have no funds for rent."

Ellie said, "Pierre, my heart breaks when I look into the forlorn eyes of those children. I lived poor as a church mouse, hungry and at times not knowing where we would sleep. I understand the fear on their little faces." Ellie took the family what little food she could scrounge up.

Days later, Ellie remarked to a fellow volunteer from the Daughters of Charity, "Thankfully a donor has paid that family's yearly rent. Those children would have been thrown out onto the streets."

The astonished friend turned to Ellie, "Didn't you know that Pierre came to the family's aid?"

Ellie felt foolish. It was well known that Pierre would lean on wealthy friends to help those who struggled to pay their rent or to find work. However, few of their well-off friends had stayed in Paris, and even the most kindhearted Parisians had little to give these days.

Ellie would search for extra rations or a donation— a vegetable or two from someone who quietly maintained a garden, day old bread or a little cheese from Gilbert—anything she could find for the neediest Parisians.

But soon strict rationing became the norm. Six-year-old Anna (as Annika was nicknamed) was often hungry. Ellie said, "Pierre, our own children and my cousin are too thin; they are not getting enough nourishment." Pierre and Ellie gave the children and Kristin some of their rationed food each evening.

Paris plunged into a hush. Only the sweet harmony of a bird's song could break the bitter silence that hung over their city. Hunger and fear prevailed. Neighbors kept their heads down and averted their eyes; Parisians no longer smiled at one another. Friendly market chit-chat had ceased.

Adding to Ellie's dismay, an acquaintance picking out a meager few strawberries and a handful of nuts at their depleted fruit stand pretended not to see her. By now, most cafés had closed.

Collaborators cooperated with the enemy in exchange for extra food. It didn't matter that petrol was in short supply; most cars had been requisitioned by the German army. A small number of taxis were licensed to drive those few who could still afford the fare.

By year's end, the golden days in the City of Light had faded away

Chapter 4

March, 1942

A deep chill permeated the city. Icicles glistened from iron street signs reminding Pierre of steel spikes that had been thrust into the heart of France. Pierre's hands slid into the pockets of his wool trench coat. A black swastika fluttered above the Arc de Triomphe.

Just blocks away, in a smoky haze the jeweler huddled with business associates in the Hotel Celtic's wood-paneled bar. Prior to the war, the quaint hotel had become a layover spot favored by airline crews who affectionately referred to its intimate bar as "the office," a name duly adopted by the locals.

Pierre ordered his weekly luxury, a "sidecar"—brandy shaken with lemon and orange liqueur. The drink became popular during the Great War when an American captain had asked the bartender to mix a drink to warm him after a freezing ride in his motorcycle sidecar.

Their stooped waiter's hand trembled; Jacques spilled a few drops when he set Pierre's drink down. "I have terrible news." Jacques's dark eyes darted around the room. Smoothing his crisp white apron, the waiter leaned in, "Dr. Morgenstern went missing."

Pierre stubbed out his Gauloise and took a slow sip of his brandy cocktail. He sank down into his chair and mulled over the disturbing report.

That evening after the children were tucked into bed, Pierre had little choice. He wanted his wife to hear it as gently as possible.

"Ellie, do you remember when Dr. Max expanded his wine cellar?"

"Yes, of course." She nodded hesitantly... "Why do you ask?"

He took her hand. "Well, as it turns out, he hid his elderly aunt and uncle beneath his floorboards." Pierre brushed a stray wisp of her hair aside. "I can barely say it aloud, but Dr. Max and his architect got caught."

Ellie dropped onto their couch. She twisted her hankie then wiped away a tear. "Dr. Max has been like a father to me, to so many of us. That poor, sweet man..."

Years ago, Dr. Maxemilien Morgenstern had diagnosed Ellie's "melancholia," a misunderstood condition which he believed stemmed from her childhood living with a destitute mother. When Ellie married Pierre, her life became stable, and the stars shone brightly for the young woman.

But Ellie's sense of safety broke when the Germans marched into Paris. She could not ignore the chaos, misery, and heartache that surrounded them. Once again, cupboards were bare, and people were starving.

Dr. Max had noticed Ellie nibble at her lower lip. He said, "Ellie, envision that a touch of anxiety follows you like a little gray bird landing on your shoulder. Try, my dear, to shoo those uncomfortable feelings away."

Nevertheless, Ellie slipped into night-time worry. Her mind could not settle down; she relived the terrifying nights when she and her mother hunkered down in the cold, dank metro as bombs exploded overhead.

With few options, her doctor had prescribed barbiturates, a common rest cure, to help Ellie relax enough to sleep through fitful nights. She had but a few pills left.

Ellie demanded... "Pierre, how will we survive if the

Nazis learn of your Jewish background? Will *you* be arrested next? What will become of our family? Let's slip away! We should join Antoine and Sophie in Saint Rémy if they will still have us. You have few customers now. And I have never needed affluence. Please! Contact Antoine!"

"Ellie, I have not attended Temple since I was a boy. Most of my childhood friends have fled. Our neighbors know nothing."

Ellie sat straight up. In a resolute voice she chided, "*Your* influence disappeared along with the French authorities. The rules have changed, and now the Germans control everything. As hard as we try, there is little we can do now. But we can still protect our children."

Pierre touched a tiny telltale scab on Ellie's lip. "Yes, I'll contact Antoine."

But it was their neighborhood bookseller, Charles Blum, who lit the fire that roused Pierre from his stubborn denial. The following day Monsieur Blum had disappeared and his shop remained shuttered. Nicknamed *Chouchou* for his love of cream-filled pastries, Blum had served tea and sweet buns in exchange for a little clever literary conversation.

His wife was right. The walls were closing in. Pierre could no longer ignore neighbors disappearing so close to his home and family. Though he sensed that getting to Saint Rémy now posed a significant challenge, he would take Antoine up on his offer to wait the remaining war out in the countryside, far from Nazi headquarters in Paris.

About two weeks later, as they waited to hear back from Antoine, Ellie felt more than winter coolness. She smiled at a friendly neighbor who abruptly turned away from her in line at the boulangerie. Ellie was no longer confused by a whisper or a cold shoulder; a web of fear and distrust had entangled their city.

That evening, Maurice Beaumont phoned. "Pierre, I regret that Marguerite is not feeling well, and we will have to cancel our frightfully skimpy dinner tomorrow."

Maurice and Marguerite Beaumont were one of the few well-established couples who had not run out of Paris. Rather, the Beaumonts mingled with the artsy crowd and musicians who performed for the French and some Germans alike. Ellie preferred to keep a distance. But Pierre cultivated the pompous couple's friendship; the jeweler gleaned useful information from the Beaumonts and their insider friends regarding German activities around Paris.

Pierre replied, "Maurice, I am sorry she is unwell. We'll make plans another time."

However, the next morning, Ellie was shocked to see a robust Marguerite enter a popular store, Galeries Lafayette. Ellie's shopping list tumbled from her hands.

Dear God... Had someone gossiped about Pierre's ancestry?

Dazed, Ellie stumbled and turned toward home.

After work, Pierre told his wife the painful truth: As hard as he had tried, he had been unable to locate their friends, the Segals.

"Sophie and Antoine were last seen several weeks ago. It is reported that an Italian officer is billeted in their home in St. Rémy." He choked on a lump in his throat. "They are missing." Arms folded and his head bowed, Pierre whispered, "Their disappearance is a mystery. And the police claim to know nothing." As youngsters, Antoine and Pierre had attended Temple classes together.

Ellie stared at the floor; her lip trembled. It was all too much... She pulled on a stray lock of hair "Oh, dear God... Not Sophie and Antoine." Ellie broke down in tears.

That night, it was the sound of heavy black boots marching toward the front door. Ellie couldn't breathe. Drenched in sweat, she tried to scream but no sound came out. She awoke from her nightmare. She shook her husband awake.

"Pierre, listen!" In a stone-cold voice, Ellie whispered,

"You will be hauled away and our family with you. Time is up…We must get to safety *now*. Our children go to bed hungry. It is too late to build a hiding place. We have no friends left who could help us!"

It was clear: exhausted Parisians had shown little energy in bucking the anti-Semitic movement.

"Pierre, we must get away now!"

He agreed. "First thing tomorrow, I'll make the call."

Chapter 5

A t nine o'clock, Pierre bundled up in his topcoat and tied a wool scarf into a French knot. He wound his way down his quiet street to an undistinguished building a mile or so away on the boulevard.

The jeweler was forced to turn to a university pal. Louis was a technician who oversaw the now German-controlled telecommunication and broadcast office. The Germans listened in on the telephone conversations of "interested persons." However, Pierre had heard rumors about a secret union of telephone workers who were aiding a struggling French resistance. He prayed that his friend would be sympathetic to his request to make the call.

"Louis, it is urgent. I *must* contact my brother. It will be so short, I promise. He is quite ill and I need to say good-bye. Ring me through, please." Pierre squeezed his friend's arm and pleaded, "I may never see him again."

Pierre's so-called brother was actually his cousin, Sir Michael Middleton, a prominent British government insider and a member of the Special Operation's Executive (SOE) known as "Churchill's Secret Army." The French La Résistance had been working hand in hand with the Brit's SOE to disrupt the occupation on French soil, and to defeat Hitler before he could cross into England.

Louis took a long look at his friend. Pierre had helped his young family when they fell into financial need during the French Depression. He placed the surreptitious call. "Pierre, you have less than two minutes."

Sir Michael Middleton heard Pierre's distressed plea through a secure speech scrambling device developed by the Americans at Bell Labs. "Michael, it's time. We need to get out. Please, execute the plan!"

Michael would coordinate arrangements with the Brits' contacts in France to get Pierre and his family from Paris to Lyon, located in the French controlled "free zone," then on to England. But with the Germans in power, it required fake documents and more time... His cousin said, "Pierre, keep your boutique open and maintain your life as normal as possible. Don't attract attention. We'll work as quickly as possible now to get you out."

Ellie had been the natural choice to facilitate the family's escape from occupied France. Pierre never wanted his wife in harm's way. But she had insisted. "Pierre, I am the only one who would not arouse suspicion at our museums." His emboldened wife looked him straight in the eyes, "I will pull it off.

The set-up was brilliant. Ellie had grown up surrounded by her mother's struggling artist friends who had lived on the scruffy outskirts of the Paris art world. Today, Ellie was an influential museum board member who shaped many cultural events for the Louvre. The jewel-like Musée National de l'Orangerie, part of the Louvre and the former winter shelter for the orange trees, would become their lifeline.

Early summer brought blistering heat to Paris. The house was too warm; the city was humid and sticky. Pierre and Ellie felt restless, exhausted and hungry. But they kept up appearances as a family attempting to carve out a little enjoyment—a cool morning stroll through the parks or a coveted ice cream at a sidewalk café, perhaps a Sunday ride on the carousel.

By late June, the anticipated envelope, disguised as a billing invoice postmarked from neutral Lisbon, Portugal, had arrived at Bijoux. A post office box number had been inserted onto the third line of the statement. The envelope included a phony invoice for an 8 x 10 gilded picture frame should Ellie's actions at the nearly empty museum raise eyebrows with German authorities. On Wednesday, Ellie would retrieve the post office key hidden that morning at the makeshift L'Orangerie gift shop.

Ellie wore a plain blue dress stitched with small embroidered dark blue flowers and sensible shoes. No high heels or colorful summer frock that could attract attention.

The jeweler's wife closed her eyes; she inhaled deeply, and exhaled. Ellie steadied her nerves and entered the gift shop. A guide working in what was left of the small gift shop called out from across the room. "Bonjour, Madame Bessette! How pleasant to have you visit us today." Board meetings had become unnecessary in this shell of a museum. In an act of defiance, the meetings continued but had been changed to Mondays. Ellie flinched when a second attendant questioned, "Madame, all is well, I hope?"

Ellie bit the corner of her lower lip then forced a warm smile.

"I'm looking for a small print. And, I couldn't wait to take a peek at our new little exhibit!"

"Madame, of course the Picasso exhibit is perfect. But I regret to tell you that Pablo's sculptures have been removed." The docent lowered her voice and said with animus, "The Germans consider his style 'degenerate.' His exhibit has been replaced with German sculptor Arno Breker's works."

Ellie fumed that an artist of Picasso's stature, and her late mother's friend, would be stifled by the occupiers. She felt emboldened to fight back. "I'm sorry to hear that... I'll browse a little and then be on my way."

A member of La Résistance had hidden the crucial key behind a stack of Monet prints. Ellie flipped through the box of 8 x 10 prints and then pocketed the postal key.

A Nazi officer on patrol had entered the room. He fixated on the pretty visitor. Ellie desperately wanted to get out of his sight and called to the museum staff, "Good afternoon, ladies. See you another time."

Ellie forced herself to casually walk away. Outside, she remembered to tie a plain gray scarf over her sunny hair. Ellie peered over her shoulder, and walked toward the post office.

She knew the neighborhood streets well: a favorite café here and the pharmacie over there. A young mother pushed her baby carriage. But today the streets seemed to whiz around her in a blur. Ellie's heart raced. She glanced over her shoulder again, uttering a prayer that she would not be followed. She had learned to cast her eyes down. Nearing the post office, the jeweler's wife picked up her pace.

Once inside, Ellie steadied her trembling hands to unlock the metal box. The Germans inspected packages. But no one noticed when she grabbed an ordinary brown business envelope that contained a forged passport and *Ausweis* (identification card) in an alias surname, Martin. She quickly stuffed the documents into the bottom of her navy-blue leather Kelly purse— a large satchel with a *haut à courroies*, a high handle. Ellie had carefully removed the stitches from the bottom of the fabric lining, and then used double-sided masking tape (ironically developed in Germany) to secure the lining back in place. She layered bills, make-up, hairbrush, wallet, hankie and her scarf over the taped false bottom.

The undercover plan had seemed easy enough. Now faced with certain danger involved in the ruse and with forged documents in her possession, the quicker Ellie walked, the faster her heart pounded. Even on an empty stomach, she felt nauseous.

At Bijoux, Pierre was pacing the floor. Ellie thrust the newly forged Martin passport and matching ID card at him. In an unusually tart tongue, "Pierre, we should not have remained in Paris!" She lowered her voice, "I'm not cut out for these spy games!"

In his back office, Pierre opened a small primitive door to the centuries-old cellar. A musty odor wafted up toward them. Forced to stoop, Pierre eased down the narrow stone steps. He shoved a suitcase out of his way. His secret safe was located inside a cramped broom closet full of boxes with outdated receipts, invoices, and ledgers. Moving the storage boxes aside, Pierre opened the creaky door to his safe. He locked the counterfeit papers in the hidden safe, known only to the Bessettes.

Pierre hoped the brisk walk and a little bite at one of Ellie's favorite bistros would help to calm his unnerved wife. He walked her to Café de Flore, a charming Art Deco restaurant on Boulevard St. Germain. A delicious smell of real dark-roasted coffee wafted toward them.

They slid into a red banquette. The occupiers kept the city's best-loved restaurants open for their own enjoyment. Ellie smelled a faint mouth-watering aroma of roasted chicken with a hint of garlic and tarragon. But she felt disgust when she glanced around the dining room filled with smug German soldiers and rich collaborators while starving Parisians lived with daily hunger and humiliation. Although her stomach rumbled, lunch was the last thing on Ellie's mind. Her nails dug into her husband's skin.

"Pierre, look at me!" She whispered, "A Nazi with a hideous jagged scar across his forehead lingered in the gift shop. His beady eyes bore straight into me; I was terrified that he would follow me. I can't get his smirk out of my mind."

Ellie looked away and lowered her head. "On my way to the post office a sobbing woman ran by me. Her head had been shaved as punishment!"

How could Pierre have put us in this dire predicament?

Pierre gently unwound Ellie's hand away from her hair. He knew what his wife was thinking and leaned forward, "I'm sorry that I waited so long to get us out." He lowered his head and shoulders. He stammered. "Ellie, I, I can no longer put you in such a risky situation. It's just too stressful. I'll retrieve the remaining passports."

Ellie took a deep breath... A moment passed. She exhaled slowly, and then she sat up determined to fight back. Pierre saw a fire light within her.

"No. The Nazis watch Bijoux. Pierre, they *know* that you do business overseas— mostly with the Americans. We have no other option. And we cannot surrender to those who may want us dead. My presence at the museum should not arouse curiosity. I am the perfect ploy. I will keep it going."

The jeweler sat straight up and looked into her eyes. Pierre's own eyes reflected the deep love he felt in his heart. "Ellie, I am truly, truly sorry. I'm very proud of your bravery."

Over the following few weeks, Ellie procured the remaining passports and the critical *Ausweis* documents. Soon, the Bessettes and Kristin would work their way undercover to the French controlled section of southern France, to Geneva and on to live in London with Pierre's cousin and family.

At the final lunch, with each of their travel documents tucked away in the cellar safe, Ellie slid closer to her husband. Exhausted by sleepless nights and the stark reality of a life on the run, she said, "Pierre, I will fight for the days when joy fills our home once again and food fills our plates. But, will we *really* be able to survive a fugitive life?"

The jeweler placed his hands over hers. He kissed his wife's hair as a lover would and whispered in Ellie's ear. "Coco always liked to say, 'The best things in life are free. The second-best things are very, very expensive.' She is right." He looked into her eyes, "Chérie, we will not live with wealth. But this is the best plan; it *will* give us our freedom back."

"Garçon!" Pierre ordered champagne.

Ellie gulped down her first glass. Pierre squeezed her hand. "Because of your courage, we will leave this dreadful Occupation behind us. Next week, we will go where we will be safe and can care for our children, d'accord?"

Ellie looked into Pierre's own moist eyes, and she nodded slowly. "I know we can't continue to live with this constant dread."

She was worn out, and toyed with the watered-down chicken fricassee. After two bubbly aperitifs, but still sick with worry over her babies' future, Ellie ate everything on her plate. Because tonight, she would give all her rations to their children.

A former customer, a loyal Frenchman, stopped by their table to greet the popular jeweler and his wife. For a few fleeting moments, life seemed normal and almost happy again.

On their walk home, the Bessettes rounded a corner and Ellie screamed, "Oh, dear God!" She turned as white as a sheet and collapsed. Pierre held his stricken wife up. The bloodied bodies of two beaten resistance fighters dangled from a tree. Pierre turned Ellie away; they ran from the gruesome execution.

Chapter 6

Pierre steered clear of Swiss banks. Although Switzerland remained neutral, it was rumored that dormant accounts had been robbed. Pierre stashed his bank notes in Ellie's mother's walnut sewing box.

Years earlier in the mid-1930s, a windfall came Pierre's way. He noticed an eye-catching ad for a Tiffany & Co. solitaire diamond engagement ring on a glamorous American movie star's finger. He took a risk and invested in the sparkling jewel that had become underappreciated following the market crash. Many wealthy clients simply did not wish to flaunt expensive diamond jewelry.

However, when economies picked up, well-to-do Europeans clamored to emulate the diamond styles popularized in America. Pierre had distinguished himself as a trendsetter mixing elegant diamonds clustered with brightly colored gems. After his signature necklace, Blossom, had been featured in *Vogue,* Bijoux became a magnet for wealthy clients in France and abroad. Pierre had cash, and he stocked up on diamonds.

Pierre had grown up fascinated by his father's riveting stories of Russian aristocrats who sewed jewels into their clothing to escape the bloody revolution. Never could he have imagined that his family would do the same. They would smuggle his diamonds and colored gems out of France.

The Duke had introduced Pierre to his dear friend, esteemed fashion designer Coco Chanel. Her first love was "costume" jewelry—faux pearls mixed with natural pearls—a fashionable look designed she said, "To decorate an ensemble not to flaunt wealth."

Coco told Pierre that she had strictly adhered to the guidelines that the trade associations enforced to disclose the marketing of synthetic stones. Her costume jewelry was clearly advertised as such. At the time, Coco had advised the up-and-coming jeweler, "Pierre, darling, you *never* want to pass fake stones off as real."

Coco Chanel now waited out the war holed up in the Ritz Hotel. She had taken a German officer as her lover and had closed her shops. However, one afternoon a few months after her cocktail party, she popped into Bijoux, "Pierre, I have heard your name come up from time to time. Some Germans envy your success. Keep a low profile, mon ami."

The Germans had ordered many fashion houses to be re-located to Berlin. Pierre believed that because his jewelry was popular with local German brass, Pierre's boutique would not be shut down. However, he took Coco's advice, and removed his most decorative pieces from the display windows where soldiers walked by on patrol. Reluctantly, Pierre also would keep away from Coco and her new friends.

Desperate to get out of France, Pierre sidestepped all of the legality and lengthy paperwork to procure synthetic gems. Instead, he paid cash to Henri, an unscrupulous vendor from a working-class neighborhood. A rough, weather-beaten brute; he smelled of sweat, fish and garlic. Henri had trans-ported genuine-looking fake stones to Paris from the docks of Marseille's slimy underworld.

Under the cover of darkness and beneath the "lover's" bridge Pont Marie, Henri pressed the bag of fakes against Pierre's chest with a cold stare. "Bessette, I'll hunt you down and plunge a knife into your heart if you utter even a word about me or my business."

Pierre never wanted to set eyes on Henri or the filthy likes of him again. He raced down the stone metro steps anxious to get home with his cache.

Pierre had taken some elaborate pieces of jewelry from Bijoux. When the children slept, he sat at the kitchen table and laboriously removed the precious stones from their settings—royal blue sapphires, cabochon rubies, diamonds, and radiant green emeralds. Ellie and Kristin then painstakingly sewed the jewels into the hems, cuffs and waistbands of their nightclothes, pants, skirts and dresses, and behind the lining of their suitcases. Ellie never yearned for wealth; with each stitch, she dreamt of a safe new life awaiting her family. Pierre replaced his precious stones with authentic looking manufactured ones. To the untrained eye, the impressive fake pieces mixed with real gems were sold to unsuspecting Germans and their collaborators. The Bessettes had worked late into many nights falling exhausted into their beds. Their life-saving jewels were hidden behind perfectly sewn tiny stitches.

Then on July 16, 1942, *"La Grande Rafle"* (raid) swept away thousands of mostly foreign-born Jewish families. The cruel, violent roundup to the Vel d'Hive sports stadium followed by transportation to the work camps jolted Pierre. He would need to place another overseas call, impossible to do from his home.

Trying not to attract attention, Pierre walked hastily to the undisclosed telecommunication and broadcast office where he begged his pal to make a call for him. Louis grappled with the notion. When Pierre palmed off a fistful of French bank notes, Louis agreed with another suspect call, "All right, but make it really short, Pierre. It's getting riskier. If the Germans find out..." Louis slid his finger across his throat. Pierre put the private call through on the secure line to Sir Michael Middleton in the Brit's war ministry.

"Michael, we cannot wait! A round-up of Jews has just taken place. I've heard that there will be more. My God, *please* make the arrangements for us to leave Paris on Monday not next weekend as we had planned. Every day that goes by puts us in mortal danger. We French-born Jews are next."

Chapter 7

The following day, a sweltering hot Friday, Pierre wove a tale of deceit to prepare his shop girl, Genevieve, for his unexpected departure.

Genevieve's husband of ten months had died on the Belgian front. With her father dead and her husband, a fallen soldier, Genevieve worked to support her mother and herself.

Genevieve was plump when Pierre hired her. But food rationing had changed her shape. Genevieve was blessed with emerald green eyes and luxurious chestnut hair. Women coveted the stunning jewelry she modeled. One day, Monsieur Beaufort had bought a bracelet for his mistress, raised his eyebrow and remarked, "Even during the weariness of war, we can count on a little fantasy at Maison Bijoux, eh Pierre?"

On this day, Pierre feigned excitement for an upcoming vacation: "Genevieve, we have been invited to visit our new neighbors at their summer house in Nice." Pierre described Auberge du Mer Bleue, the glistening whitewashed Mediterranean villa in southern France with its red tiled roof and blue shutters that jutted out over the azure sea. With a faraway look he said, "We will swim every day, and dine al fresco under the shade of their lemon grove. In town, we'll sip aperitifs under a canopy of palm trees on the Promenade des Anglais."

The jeweler could not miss Genevieve's downcast expression. Masking her true feelings, she said, "Pierre what a fantastic trip!" Considering his less than jovial mood and the tiredness on his drawn face these past months, perhaps Pierre needed this last-minute vacation after all.

Genevieve understood that Pierre truly loved Ellie. But the jeweler's smile melted the young woman's heart. Over time, missing the attention and warmth of a man in her bed, Genevieve's heart ached for her handsome boss in a way that she could not deny. She hoped this upcoming vacation would rejuvenate him to his old charming self. "Pierre, you will come home rested and relaxed!"

Pierre had acquired a rare antique pearl necklace, interlaced with diamonds, to give to Ellie as an anniversary gift. He added a heart charm that dangled from the clasp. Ellie's charm was encrusted with diamonds. He placed the iridescent necklace into a handsome signature cream box with an elegant **B** scrolled in black and tied it with a gold ribbon.

Pierre took Genevieve squarely by her shoulders. "Listen carefully. On Monday my family and I will leave for Nice. Please keep Bijoux open in my absence. I have set aside the sapphire necklace that *Comtesse* Irena Montebourg admired last week. Genevieve, it is important that you keep the shop open. The *Comte* plans to pick up the necklace for his wife next week." Pierre knew that Genevieve would need this lucrative sale.

He took her face in his hands, looked into inquisitive green eyes and kissed her gently on the forehead for the first time. Genevieve's heart skipped a beat.

Pierre placed the chunky bronze key in the young woman's hand and squeezed it shut. He whispered, "Goodbye, dear Genevieve," turned and walked toward the door. She yearned for this man who did not look back.

Friday afternoon her boss walked away toward his home and an uncertain future. Genevieve did not understand that Pierre was leaving behind not only his business, but the cherished life he had built. If the Germans came for him, Genevieve would give the authorities false information as to the whereabouts of the Bessette family. Auberge du Mer Bleue did not exist, nor did the charming neighbors with a summer home on the dazzling French Riviera.

The Bessettes were not heading south to Nice but across the Channel to Pierre's English cousin in London in a desperate attempt to escape imprisonment or death at the hands of Hitler's Third Reich.

Chapter 8

On summer evenings, Pierre would stroll home to enjoy the ambiance—the historic stone architecture, stylish boutiques and graceful arches—and their neighborhood camaraderie. These days, he forced himself to look past grotesque swastikas now hanging from former palaces. It pained him to see filthy tanks parked in front of revered monuments.

Fridays after work, Pierre often would linger at Fleurir, the corner florist located in a periwinkle blue cottage. He would tease the portly owner, Madame Marie Bonheur, known as the neighborhood's "grande dame." When she arranged her bright flowers in tin buckets, Pierre would pick out a weekend bouquet for Ellie and remark, "Madame Marie, you are lovelier than your flowers," and blow a kiss to the blushing matron.

Madame Bonheur's husband, Bernard, was one of the finest bakers in Paris. On occasion, Madame presented Pierre with a small box tied with string.

"Pierre, please take these sweet treats home to your family."

His children delighted in the small sumptuous cream-filled éclairs brushed with a rich Belgian chocolate or the flaky pastry cups filled with a tart lemon curd filling.

On this afternoon, Pierre walked by Fleurir without stopping for flowers. He would prepare his family for a risky escape.

Closer to home, from across the road and up the chestnut tree-lined street, Pierre's pace slowed but his heartbeat quickened. Two Nazis approached his tranquil street. They veered into a local tabac most likely for cigarettes. Pierre exhaled; he would stick to his routine.

Seemingly without a care, Pierre whistled softly and crossed the cobblestone street. As he did every evening, he stopped at Pascal's tabac where magazines and propaganda newspapers were displayed under a bright red awning. Pierre took a deep breath and willed the soldiers to stay inside while he picked up his censored newspaper.

Jean-Luc Pascal twirled his handlebar moustache with panache and smiled upon seeing his neighbor. He called out, "Eh, Pierre, the Cuban Montecristos you ordered just arrived. Come inside and take them home with you?" (Even during the rigors of war, if you knew the right people you could still find Cuban cigars in the city). Usually, Pierre shared a light moment or two with the jovial tabac owner. Tonight, Pierre would not linger.

Anxious to get away, Pierre gave Jean-Luc a neighborly pat on the back. "I'll stop by tomorrow, my friend. I'm running late for an anniversary dinner with my wife."

When Jean-Luc mentioned Pierre's name, the soldiers, just emerging from the tabac, glanced in the direction of Pierre's home. Dear God, they knew exactly where he lived; *he was under surveillance.*

Pierre swallowed hard and indicated the jewelry box tied with its fluffy ribbon. He forced a smile, then tipped his hat and gave the three men a solicitous wink that suggested an evening of romance. Jean-Luc chuckled. "Ahh, Pierre you are a lucky man!"

The Nazis did not share in the light-hearted exchange. Cold eyes seared into the jeweler. The soldiers whispered back and forth. Pierre hurried toward home.

The soldiers marched behind him. Their jackboot hobnails struck the cobblestones with an ominous *click, click, click* that reverberated over and over in Pierre's ears. The jeweler squeezed his eyes shut and his heart beat more loudly with each step. Pierre gulped air. He needed time to think.

Will they stop me and question me, or should I run?

Closer to his home he slowed his pace.

Will I be arrested in front of my family?

Late afternoon heat radiated off the 19th century cream-colored limestone. The mahogany front doors, embellished with bronze lion-head knockers, were flanked by two topiaries. Reminiscent of happier times, cascading ivy, petunias and red geraniums overflowed window boxes.

I have no choice but to confront them.

Pierre turned to face the enemy. By now, the only sound he heard was a gentle wind shimmer through the aspen trees. The tall soldier was steering the reluctant, stocky one toward the park.

Pierre hurried through the small courtyard, unlocked the door and took the stairs to the second floor. He bolted inside his apartment and locked their front door.

"Ellie, we have to get ready, *tonight!*"

Ellie sank down onto their couch. "All right." She crossed her arms. "But we still have so much to do?"

Pierre pulled the drapery aside. He peeked behind silk drapes and watched the soldiers walk further into the park.

"The planning is over. I was followed on my way home. We have no choice but to get out now. They *will* return."

"Oh, dear God! Pierre, are you okay?"

Pierre knew well the Gestapo tactics used to address the so-called "Jewish problem." The Nazis discreetly watched daily habits and looked for hints of escape. From conversations with clients in his boutique, and through his relationship with Nazi sympathizers Maurice and Marguerite Beaumont, Pierre understood the ghastly details.

By early Monday morning, the holding cells would be clear of rowdy troublemakers and the weekend drunks who pissed in the streets. The Nazis would strike with precision and with as little commotion as possible to avoid complaints from sleeping neighbors or any potential neighborhood uprising. Groggy Jewish families would be slow to awaken or to create a fuss when being dragged from the comfort of their warm beds. Pierre would be taken in for so-called "questioning." Then the local *gendarmes* would be forced to round up his family.

Pierre believed that his actions outside Pascal's appeared normal and would buy them a little more time. Since they had not grabbed him when they had the chance, most likely the Nazis would not return tonight. On weekends, many German officers traveled home to visit their families. Or they brought their wives or girlfriends to Paris, a city made for bubbly champagne and sex. However, by Monday morning, the Nazis would be ready for their nasty business. They could not wait. Pierre must get his family out of Paris immediately.

Chapter 9

Pierre was on the list and the clock was ticking.

He checked up and down his street again and left his home. Pierre didn't ask; he thrust a hefty wad of French bank notes at Louis who gave the jeweler an unsettled look. Louis hesitated... Then he whispered, "The very, very last time, mon ami." Pierre held out a piece of paper, and Louis dialed Michael's telephone number at 64 Baker Street, London. The address for British Intelligence.

After hearing about Pierre's encounter with the soldiers, Michael agreed. "Pierre, your instincts are spot on. Stick with your plans to pick up your travel documents. *Be on those first trains early Saturday morning.* A resistance operative will bring the train tickets tonight and slide them under your door. We will alert our people who will watch the trains for your arrivals in Lyon. Unless told otherwise, you will check into the Grand Hotel. Once you rendezvous with our contacts, you will be given more details."

Cousin Michael Middleton had arranged for the forged passports and the prized Ausweis ID cards that would allow the Bessettes to cross the demarcation line between the German-controlled north and the southern Vichy "free zone." Their documents had been perfectly forged thanks to double agent Fritz Kolbe who worked in Hitler's Foreign Ministry. Kolbe conspired against Hitler's government when he discovered the Nazi euthanasia program. He stole intelligence documents and passed them along to the British and American offices in Switzerland.

Michael reiterated, "Pierre, a businessman with a briefcase will observe and track you and your family when you embark from the trains in Lyon to ensure that you are not followed. The agent will know if anyone watches you too closely. He will be a Frenchman recruited and trained by the British SOE (Special Operation's Executive.) The hotel on the village square is large and you will blend in with the festival crowds."

Michael continued, "Days later your family will take refuge at a Benedictine Monastery on the eastern shore of Lake Annecy. Your final leg to freedom will be a short drive to Geneva airport to board a Red Cross plane bound for England. We will have to wait for the availability of a plane and for good flying weather." Two minutes were nearly up. Michael quickly added, "Safe travels, cousin."

The Bessettes would fly on a DC3 as British citizens supposedly returning to London. The mercy planes, with their unmistakable Red Cross insignia emblazoned on the tail, usually flew untouched by opposing air forces. But first, they would have to evade tight German security as they fled Paris.

Chapter 10

Pierre gathered Ellie and Kristin. "The day we hoped would never come is here." Ellie held her emotions in check and put her arms around Kristin when tears welled in the young woman's eyes.

"Tonight, we pack our essentials and go over the plans once more with the children. Ellie and I will pick up our Martin passports from the Bijoux safe. German soldiers had been listening at Pascal's. To keep up appearances, we must follow through on our dinner plans."

Ellie added, "Kristin, please bathe and put the children to bed. Make certain that Michi's folded belongings and his toys for the train are packed in your suitcase. Early in the morning we will depart Paris separately in pairs taking one train through Dijon and another train directly to Lyon."

They called the children together to break the disheartening news as simply as possible. Pierre caught hold of his eight-year-old daughter, a vision of pink cotton candy swirling through the house in her tutu.

Pierre hugged Anna and put her down. He announced, "Children, tomorrow we are traveling to Lake Annecy, which will be delightful and cooler than the city."

Anna was a little young, but Michi understood what was happening. They would travel separately to throw the Germans off course. Kristin would travel under her own Swedish passport, and Michi would travel as her son, Mikael Larsson. Twice the family had vacationed in Kristin's hometown and had shown the children Grand-mère Annette Lindstrom's ancestral farmhouse. To boot, Michi grew up speaking fluent Swedish.

Pierre took his son gently by the shoulders. He said, "Michi, remember never mention England. Kristin will do the talking. But if addressed, just say that you and your *moder* have been called home to Marieberg in Sweden."

For months, they had prepared Anna for this day. They insisted that she practice writing her new name, Annabelle Martin, a typical French surname.

Anna cried after she was reminded, "For now, pretend that you do not have a brother." By Monday, the Germans could be on the lookout for a family with two children, a 12-year-old boy and his younger sister.

Pierre knelt down and soothed his little daughter. He smoothed her hair. "Annika, *ma petite*, remember you must pretend and never say that you have a brother. Do you understand?" She nodded. Pierre wiped away a tear and promised her, "You will see Michi again soon, okay?" He sighed and whispered, "God willing," praying that none of them would be stopped, interrogated and separated, or worse.

The moving and storage company, Maison Entreposage, had been scheduled to clear the apartment the following Thursday to store their personal goods. However, no longer under Pierre and Ellie's supervision, Maison Entreposage would carefully pack and crate the furniture including antiques, silver and china. Artwork would be expertly crated for climate-controlled storage until they returned after the war to resume their lives. Recently, Pierre had photographed their valuables with his Fex camera should he find damage later.

The Germans traveled in spacious first-class compartments. With the train's small second-class compartments, Ellie was allowed to take only their steamer trunk with the hidden gems sewn into their clothes, a few favorite toys, and her small personal valise.

Anna had chosen watercolor paints and three of grandmere's art brushes, a sketchpad and art pencils, a botany book and the book *Madeleine*, her doll Lillie, and a miniature white tea set with tiny blue flowers. The children's clothes had been washed and folded. Everyone would wear worn clothes and comfortable shoes. (Kristin and Ellie had rubbed and frayed their clothes to look commonplace). Anna wanted to wear her tutu but it would be packed. In her small valise, Ellie had packed a few personal items: a small bit of simple jewelry, toiletries and snacks. Kristin would carry her own scraped-up suitcase with clothes for her and Michi, and a few books and toys. He had requested his shiny red model triplane and his toy boat, his reader and a set of miniature toy soldiers. Pierre and Ellie specifically insisted that Anna carry her teddy bear so she would appear younger. They were forced to leave all other possessions behind until they returned after the war.

Pierre was eager to help his beleaguered wife forget the turmoil of war for a few scant hours before escaping their home and city. "For old time's sake, let's make an anniversary stop at the Ritz? Chérie, we'll sit at our table at Bar Hemingway—for a French 75! What do you say?"

Ellie looked up as she and Kristin emptied their small white refrigerator. She could almost taste the elegant, golden bubbles in the champagne martini – sensual, sweet and aromatic. "Pierre, I would love champagne about now. But we have too much to do in so little time." She smiled at her disappointed husband, "We'll go out for a simple dinner then pick up our passports. Bar Hemingway will be our first stop when we return to Paris, d'accord? I promise, and by then, Federico will have returned, and we will celebrate all together!"

In her dressing room, faintly scented with tea rose and a touch of vanilla, Ellie dressed for dinner. Textiles like silk were needed for parachutes so she pulled an older Nina Ricci pale yellow silk dress with a scooped neck and a full skirt from her closet. Everything Ellie owned hung loosely now.

She stepped into navy pumps and sighed... Even her shoes felt too big.

Ellie applied make-up. She clasped her beautiful anniversary pearls; their delicate luster and the dangling diamond heart made her smile. She took comfort in all the good years spent with her kind and devoted husband. She dabbed Chanel no. 5 behind her ear. Pierre was right. She would put this escape out of her mind for one last evening in Paris with the man she loved.

Ready to go, Ellie stood up then dizzily clung to her dressing table. For weeks, she knew this moment would come. She had tried to dispel the chilling thoughts of her family being separated, and she could barely hold down what little food they were allowed. Ellie slid to the floor with an aching heart; deep sobs wracked her body.

After several minutes, she willed herself to get up. She regained her composure. From the tabletop, she took a simple painting of the Lindstrom's red-framed Swedish farmhouse where she was born. It pained Ellie to leave behind keepsakes of her mother and now to leave their apartment, the only stable home she had known. Tonight, she would be forced to go over last-minute details to escape this life that had given her happiness and security.

Ellie dabbed on fresh make-up. *We will risk everything if we stay in Paris. I must push forward for my babies. God help us...*

Chapter 11

Pierre reserved their favorite table at Allard, an old-world Paris bistro. The wood beams and warm Provencal décor provided a homey atmosphere but little comfort. Tonight, they would go over last-minute plans to escape a life and a country they loved.

Philippe, Allard's thin, wiry maître d,' greeted two of his favorite customers. "*Bonsoir* my friends! I am pleased to see you. It's been too long!"

Seated at their table, Ellie pushed the white lace curtain aside and stared out the window only to turn away from her worn out reflection.

Philippe bowed slightly when Pierre mentioned their anniversary. "I am honored to prepare two special meals for this evening." Restaurants were strictly regulated and dealt with severe shortages. Meals that contained meat would cost hundreds of francs. Allard's owner maintained a patch of land in the countryside. Cleverly, he kept some vegetables and poultry from the Germans.

The small portions of a rich chicken chasseur and a fragrant cassoulet, a rustic white bean and pork stew, were mouthwatering. The couple had eaten a few bites when, at this early hour in the near empty restaurant, a German officer gestured to a table near the Bessettes. He steadied his rifle against his table; it pointed straight at Pierre and Ellie.

Ellie searched Pierre eyes. "Good Lord, could *he* be following us?"

Pierre could only stare at his plate: he shrugged wearily... "I don't know." Their stomachs tied in knots, neither Pierre nor Ellie could dredge up any more than a scant appetite.

Pierre glanced at the Nazi gulping his wine. He whispered, "Ellie, we will start a new life in London and someday return home when we can live without fear day in and day out. But we must act as though we are enjoying an anniversary night out, d'accord" Ellie nodded and took Pierre's hand.

"I paid Maison Entreposage in advance to clear our apartment. Paul Roux, the owner of the storage company, is my friend. He assured me that he would make certain that our belongings are stored properly." Ellie squeezed his hand.

Tonight, I will reason with Pierre about what I need to do.

Philippe hovered near their table. Concerned about the fidgeting with their dinners and the half-full carafe of table wine, he asked, "Everything is good? Your meals are flavorful, oui?"

Philippe knew from experience that the Bessettes enjoyed hearty appetites and typically savored his cuisine. It was most unusual: Parisians were hungry. Yet, Pierre and Ellie picked at their meals. Despite Pierre's assurance, he scurried off to his wine cellar. Philippe returned with an excellent Chateau Lafite Rothschild, a rich, full-bodied Bordeaux to celebrate their anniversary.

He announced with a smile, "Please, enjoy the wine to enhance your dining pleasure." But, even with its smooth taste of sweet berries and spices, much of the remarkable Bordeaux remained.

Philippe scratched his head when, for the first time, Ellie did not order a slice of his creamy chocolate mousse charlotte cake. Ellie reassured him. "Philippe, please excuse us. Your meal is perfection; I am so sorry but this uncomfortable heat has even diminished my appetite." Philippe exhaled. Perhaps his reputation was still intact.

As they prepared to leave, Pierre slipped his hand into

Ellie's. He traced her finger over a crudely etched letter "V" which he had carved into their table. Ordinary citizens were carving the French Résistance victory letter onto German police cars, on bridges, pavements, light posts, tables, and chairs. Parisians gave the occupiers daily reminders that they were not welcome, and that ultimately, they would lose. Pierre dropped his napkin to cover the faint "V." He whispered in Ellie's ear, "Hitler *will* be defeated, and France will be free. We will live happily at home again."

At the door, Ellie smiled and complimented Philippe on his meal and surprised him with a hug. Pierre shook his hand and said loudly, "Au Revoir mon ami. See you another time."

Once outside and away from earshot of the soldier, Ellie admonished her husband. "How could you take such a risk and jeopardize our safety with that carving? What if the German had noticed?"

Pierre and Ellie crossed the sixteenth-century Pont Neuf Bridge. They leaned on the railing, mesmerized by a barge drifting slowly under stone arches. At twilight, the boat meandered gently down the Seine; couples strolled beside lush river banks.

Out of a warm night, chilling words broke the spell. Ellie and Pierre were startled by two Nazis who brusquely demanded their papers.

A fair-haired young soldier looked Ellie up and down. He suggested to his comrade that she might prefer a younger stud like himself. Pierre smelled liquor on their breaths. His hands curled into fists by his sides. Remembering Ellie's recent precaution, Pierre held his anger. However, he widened his stance just a bit, balanced himself and lowered his chin ever so slightly. He was prepared to fight if these men came near his wife. Meanwhile, the soldiers scrutinized their papers.

Calling his partner, a "schwein," the senior officer laughed and reminded the oafish kid, "two lusty French whores are waiting for us when we got off duty." He thrust their papers back to Pierre who slowly unclenched his fists.

The soldiers bumped against Pierre and Ellie when they topped off their departure with a "Heil Hitler." A bell tolled from a church steeple; their City of Light had plunged further into a dark abyss.

Pierre and Ellie held hands and walked quickly. Curfew was approaching. Pierre unlocked the wrought-iron gates to Bijoux's front door. In the backroom, he hurried down the ancient stone cellar stairs. The dank odor reminded Ellie of the dirty cabaret where she and her mother hid when they had been evicted from their tiny apartment during the First World War. Ellie drew what strength she had left from her mother's own struggles during the previous war.

Pierre removed their travel documents and emptied the safe of most of its cash. He left behind a few modest pieces of authentic jewelry for Genevieve to sell. Pierre locked the safe and placed the boxes back on the shelf.

Upstairs, he handed Ellie half the cash and their son's forged travel documents in addition to Kristin's Ausweis card to go with her Swedish passport. Ellie hid the documents under the false bottom of her handbag. She tossed Bijoux invoices and papers on top of her personal belongings. Pierre kept some cash for himself and the passports and Ausweis IDs with the counterfeit names Philippe, Marie, and Annabelle Martin. He buried them in a hidden pocket deep within his leather briefcase. Papers, drawings and invoices filled the briefcase.

"I called a taxi. We can't arouse suspicion by traveling together carrying false papers. There is time enough that you won't be stopped. I will go separately on the Métro."

Pierre kissed Ellie and handed the taxi driver the fare. She turned back to look at Maison Bijoux. A single tear fell and she whispered softly to her husband, "God speed." The taxi pulled away.

Back inside, Pierre locked the cellar door. He removed

from his upstairs office safe a simple gold necklace with a small diamond center stone flanked by two emerald baguettes the color of Genevieve's eyes; he placed the necklace in a gift box with two small matching earrings. Hastily, he scribbled a note to Genevieve and laid the package with the envelope on his desk. The note detailed the whereabouts of the cellar safe and instructions during his absence.

A scraping noise then the sound of breaking glass outside. Pierre locked the main office safe. He grabbed his briefcase.

Pierre also took a painful last look at his boutique. He switched off the light. Listening carefully, he slowly opened the front door and peeked outside. The Siamese cat from the café next door swished up against Pierre's leg. A shattered glass lay on the ground. Pierre locked his front door and he slid the wrought-iron gate into place.

Pierre sprinted down the steps to the Métro. He recognized a Nazi officer who patrolled the neighborhood and perused his boutique windows. The Nazi nodded briefly at Pierre before his attention was diverted to an elderly man and woman with a yellow star sewn to the left side of their garments marking them as Jews. They waited to enter the last car. The guard walked along the platform toward the anxious couple; he struck the old man's back with the butt of his rifle before turning and walking away. Pierre bent over and threw up on the tracks.

A lamppost flickered off just as Pierre unlocked his apartment door precisely at nine o'clock. He picked up a brown envelope packed with five train tickets and a schedule.

Chapter 12

When Ellie arrived home, she distributed some jewelry and cash to Kristin and handed over Michi's and Kristin's travel documents. She hid her personal jewelry in her valise. She checked on the children and made certain their bags had been packed.

When Pierre returned home, they argued. A frustrated Pierre was adamant that they could *not* take heirlooms on a supposed outing to Lake Annecy.

But Ellie insisted, "Then at least we can hide my mother's painting of Anna under floorboards or in a wall behind furniture!"

Pierre pleaded, "Ellie, *please* listen to me. It is too late to dismantle our home. It would create noise and we have precious little time now." Pierre held her gently by her shoulders. "We are being watched. Think about the probing questions if paintings or silver picture frames were stashed in our trunk! We could be detained."

Ellie's dearest possession hung in the living room, *Portrait of Anna as a Young Girl*, painted by Ellie's mother, an unknown deceased artist, Annette Lindstrom.

Pierre softened his tone and promised, "Look, I will call Paul Roux once we have safely left the country to make absolutely certain our belongings are stored. Let's remove the small photograph of your mother from its frame and you can take it with you.

Ellie agonized through another sleepless night; she

knew unscrupulous Germans stole from museums and Jewish homes. After all, Pierre was fleeing *to* his family in London. Ellie was leaving everything of her ancestry behind.

Very early Saturday morning, Ellie summoned the courage to defy her obstinate husband. She would ignore Pierre and would remove not one, but two sentimental paintings from their carved wood frames. She would give the least cherished painting to Kristin. As a neutral Swedish citizen, Kristin's bag was not likely to be scrutinized.

The Nazis would not find fault; they stole artwork all of the time.

Ellie could not leave behind her mother's amateur *Portrait of Anna*. The bottom of their Louis Vuitton trunk was flat. Since Anna was taking a few paints and brushes, Ellie did not think the painting would arouse suspicion. *Yes, this idea would work.*

With her head held high, Ellie walked steadily to the living room. She turned on the light and smiled at her mother's artwork. Anna was just four years old, sitting on their window seat. In the distance, a cherry tree blossomed. The sun filtered through, lighting Anna's sweet face. Her daughter's wavy blonde hair was tied back with a ribbon that matched her cornflower blue eyes. Anna was wearing her favorite rose-colored dress with a satin sash and a lace collar. Anna's stuffed brown bear sat in her lap.

Ellie removed the painting from the wall. She began to dismantle the canvas from the carved frame. To her utter disbelief, the telephone rang. She jumped at the shrill tone in the predawn hour. The painting slid from her hands.

Pierre was quicker to react. He raced past a stunned Ellie, picked up the telephone and listened carefully. "Thank you, my dear. Please take care of yourself. We'll be fine."

Chapter 13

The Bessette's neighbor, Madame Brigitte Simone was a buxom white-haired widow who arose early. With little to do in life, she felt responsible to "oversee" the goings-on in their small apartment building. Madame Simone was nosy.

Last night, she heard a rapping on the Bessette's door. Kristin did not answer. Ellie and Pierre had left their apartment earlier. Madame Simone had opened her door just a crack to see what the commotion was about. Two tall heavy-set Germans politely asked her if the Bessette family was home. "We are inquiring about a gas smell in the building. It is nothing more." Without as much as a whiff of odor, Madame Simone lied. "The family has gone out for the evening."

She heard them whisper to each other in German, "We'll report to headquarters and return tomorrow morning. We have better things to do with our Friday night than wait for their return." With the family supposedly away for the evening, the older soldier remarked. "It is unlikely any resistance activity would be going on." They bade the matronly neighbor a *"guten Abend,"* good evening, and left.

Madame Brigitte Simone was born in Berlin to a German mother and her French journalist father. The family relocated to France when Brigitte was eight years old. German was her native tongue and she clearly understood the soldiers' conversation. Madame Simone decided that she would call Pierre as soon as they arrived home that evening. She did not believe for one minute the reference to Pierre and "La Résistance." It was nonsense. Surely, she would have noticed strange men and women coming and going from their apartment. Frankly it would have been fine with her. Madame Simone had lived in France most of her life and did not care for the brutish manner of the German Occupation.

Brigitte was fond of the Bessette family. She never had children of her own. She could almost hear little Anna's sweet laughter while she chased her brother around the courtyard fountain. As a toddler, Anna had followed Michi like a faithful puppy. In turn, he intuitively looked after his little sister.

Madame Simone baked apple strudel for the children who devoured the sweet pastry seasoned with cinnamon and dotted with plump raisins soaked in vanilla; powdered sugar dusted their adorable faces.

But last night she'd fallen asleep on her sofa. She never called Pierre about the two Germans sniffing around their apartment. She awoke just before five o'clock Saturday morning. Forgetting about last night's encounter, she wrapped her mother's crocheted shawl around her shoulders and brewed a piping hot coffee mixed with chicory. Bitter, but better than none at all. She buttered a piece of dark toast and spread it with a smidge of the lemon curd. She found a little canned fruit in her pantry and spooned it onto a delicate Rosenthal porcelain saucer.

Madame Simone sat down in her living room to read. When she looked out to her courtyard, she noticed a light illuminate the Bessette's apartment. She realized that she had failed to call Pierre last night. "My goodness, they are up so early. Something is not right" the concerned neighbor muttered to herself.

Pierre picked up the jarring phone almost immediately. Brigitte mentioned the prying Germans from the night before. She told him they planned to return "early tomorrow morning."

Pierre masked his alarm and told her, "Please don't worry. We'll be fine, my dear."

Pierre reeled in disbelief when she mentioned the soldier's vague reference to the French La Résistance? Nevertheless, there was no time to reflect on it now. He was a wanted man; they had to get out. "Thank you for telling us. Please stay safe, too."

He hung up the telephone. "Wake Kristin and the children now! Take only what is packed. Leave everything else. I will call the taxis. Ellie, move, quickly! We are out of time. Dress the children." Pierre shouted, "They are coming back for us. Let's go!"

The distinguished socialites were now fugitives.

Chapter 14

That same Saturday, Pierre's shop girl strolled to work. The horizon radiated a pinkish glow, and the sky was laced with puffy white clouds. The refreshing early hour would give way to a warm morning and a day poised to become hot again. Customers would shop early in the cooler part of the day.

Genevieve stopped at the charming café next door to Bijoux. Although three German soldiers on patrol sat nearby, she lingered at a copper bistro table eager to enjoy her coveted *café crème* and a plump buttery croissant. Genevieve closed her eyes to savor the luxury of real dark espresso warmed with milk.

With a little pout she confided in her waiter friend. "Albert, it will be so dull at Bijoux. Working alone will bore me. *Please* come to visit often and cheer me up." A sleepy Albert perked up at this news and happily agreed to visit the pretty young woman working next door.

Genevieve unlocked Bijoux's wrought iron security gate. In the back office, she hung up her cream sweater and her red and gold Chanel scarf. Unbelievably, could she still smell the lingering scent of Pierre's cologne left over from yesterday afternoon? The scent was fresh, like talcum powder mingled with jasmine and a touch of citrus. She closed her eyes and pictured her handsome boss.

Genevieve would need to ready the boutique alone. She pushed open the shutters. Rays of early morning light streamed into the showroom as she cleaned the glass counters. A lavish bouquet of flowers graced the round center table. Several white rose petals had fallen onto the polished wood. She changed the water and removed a withered stem. Madame Bonheur would deliver a fresh floral arrangement first thing Monday morning. Pierre no longer displayed an abundance of his jewelry. Genevieve set out several unique pieces and would bring out jewelry as needed.

She hummed *La Vie Parisienne* while she swept the front stoop. A black Mercedes Benz pulled up to the front door. With an abrupt screech, the driver slammed on the brakes. Two uniformed Nazis emerged from the back seat and approached Genevieve. They ushered her back into the shop, shut the front door, and closed the shutters. It was too early for customers... Confused, she looked from one soldier to the other. *Perhaps she would sell a necklace or bracelet and make a good commission after such a brusque intrusion?*

After glancing around the boutique, the stocky one's watery eyes bore into her. "Where is Monsieur Bessette?" His brass nameplate identified Oberleutnant Otto Heinrich. He stood medium height with broad shoulders, brown hair, a large nose and full jaw. His skin was pock-marked. His mustache could not hide crooked, tobacco-stained teeth. Genevieve could tell that despite his younger age, he was the superior officer with assorted medals and a braided epaulet; he puffed out his chest.

"Well, tell me! I'm waiting...When does Bessette arrive at work?"

Genevieve replied. "He is not coming in today. He is taking a vacation with his family." Genevieve forced a small smile. "But I am happy to be of assistance."

Heinrich edged closer pinning Genevieve against the display counter.

"And, how long will Bessette be on this vacation?"

Genevieve smelled stale tobacco on his breath. She felt uncomfortable and tried to move aside and answered. "He is not expected until August, Monsieur. Why do you ask?"

Heinrich slapped her across the face. "*I'm* asking the questions. Now, where is he taking this vacation?"

Stunned, Genevieve shivered despite the warm morning.

He slapped her across the face once again, cutting her lip. Her face stung, reddened with the imprint of his hand.

The tall, blond officer gingerly spoke up "Hey, Otto, back off, eh? Give her a chance to answer." But Otto Heinrich turned back to face Genevieve with a hard stare. He raised his hand once again...

Terrified, Genevieve put her hands up in defense. "They are leaving for the south, for a family vacation. Their neighbors own the villa... I, I don't know their names." Genevieve understood that Pierre and his family were in terrible trouble. At a loss, she tried to think of a way to help them. Then quickly she added, hoping a lie would distract them. "The neighbor's summer house is in Cannes."

Heinrich stared at the cowering young woman and he inched up against her.

"Otto, come on... she's telling the truth," pleaded the tall soldier nervously watching Heinrich's next move. "We'll head to the Bessette's home. They were in town last night. It's very early, they probably have not left." He grabbed Otto's arm. "Let's go."

Otto yanked his arm free. "Let *go* of me, Stefan!" Heinrich eyed Genevieve, sucked in his breath and muttered in German. "We are not done with this little French confection. I will take her first. And then you can have your turn."

Heinrich pulled her by her long hair into Pierre's office. Genevieve screamed hoping her waiter friend would hear her pleas. "No! Help! Albert!"

"Lock the front door, Stefan," yelled Heinrich.

"Otto, let's not waste more time!" Stefan Schafer demanded and yelled; his arms thrown up in the air in exasperation. "We should head to their home, *now*. We may still get to Bessette."

Heinrich ripped the buttons from Genevieve's blouse while the young woman screamed and twisted away from him. He hit Genevieve again. The blow stunned her. He pushed her onto Pierre's desk swiping its contents onto the floor. The brute rubbed against her and lifted her brassiere. His large hands fondled full, young breasts. Genevieve pushed him and tried to break away. He kissed her lips; Genevieve's struggling aroused him further. He raised her skirt and tore at her undergarment. His hands wandered over her body and between her legs. He raped her on top of Pierre's desk.

Across town, Pierre had put down the phone after taking Madame Simone's call and screamed commands: "Ellie, we must hurry. Hurry! Good Lord, they are coming back for us!"

Ellie ran to Kristin and the children. "Kristin! Help me dress the children! Quickly!" Kristin threw on her clothes while Ellie tucked in Michi's shirt. She fought back tears and embraced her son and her cousin.

Buckling his belt, Heinrich laughed and approached his partner. "Eh, Stefan, that delicious tart is all yours." He snatched Schafer's handkerchief from his jacket pocket and wiped the sweat from his brow. "Don't take too long." Tossing the cloth back to him, he snapped, "Hurry up."

Schafer found Genevieve dazed, whimpering and cowering in a corner. She tried to cover herself.

Hands held up, he whispered, "I won't hurt you." But he raised his voice just enough for Heinrich to hear and yelled. "Lay down." Trembling and sobbing, she scooted back away. Handing Genevieve his handkerchief for her bleeding lip, he said, "Shh, I promise... I will not touch you." Then he said loudly for Heinrich to hear, "Lay back down, *now*."

Stefan helped her up. Again, he whispered in the trembling woman's ear, "I *won't* hurt you." Still, she could only stare at his nameplate, Leutnant Stefan Schafer.

"Please. You must listen to me." Stefan said gently turning her face up toward him. Genevieve stared blankly into bright blue eyes. "As *soon* as we leave, call your boss, Bessette. Tell them to leave their house *immediately.* They should not waste time!"

A few miles away, Ellie dressed Anna. Her fingers trembled, and she fumbled with the tiny mother of pearl buttons on her little girl's blouse.

Meanwhile, Pierre kissed his young son. He took Michi squarely by his shoulders and hugged him, "Remember, it is important to speak *only* in Swedish from now on... We will meet up soon in Lyon." Michi nodded.

Outside, their taxi pulled up. Once more he hugged his son and then Kristin. He held their suitcase and guided them toward the taxi. Kristin was tall with sun-streaked light brown hair and blue eyes. She would be noticed. Because of her slight limp, he reminded Kristin, "Walk slowly so you don't attract too much attention." He hustled them into the waiting taxi and directed the driver to hurry to the Gare de Bercy train station.

Stefan Schafer left Pierre's office slamming the door behind him. A smug and smiling Otto Heinrich knocked over the flower vase that crashed to the floor. He unlocked the front door, pocketing a sapphire necklace on the way out. Heinrich ordered his chauffeur to light his beacon and drive quickly to the Bessette home.

Tears streamed down Genevieve's cheek. She held her torn blouse over her chest. A moment later, she picked up the telephone that had fallen to the floor. Pierre's line was busy.

Pierre was calling to ask where the second taxi was. The dispatcher remarked, "There is construction for new barricades. There will be a slight delay, monsieur." Pierre pleaded.

"Please, *please* hurry as fast as you can." He hung up the phone. He uttered, "Come. Come quickly, family! Let's move along." Ellie picked up Anna's teddy bear and tightly clutched her daughter's hand.

Pierre ushered a drowsy Anna and her fearful mother out of their home. Pierre turned around taking a last glimpse. He steadied his hand to lock their door. He carefully placed the key in a hallway umbrella stand for the storage company, Maison Entreposage.

They hurried through the courtyard. He looked up and down his deserted street. Under his breath he murmured, "Where is that taxi! Please hurry." The air was already warm. Yet, Ellie pulled her old sweater tight to contain her shaking body. She pulled her little girl closer.

Genevieve pleaded with the operator, "Please try again. Keep ringing the apartment!" But after no answer, she gave up. She prayed the family had left for their journey to Gare de Ville Nice train station and that her deception had worked. Genevieve believed the Germans would search Cannes rather than Nice.

Genevieve grabbed her sweater from the hook to cover her chest. Unable to bear wearing her torn blouse, she wrapped the bloodstained, sweat-soaked handkerchief, blouse and her undergarments in plain brown paper tied with string to throw them all away. Still crying, she buttoned her flouncy skirt and wrapped her scarf over her matted hair. In a trance, she placed the *fermé* sign in the front window, and locked the front door. She slammed the shutters closed. Genevieve retrieved the jewelry pieces that she had displayed and returned them to the safe. In the back office, she left through a service door into the alley. Not wanting to leave her package on the top of an overflowing trash bin, she held on to it. She locked the rear door and walked quickly home, avoiding the eyes of strangers who stared at her disheveled appearance and tear-stained face.

Genevieve stumbled through her surprised mother's front door and collapsed into her arms. Trying to comfort her distraught daughter, Madame Caron brought her tea laced with brandy, and then she called their family doctor. Genevieve pleaded with her mother not to do it... But her mother insisted that the French police needed to know about the occupier who had raped and battered her daughter. Before Genevieve cried herself to sleep, she begged her mother to throw away the package of ruined clothes.

In the distance, a siren wailed. A taxi crept onto their street. The Bessettes quickly loaded their packed steamer trunk and Ellie's small valise into the car. *"Putain,"* their driver cursed as he attempted to maneuver back onto the choked boulevard on the way to Gare de Lyon train station.

The taxi inched its way around newly constructed police barricades and congestion. Pierre and Ellie sat in stunned silence. Anna held her teddy bear and cuddled up against her Maman. The scruffy, worn brown bear gave Anna a younger appearance, which her parents hoped would throw off Germans on the lookout for a family with an eight-year-old daughter.

Pierre was confident that a vigilant search would begin throughout all cities and checkpoints. He prayed that they had enough time to get to the safer French-controlled Vichy section before the alarm was sounded.

Pierre was particularly troubled by Mme. Simone's remark about "resistance." For what reason would Pierre be hunted? My God, not because he was Jewish, but the Germans believed that he colluded with the French La Résistance group? If that were the unfortunate case, there would be a full-blown manhunt for him believed to be an enemy of the Nazi regime.

Chapter 15

They arrived at the Gare de Lyon train station. Pierre glanced up at the clock tower reminiscent of London's Big Ben. Another stab at French sovereignty, the Nazis had set the clocks to German time. Pierre put his arm around Ellie. He whispered encouragement to his terrified wife whose son and cousin had fled on their own. "The British style clock is our good omen? We will be more secure and happy in England."

Ellie sat in silence. She had known this day was coming, and she could not turn back that clock. She had no other choice but to board a train that led to an uncertain future. Ellie held Anna's hand and they walked toward the entrance.

"Ellie, soon we'll be out of harm's way. Let's act as though we are looking forward to our vacation. Michi and Kristin will do fine." Ellie did her best to venture a small smile.

They entered the crowded train station and approached the first checkpoint. The ornate terminal was hot and stuffy, reeking of brake pads, grease and stale perfume—Pierre began to feel off-balance. But he stood tall and handed their Martin passports and papers to the guards.

Ellie held her head high. She winced when the first guard yelled in a booming voice as he checked their Ausweis papers, "Naaaames, please,"

"Martin," swallowed Pierre. "We are the Martin family."

Another soldier came over and stood so close to Ellie that she felt his hot breath on her neck. She looked up at a repulsive smirk. Ellie felt bile rise in her throat. She forced herself to smile sweetly.

The first guard thumbed through Pierre's travel documents. "What do you do for a living, *Herr* Martin?"

Pierre did not hesitate. "I am an accountant with my own business. However, my clients, well, many of them are no longer working."

The German looked up and replied sarcastically, "Well, isn't that too bad... And now what is the nature of this trip?"

"We have family living outside Lyon in the small town of Perouges. We plan to attend the music festival." Pierre smiled nonchalantly, "Paris is much too hot, eh? And, we have time to get away to the lake region."

Anna had been told not to speak to the soldiers. Ellie reminded herself to breathe. The guards opened their steamer trunk and searched its pockets, underneath and along the inside of the trunk, as well as Ellie's small valise. She stiffened when they fingered her garments, and she nibbled at the corner of her chapped lip. Anna clung to her teddy bear. Unbeknownst to Anna, her worn bear was stuffed with precious gems. Finally, the guards passed them through to the main section of the railway station. Pierre exhaled.

A little distance away, Ellie stopped and faced her husband who read terror on her face. "Pierre, that first guard is the same soldier who lingered at the museum and watched me so closely. I recognize that awful shrapnel scar on his forehead. Dear God..."

Pierre put his arm around his wife. "Ellie, he appeared intent on scrutinizing our papers. I'm sure that we are fine, or we would have been detained by now, oui?

After leaving the stunned shop girl, Otto Heinrich and Stefan Schafer's car had maneuvered around construction and arrived at the Bessette's apartment building. Furious when their apartment door went unanswered, Heinrich beat on it. Madame Simone opened her door slightly and peered out. His face was red with exertion, Heinrich shouted at the elderly woman and demanded, "Where are they?"

She said in an indignant tone, "I have not seen them in days. I do not know their whereabouts." She closed her door. The soldiers battered the Bessette's door and stepped inside.

A painting lay face down on the floor and nightclothes were strewn about the disheveled bedrooms.

Heinrich screamed at Schafer. "This is your fault, you damn fool! We could have detained him yesterday!" Heinrich radioed an alert to the General Command, "Immediately watch all stations, the trains and check points. Look for the jeweler, Pierre Bessette, and his family!"

In a rage, Heinrich smashed Chinese porcelain and crystal stemware, and he stripped the apartment of whatever he could carry. He forced Schafer to trail behind carrying a pair of silver candelabras.

Pierre's mouth was dry; he needed a drink. He wiped his damp brow and steered Ellie and Anna through massive arched doorways into the sumptuous Le Train Bleu bar and restaurant. The walls and ceilings were adorned with gilt. The elaborate paintings and mahogany panels were deemed appropriate for a former grand exhibition hall.

The Bessettes settled into a leather booth. Pierre steadied his hand to light a cigarette. Ellie ordered Anna a soft-boiled egg, a croissant and an orange juice. Ellie asked for a Mariage Frères black tea with warm milk. Coffee would be too bitter. She needed to keep her stomach settled. She nibbled on a pain aux raisin pastry. Despite the early hour, Pierre ordered a cool pastis drink. The waitress brought water to mix with the strong milky yellow liqueur. He ate a croissant with butter and a pain aux raisin and drank down his black coffee.

The station was crawling with Nazis. The licorice-tasting drink helped Pierre to relax as they made their way to the train. In order to board, they were asked once again to present their travel papers and easily were passed through to their car.

Ellie's mind drifted to their son and Kristin all alone at Gare de Bercy.

The first passenger car had been requisitioned for military. The German soldiers stared as the attractive family passed through the cabin. Ellie steadied herself against the seat rests and trailed behind Anna who skipped down the narrow aisle. The second car held a mixture of military and a few civilians.

Finally, they reached their small compartment in the third car. It consisted of two red cracked leather divans opposite each other with storage racks overhead for their luggage. Once inside the stuffy cabin, Ellie removed Anna's sweater and checked once again that Bonbon was nestled with Anna. A porter had stored their trunk overhead. Thankfully, it was still locked.

Ellie took a deep breath and settled in to read to Anna. Pierre took out apples, and some hard-aged cheese they had packed last night. "I don't want to risk going to the dining car." At last, the whistle blew and doors slammed shut.

Moments later, Pierre fidgeted with his gold Patek Philippe pocket watch. He carried it for good luck—it had been his father's. On the back, his mother had inscribed, *"Wherever you go, travel with my heart."* He glanced at the time; they were a little behind schedule.

Seconds later, the doors to their compartment slid open. Pierre's mouth dropped open. Ellie stared straight up at an ugly forehead gash and cold gray eyes that met hers when he said, "It seems there has been an inquiry."

Two Nazis brazenly crowded into the small space and demanded to see their papers. Once again, the officer with the jagged scar scrutinized the documents. A young handsome soldier with a friendly smile knelt down to talk with Anna.

"What is the name of your cute bear, fraulein?"

"I am not fraulein. I am Annabelle," she giggled. "My bear is Bonbon!"

"He is *very* handsome," said the boyish soldier as he pets

the teddy bear. "And where are you and Bonbon going today?"

"To visit my cousins," giggled a besotted Anna.

The guard inquired a little more, "But don't you have a brother, Annika? He is not with you?"

Pierre stiffened and quickly answered, "Her name is Annabelle. And why are you troubling her with your ques tions? *I* will answer them."

But Anna smiled at the question and gleefully said to the friendly soldier, "I have a brother. I'm going to see him again!" Ellie gulped, unable to take in enough air.

Pierre started to speak, but the third guard jerked his arm and pulled him away. He held Pierre back with a tight grip; the guard eased a Glock pistol from its holster.

The playful guard continued to question Anna.

"Wonderful! And when will you see your brother?" He smiled while Bonbon pirouetted into the air. "Soon?"

In an exuberant voice, Anna exclaimed, "Someday in heaven. Papa said I will see him. He is with God." Ellie let out a mournful cry like a wounded animal.

Pierre yelled at the first guard. "I *hope* you are happy now! Look at my wife's distress at the loss of our son two years ago." He pulled Anna away from the young guard; Anna lunged for her mother.

The soldiers left without apology, slamming their compartment door shut, metal grating against metal. Pierre rushed to comfort his stricken wife. Ellie had held up, but her nerves had been stretched too far; she rocked back and forth.

Pierre whispered just loud enough, "Anna, why did you say Michel was in heaven?"

"Papa," she returned the whisper, "You said I would see Michi again someday, *God willing*." Pierre hugged his little daughter.

"Did I do good, Papa?"

He kissed the top of her head, "Yes, baby, yes!"

The train lurched forward and pulled slowly away from the station.

Chapter 16

Pierre placed a pillow under Ellie's head. In the warm, stuffy compartment, she said, "I'm so cold." Pierre wrapped a sweater around Ellie. He removed his suit jacket and placed it over his wife. He stroked her head. "Rest comfortably; we are safe."

The rhythm of wheels and Pierre's reassuring words were the last his distraught wife heard before drifting to sleep. Following a troubled childhood, once again her emotional well-being was tested to the limits. Their lives dangled by a thread.

Anna snuggled against her papa who read to her while she crunched on her apple. Eventually, Anna also fell asleep to the gentle hum of the train winding along the tracks.

Looking out at the hazy blur of the French countryside, Pierre thought about his family with a heavy heart and a gnawing pit in his stomach. They had been living an advantageous life. Now his wife was in a state of shock and they were fleeing their home. He prayed Kristin and Michi's trip from Paris to Dijon then on to Lyon would go without a hitch. Like the captain of a ship navigating stormy seas, he had no way to forecast their uncertain future.

Pierre, Ellie and Anna would remain undercover in Lyon waiting to reunite with Michi and Kristin. They would sleep at the Grand Hotel. A university town, Lyon would be filled with students attending summer classes as well as vacationers enjoying summer concerts and plays. The family should blend in with summer holiday crowds.

Pierre knew the German secret police were vigilant. Also, some French police could be cold-hearted or indifferent by cooperating with the Nazis.

Pierre considered their formidable journey, and his head dropped. He slumped over in his seat.

Chapter 17

In his Paris living quarters, Leutnant Stefan Schafer paced. He shut his window when the sky darkened to a somber gray, and an early afternoon thunderstorm rumbled. His apartment was located above a popular brasserie, Chez Jenny. Despite the approaching storm, classical music and a little laughter floated upstairs above the crackle of lightning.

Schafer was a German intelligence officer who lived among everyday Parisians to listen and watch for signs of resistance or retaliation.

His studio was snug yet cheerful. Under the eaves, a brass bed was covered with a colorful down duvet. A comfortable couch and an end table were set up in a separate reading alcove. The apartment included a kitchenette where Schafer could prepare simple meals. He was lucky to have his own small washroom.

The restaurant's chef-owner was born in Strasbourg and specialized in Alsatian cuisine. Even with the anti-German sentiment and strict rationing, Chez Jenny remained a popular gathering place known for cellar-chilled beer and a warm welcome where the cares of the Occupation and the outside world were left on the doorstep. Some days, the smoky fragrance of a small roasted pork, sauerkraut, and *flammekueches* (thin crust pizzas) wafted upstairs, reminding Schafer of home.

Today it was not La Résistance that heightened Schafer's unease. Something had to be done about his commanding officer, Oberleutnant Otto Heinrich, a brute whose vicious behavior had escalated: Twelve days ago, Heinrich had cornered a teenage girl coming home from a *boulangerie*; he forced her into an alley and fondled her. The following Friday, in a rage, Heinrich had bashed in the head of a prostitute. The young woman lay unconscious in a hospital bed. This morning, he battered and raped the shop girl at Bijoux when it became clear that Bessette would not be coming to his boutique.

Heinrich feared that Bessette had escaped. Unless the family could be found, they would fail to capture a suspect that Heinrich believed to be a well-connected member of the Free French Résistance (FFL). But Schafer knew of no evidence against the jeweler. What was definitive, Otto Heinrich was out of control; he had become a tyrant. Heinrich had put out a city and statewide search warrant for the Bessette family with a significant reward if Pierre were captured. Additional men were diverted to Gare de Cannes Ville train station.

The jeweler's name had come up in a report stating that a captured member of the Résistance had been a customer of Bijoux. However, as the local police argued, Pierre's boutique had *always* been a popular rendezvous for shoppers and for neighborhood camaraderie. Then Pierre was spotted having drinks in the Hotel Celtic bar where just weeks ago two members of a local resistance group had been arrested. But again, the bar was a long-standing watering-hole for local businessmen.

Otto Heinrich looked for trouble. Commanding officers had specifically told Heinrich, "Back off until after a formal investigation into Bessette's background is completed and you are given orders. Bessette is a popular figure." The Nazi hierarchy did not want to stir up populace trouble by going after a distinguished, well-connected citizen. Bessette's jewelry designs were in demand outside of France. Any unwarranted harm to Bessette could create uproar beyond French borders and especially from America.

One night about a month ago, a young policeman, the nephew of Pierre's good friend, Antoine Segal, drank too much and tried to earn a little favor with the Germans. The lad mentioned that the Paris jeweler might be Jewish. Heinrich, who loved to take advantage of wealthy Jews, was intensely jealous of Pierre's stature and success. The kid's rumor provided Heinrich the impetus to monitor Pierre. Heinrich sent soldiers to discreetly watch Bessette's home and to look for any resistance activity or happenstance which could put the jeweler in a bad light and give Heinrich a green light to arrest Bessette.

Sabotage had become dangerous for the German war movement. Local La Résistance groups like the Maquis blew up or derailed portions of railroads that the Germans relied on to transport their supplies and soldiers. Communication lines were disrupted. A London film director managed the Camouflage Section where lethal devices were crafted out of papier mâché or plaster. A realistic looking clump of manure or a rock often hid a booby trap or dynamite

Heinrich specifically wanted revenge after eight German soldiers had been lured into a smart set-up and killed. At the heart of the cat-and-mouse trap were two young resistance women who met naive German soldiers patrolling at night. Wearing suggestive dresses and high heels, the women shared a cigarette outside the popular Club Mademoiselle tucked onto a side street behind Blvd. St. Germain. Glamorous and sexy, their French perfume and bright red lipstick attracted the soldiers to the women like flies to honey. Lighthearted conversation flowed, enhanced by demure smiles and the suggestion, "Hey *kumpel* (fellas), come inside and buy us a drink." After a few drinks, an exchange of sex for money or ration coupons would be suggested. The women lured the soldiers to a nearby apartment. Once inside the tiny walk-up, the confused soldiers were ambushed and killed by waiting men from La Résistance.

The dead Germans' papers were handed over to the

Allies False Documents Section where bogus identifications were created. Nazi uniforms were removed from the dead soldiers. With the authentic uniforms and perfectly minted fictitious ID, La Résistance lured additional unsuspecting German soldiers away from their posts around the city. Killing a two-star and a three-star commander had been a real coup. Their official papers were copied; insignias and medals were used over and over to deceive enemy soldiers throughout Paris. One German soldier escaped despite a severe blow to his head. After the injured soldier got away from the ambush, the team was forced to temporarily close down the apartment and stop frequenting Club Mademoiselle.

However, weeks later a slightly different scheme was established on Montmartre within view of the Basilica Sacre Coeur. Club management advertised "first beer free to soldiers." Once inside, the showgirls, displaying long shapely legs, would strike up conversations with interested German soldiers—those men who were not interested in *les putes* who walked the streets of Montmartre late at night. Often, a lonely soldier happily escorted a young lady home only to fall into the unforgiving arms of La Résistance.

A bold rising star in the Hitler Youth Movement, Hitler-jugend, Otto Heinrich advanced as the youngest Oberleutnant in the German army. He earned his rank early on by capturing a leader of the Paris Liberation Group and severely limiting that group's efforts. Heinrich's intelligence gathering had shut down a rural gang that had derailed two German freight trains. Heinrich had become an eager soldier, a cunning stalker hunting his prey for the Third Reich. He was a natural predator who fancied himself as the Fuehrer's conquering gladiator. On the other hand, Leutnant Schafer believed the commanding officers should know that, in his fervor to make a name for himself, Otto Heinrich had become a dangerous brute. Schafer feared Heinrich was poised to kill an innocent woman or worse, a young girl.

Leutnant Stefan Schafer had no taste for war, particularly when unarmed civilians were injured or killed. Schafer began his career as a police officer. He had developed a security company in his hometown, Mainz. There was no evidence that Bessette was a threat to the German war machine. Another quandary gnawed at Schafer: Otto Heinrich ransacked French homes. He pilfered valuable personal items that he sold on the Black Market. He stole "abandoned" artifacts and paintings from well-to-do Jewish families, and art patrons like the Rothschilds and celebrated art dealer, Paul Rosenberg. To gain prestige with German Oberkommando, Heinrich personally delivered stolen art to the Jeu de Paume Museum. Goring himself visited the museum to claim stolen masterpieces for his own collection. Private art collections were sent to Bavaria. A department store had been set up as storage for looted Jewish property. Valuables were transported to high profile Germans, many of whom were particularly fond of Impressionist paintings.

Schafer realized that he was putting himself at risk by speaking out against his partner. The commanding officers might turn a blind eye to Heinrich's barbaric treatment of women to keep the steady stream of luxury items and valuables flowing into Germany or personally into Goring's and Hitler's dirty hands.

The Third Reich had envisioned the two resistance officers as likely partners. Nothing could be further from the truth. Schafer was a man whose life work had been devoted to protecting people and property. As a bitter consequence, he had to stand by as his younger, commanding officer stole from victims. His emotions over his duty to serve his country by protecting German soldiers and the moral dilemma of Heinrich's brutality, together with the overall plight of Jews, had overwhelmed the soldier.

Leutnant Schafer had come to an ethical crossroad: He felt that had no choice but to approach the generalmajor on Monday concerning Heinrich's overreaching and sadistic behavior. Oberleutnant Otto Heinrich may be dedicated to his country. But his renegade attitude and cruel behavior must be curbed; his brutal authority was a threat to vulnerable French girls and women.

But on Saturday afternoon Schafer was forced to accompany Heinrich as they resumed a sweeping search for the Bessette family. They continued surveillance in a café next to the jewelry boutique. Maison Bijoux remained shuttered after the shop girl's attack. Heinrich sent a team to hold surveillance and talk with tabac owner Jean-Luc Pascal and other neighborhood merchants.

Several doors from Bijoux stood a luxury men's shop, Chez Marcel. Heinrich's men spoke with Marcel's assistant and planned to question Marcel on Monday when the owner returned from his business trip. Meanwhile, they interviewed the proprietors of the family's favorite bistros and restaurants. So far, neighbors had shed no light on the family's whereabouts. The Bessettes had simply vanished.

Otto Heinrich was furious. They had lost their chance to detain Pierre Friday night outside Pascal's Tabac. It would have been an easy request to ask Pierre to come down to the station to answer a few questions concerning his associates at the Hotel Celtic's bar. But Stefan Schafer urged him not to detain Pierre in front of his home and family.

Schafer had made a few good points: As yet, they had no *proof* of Bessette's involvement in any anti-German activities. It was also true that Friday night was not an opportune time for a "conversation." Pierre Bessette was popular even with some German hierarchy. A public uprising would not sit well with Heinrich's commanding officers who would expect to enjoy an upcoming Paris weekend.

But now, Heinrich berated Schafer that their outstanding reputations as protectors of the Third Reich could be tarnished. The jeweler had been tipped off that he was being investigated and the family had fled which pointed to Pierre Bessette's possible Jewish ancestry.

The rail stations were being watched. Several families

resembling the Bessette family were stopped and questioned without success. Full search teams were dispatched in Cannes; villas and hotels would be checked for any signs of the family although none of Pierre's neighbors knew of a family with a vacation villa in the south. They would monitor stations in Nice as well as the smaller towns along the coast.

Perhaps the shop girl was not telling the truth? Perhaps Bessette was hiding out with friends in Paris? Nevertheless, Heinrich would enlist the help of all Nazi and French security patrols in the major cities: Dijon, Nice and Marseilles, giving special attention to cities and villages bordering neutral Switzerland like Lyon, Annecy and Grenoble. Patrols were instructed to remain vigilant and keep an eye out. Any family resembling the Bessettes should be reported to the local authorities *immediately.* A significant reward had been posted throughout France. Heinrich wanted to capture the jeweler. He told Schafer that he fantasized about Bessette's blonde wife. "She will become my very own prize."

Chapter 18

Lyon

The train from Paris made its slow approach onto track 12 at Gare de Lyon-Perrache. Now awake, Anna shook her mother. "Maman, Maman make Papa wake up. He won't wake up, Maman!" Ellie blinked her eyes open and reached across to nudge Pierre. He did not move. The train edged closer to the platform. Ellie got up to sit next to her husband. She stroked Pierre's cold forehead. Ellie whispered, "Cheri, we have arrived in Lyon. Please, it's time to wake up. Pierre, you must wake up now!"

Pierre stirred. Disoriented from a deep pastis-induced sleep, he yawned, "Where are we, Ellie? Is this Lyon?"

"Oui, the train is pulling into the station. We have arrived."

Pierre sat up slowly and stretched. He spotted German soldiers milling around the platform. He leaned forward, "Anna, remember my girl do *not* talk about Michi. We are pretending that he is with God. Remember chérie? Our secret; you will see Michel soon."

"Oui, Papa! I can pretend. It is make-believe."

"Remember, Anna, we are here to take a trip to the lake for our vacation, d'accord? Let us go to our hotel."

Pierre straightened his tie and smoothed his rumpled hair. Still feeling unsettled; nevertheless, he stood tall and remained alert leaving the train. Pierre's eyes roamed the station watching for anyone who seemed interested in their movements. Few appeared to notice the mother, father, and daughter. Their travel documents were stamped, and they moved easily through the station. He glanced over his shoulder several times...

Pierre's stomach rumbled. He said, "I feel guilty thinking about food when Michi and Kristin are still unaccounted for..."

"Papa, I'm hungry."

The taxi pulled up to the Grand Hotel. Stately stone lions, the symbols of Lyon, flanked the palatial entrance. Two alert bellboys commandeered their trunk and Ellie's valise while the uniformed doorman, wearing a gold-trimmed cap and braided epaulets, bowed slightly and opened the tall brass double doors etched in glass. The Bessettes stepped onto marble floors and entered a luxurious lobby softly lit with glittering Murano glass chandeliers from Italy.

Pierre checked in at the mahogany front desk and necessarily surrendered their Martin passports. They were shown to a pleasant Provencal room. It contained two antique iron beds adorned with scrolled brass fleurs-de-lys, pale yellow quilts with sprays of blue flowers, a bedside table, writing desk and a hand-carved oak armoire. Bonbon would wait on a bed for Anna.

The family made their way to an old-world dining room. The Germans' favorite hotels did not suffer food shortages as severely as the local population. Pierre ordered a traditional, though it would be small-portioned, Lyonnais meal beginning with a specialty from the days when Lyon was a silk weaving center, a creamy cheese spread made with fromage blanc seasoned with chopped herbs, shallots, salt and pepper, olive oil and vinegar spread onto pieces of crusty baguette. For their main course, Pierre requested coq au vin, dauphinoise gratin potatoes with a small amount of creamy cheese, ending the meal with a salade Lyonnais. Pierre purposely ordered an increasingly rare, fruity wine from the Domaine Huet vineyard.

They relished their meal, although Ellie was preoccupied and deeply concerned for her son and cousin. Pierre kept the conversation light, "Chérie, do you remember the young man, Gaston Huet who we met before the war? He was in Paris to introduce his father's wine to Maxim's, and we met him again at the Rosenberg's gala."

"Yes. And I do recall that Gaston was very excited about his father's new vineyard."

"Well, Gilbert, the steward at Maxim's, told me an interesting story. Unfortunately, Gaston had to surrender in Calais while trying to escape. But he is one clever wine producer."

"Why do you say clever?"

"Well, before leaving for the war, Gaston hid their best cases of wine in caves in the Loire Valley. In front of the caves, he built a fieldstone wall designed to look very old by placing mature plants in the front and rubbing dirt into the cracks." Pierre chuckled. "Huet then transported spiders from their cellars to the newly built wall. It was clever, oui? The cobwebs created the deception of a centuries-old stone wall to hide their wine from the Germans."

Ellie smiled, "Now, hearing Gaston's story of retaliation, I'm enjoying this wine even more." Savoring the honeyed notes of apple and pear, Ellie gave Anna about an ounce of the wine mixed with a splash of water.

Ellie replied, "Well, it appears that the Nazi weinfuhrers not only stole France's best wine to sell for their war efforts, but they drew their demarcation lines carefully, didn't they? Our Bordeaux, Champagne and Burgundy regions are located in the now German zone. I suppose the invaders plan to keep their troops well-fortified." Ellie raised her glass, leaned in and softened her voice, "Well then… Cheers to Gaston and his family! May his best wine be kept from the enemy."

Pierre took her hand, "Ellie, it is so good to see relax even just a little."

They shared a small portion of fresh fruit and real coffee. A waiter arrived with a silver tray carrying a note for Monsieur Martin. The note requested that Pierre meet two businessmen in the lobby. Pierre asked Ellie to take Anna to their room where they could bathe and Anna could play with her toys from the steamer trunk.

Ellie said, "First, I'm taking Anna on a walk. She needs fresh air and exercise. No one will suspect a woman walking with her little girl."

Mustering his composure, Pierre returned to the formal lobby. Three German soldiers were standing tall near a massive unlit stone fireplace. An older officer pointed his finger accusingly at the two younger soldiers. The senior man looked over at Pierre who quickly turned away to avoid eye contact.

Pierre approached the concierge about his gentlemen callers. He nodded at two men dressed in suits and seated in silk club chairs. Nearby Louis XV armchairs, plush sofas and oriental rugs were arranged in various conversation groupings. An assortment of strategically placed palms created a more intimate feeling in the spacious lobby.

Pierre made his way toward the men when he was shocked to hear a familiar booming voice, "Pierre Bessette is that *really* you?" All three soldiers turned toward the commotion.

A boisterous Marcel Girard stepped forward, blocking Pierre's way to the two seated gentlemen. Marcel owned the famed men's haberdashery, Chez Marcel, located three doors from Bijoux. Pierre never understood how such an uncouth man could own one of the most refined and luxurious men's boutiques in all of Paris.

"Well, hello Marcel," Pierre replied, steering Marcel further away from hearing range of the Nazis. Forcing a smile, Pierre quietly said, "What brings you here to Lyon?"

"I was going to ask *you* the same question," Marcel exclaimed. "My assistant told me that the police came to my shop this morning to ask if I knew where you were these days!" With a devilish smile, Marcel asked, "So, are you up to a little mischief, eh, mon ami?"

Pierre's gut wrenched, but he forced a chuckle. "It's a silly mix-up. It seems that a criminal shares my family name. Fortunately, it's been cleared up. I am here on business. And, you, Marcel, how is your business doing these days? What brings you to Lyon?"

With a wide grin, Marcel replied, finally in a hushed tone. "Well, between you and me, Pierre, I met a student from the university when I was on a business trip." He glanced around and gave Pierre a quintessentially French wink and a couple of pointed jabs to the ribs with his elbow. "I'm enjoying a little extracurricular activity, if you know what I mean."

"Of course." Pierre remarked as he forced a little smile and tried to get away. "Well, good to see you Marcel! I have a meeting myself to attend. What do you say we scrounge up a little lunch back in Paris, eh?"

"Au Revoir, my friend. Stay out of trouble!" yelled the clothier. The senior Nazi glared at Marcel and Pierre with an even greater degree of annoyance.

Marcel watched the jeweler approach two men who rose to greet Pierre. Marcel glanced at the three Nazis, then back to Pierre. Interrupting Marcel's train of thought, the desk clerk cordially asked Marcel, "Sir, do you have a reservation for a room? Will you be checking into the hotel?

Pierre wiped sweat from his brow as the two business-men rose to shake his hand. They wore suits cut to the popular continental style. They did not give their names.

"Take a deep breath, Pierre. No one appeared to have been watching your family coming off the train." Pierre stud-ied the mild-mannered middle-aged man with gray temples in the tan suit. He stood medium height and carried a notebook and newspaper. He directed Pierre to a comfortable leather chair. Pierre realized that the gentleman in the tan suit had purchased his newspaper at the tabac outside the train station. However, the trim younger man in the charcoal suit and carrying a briefcase did not appear familiar.

They reported that the baggage handler, one of their men, watched as he trailed behind Pierre, Ellie and Anna with a luggage cart. The younger man in the gray suit had walked behind all of them casually assessing the surroundings and the crowd. He grabbed the taxi behind Pierre's and followed the family to the hotel. He watched and waited while the Bessettes checked in and kept an eye on people coming and going. Meanwhile, tan suit had maintained surveillance looking for any unusual police activity outside the station. The two surveillance men met up at the hotel lobby while Pierre, Ellie and Anna finished lunch.

Pierre carefully watched the three Nazis finish their conversation. He flinched when the senior officer waited directly in line behind Marcel.

The younger man in the elegant gray suit kept talking. "I will remain at watch in the lobby area, especially with the unexpected arrival of the loud shopkeeper."

Pierre's shoulders tensed when he told them about Marcel's comments; "Soldiers came into Marcel's shop today asking about my whereabouts. I hope Marcel accepted my explanation." Pierre shrugged. "He seemed more preoccupied with his upcoming rendezvous with a young woman." The men nodded.

Checking his watch, tan suit got up to return to the train station to meet the arrival of Kristin and Michel's train from Dijon. He said, "We will use a similar procedure with the help of our baggage handler. I doubt that a young woman and your boy would attract attention."

"Pierre, stay in the hotel for the remainder of the evening. Do not be seen all together outside of your hotel rooms, especially now with the unanticipated arrival of your curious neighbor. His disturbing comments that the police in Paris are searching for you are troublesome."

In light of this new complication, the two watchers decided to alternate surveillance on their floor and in the lobby to watch for any unusual German police activity.

Gray suit leaned in. "Pierre, now that Marcel knows that you are staying at the hotel, our team must locate another hideout for you and your family. It will be difficult during this festival week; hotels have been booked far in advance."

Fortunately, as its name suggested, the Grand is a very large hotel with hundreds of rooms and they were booked under the Martin name. Kristin and Michel would be checked in under Kristin's surname, Larsson.

Pierre was given instructions as to the time and place to meet his contact tomorrow morning to receive their British travel documents. Arrangements would accelerate with Marcel's latest information out of Paris about a very active manhunt for Pierre.

Chapter 19

E arlier, on their morning call, Marcel's shop manager in Paris had delivered shocking news: "Marcel, I can hardly believe it? There is a manhunt and a reward for information about Pierre Bessette's whereabouts. The German police came to the shop inquiring about him!"

In the hotel lobby, Marcel noticed that Pierre kept glancing over at the Nazis; small beads of sweat had broken out on the jeweler's forehead.

Marcel's business was not doing well. What had happened to Parisians? Gentlemen were now content to patch the elbows of a cashmere sweater rather than to purchase new. Of course, tourists no longer flocked to his boutique for custom-made shirts, suits and exquisite French ties. Textiles were difficult to come by... especially silk needed for German parachutes.

Marcel knew it was the damn war. But Paris haberdasher Marcel Girard was desperately in love and desperate for money. In these tight financial times, how could he maintain his family in Paris, and his exciting romance and gourmet indulgences in Lyon? Marcel would need to think more about this new revelation concerning Pierre... and a reward.

Disheartened by the unexpected encounter with Marcel and his unwelcome news, Pierre hauled himself to the elevator cage. He joined Ellie and Anna who had returned from their walk. Ellie took comfort in that more than one agent would watch over them. Pierre did not divulge his chance meeting with Marcel or about the intense manhunt underway throughout France.

"Ellie, please don't unpack. Keep our belongings well organized and ready in case our flight is moved up."

Tomorrow, Sunday, Pierre would retrieve their new travel documents—British passports, International Red Cross identification and last-minute flight details. By Monday the family may be on their way to the monastery on Lake Annecy near the Swiss border. If so, they would hide with the Benedictine monks until their Red Cross plane arrived to fly them to England.

Pierre ran a deep bath and after a good, long soak, he changed into fresh clothes. Soon after, he heard a light rap. He opened the door cautiously and to his great joy Michel leapt into his arms. He pulled his son and Kirstin into the room. Gray suit followed them into the room and locked the door. Ellie was overcome with joy to see her son and cousin, hugging and kissing them both at the same time. Anna ran to join the welcoming party, crying "Michi!"

Michi gave Anna a little coin purse with a picture of a fluffy kitten on the front. He purchased the gift in the Dijon station. Michi and Kristin had had a long day but an uneventful voyage.

"Fortunately, there were no questions or interrogations. We strolled around the train station. We ate our meal in the dining car but spent the rest of the trip in our compartment, reading and napping. I walked slowly and was careful not to limp."

Pierre ordered room service, a novelty for his son and Kristin. To top it all off, the meal ended with a Bessette family tradition, a bowl of ice cream to share.

Chapter 20

On a perfect sunlit Sunday morning, Paris shopkeeper Marcel awoke a conflicted man. He glanced at the naked young woman sprawled next to him and felt stirrings of an erection. At forty-seven, Marcel had grown tired of his nagging wife, tired of the war, and tired of selling ties. Juliette was tall with spectacular legs, mahogany colored hair and wide doe-like brown eyes. He loved to watch men look at her when they entered a room and then regard Marcel with envy. His foolish infatuation with the beautiful young student who had expensive taste in clothes, jewelry, restaurants and travel would bankrupt him at this pace. But, when he was with her, Marcel felt so alive and young again. Marcel lit a cigarette and pondered his predicament.

Yesterday, after checking in to the Grand Hotel, Marcel left to meet Juliette on the steps of the university. Marcel saw her talking with a handsome, younger man. Taken aback, Marcel watched as Juliette touched the man's arm and the two shared a laugh. But, when she noticed Marcel, Juliette smiled and broke away from her friend with a kiss on each cheek. Yes, no doubt a classmate.

It had been a divine evening. They took a lover's stroll beside the rippling Rhône River and then meandered across the elegant Place Bellecoeur. Arm in arm, they wandered over to upscale rue Émile-Zola to peruse the shop windows. Juliette stopped to gaze at a lacy diamond necklace apparently the latest in fashion. "Marcel, look how it sparkles!" What else could he do? She squealed with delight and touched his hand as he placed the delicate necklace around her slender neck. She leaned toward him and blew a kiss into his ear. While, he fastened the clasp his mind drifted to the sexual delights in store for him that evening.

Following a candlelight dinner in a cozy corner of the romantic bouchon, Le Jura, the lovers strolled arm and arm past the illuminated Lyon Basilica de Notre-Dame.

In the Grand's tapestry-appointed cocktail lounge, the gentleman and the college student sipped brandy while listening to Parisienne starlet, Edith Piaf, sing of love and loss. Under the round marble and brass cocktail table, Juliette ran her fingers up along Marcel's inner thigh sending a thrill through his body.

As Marcel had been forced to do in the past, he had bribed the concierge for an extra key for his "niece." The manager temporarily left his post, and after a complicit nod, the concierge held the elevator cage door open for the unaccompanied young lady. After a respectable amount of time, Marcel returned to his room.

Juliette undressed slowly, exposing her exquisite body. Her fingertips touched Marcel so lightly that he could barely stand it—she teased and toyed with him. He had never before experienced the pleasures of lovemaking that this sensual woman had aroused in him.

On Sunday morning, a distant church bell rang. Sun streamed in through the shutters. Marcel knew he could not give up the beautiful woman lying next to him and the erotic pleasures of her company. But he could no longer afford her.

Yesterday, his shop manager had revealed, "Marcel, a significant reward has been offered for the capture of Pierre Bessette!"

But what if she was wrong and the Nazis did not want his neighbor after all? Marcel would be run out of Paris for such a mistake. Pierre was charming; his jewelry was popular with some German officers and the fashionable Parisian set. Ellie was practically a saint for her work to help the disadvantaged while his wife sat home devouring bread or chocolate when she could get her hands on them. Well... he had no choice. Out loud, Marcel said, *"It is my honorable duty after all to cooperate with the authorities! Whatever Pierre has done, or not done, it is not my problem."*

After taking his morning pleasure with Juliette, Marcel exhaled and said aloud. "Anyway, I never believed that story about a name mix-up." He extinguished his second cigarette and picked up the phone. Marcel asked to be connected to the local *gendarmerie*. Hopefully, he would collect his reward from the police. He had planned a delightful little adventure with his coed for early October in Milan.

Chapter 21

E arly morning, the cooped up, restless children jumped up and down on Kristin's bed. Pierre reminded the women, "Skip excursions together. Each of you can take a child, one at a time, for a short outing."

Meanwhile, Pierre would meet the courier who would hand over their British travel papers to escape across the border to Switzerland.

It had not been an easy task. The International Red Cross remained neutral, and it took several British channels to secure their passage including help from Margaret Middleton, Sir Michael's sister and also Pierre's cousin. Margaret had donated her London townhouse to the Red Cross for use during the war. She had married an American diplomat and now lived in New York.

Pierre whistled for the first time in weeks on this radiant morning, Lyon's Gothic and Renaissance architecture seemed awash in a bright lemony hue. The Sunday market bustled with villagers carrying baskets that they hoped to fill with a little fresh produce. Farmers brought some eggs, dairy products, garden vegetables, and a clandestine chicken or ham (which had not been seized by the occupiers) that would become a lucky family's dinner. Parents browsed, shopped and gossiped while the children played with marbles or ran along the streets chasing their hoops and playing tag. Soldiers appeared conspicuously absent from town.

After a brisk twenty-minute stroll, Pierre met up with gray suit who reported that Pierre had not been followed. On a remote side street, they stepped into a café that smelled of freshly baked bread and pastries. Each man ordered a rich, dark café espresso and a flaky croissant warm from the oven. An older couple sat at a table near the back; they held hands and paid little attention to the newcomers.

Pierre was never given the names of his handlers and he tried to learn more. Gray suit revealed a few sketchy bits of information. "We are university co-workers with English backgrounds and we speak several languages." Gray suit quietly divulged, "I was born in Bourg-en-Bresse, north of Lyon. I have family ties with British associates at the SOE. Monsieur, my partner and I have been well trained to fight with the underground. We are part of the Lyon resistance movement."

When war broke out Prime Minister Churchill called upon Sir Colin Kingsford, a high-ranking member of Churchill's Cabinet, to conduct a strategic underground war against Hitler's army to derail the Wehrmacht, German war movement. Then the SOE was born: Cagey men and women were trained in the dark world of espionage and sabotage. A recruit could kill with his bare hands or shoot from a slender pistol camouflaged as a pen or cigarette. Pierre's cousin, Sir Michael Middleton, had attended Oxford University with friend, Sir Colin Kingsford.

Waiter Jean-Paul brought a plate with what appeared to be the check. Rather, it was a note instructing gray suit to go to the toilette—no more than a stinking back room closet with a hole in the ground. Inside, an envelope was taped behind an antique mirror; its silver had flaked onto the floor. Gray suit placed the envelope inside his jacket. Back at the table, with the one couple now gone, the door locked, and a *fermé* sign placed in the window, gray suit handed over British passports and Red Cross identification for Pierre, Ellie and Anna. Gray suit placed the other set of documents for Kristin and Michel into his attaché. "I will hand these to Kristin back at the hotel," he said.

He instructed Pierre, "Listen, walk straight back to the Grand, pack and wait with your family. We have been working feverishly with London to get all of you out of Lyon as soon as possible. The arrival of shopkeeper Marcel Girard has complicated things. Pierre, unfortunately, a fervid search for you is well underway *all across France*."

When Pierre returned to his room, bedlam had ensued. Tan suit barked the orders. "Hurry, hurry!!" Anna was sobbing.

While Ellie feverously gathered the remainder of their belongings, she pleaded with the man, "Please do not scream at Anna. She is just a frightened little girl!"

Tan suit delivered dire news: "A police secretary, luckily one of our informants, took a call this morning from a gentleman staying at the hotel. We can guess who... The caller insisted that the fugitive, Pierre Bessette, was a guest at the hotel and the caller had asked for the reward. Alone at the time, the secretary quickly alerted Lyon resistance leaders. Fortunately, the police captain was away from the station. We caught a break. But have to move now *without delay!*"

The police secretary, Jeanne Charbonnier, was sympathetic; her best childhood friend had been Jewish; Hannah and her family had been extradited to the camps.

Jeanne Charbonnier had "attempted" to locate her captain. The secretary surmised that he had taken an hour or so of intimacy with his bride, as he did last Sunday. Some of the police officers, knowing that the captain was not at the station, also went home or stole a little time with a mistress on this laid-back Sunday morning.

First, Jeanne scurried over to the popular Café Fleur de Lyon. Continuing the subterfuge of looking for her boss, she ran over to the local patisserie where the captain was known to take his coffee and a sweet. But Jeanne had no choice when minutes after her return to the station, Captain Bettencourt arrived back at work. Jeanne relayed the urgent telephone call from the guest staying at the Grand. "Captain, I tried to locate you at the café and at the patisserie."

"Damn!" shouted Captain Philippe Bettencourt. Using his German telefunken radio, he alerted his police officers out on patrol.

"Head straight to the Grand Hotel and hold a Monsieur Pierre Bessette, who is under suspicion of aiding La Résistance. Detain Bessette and anyone traveling with him until I make the arrest. *Vite!* Go quickly, this is the highest priority." Bettencourt would love the prestige and privileges after helping the Germans capture a wanted criminal, especially in Lyon, the very heart of resistance.

Gray suit arrived about a minute behind Pierre and helped to rush their departure.

Tan suit implored the bellboys "Hurry up. As quickly as you can, deliver the trunk to the waiting taxi stand. Go!"

They hushed Anna and tried to comfort her as the family once again left the hotel separated from each other. Michi hugged his sister and promised they would be together again soon, saying, "Anna, you must not cry or attract attention."

The taxi driver dropped Michi and Kristin off at the train station. Last night, tan suit had reminded Kristin that the Germans had been looking for a female spy who had been injured while parachuting into France. They called her "the limping lady." Now, once again, Kristin repeated to herself, *"Don't limp, don't limp."*

Kristin and Michi entered the bustling station, paused a moment in the waiting room, then left the station through a side door. They veered just across the street to a car pulling up. Tan suit opened the doors ushering Kristin up front and Michi on the back bench. He said as he donned a cap, "Listen carefully, I am your vacation driver taking you on a tour, okay?" Kristin and Michel were driven to a farm "safe house" in the country town, Thurins.

The police secretary's sister and brother-in-law, Emma

and Thomas Fermier, owned the farm. (Emma's family and police secretary Jeanne were members of the Lyon résistance). Thomas and Emma farmed their plot and sold what little the Germans did not confiscate—eggs, butter, milk, seasonal produce. When able, they sold a French ham to a restaurant or split it among local families. Thomas had just returned from making a delivery to the Sunday market when Kristin and Michel arrived. Tan suit was given an egg and a slice of bacon, coveted luxuries during the war. He drove away, separating himself from the hunted fugitives.

Emma said, "Kristin and Michel, you will be hidden if the authorities come looking for you in the dark. Let me show you around and where you will sleep at night. You should be comfortable sleeping on mattresses in the stone cellar."

Michel and Kristin were taken down to a root cellar hidden behind a rustic pantry faced with a vintage armoire door. (The original hinges had been melted down for bullets during the French Revolution). The pantry contained home-canned fruits and vegetables, jams and jellies, a little flour, a bit of sugar and some cooking pots. However, the third shelf could be removed allowing a finger to unlock a bolt so the entire pantry door would swing open revealing a hidden staircase. A person could move his body sideways behind the pantry, and take stone steps down to the cool cellar. Kristin and Michi left their belongings in the hideaway.

For now, the fugitives could remain upstairs in the house. The stone farmhouse with light green shutters sat prettily at the top of a hill at the end of a long gravel driveway. It was easy to spot a car or hear one approaching as it drove up the road.

Michi stroked their cream and white Angora cat. Accustomed to city life, he said "Can I help milk the cows? I can feed the chickens and gather eggs!" Kristin offered to help Emma prepare meals.

Now that Paris Central knew Pierre, and most likely

his family were in Lyon, all attention would be directed toward routes into Switzerland, including Lyon's famous underground tunnels that centuries ago were used to transport delicate silk fabrics across town in rainy weather. The Résistance used the tunnels to help Jews escape. However, they would not chance using the underground passageways during an active manhunt when the fugitives could be trapped.

Pierre, Ellie and Anna also had followed quickly in a taxi to the train station. Toward the rear of the station, gray suit had waited casually beside his car and smoked his cigarette. Tilted to the side, a wide-brimmed light khaki straw fedora hat covered most of his clean-cut face. After the taxi dropped them off and pulled away, Pierre and gray suit loaded the steamer trunk and valise into the waiting car. As gray suit's car pulled away from the side of the station, soldiers and police stormed the front entrance.

A safe distance away, gray suit parked behind a black rental car. The Germans had confiscated most rental cars. However, they allowed the Sixt company to keep several cars on hand for the July Festivals. "Quick, Pierre, give me those passports that I handed over to you this morning." It would be disastrous for the French Martin family to be stopped with British passports in their possession. Gray suit said, "Take the car. Jean-Paul, the young man from the café, will deliver your trunk and passports to the monastery. The trunk will be hidden in a false compartment of his rickety brown truck, beneath a load of hay, farm supplies and implements slated for the monastery. Jean-Paul will spend the night in the monastery before returning to Lyon very early Monday and returning with wine and pear brandy for his café. Don't worry... This is his typical route."

Pierre nodded and hurried his family into the waiting getaway car, a Citroën sedan, placing Ellie's small valise in the trunk. Pierre's fingers dug into the steering wheel as he drove his wife and daughter away with a map to guide them. Once again, Pierre reminded Anna, "My pet, you are Annabelle Martin and today we are on our way to visit Lake Annecy. Do you understand?"

Anna was dressed in a cotton summer dress with lilac flowers. She clung to Bonbon and nodded importantly. "Oui, Papa!"

Meanwhile, gray suit drove his own car to a discreet meeting point away from central Lyon where he delivered the steamer trunk containing the British passports. As promised, gray suit and Jean-Paul hid the Bessette's trunk under a stack of hay on Jean-Paul's rusty truck.

Pierre drove to the Benedictine monastery located on Lake Annecy's stunning northeastern shore. The verdant countryside with canals and lakeside villages was spectacular and their journey so far proved uneventful. After the morning excitement, Anna slept curled up on the back seat.

Ellie and Pierre stopped in the small village of Saint Genix-sur-Guiers. They found a pleasant outdoor café on the church square and ordered some bread, a pâté sampler and a salade mixte. They took a walk about the sleepy town, and Anna played with two local children in the town park.

Thanks to her artist mother, Annette Lindstrom, Ellie knew the history of the 15th century monastery— the Abbaye where the monks lived and prayed. Decades after the monastery was built, a nearby inn had become popular with French artists, like Paul Cezanne, who painted the shimmering lake and its rich golden hills that had been sought for inspiration to study light, color and texture.

During wartime, the monks' simple tunics hid other than ritual. They sheltered escaping Jews; among them, orphaned children left behind by deceased or arrested parents. Jeanne Charbonnier, the police secretary, attended prayer retreats at the Abbaye. Today was not the first time that her son or husband had driven to the Abbaye with hidden cargo.

Chapter 22

The Bessettes arrived at the centuries-old Romanesque limestone Abbaye surrounded by apple and pear orchards. Pierre tapped the large metal door knocker shaped like a wreath of leaves. The ancient wooden monastery door, with its forged iron hinges, creaked open... Pierre, Ellie and Anna were quickly ushered into the hallowed halls.

They were welcomed by two monks and a mouth-watering aroma of freshly baked rosemary bread. The brothers cultivated grapes and made brandy, wine, cheese, brandy-dipped fruit cake and various breads that they sold to sustain their contemplative lifestyle.

The cloister, designed with pillars and arched colonnades, led to the main common room enriched with colorful inlaid clay floors, a kitchen, and dining hall containing a refractory table, a dormitory and an extensive wood-paneled library. A simple white chapter room was attached to a cozy chapel with dark stained fir beams, stained glass windows and a bell tower.

One of the monks requested, "Follow me. Jean-Paul and two younger monks have carried your trunk to the old wine cellar where you will sleep. It is located next to the buttery where our liquors are stored and where Jean-Paul will rest for the night." Jean-Paul would leave before dawn to return to Lyon with wine and brandy for his café.

Brother Baptiste informed Pierre, "Your rental car is being driven into town and left in the inn's parking lot. It will be retrieved with the first morning light and driven back to Lyon. There will be nothing to connect you with the monastery."

Several monks moved huge oak barrels aside and unlocked the wine cellar door. Famished and tired, Ellie and Pierre had one thing on their minds. They could not relax until they had located their gems and British passports.

Ellie removed a few bits of hay that had stuck in the hinges of their trunk. She and Pierre dug around the contents looking for their jewels, the assets needed to sustain their future. The seams appeared intact; they felt the gems. They located their British passports that had been tossed into the bottom of the trunk.

Ellie and Pierre now looked around their hideaway. The sparse quarters contained two single iron beds, a cot, a table with two chairs and an age-old painted dresser. On top of the worn dresser was a pitcher of fresh water, glasses, crisp white towels and a basin.

Reassured that their belongings were safe, the hungry family devoured a beef stew braised in red wine, some fresh baked bread, and cheese. Pierre and Ellie shared a carafe of the monk's fragrant Beaujolais. Exhausted, they fell into their beds. A cot had been set up for Anna. Unsure of their rustic sleeping quarters, she insisted on sleeping with her Maman and Bonbon. Before falling asleep, they prayed for Kristin and Michi's safety.

Ellie slept soundly and awoke to the sublime sound of carillon bells. She barely heard faint Gregorian chanting through stone walls; the monks were singing morning prayers. The Bessettes washed up, and soon after they were brought a tray with hot milk to blend with dark roasted coffee, fresh baked rolls with butter and jam, a cheese omelet to share, and a carafe of orange juice.

After breakfast, a young monk tapped gently again on their door, "Abbé Charles, our prefect, would like to welcome you. Please follow me upstairs."

Abbé Charles greeted the family with outstretched arms and soft brown eyes. He smelled of shaving soap and lime. He smiled, "Please forgive the brusque welcome yesterday. Anna, why don't you help Brother Gilbert pick some apples right outside our library window."

Once Anna left the room, Abbé Charles turned to Pierre with a concerned look.

"There is a wide and determined search for your family, and we could not take any chances but to hide you immediately. When Brother Gilbert brings Anna back, I prefer that you stay inside or right outside very near the monastery. Please do not wander away from our immediate vicinity."

At least in the daylight, from their high vantage point they could hear if cars were approaching. To help them pass the time, the prefect offered his library and any books they wanted to read.

Chapter 23

In Paris, Kapitanleutnant Stefan Schafer awoke to a gloomy Monday. His conscience allowed little choice but to speak with the generalmajor regarding his partner, Otto Heinrich. Overcast skies and a drizzle kept him company as he walked to Nazi military headquarters located in the elegant Hotel Meurice.

He was granted an appointment with Chief Personnel Officer Kapitain Fritz Adler. Schafer was ushered into Adler's private office, an elaborate room with silk draperies, and carved gold and cream columns. The red and black swastika hanging on the Kapitain's door seemed out of place against the historic elegance of the hotel. Adler was tall and lean with bird-like features.

Schafer stood erect. In a strong voice he thanked the CPO for seeing him on short notice. Kapitain Adler replied, "Of course. How can I help?"

Schafer cleared his throat. "Herr Kapitain, I have witnessed alarming behavior by my partner, Oberleutnant Otto Heinrich, that is harmful to females and which causes great acrimony toward the Third Reich." He described Otto Heinrich's escalating brutal attacks on innocent girls and women including the recent rape of the shop girl at Bijoux. Schafer further asserted, "Despite Heinrich's accomplishments, his behavior is a disgrace to the German army. It is likely that, in a rage, he will kill a defenseless female."

Kapitain Adler listened to Schafer's portrayal of Heinrich: his obsession with Ellie Bessette and his increasing animosity toward the jeweler without proof of any wrongdoing by the jeweler. Schafer did not mention Heinrich's thefts believing that the stolen art had become just too important to the Third Reich.

Kapitain Adler dismissed Stefan saying, "Thank you for bringing these incidents to my attention. I will speak with the generalmajor who can look into your concerns."

He bade Schafer a good day and ended the short meeting with a "Heil Hitler."

In a dreary rain, Stefan Schafer walked back to his room; he felt an ache in the pit of his stomach. Thunder rumbled in the distance. Stefan feared that Heinrich would not be stopped. Adler had not taken notes regarding dates, places or names.

Chapter 24

Ellie set up Anna's paints outside the library window situated in the rear of the monastery and out of view from the main drive.

Sitting on a large boulder, Anna painted the white Abbaye with the red apple orchard and a magnificent Alpine vista in the background. As the hour wore on, monks deviated from their chores to gather around and watch Anna recreate the breathtaking beauty surrounding their Abbaye. Round-faced Brother Bernard, a painter himself, gave Anna a few pointers. Soon the monk was learning from Anna how to capture the splendor. Brother Bernard told Pierre, "Monsieur, if I may say, Anna has the talent of a true artist." Anna smiled with delight at the compliment.

Large gray clouds darkened the sky. A thunderstorm forced Anna back into the library where she presented her painting to Brother Bernard, "This is a gift for you!" He accepted it graciously.

Abbé Charles called Pierre to the telephone. Through noisy crackle, Pierre heard his cousin's distant voice over the Brit's secure scrambler phone. "I have news."

Sir Michael told Pierre that a strong weather front that had cleared England earlier was now moving through France. "We expect thunderstorms to skirt southern France today." Pierre looked out the library window as thick raindrops beat against the leaded glass panes. Michael told Pierre that their "package" would arrive by "air mail" early tomorrow in better weather.

Geneva airport was about twenty-five miles from Annecy. Technically, all Swiss airports were closed for commercial travel during the war, but remained operational for supply movement and emergencies. Most POW relief supplies and food boxes were shipped to European ports and then transported to camps by rail. The International Red Cross utilized the airport to transport critical supplies and medical personnel.

The family's departure had been moved up. A plane had been scheduled to leave Geneva early tomorrow morning with medical supplies. Tomorrow, weather should be excellent and with the intense search for the family, the British SOE had wasted little time. All the necessary paperwork had been completed.

Pierre would be listed as Peter Ambrose, a high-ranking International Red Cross official traveling home to London with his wife Emma Ambrose and their children Annette and Blake. Pierre had suggested the name Ambrose, a comfortable name for Ellie and the children. Ellie's French grandmother's maiden name was d'Amboise. Peter Ambrose supposedly was returning to London after living in Switzerland and completing International Red Cross business.

Michael explained, "Listen. Kingsford's SOE group is spreading behind-the-scenes rumors. German intelligence in Lyon has intercepted our fake radio transmission stating that the Bessette family purchased train tickets in Dijon to Zurich via Bern. Therefore, Annecy and Lyon police are being diverted from Lyon and its surrounding areas. German and French police are concentrating their efforts on escape routes between Dijon and Bern, Switzerland. So, before daybreak you will be driven to a hidden rendezvous site adjacent to the Geneva airport."

Straining to hear Sir Michael's distant voice above static, Pierre shushed Anna who was chasing Brother Bernard around the library. She laughed hysterically when she tagged the chubby monk. Pierre winced at the stern look of admonition he received from his wife who took comfort watching Anna joyously run around the room.

Pierre thanked his cousin and said, "I understand and will follow." He replaced the receiver. Pierre felt relieved yet unsettled. As fugitives, soon they would attempt to leave French soil as enemies of the Nazi regime on their daunting journey to England where Pierre had lived during much of his youth. He looked up at Abbé Charles, and simply said, "God willing."

Pierre and his cousin, Michael Middleton, had spent their childhood summers together. Pierre's mother, Elizabeth, was the daughter of Captain Henry Middleton, Commander of the Royal Navy. Pierre's father, Alain Bessette, had been commissioned as the French under-attaché to England.

In 1902, France's Ambassador to England, old and growing tired of the long voyages across the Channel, sent the young Alain Bessette to a British state dinner in his place.

Alain was considered to be quite the skilled lady's man; he loved the chase. Who could be more alluring than a handsome Frenchman with a bottle of silky Rémy Martin cognac to warm a chilly evening? A stolen kiss brushing a creamy neck; Alain often would entice an eager young lady to his bed.

At the state reception, Commander Middleton had introduced his daughter, Elizabeth, to under-attaché Alain Bessette. Elizabeth was intelligent and charming. Alain courted Elizabeth who firmly resisted his advances.

With a smile, Elizabeth chided. "Monsieur Bessette, the warmth of cognac will not melt *my* heart."

But Alain fell head over heels and professed his love to this beautiful English rose; he simply refused to leave London without her.

Six months later, Elizabeth Middleton and Alain Bessette married at London's St. Paul Cathedral and made their home in Paris. Their son, Pierre was born ten months after the wedding.

Growing up, Pierre and his mother sailed to England every year to visit her family and Pierre's two cousins, Michael and Margaret Middleton whose maternal grandparents owned a sprawling country estate in Northamptonshire. Michael and Margaret were like siblings to Pierre, an only child. Every July and August, Pierre and his robust cousins swam, played lawn tennis, and rode horses at their Laurel Manor estate. Pierre learned to fish and to hunt with the hounds. His childhood summers were filled with the love of the outdoors in the lush English countryside.

Every other year, the Middletons traveled to Paris to spend a holiday with their French kin. They skied in picturesque Chamonix.

Michael Middleton adored France. "One day, Pierre, I will work in a government post like my father. Then, I will visit you and enjoy your French culture." Ironically, now Pierre's knighted cousin, a distinguished member of the English war department, would establish the way *out* of France for Pierre and his family.

During one summer, tragedy struck when Pierre was eleven years old. His mother, Elizabeth, died of pneumonia. Overnight, Pierre's world fell apart. Over the course of a year, his father Alain nearly drank himself to death. Pierre had been sent to stay with his Middleton grandparents in London where he attended the prestigious St. Stephen's lower school with his cousin Michael.

Eventually, a grief-stricken Alain woke from his stupor to realize that young Pierre needed his father. Equally important, Alain needed his son. Alain brought Pierre home to Paris. They attended Temple together. Father and son traveled far and wide during Alain's Cultural Affairs post. He educated

Pierre about art, music, fine food and wine.

Alain wisely kept the vacation ritual with Elizabeth's family. He sent Pierre to visit his English grandparents and cousins every summer for the remainder of Pierre's youth. Many years later, leaving a restaurant after dining with friends, Attaché Alain Bessette had been hit by a car and died of his injuries.

Now, Pierre's cousin and best friend, Sir Michael Middleton, would help Pierre and his young family to escape and evade imprisonment in a concentration camp or possible death at the hands of the Nazis.

Chapter 25

Before dawn, and even before farm life stirred, Michi hugged Madame Fermier, who kissed the top of his blond head and whispered, "Safe travels my pet." Kristin exchanged a traditional kiss on each cheek with the kind couple.

In the farm's wobbly field truck, laden with garden implements and supplies for the monks, Kristin and Michel were covered with blankets and hay and driven by Monsieur Fermier to rejoin their family at the monastery.

Although grateful to be reunited, the fugitive family was considerably worn down by the persistent manhunt. Following a quick breakfast of bread with homemade raspberry jam, hard-boiled eggs, thin ham slices, coffee and juice, the Bessettes expressed their deepest gratitude to Abbé Charles and his monks. With a hug, Ellie said, "Thank you for the kindness you have shown us, Abbé. You have rekindled our faith in the goodness of people. The brothers have given us the courage we need."

The prefect returned Ellie's embrace, and wished them all, "Godspeed." Brother Gilbert handed Ellie a basket packed with cheese, apples, pears and dates, warm bread and chilled butter to sustain them on the last leg of their journey. Brother Bernard presented Anna with a small prayer book. With a bear hug, picking her up off her feet, and prompting peals of giggles from Anna, he said "I will miss you, little one!"

Tan suit drove Kristin and Michi on the short drive to

the Geneva airstrip. At this early hour the roads were empty and eerily quiet. Thanks to the SOE's trickery, the Lyon police had been diverted toward the Swiss border near Dijon about two hours north. The Annecy police had also joined the fictitious manhunt for Pierre Bessette who they believed was en route to Bern, Switzerland.

With night still hanging in the air, Michi snuggled against Kristin to stay warm and drifted off to sleep. When they reached the outskirts of the airport, they veered from the main road and drove slowly down a hidden dusty gravel road into a thicket.

Gray suit had followed shortly behind with Pierre, Ellie and Anna after he received a radio call from tan suit signaling the "all clear." If the Bessettes were stopped, their new International Red Cross papers were their only security.

The local resistance had cleared tangled brush and bushes to create a secret lane leading to a holding space on the edge of the airport. Soon they expected to board the plane bound for England. Since she was hesitant to use aircraft lavatories, Anna had to be persuaded to go with her mother to relieve herself in the bushes. Michi was thrilled with this unrefined task.

With deep emotion, quietly, they said goodbye to the two men who had risked their own lives to get the family to safety. Anna tiptoed to hug tan suit while Bonbon dangled by his ear from her other arm. Anna insisted on continuing to do her part by holding tightly onto her teddy bear. Ellie choked back tears, "Thank you from the bottom of my heart," she said, embracing gray suit and giving him a formal kiss on each cheek, then turning to thank tan suit as well.

From the front seat of a dark green Peugeot hidden behind dense brush, an inquisitive pair of blue eyes swept the airport, searching for signs of activity; patiently he watched and waited.

Soon, the first rays of morning sun illuminated the bright red cross painted on the tail of a DC-3 when the plane emerged from a hangar. The plane was being fueled and readied for departure. Despite the chilly morning, Pierre's forehead glistened with sweat. His heart rate began to rise; this was the moment they had planned for so many months. From the Peugeot, he watched their steamer trunk be carried onto the plane's cargo hold, surrounded and covered by mailbags and boxes of medicine and supplies bound for POWs. Finally, a few stretchers were stacked alongside seats usually filled with International Red Cross nurses and personnel.

Meanwhile, the children waited with Kristin and tan suit. Now fully awake, the children wrestled with each other. Both cars were ready to drive off if trouble arose. The adults held their breaths.

In the aircraft, the captain and first officer read their checklist. Captain Reynolds commanded the co-pilot, from the left seat. "It's time. Let's go, old chap!"

"Straight away, sir." The co-pilot got up from his seat and exited the aircraft. He stood on the tarmac in front of the plane where the captain could see him. The co-pilot checked to make certain the area around the ramp and the propellers was clear. Using his hand, he signaled the captain. He raised his left hand with two fingers extended, and with a turning motion of his right hand signaled that the area was clear to "start the engine." Pierre lined his family up. After what seemed like an eternity to Pierre, the propeller rotated and the engine rumbled to power.

The start of the right engine was the family's cue to run to the plane. Taking one last look around, Pierre shouted, "Let's go now!" Following Pierre, Anna, Ellie, Michi and then Kristin ran from their cover to the plane's passenger door.

Pierre helped them jump on board through the rear

door of the "tail dragger" as the co-pilot raised one finger of his left hand and rotated his right hand to signal the captain to start the left engine; then he ran to the passenger door.

The co-pilot followed the family onto the plane. Closing the door, he spotted Anna's teddy bear lying on the tarmac. With both engines running, he debated whether he should stop for a child's scruffy old toy and decided to close the aircraft door. He turned to make his way to his seat. In a split second, he turned, opened the door, jumped down and scooped up Bonbon. He locked the cabin door just as Captain Reynolds started toward the runway. While the plane taxied into position, the co-pilot grabbed his cockpit seat and buckled up for take-off.

The plane lifted off the runway. Watching it climb, the two suits smiled and shook hands. In the air, the plane tilted into a gentle "wing wave" as a salute to the two brave resistance fighters below. The men burned the Martin passports and buried the ashes.

Tan suit drove carefully down the narrow path that had been cut into the woods to the main road. Then gray suit eased his green Peugeot out of the hidden bower.

Stopping on the main road, gray suit raised the hood of his car, appearing to have engine trouble if a stray police car happened by. Laboriously, the men rolled one huge boulder in front of the opening to the path and placed a few big rocks randomly to better obscure the entrance. They rearranged large, tangled bushes and tree branches that had been haphazardly strewn along the side of the road and carefully placed them back in front of the entrance to their carved-out path.

Satisfied that their airport hiding place had been well concealed, a relieved tan suit drove away. Elegant gray suit, now with smudges of dirt on his pants and with a broad smile on his face, drove back through Annecy and to his home near Lyon.

Chapter 26

Pierre hunched his shoulders; he whipped his head back and forth from one side to the other scanning the airspace. Even though the fuselage of the International Red Cross plane was painted "Sisters of Mercy" in bold crimson red, planes had been shot down by the Luftwaffe if Germans even suspected that spies or British officers were on board. Ellie's eyes were tightly shut. Pierre squeezed her cold hand. They understood the ultimate price of fleeing France in the midst of war with Germany.

The plane cruised northwest, and Pierre ventured a look down. He could not help but smile at the thought of the German and French police swarming the Dijon train station below while searching for him and his family. When they flew over Paris, glimpsing the Eiffel Tower through broken clouds, Pierre nudged Ellie. They looked at each other with a tinge of sadness but also hope for the future. Ellie squeezed Pierre's hand.

After recent thunderstorms, the flight was smooth with just a few ripples. In the back seats, Michi and Anna each demanded to be in charge of the monks' picnic basket. Kristin took over and unpacked the food. The children giggled as they tried to drink from a thermos during an occasional bounce.

Finally, Captain Reynolds announced that they had crossed the English Channel at Southampton. The plane was bearing northwest toward Bristol airport. Pierre looked at Ellie who smiled. After years of living in fear every day, she felt that her family was nearly safe… Pierre pulled her into his arms.

∞∞∞

On the ground, British operative Sir Michael Middleton watched the Red Cross plane bounce onto the grass runway. He shifted from leg to leg waiting for his French family to disembark. Michi and Anna ran toward their gregarious, tall and lanky "uncle" and danced around him. He ruffled Michi's hair. Ellie beamed as cousins Pierre and Michael embraced. Pierre said, "Michael, I am so relieved. I feel that I am walking on air!"

Michael hugged Pierre again, "Welcome cousin! Welcome to Great Britain, at last!" Turning to embrace Ellie, he told her, "Beatrice and I are delighted that you are all here safe and sound. Charles is excited to see Michi and Anna. Welcome, Kristin, it is good to have you with us. Come! Let's load up the cars, shall we? I know you are weary, so let's get you on the road to your new home. We will have a rest and a small bite at a traveler's stop along the way." Pierre and Ellie profusely thanked their pilots. Ellie placed Bonbon in her valise.

Pierre, Michael and an aide loaded the cars with the trunk and two valises. Pierre and Ellie rode to London with Michael. Following closely behind, Kristin and the children rode to the Middleton's townhouse with an aide.

Sir Michael's wife, Lady Beatrice, had inherited a spacious townhome located in London's Belgravia district where they lived with their son Charles, about six months younger than his cousin, Michi.

Ellie closed her eyes and smiled at the thought of spending the remainder of the war without constant tension. Despite the ensuing repercussions of war on everyday life in Britain, she felt relief and even hope.

Ellie, Pierre and the children had last visited London in 1938. Now, just four years later, they were shocked at the devastation. Pristine villages were battered by bombings that covered England with a gritty patina. In London and the larger cities, some factories and buildings were in ruins, with crumbling walls and debris everywhere. The scale of bombing destruction was difficult to comprehend. The children could not believe their eyes when they saw half a building standing while the other half had become a pile of rubble. Cars were conspicuously absent because petrol was in dire supply.

Chapter 27

Beatrice welcomed the Bessettes with open arms. She had beautiful English skin, a sweet face and a plump figure.

In Paris, the Bessette's home was charming and well appointed. But it could not compare to the Middleton's grand estate perfectly situated across from a manicured park and gardens. Belgravia was the most distinctive district in London. Michael would walk to 64 Baker Street where the Special Operations Executive (SOE) spy team, known locally as the "Baker Street Irregulars," had set up shop.

Designed by renowned architect, George Basevi, Jr., the Middleton home on Belgrave Square was a white stucco mansion with a mansard roof, dormer windows and pillars. Cut stone steps led to a gracious portico entrance enhanced by a wrought iron railing.

An elegant white and emerald green Carrara marble entrance hall contained an impressive scrolled iron staircase. A 19th-century English flamed-mahogany pedestal table graced the entry hall. A decorative caged lift stood ready to deliver its occupants to the upper floors.

On the ground floor, a gracious parlor designed for afternoon tea, overlooked the gardens, as well as a wood-paneled library with a marble fireplace where the men would enjoy brandy, cigars and poker. In the wainscoted dining room, a rich mahogany George III dining table would seat thirty guests. A spacious kitchen and an adjacent butler's pantry were tucked off the dining room. A ballroom on the second floor included a salon and game room for bridge, mahjong or chess and a children's play room.

On the third floor, Pierre and Ellie were given the largest guest suite. Michi roomed with his cousin Charles, and Anna was given a smaller guest room of her own. The housekeeper placed Kristin in a spare room in the maid's quarters. However, Ellie immediately asked to have Kristin moved to the guest room next to Anna's. Another guest suite remained vacant.

Like her husband, Sir Michael, Beatrice had come from wealth. Beatrice was given the title "Lady." However, she preferred to be called Beatrice or Bea, a trait that Ellie liked about her hostess. Bea was down to earth, and she embraced the changing customs of the British aristocracy. She did not expect to be waited on day and night by servants.

When Ellie saw that a bomb had destroyed one of the Belgravia mansions, she realized the foolishness of her initial unease living in the richness of such surroundings. If a bomb had hit the Middleton's home, they would not have a place to live and worse, the Middletons could have lost their lives. Ellie accepted their good fortune. She told Pierre, "Every day I thank God for our safety and your family's generosity."

Throughout their marriage, Ellie and Pierre had visited London on numerous summer trips. For two weeks they would enjoy the London theaters, parks and museums. Typically, the Middletons and Bessettes would caravan with a cook and housekeeper to Laurel Manor, their summer estate in Northamptonshire. There, the children enjoyed an outdoors country vacation much as Pierre experienced growing up with his cousins, Michael and Margaret. Now Laurel Manor was off limits. The estate had become a hospital and rehabilitation ward for wounded soldiers and burn victims. Petrol was in short supply and country drives were out of the question.

The children played in nearby London parks. Though food was scarce, on occasion they were treated to a "petit picnic" made from whatever food could be scrounged up and enjoyed under the Peter Pan statue in Kensington Park. The Serpentine Lake in Hyde Park became a favorite for Michi who took his toy boat, given by his late Grand-mère Annette Lindstrom, and sailed it around the lake.

Michi joined his cousin, Charles, and other neighborhood chums to play rugby and cricket. Michi was athletic and loved the games. And, because the national leagues were on hold due to the war, the boys pretended they were the pros. Michi made certain that Anna was not left out of the fun. She got into the action when Michi told the other boys, "Even a girl will give our team enough players." Thinking it over, the neighborhood boys decided it would be okay for Anna to play and even-out their teams.

Chapter 28

The first week in August, London was awash in summer. The Bessettes basked in the pleasant, sunny days and the warm glow of not looking over their shoulders or listening for heavy footsteps deep into the night.

Pierre was asked to pay a visit to the headquarters of the Free French in London at Carlton Gardens. The written invitation stated that the Forces Francaises Libres (FFL), France's government in exile, was anxious to meet with the jeweler regarding his knowledge of French citizens living under the tyranny of occupation.

To Pierre's surprise, Ambassador Francois Charles-Roux stood beside the imposing figure of the leader of the FFL Résistance, General Charles de Gaulle. Ellie and the children, along with Kristen and the Middletons beamed as General de Gaulle ceremoniously placed the *Croix de Guerre,* French military Medal of Honor, around Pierre's neck. "Pierre Bessette, with deepest gratitude, I honor you with France's medal of valor for your bravery, dedication and immense contributions to La Résistance in Paris."

Nazi Otto Heinrich had been correct in his suspicions of Pierre's role in the resistance. After de Gaulle had escaped to London with barely any funds, the prominent jeweler was contacted by the Free French. Pierre had recalled de Gaulle's emphatic radio plea from London to his fellow countrymen: *"The flame of La Résistance must not and shall not die."* Pierre hated the Nazis—invaders who had brutally overrun his country and who sought to destroy their heritage. He would do whatever he could to thwart the enemy.

At first, Pierre simply donated money to resistance causes. But then, the jeweler altered a few of his designs by replacing some authentic gems with beautiful but worthless lab-produced stones. Pierre took pleasure in selling the fake jewelry to Nazi officers and collaborators like Monsieur Beaufort, a despicable black marketer who preyed on Jewish families. The duped men never suspected that a bracelet purchased for a wife, or mistress, contained a faux gem or two. With the Fuhrer's own money, Pierre aided the fledgling resistance.

Bijoux had been a perfect set-up for clandestine chats. After a sale, Pierre would invite a loose-tongued collaborator into his back office. Pierre was charming, a smooth talker and a very good listener—a formidable informant. Men felt noteworthy in the esteemed jeweler's presence. Two or three cognacs later, a German sympathizer, or even a Nazi, might regale Pierre with a snippet regarding an up-coming military plan. Pierre had been given a radio to transmit crucial information that could become useful. Then, he became more involved.

Often on Fridays after work, Pierre would be handed a military secret from florist Madame Bonheur. Marie Bonheur's husband, Bernard, was a master pastry chef who had baked for French President Lebrun at the Élysée Palace. When French government leaders ran away, the German commander, Dietrich von Choltitz, ordered Bernard to remain in his job. Bernard kept his eyes and ears open to German business. Prior to the war, sometimes the baker would send a petit sweetheart box of his delectable pastries to his wife. During the Occupation, a discrete love note, tucked under layers of fine lace doilies, would become a purloined military secret. Mme. Bonheur would gift the box of sweets to Pierre Bessette (after taking a little sample). Like poetry in motion, German war plans flowed from the baker to the florist, to the jeweler and finally to fellow compatriots at the Hotel Celtic bar where Pierre discretely handed over the confidential information to their waiter, Jacques.

Madame Bonheur would deliver her weekly flower arrangement to Bijoux every Monday. Sometimes her invoice included crucial information that Pierre radioed to resistance leaders.

Bookseller Charles Blum had not been so innocent either. Before the Germans closed him down, his book shop had become a safe haven for secret nighttime meetings.

The Bessette's private funds and Pierre's growing network of intelligence had been responsible for several major disruptions that thwarted German operations: a supply train filled with German guns had been derailed and the guns confiscated, a critical power station had been blown up which halted electric railways for miles. Pierre felt euphoric by the challenge. He had told Ellie, "As a Jew, I feel a strong resolve to help defeat the tyrants."

To top it off, the famous *Maquis Résistance* group had been given critical timing information that allowed a bridge in the Périgord region to be blown up in order to stop German advancement. However, Pierre was disheartened and Ellie was sickened when they learned that innocent citizens had been rounded up and executed in retaliation for the destroyed bridge.

Most of the Bessettes' wealthy friends had abandoned Paris before the Germans invaded France. When Antoine suggested they leave for the south of France, Pierre stalled; he never believed the Germans would make it as far as Paris. Once the shock wore off, Pierre found himself in a strategic position. The jeweler enjoyed phenomenal business success bestowed mainly by the Americans. His fortune and contacts had allowed Pierre and Ellie to aid not only the resistance but everyday Parisians who suffered terribly from lack of food or housing during the German Occupation.

Ellie felt proud; Pierre was a patriot and a man of conviction who, she had known, would be very, very good at thwarting German endeavors. Pierre had Ellie's blessing, and she yearned to help the struggling families especially of the men who had been sent to war.

Pierre turned to his wife, "But this honor belongs to you Ellie. I love you and admire you more than you can ever know. We would not have made it out alive if not for your courage. Nor would we have been able to help so many of our fellow countrymen."

Pierre then placed the medal around his wife's neck and kissed her cheek. General de Gaulle beamed and the family clapped at his surprising revelations: Ellie had taken it upon herself to get urgent messages to Pierre from suspected resistance members who could not be seen near Bijoux like their neighbor, operative Gilbert Dupont. At times, a map, a train route or a last-minute change in plans would be handed off to the jeweler's wife. Ellie would walk to Bijoux with the covert plans; she carried notes in her false handbag or a market bag. Pierre would then radio the urgent message to resistance leaders. The walks terrified Ellie when German soldiers searched her belongings. Too often, Nazis would stroke her hair or fondle her. For her country, Ellie had bravely endured their liberties and salacious comments.

Not only had Ellie scoured Paris for extra rations for hungry families; she found secret rooms and basements for Jews hiding from the Nazis. As she and her mother were forced to hide from a hostile landlord and the police, Ellie helped vulnerable Parisians escape the camps or death. She begged Monsieur Blum to allow a young family and their little boy to live in his upstairs apartment. Around the city, Ellie's "resources" hid resistance members who had fallen into German crosshairs.

Knowing that Pierre's boutique was being watched had unnerved Ellie. She pushed herself into the risky venture to procure their fake passports. Then, there came a point when

Pierre and Ellie's clandestine activities had compounded her fear for her own children's safety.

"Ellie, in my fervor to fight for France, I had turned a blind eye to the chilling danger we faced. I never dreamed until it was almost too late—when Jewish friends in our neighborhood began to disappear—that we would be forced to run for our lives and to flee our homeland overnight. Ultimately, you knew when it was essential that we pack it up and get out. And, it was your bravery that gave us our freedom, in the nick of time."

General de Gaulle invited the Bessettes and Middletons, "Please be my guests for a well-deserved celebratory luncheon at the Connaught Grill. Food will be sparse but nonetheless, we will dig around the cellar for a decent bottle of French champagne to celebrate these two courageous resistance fighters."

The following day, Pierre met, and with all measure of humility, thanked the British SOE who had executed his family's escape. Pierre stood, "My friends, I am deeply grateful and can never thank you enough for your expertise in coordinating my family's escape. Beyond a doubt, my capture was imminent and we got out just in time. Allow me to help the SOE in any way I can to end this cruel war." The men and women of 64 Baker Street clapped and welcomed Pierre and his family to London.

England was fighting at every level to remain free. In 1940, Prime Minister Winston Churchill established the SOE, the precursor to today's MI6, Britain's secret intelligence service, to sabotage the German army from behind enemy lines by blowing up bridges, trains and factories. "Churchill's Secret Army" developed tactics to go underground and "set Europe ablaze" in order to weaken Hitler's army. Pierre would work from Baker Street to advise the spy team as they increased their resistance work throughout France and Europe. General de Gaulle's loss in Paris became Churchill's gain in London.

It began with a rag-tag group of field agents from all walks of life—butchers, bakers, journalists, clerks, electricians, students, and some brave women and foreign nationals like the Poles. After intense training at British country houses, the volunteers became more sophisticated at employing spy craft that included disguises, poison pens, plaster props such as a dead bird designed to hide munitions.

Senior officials organized the SOE spy school headquarters on Baker Street. At times, they plotted the resistance strategies in classy clubs like Boodles on St. James Street. Here, the original James Bonds were born! Writers Roald Dahl, Ian Fleming and others became part of a cozy undercover spy network that Churchill had set up squarely in Washington, D.C. With their good looks and wit, these bright, charming spies infiltrated the highest political and social circles. From cocktail parties to the bedrooms, they cajoled senators and powerful American women into supporting the British war effort.

By the time the Bessettes escaped to London, nightly air raids and Blitzkrieg bombings had ceased. Children evacuated to the country for safe-keeping during the bombings had returned home to their parents. Laurel Manor country estate was one such refuge for London's children before becoming a surgical recovery ward. Young Princess Elizabeth and her sister, Margaret, broadcast encouraging messages to Britain's children.

Charles and the Bessette children were allowed to play outside in the parks, but were sternly instructed not to enter any closed-up houses or bombed-out buildings which could be unstable and dangerous. By the best of luck, their immediate neighborhood had been spared the worst of the bombings.

Life in war-torn London was filled with daily ups and downs. Fire drills were common and families were encouraged to practice. Every household was instructed by the fire brigade how to pump water from buckets to protect their house. With newfound strength from their developing bodies, Charles and Michi became experts with the hand pumps. The boys extricated iron garden railings from homes and turned them in as scrap metal for war armaments.

Everyday items like nylon stockings, cigarettes and petrol had long been rationed. German U-boats in the Atlantic torpedoed American ships that were laden with supplies, creating extreme food shortages and a major problem across Great Britain. Food scarcity went from painful to severe. Rationing forced everyone to share in the restrictions. Meat and lard were difficult to live without.

Thankfully, fish seemed to be plentiful and the Middleton's cook was adept at frying, poaching and grilling fish. Sweets were allowed just once a month. Kristin adapted her own baking skills. If they had *any* flour, for a special celebration, she would bake a small fruit tart latticing it with dough scraps. The Bessettes craved French au gratin dishes; they appreciated the rare occasion when they had potatoes or cheese at all with their meals. Kristin taught Cook how to enrich their meals with a tiny amount of mouth-watering sauces like Hollandaise and Béarnaise with just a smidge of butter, a pinch of flour and an egg. Eggs of course were rationed, but powdered eggs imported from America were a useful though distasteful substitute.

When Michael rode out to check on Laurel Manor, he asked the workers at his summer estate-turned hospital, "Hide a fresh egg or two for me, if you can." To everyone's delight, he occasionally came home beaming his mischievous grin and holding up a small bag of flour or sugar that had somehow "fallen off a lorry," or he gave Cook eggs stolen from the chickens at his Laurel Manor estate. Though they had lost weight, everyone living in the Middleton household felt luckier than most.

Chapter 29

E llie felt grateful that her family was safe and protected. Soon after they settled in London, she had asked Pierre, "Please contact Maison Entreposage to make certain that our belongings have been safely packed and our furnishings stored." She was most concerned about protecting her mother's artwork.

Ellie's mother, Annette Lindstrom, had been the youngest of four children born to a poor Swedish farmer and his wife. Annette hid from her responsibilities in order to sketch landscapes and farm life. Every day when she was a child, it was the same story. "Annette, where are you? Come out now and take care of your chores!" In 1903, Annette won an art scholarship to the Salon de Paris.

Barely twenty years old, Annette was enthralled with Paris—the lavish architecture, wrought iron balconies and mansard roofs. Chestnut trees stood tall alongside wide boulevards; flowers overflowed their window boxes—it all contrasted with the simplicity of Sweden.

At the prestigious art Salon de Paris, Annette befriended American artist, Mary Cassatt, who took the young woman under her wing. At first, Mary protected Annette. "You are simply too young to mix with the older art crowd. Give yourself a year or two..." But iron-willed, Annette begged to go with the older artists to glamorous nightclubs and the more risqué cabarets.

"Nettie," as her friends called the exuberant young Swedish painter, loved the Bohemian lifestyle practiced in Montmartre cabarets, the Folies-Bergère and a hidden opium den. Annette was drawn to the new Impressionist art crowd. She posed nude for the artists from the *Societe Anonyme*. Affairs of the heart were not uncommon. In 1905 she had become pregnant by a young American painter passing through Paris.

Annette had little choice but to return to the Lindstrom family farm in Halmstad where her pregnancy was kept quiet. Her daughter, Elsa, nicknamed Ellie, was born in 1906. Life on the farm was dull, and Annette longed for her free-spirited Parisian days.

With her toddler in tow, Annette found a bare room to rent in Paris. The room was dreary and drafty in winter. Mother and daughter often were cold and hungry living on pennies and later, war rations.

One time, Ellie's mother did not budget rent money. The evicted artist and her little girl had been smuggled into a cabaret and allowed to stow away in the dressing room where the heat was turned off at night. Annette had soothed her crying daughter, holding her close for warmth, "It will be okay, my pet." But Ellie shivered and shook with fear. Strange men who reeked of cheap liquor touched the little girl's golden hair. Stale cigarette smoke stunk up the moth-eaten furniture and tattered curtains. The misery of eviction became a defining moment in little Ellie's life. Nightmares interrupted her sleep

When Nettie finally found an affordable apartment on *Montmartre*, the youngster learned to keep a calendar to remind her mother when rent was due so they would never be evicted again. Ellie had never forgotten the fear of not knowing where they would live during those dreadful, cold nights without their own bed and with rarely enough to eat.

Ellie knew that when her Maman sang likely a painting had sold. Life would feel more comfortable with her tummy full, a least for a while. As early as she could remember, Ellie relished summer when the warm sun washed over her skin...

Annette's American friend, Mary Cassatt, had returned to Paris from overseas. Annette still struggled to care for Ellie while trying to earn a living. "Aunt" Mary visited, read to the little girl and taught Ellie American songs. She brought some food for their pantry.

Annette's impressionistic paintings were better than sentimental "pot-boilers," painted merely to sell to tourists. But her work never captured the awards, acclaim and broad appeal that some Impressionists enjoyed. Annette always believed her paintings would catch on. Privately, Mary told people, "Annette may always be considered an unlucky "petite-maître" (little master) and never achieve the acclaim of a true Impressionist."

Eventually, Annette confessed, "Mary, as hard as I try, I may never be able to support Ellie properly. I am tired of seeing my sweet girl live with so little." Annette lamented that she was "desperate to find some way to better care for my daughter, whatever I have to do..."

Mary took pity on Annette and her daughter. She invited them to live with her so that Annette could save for future living expenses. Although Mary had to give up painting due to failing eyesight and arthritis, the American's comfortable home had become a congenial gathering place for aspiring artists and for her more established friends, Degas, Monet and Pissarro.

When Oscar-Claude Monet came to Paris, he brought an occasional toy and sweets for Ellie who delighted at these small pleasures. Life became easier. Memories of those secure years helped to blur the terrifying times of Ellie's earliest childhood—shabby cold apartments, and gnawing stomach pain compounded by the First World War that raged in 1914.

Ellie Lindstrom attended the Sorbonne on a scholarship to study early education. In 1925, she met an ambitious, charming young man studying business and economics.

Pierre Bessette was smitten with the lovely Swedish woman with the sweet disposition and kind heart.

The young couple toured the museums and picnicked along the verdant banks of the Seine surrounded by stunning views of Paris. They strolled the Left Bank hand in hand and scoured "Chouchou's" book shop for literary finds. Pierre shared his dream of opening his own jewelry boutique. He had been dazzled by the crown jewels from the houses of the Habsburgs, Bavaria and United Kingdom while traveling abroad with his father. The young Pierre Bessette was guided by the memories of his glamorous English grandmother who wore estate jewelry at formal dinners.

Pierre proposed to Mademoiselle Elsa Lindstrom at the restaurant, Cristal, with its glittering chandeliers and a view of La Tour Eiffel. Pierre cleared his throat, "Ellie, I love you dearly. I hope to spend my life with you. Please be my wife." Ellie said yes and Pierre placed a solitaire diamond engagement ring on her slender finger. Many women preferred an engagement ring designed in the Victorian art deco filigree setting, a diamond stone with sapphire or ruby baguettes. But Pierre knew Ellie would be more comfortable with simplicity.

Annette wept tears of happiness at the news and hugged her daughter. "I am so thankful. You will have real security in life with Pierre."

Ellie Lindstrom and Pierre Bessette married at the *église* Madeleine. Ellie's "Uncle" Oscar-Claude Monet had walked the beautiful bride down the aisle. As a wedding gift, he gave Ellie one of her favorite childhood paintings from his *Morning on the Seine* series.

Claude Monet passed away little more than four months after the wedding. Several of Monet's sketches and a few cast-off etchings from Nettie's other friend, Pablo Picasso, also hung in Pierre and Ellie's salon. But it was the softness of Monet's cool blue and green painting with the dawn mist shrouding the river, *Morning on the Seine,* hanging on the wall of their living room that gave Ellie peace. Monet's wedding gift instilled warm-hearted memories living with "Aunt" Mary; but most important, the wondrous day when she married the love of her life, Pierre Bessette. After her marriage, Ellie felt safe and protected for the first time.

In 1930, Ellie gave birth to their son, Michel Claude, (Michi) named for Cousin Michael Middleton and Claude Monet. Their daughter, Annika Elizabeth, (Anna) named for both grandmothers, was born in 1934.

Ellie's mother, Annette Lindstrom had lived with Ellie and Pierre. She spent hours taking grandson Michi to the park to sail toy boats in the Luxembourg Gardens, and to the Paris art museums. She proudly showed him paintings by her friends and told him stories about the "good old days." Michi dearly loved his Grandmother "Nettie," and over and over begged his sweet Mémère, (Gram) "Tell me again the stories of life on your farm in Sweden." The children implored her to describe the gaiety of Paris when she was a young artist. Annette taught little Anna how to paint, and together they painted the park near their home.

The children's beloved Mémère Annette had passed away in her sleep in 1939 after a bout with a nasty flu that had led to pneumonia. It had broken Ellie's heart to flee while forced to leave behind *Morning on the Seine* and above all, her mother's own *Portrait of Anna.*

As Ellie had requested, Pierre contacted Monsieur Paul Roux, the owner of the moving company, Maison Entreposage. "Pierre my men went to your apartment on Thursday morning. We located your key in the umbrella stand but the door had been battered and the locks changed. I am very sorry but, under the circumstances, we were unable to enter your home or store your belongings. We asked several neighbors who knew nothing of your whereabouts. Pierre, where should I send your refund?"

Pierre reeled from this distressing news. But Pierre

would not give their address to anyone in Paris. He hoped that his home would remain locked up until their return. Pierre replied, "Paul, I am asking a favor. Please keep the refund until a later date and either I or someone else, perhaps my assistant, Genevieve Caron, will be in touch. I will look into it and get back to you at some point, d'accord?"

Thinking it over, Pierre did not contact Genevieve. Doing so might put his young assistant in danger if she had any knowledge of their whereabouts or even knew that Pierre was alive.

After explaining the situation, Pierre asked Sir Colin Kingsford, "Colin, could I impose upon your contacts in Paris to discreetly inquire into the disposition of our home?"

Two weeks later, Kingsford said, "Pierre, I am very sorry but my men tell me that a German officer is now living in your 'abandoned' home with his wife and two sons."

Crestfallen, Pierre did not have the heart to tell Ellie. When they returned home after the war, their possessions could be gone. However, it was still possible that Ellie's most cherished belonging, her undistinguished mother's portrait of Anna, might have remained in their apartment. Pierre held out hope that the German would have a heart and leave the amateur painting of their daughter in its rightful place. Pierre would not share with Ellie this disturbing information because he had no recourse. Right now, Ellie appeared more at peace. When she asked about her heirlooms, Pierre kept his deception simple. With a heavy heart he crossed his fingers behind his back.

"Ellie, I contacted Maison Entreposage, and Paul told me his men went to our apartment the following Thursday *as planned.*" Satisfied, Ellie never asked Pierre pointedly regarding any particular details. Pierre felt sick with his lie, but he could not shatter Ellie's stability by telling her the truth now. He prayed that when they returned to Paris after the war, though lived in, their home would be intact and at least Anna's portrait still hanging. For now, Pierre felt it foolhardy to bring more sadness into their disrupted lives. Meanwhile, Pierre would hire a detective to look into whether their belongings had been removed and stored by the authorities or left in their home.

Life for the Bessettes and Kristin took on a day-to-day normalcy that replaced the daily fear and upheaval living under the Occupation. Ellie and Anna were disappointed that the London art museums had closed due to the bombings. Their great works of art were hidden deep in the countryside just as the Louvre in Paris had done… Musicians were drafted into military service and ballrooms closed as did many restaurants. It was difficult to live with bombed-out debris, and misfortune around every corner of the city. Yet the Bessettes were eternally grateful for their freedom from the Nazis and the extreme hardships thrust upon Parisians.

The cheerfulness of the Brits during the war had become a national rallying cry. Everyone in the Middleton home embraced the winning attitude of Londoners invoked by Churchill's staff. A precocious Anna slid down the lower end of the banister yelling, "Here I come. Don't worry, Maman, just keep calm and carry on!"

Each family pitched in for the war effort. Beatrice gathered clothes and personal care items for the ever-increasing homeless. Bea took Churchill's advice and wartime motto to heart: *To DRESS extravagantly in wartime is worse than BAD FORM it is UNPATRIOTIC.* She refused to wear her designer clothes. With Anna's help, Michi and Cousin Charles volunteered to clear rubble from areas in the city that were deemed stable by the buildings committee. The children tended vegetable gardens for the elderly.

Ellie threw herself into the ladies' wartime auxiliary; she fed and comforted the wounded in hospitals. In the evenings, she and Kristin sewed bandages for the Red Cross. Eventually, Ellie spent much of her time reading to children in orphanages and rocking them to sleep. Soon it became a calling. Anna begged to accompany Ellie. "Please Maman; I can organize crafts and games. I will teach them how to paint. Even if we don't have brushes, we can use our fingers."

Ellie often stayed with the children well into the night, singing until their little eyelids fluttered and closed. She sang the soothing American lullabies that she remembered as a little girl being sung by Mary Cassatt, "Twinkle, Twinkle, Little Star," "Hush, Little Baby," "Rockabye Baby," and the sweet Swedish lullaby her mother sang, "I Know of a Lovely Rose." Some little ones who had lived through the bombings screamed or trembled with fear during their nightmares. Some nights, the only way Ellie could rest was to cry herself to sleep.

Michael worked directly with the SOE Intelligence Services to thwart a German attempt to invade England. With his multi-lingual proficiency, Pierre deciphered non-secret conversations, routine French and German talk containing information pointing to possible resistance activities, concentration camps, etc. Colin Kingsford advised Pierre, "If you find compelling information that could affect the success of the resistance, pass the information on for potential action."

In October, golden and crimson leaves drifted into piles. The children had returned to school. Young Charles and Michi attended Westminster Upper School and Anna, St. Elizabeth's School for girls.

By 1943, a year after their escape to London, the Ambrose family had taken root in London. Birthdays and holidays were celebrated simply. Though underweight, the children were growing; their lives were nurtured by family and new friends. They took satisfaction in that they were doing everything possible to help Britain and France to win the war and to keep the Nazis out of Great Britain.

An influx of American GIs and intelligence personnel

worked on assignment in London. Baker Street became hectic with British spies, officers and soldiers or "Tommys," some working side by side with American military officers. The Brits enjoyed the freewheeling Americans and the Yanks liked the more proper English congeniality— an amicable clash of cultures some would say. Americans were invited to neighborhood pubs, or as the Brits would call one, "the local." The Americans loved the camaraderie, a game of darts and the pub atmosphere. However, American GIs could never get used to warm ale.

Pierre worked with a mathematician and American businessman, James Turner, whose consulting time rotated between SOE headquarters on Baker Street and Bletchley Park, the secret decoding site. A retired captain in the Air Force, James was a successful IBM business analyst in New York. He earned a master's degree in statistics from the University of Pennsylvania, Wharton School of Business.

In1937, James Turner had been assigned a seat next to brilliant British mathematician, Alan Turing, at a statistics and global economics seminar in New York City. Alan Turing and James Turner continued to meet from time to time to debate mathematical theories.

Turing returned to Britain's cryptanalytic headquarters at Bletchley Park. He and analysts worked around the clock to crack the portable German electromechanical device known as the Enigma which protected German communications on the battlefield, on the seas, and in the war rooms. Turing and his colleagues devised the techniques that broke the U-boat codes which allowed the British Navy to protect critical American supplies en route to England.

Alan Turing had arranged for James Turner, to lend his expertise to the U.S. Intelligence Service in London. In doing so, James taught Pierre how data was compiled using punch cards. The men created a data processing method that could help surviving Jews to locate and reunite with their loved ones once the war ended.

James Turner and Pierre's work relationship grew into a warm camaraderie. They shared common interests including rugby, which Pierre had played growing up, and its counterpart, American football, that Turner played as an undergraduate at the University of Southern California. Turner lived in Scarsdale, New York with his wife and two young sons. Both families were avid skiers. James became a welcome dinner guest at the Middleton home. He was mindful to eat sparingly so as not to use up scarce rations.

James invited Pierre to dine with him at the American officers' plush Columbia Club on Bayswater Road near Marble Arch. A grand white stucco building with views of Hyde Park and Kensington Gardens, the club contained a wood-paneled gentleman's bar, a gracious formal dining room with crystal chandeliers, and a small casino. James and Pierre mingled with American naval officers and airmen. James also invited Pierre and Ellie, Michael and Beatrice to a dinner dance at the Columbia Club when his wife, Mary, joined him in London.

Ellie looked forward to a dressy evening out with Pierre and his friends in the intelligence community. Ellie worked day in and day out to comfort orphans. She assisted Bea's ladies' auxiliary and gathered supplies for disadvantaged Londoners. Ellie was ready for a carefree night on the town.

The men would wear dinner jackets. Ellie borrowed one of Bea's cocktail dresses, a chic Jeanne Paquin crepe dress with black sequins and a V-neckline. The dress was sizes too big and Bea insisted that Ellie take in the dress to fit her thin shape. Ellie wore her pearl and diamond anniversary necklace. *Damn the war!* She wore a bright "heart red" lipstick by Coty. Pierre's own heart skipped a beat when his wife walked into the room.

Mary Turner, the American's wife, and Ellie shared a love of art and the evening was a smashing success for everyone. Promises were made... "Pierre, after this miserable war ends, you must bring the family to New York as our guests. We will take our families skiing in Vermont. Ellie will love the Metropolitan Museum of Art. Come visit, my friend and bring your family."

Chapter 30

December, 1943

C hristmas had always been Bea's favorite time of the year. From the mantles to the rafters, fragrant evergreen and holly arrangements had dressed their home. Winterberries and sumptuous cedar garland would entwine the staircase. Crystal bowls overflowed with fresh tangerines, and the intoxicating scent of clove-studded oranges. A formal Christmas tree would be placed in the front window, and a children's tree would be decorated with strings of sugar plum fruit and toy ornaments. Also, in the playroom, the sweet, spicy aroma of a grand gingerbread house would fill the air.

Last Christmas had become a meager war-time affair. In 1943, the holiday was about to be austere. But Bea promised festivity. The women and children cut fresh greens from the property and arranged Bea's crystal bowls with holly and aromatic mixed pine greenery.

The women made a kissing ball, tied with fresh holly and greens from the property and mistletoe purchased from a teenage girl bringing in money for her family. The kissing ball was hung by a festive plaid ribbon from the entrance hall chandelier. Bea smiled, "Ellie, it is an English tradition that when all the berries are gone from the mistletoe, the kisses were gone as well." Candles were plentiful due to previous bombing power outages and blackouts. The spice-and-pine-scented home was filled with candles illuminating the comfortable rooms with a warm glow.

Michael and Pierre dragged a small fir tree in from Laurel Manor. Flour and butter ration coupons were saved up so that Kristin could bake a few Swedish butter cookies and two gingerbread boys and one girl. She also made three pepperkaker heart-shaped cookies, and then cut a hole near the top of each one. Once baked, she threaded a red ribbon through the hole and the children decorated and then hung their cookies on their evergreen tree. Cook saved a few eggs, one apple, an orange, currants and a smattering of nuts to make a small traditional Christmas pudding.

Wrapping paper was non-existent. The children were tasked with decorating ordinary butcher paper. Although the boys hated the chore, Anna spent hours drawing Christmas scenes —painting Father Christmas, winter snowflakes, mittens, stars and bells. She wrote Joyeux Noël on the paper. The children arranged the crèche and fought over the placement of the three wise men and the animals.

Factories were retooled for the defense industry, and new toys were out of the question. Bea and Ellie spent weeks collecting old toys and clothes for those left without homes or work during the war. The children collected used toys from school mates. The women filled boxes with the refurbished toys and hand-made cloth dolls, knitted scarves and mittens donated by Bea's church auxiliary. They cleaned and pressed old clothes and whatever "goodies" and sweet candies they could find. When lucky, they added fresh fruit, a true luxury. They would deliver their gift boxes to the orphanages and hospitals.

Anna had fallen in love with one doll with blonde braids and a Scottish plaid skirt and plaid scarf. It even held a little brown bear in her arms.

Anna begged for the doll, "Please Maman, I love her. I will call her Annabelle!"

"*Non, ma bichette*, (darling) we are collecting toys for less fortunate children. Let's think of others because we have been given so much. Now, help me pack these boxes, oui?"

After a disappointed Anna left the room, Ellie plucked "Annabelle" from the gift box and wrapped her for Anna's Christmas gift. A new paint brush, a few tubs of paint and canvas rounded out her gifts. The boys would receive cricket bats and used rugby gear. Michael brought home two discarded army-issued walkie-talkies for the boys. With help from Kristin, using a French hook, Anna crocheted a bookmark for Michi's favorite reader to save his place when lights were turned off each night. Michi read his *Boys Book of Heroes* by light of an old flashlight. She wrapped the bookmark with her personally designed wrapping paper decorated with boats, airplanes and rugby bats.

Several days before Christmas, Michael trudged through the back door in his hunting boots and proudly held up a plump turkey shot in the woods at Laurel Manor. As if the turkey was a trophy he announced, "Look everyone! We will have a savory Christmas dinner after all."

Michael introduced his companion. "Meet Ian Fleming, a clever chap who works in Royal Navy Intelligence. We went hunting today." He clapped Fleming's back, "Good shooter he is, too. Look here!"

Michael surprised the family with burlap bags filled with seven game rabbits, five turkeys and four pheasants. One turkey would be served with maple roasted parsnips, stuffing, gravy and Christmas pudding. The remaining rabbits, turkeys and pheasant would be donated to the Red Cross Auxiliary. The organization would prepare Christmas dinner for those who had lost their homes in the bombings.

Michael asked Ian, "Care to stay and join me in a drink, ole chap."

"I'd be delighted," Fleming said as they removed their muddy Hunter Wellington boots and made their way to the library. "I'd prefer a medium dry vodka martini, if you don't mind, with a twist of lemon peel, shaken and not stirred."

Cook called out to Sir Michael, "Oh, sir, before you go...

May I have one rabbit? I will marinate it in red wine, garlic and an herb bouquet as my grandmother did for a winter stew."

Although tired of war, the family enjoyed a festive mood that enveloped the home on Christmas Eve. It was cloudy and 39 degrees. The families bundled up in their bright plaid scarves and warm gloves and walked the short distance to St. Michael's Anglican Church on Chester Square. Church bells and carols rang out as neighbors spread Christmas greetings with renewed anticipation for peace in the New Year. Lights in the church were not permitted; candles glowed with hope. The ladies church auxiliary had woven greenery that symbolized life. The wreaths hung from each stained-glass window.

After church, the families shared Cook's savory rabbit stew for *Le Reveillon* (a symbolic Christmas Eve dinner — "the new awakening" or passing of the winter solstice and the arrival of Christmas) accompanied by roasted carrots, and much to the delight of the Bessettes, a small cheese course. After the simple dinner, Kristin and Cook surprised everyone with a petite *Bûche de Noël* "Yule log" sponge cake with chocolate icing and tiny white fondant mushrooms.

Ellie smiled when Pierre stood and toasted his family members. His eyes were moist; he looked at the women he cherished, "With all of us together and safe, this is the most heartwarming Christmas Eve of my life."

Everyone, including Cook, retired to the living room fireplace to enjoy a Swedish cookie, wassail, and hot mulled wine. Anna had decorated a heart shaped cookie for each family member.

Before returning to New York for the holiday, James Turner had given Pierre a bottle of Wild Turkey American bourbon. He said, "Merry Christmas! Let's celebrate the end of the war in New York."

Pierre remarked, "James, alcohol is nearly impossible to come by. It is *so* scarce now that only one person had been arrested for drunkenness over the entire previous Christmas holiday! Thank you, my friend."

Pierre brought out the Kentucky bourbon for a toast; he allowed the boys to taste their first sample of whiskey. Anna was given the privilege of laying the infant Jesus in his crib as everyone settled in for the night before Christmas. The children made certain to place their stockings on their bed-posts in hopes of waking to find a sugary treat and perhaps an orange or a tangerine from Father Christmas. Although Anna no longer played with Bonbon, stitched together after Ellie removed the gems, he remained an old faithful friend perched at the foot of her bed.

On Christmas Day, the aroma of roasted turkey filled their home, and Cook's Christmas pudding, made on "Stir it Up Sunday," the last Sunday before Advent, stood on its cake plate on the sideboard. In late November, each family member had taken a customary turn stirring the pudding and making a wish for an Allied victory.

Bea had set the Christmas dinner table with her best Royal Doulton bone china and her mother's English King sterling flatware and crystal goblets. Candles radiated a soft glow. When they sat down for Christmas dinner, Anna called out, "Everyone, look!" Fluffy white snowflakes floated through the still night and dusted the barren trees and gardens.

The children realized that their stomachs felt full for the first time in many, many months. Despite the bleakness of war, this year's Christmas, filled with hope and joy, had become a simple, yet merry infusion of English, French and Swedish traditions.

Chapter 31

The tranquil Christmas season dissipated into an endearing memory. By January 22, 1944, Germany's air force, the Luftwaffe, pounded London in what began as the "Baby Blitz." The ramped-up Germans retaliated after the Allies had bombarded prestigious cities, including Berlin.

Night after night, central London was particularly hard hit. Unaccustomed to the blaring nighttime air raid sirens, Ellie and Pierre soothed their terrified children as they waited out the bombings in their basement shelter. The sound of exploding bombs above and the loud thunder of continuous blasts rattled windows and everyone's nerves. Anna failed to hold back tears. Ellie wrapped her daughter with a blanket and stroked her head. As her own mother had done, Ellie whispered, "It will be okay, darling, don't worry."

When dawn broke and the bombings finally stopped, they trudged up the stairs through fine dust and chunks of stone that littered the floor. They smelled the stench of smoldering buildings. Fire trucks wailed and ambulances raced through the streets with the wounded and dying. The Bessettes were shaken to their core by at the painful sight of misery and new destruction all around them.

The Luftwaffe blasted London throughout February. Nearly a thousand were killed and thousands more were injured. Bombs damaged Scotland Yard and the Houses of Parliament. The windows were blown out at 10 Downing Street, the Prime Minister's residence.

Ellie slipped into renewed bouts of sleeplessness and anxiety. She jumped when a dish crashed onto the floor but then slumped to the floor and broke down in tears. Pierre held his exhausted wife in his arms. After weeks without sleep, as Dr. Morgenstern in Paris had done, an army doctor prescribed barbiturate to help Ellie sleep on the nights uninterrupted by air raids.

Morale sagged at home and on Baker Street. Ellie said, "We never know when those dreadful bombs might fall next." She wrung her hands, "Pierre, even when I console Anna, I am frightened for us all." Pierre held his wife and stroked her hair.

Relative calm did not return until early March, over a year and a half after the Bessettes escaped Paris. Sir Michael tried earnestly to encourage the weary families by relating the success in intelligence and exalting the latest news from Baker Street. "Hang on everyone. Very soon the Germans will be defeated by "Operation Overlord" (the intended invasion of Normandy).

With the let-up of a constant drizzly winter, March brought a welcome renewed peace. Finally, nights became peaceful once again. Exhausted Londoners awoke to a touch of optimism in the spring air. The children returned to school. Beatrice and Ellie volunteered in the overflowing charity wards while Michael and Pierre worked overtime at their war departments.

After weeks of bone-chilling weather, London turned pleasantly warm. Finally freed from the dreary, wet weather, Charles called to Michi and Anna after school, "Let's round up the team and head to the park!"

Anna grabbed her sweater and followed the boys outside, running to catch up with them. "Wait for me, I'm coming." she yelled. Anna never made it to Hyde Park.

Her body was found beneath a pile of rubble. The teenage boys had run ahead of her. Falling behind, Anna had stopped to join neighborhood children in a game of hide-and-seek in an abandoned building. Despite multiple warnings, the children played in the bombed-out building, and teenagers used it to rendezvous with sweethearts. Shaking from recent bombings had likely caused greater instability and a wall had crumbled.

One of the children witnessed the tragedy. The youngster sobbed, "A big chunk fell and hit Anna on the back of her head." She had been knocked unconscious before the remaining building collapsed on top of her. Another child, who ran further away from the falling concrete, had suffered a broken arm and a concussion.

Words cannot describe the grief felt in the house on Belgrave Square and that reverberated throughout London's intelligence community. Ellie's anguish was primal and horrible. She wailed as though her heart had been ripped out of her body.

Anna was buried in a small cemetery at Laurel Manor with Bonbon in her arms and Brother Bernard's prayer book placed in her small hands. Sedated, Ellie was in such shock that she was barely able to stand at the funeral. She came home and took to her bed wrapping herself in a cocoon of despair. When the sedatives wore off, Ellie would suddenly scream in anguish. For days, Ellie would not talk or communicate. Bea tried to feed her soup which she refused. Ellie gnawed her lip until it was red and raw.

Pierre's own shock and grief was immeasurable. But he understood that somehow, he had to keep his family from falling apart. Michi would cry with an indescribable emptiness and remorse in his young heart. *Why had he not waited for his little sister to catch up*, painfully he asked over and over and over? Michi had always taken care of Anna... "A part of us has been torn away, and we will never be whole. It's entirely my fault." Pierre insisted that it was a tragedy, an accident, But Michi blamed himself. "Don't tell me it's an *accident!* He screamed, "I didn't wait for my little sister!"

Tortured by his own anguish, Pierre said, "Michael,

how do I raise Ellie from the depths of this tragedy? My son is going through pain like I experienced when my mother died… but to make it worse, he feels guilt."

Although Kristin knew her parents loved her, they had not been outwardly affectionate to her or each other whereas the Bessettes' home exuded warmth. Ellie had become like a big sister. Now Ellie was somewhere in a dark hole. Anna's death and the uncertainty of Ellie's recovery filled Kristin with heartache. Kristin told Cook, "I feel so alone and lost." Beatrice and Cook offered Kristin solace as best as they could in this darkest hour in all of their lives.

Every morning, Pierre brought Ellie a cup of tea and a biscuit. He kissed her forehead and held her hand until Michi joined them. Michi sat on his mother's bed for hours waiting for her eyes to open. Almost a week went by, and still she did not speak. Some days, she just rocked back and forth.

Then one morning, Pierre was shaving when Michi ran into his bathroom, "Papa, Papa, come quickly, Maman is talking!" Pierre ran a towel over his soapy face and sprinted down to her room.

Pierre stroked Ellie's head, and she spoke, "Cheri, bring Anna to me so that I can braid her hair before school?" Sadly, Pierre held her hand and told Ellie that Anna was no longer with them. "But Pierre, I must braid her hair today." Tears welled in Michi's eyes, and he ran from the room. He had lost his sister and his mother was slipping away.

The heartbreaking scene was repeated over and over. Often in the middle of the night, Ellie screamed in a nightmare. Michi stayed home from school, sitting with his mother, waiting day after day for her to pull out of her overwhelming grief.

One day, Ellie reached for Michi's hand. *Life has no meaning for me. But Michi, please forgive yourself.*

Numb even to occasional new bombings, Pierre and Michael carried Ellie to the shelter.

With no significant change in sight, Michael asked their

surgeon-general to examine Ellie. The doctor recommended electroconvulsive treatments to shock Ellie out of her deep despair. Pierre and Michael thanked the doctor and showed him to the door.

Pierre feared that psychiatrists would commit his wife to an institution. Although Ellie had never experienced such a devastating trauma, she had always pulled herself out of her "melancholia" in the past. Pierre believed that Ellie just needed more time.

The following morning, Pierre brought Ellie's tea. Her empty bottle of barbiturates was lying on the floor. Ellie was unconscious; her breathing shallow. Pierre raced to the telephone and called for an ambulance. The medics gave her charcoal granules and water. She barely survived.

After Ellie's suicide attempt, Pierre asked his cousin to call the most well-known psychiatrists in London. Several therapies were discussed. The most prevalent diagnoses were traumatic neurosis, severe psychological trauma, and "shell-shock," a likening of Ellie's trauma to what a soldier faces on the battlefield. However, one doctor in particular stood out.

One of London's most esteemed psychiatrists, Dr. William Macpherson applied a salve and bandage to Ellie's shredded lower lip. Off to the side, the doctor said, "Pierre, your wife's condition, as you know, is very serious. But I do not believe in shock therapy or placing Ellie in a mental hospital. Certainly, I do not recommend a lobotomy which is unreliable and often does worse damage. Our traditional hospitals are packed with the war-wounded and victims of the latest bombings. There are simply no beds or enough adequately trained mental health personnel to help someone suffering from such a severe emotional shock."

Dr. Macpherson said, "I watched Madame devote nearly two years tending to the war-wounded and orphans. I simply cannot allow her to languish in a mental ward where severely mentally ill or dangerous individuals are housed. She needs rest, compassion and time to heal. But Madame also needs professional psychiatric care, and soon. Or she may try again to end her life."

Pierre pleaded. "But, what can I do, doctor?" He threw his arms in the air and whispered out of Ellie's earshot, "I am desperate to help my wife. I have no idea where to turn!"

Dr. Macpherson placed his arm on Pierre's back, "Listen, after the Great Depression, care in mental hospitals declined. There simply were no funds. Psychiatrists in the United States looked for alternative ways to treat those experiencing a reactive breakdown or mental shock. I may have a solution for you."

Dr. Macpherson was strongly in favor of a recent American phenomenon. "Doctors in America have developed a practice termed "outpatient" in which doctors treat mental health issues on a weekly basis rather than to house patients in large, impersonal mental wards. Doctors treat their patients on a one-to-one basis for a set period of time each week. Pierre, this is a bold new process available to treat people with a mental state that we no longer refer to as "melancholia" but what the Americans have termed "depression." Patients live at home rather than in an institutional environment. They have had good success. I believe this treatment would be most appropriate for Madame."

Pierre mulled it over. As an enemy of the Nazi regime, Pierre could not return to France for help. Dr. Macpherson was adamant that returning to Paris with the likely loss of their home and belongings could permanently devastate a recovery.

Dr. Macpherson asserted, "The United States can offer the best psychiatric care away from these rigors of war. If you like, I will make some calls to psychiatrists in New York to get Madame the best help possible. If I were you, Pierre, I would not wait."

Michael called his recently married sister who currently lived in upstate New York. "Margaret, can you and Andrew assist Pierre to get situated? They will need housing and help acclimating to life in the States."

After tearful goodbyes to Michael, Beatrice, young Charles and the small staff at Belgravia, and their many new-found friends in the intelligence community, Pierre, Michi and Kristin boarded a BOAC plane, a Boeing 314 flying boat named "Speed Bird," from Southampton bound for the United States. With deep sadness, they departed with a very sick Ellie and without Anna. Once again, they would leave a home filled with warmth and love in exchange for a daunting future.

They would arrive in the United States as Peter and Elsa Ambrose, Michael Ambrose and Kristin Larsson, determined to rescue Ellie from her depression over the painful loss of her daughter and to push the dreadful war as far from their minds as possible.

Chapter 32

Spring, 1944

The Boeing B-314 clipper flying boats were extravagantly well-equipped with comfortable beds and a dining room where meals were prepared by four-star chefs and served by white-coated stewards. However, the Bessette's were not destined for such luxury. Sir Colin had arranged for the first available passage to New York which was a bare-bones BOAC flight used to transport troops and military personnel.

The newcomers set foot in Port Washington on Long Island. Pierre's family disembarked on a misty London fog day. With British passports they easily cleared Immigration.

Michael's sister, Lady Margaret, Americanized as Maggie, spotted the family emerge from Immigration. Her heart broke when she did not see Anna cheerfully run toward her. Maggie's sadness intensified when she encountered Ellie's vacant eyes and listless demeanor.

Maggie did her best to smile and welcome her extended French family to America. With arms wide open and in a subdued tone she hugged the newcomers. "Bienvenu. Welcome to America, dear cousins."

Cousin Maggie had brought a small entourage: her American husband Andrew, along with baggage handlers and a nurse. Maggie still seemed the girl from Pierre's youth— tall with a crop of light reddish blonde hair, a sprinkling of freckles and an exuberant personality; she was full of life and ready for action. As children, it had been hard to keep up with her energy and enthusiasm. Her husband equaled her vigor. Andrew shook Pierre's hand, and Pierre noticed that Andrew too was tall with boyish good looks and extremely likable. He and Maggie were almost like a matched set.

"Mags," as Andrew called his wife, had found a tastefully furnished chocolate color brownstone near Central Park. The stately home, located on a tree-lined street, was an excellent choice with its pleasant solarium in the rear of the house. Glass French doors opened onto a private patio enclosed by an ivy-covered stone wall. Purple crocuses and yellow daffodils hinted at the splash of color that would brighten the garden during the summer. A small wrought iron table and four chairs were positioned beneath a pink dogwood tree. Maggie told Pierre, "Ellie can take afternoon tea here and benefit from sunlight and fresh air. I hope that the family can enjoy their meals outside on warm days."

Pierre smiled at his cousin. "Maggie, it would be wonderful for us to spend time together in this pretty garden."

I wonder if anything as delightful as sharing lunch together under a tree will ever happen again.

Maggie settled them into their gracious new home with 12-foot ceilings, extensive woodwork, bow windows and an ornate cherry fireplace opposite plump sofas.

Maggie showed Pierre and Kristin around their Upper East Side neighborhood. Central Park was close by where Michi could learn to play American sports—baseball, basketball and football. Maggie had enrolled Michi at the academically acclaimed Horace Mann Preparatory School, Andrew's alma mater. Pierre had been disposed with diplomatic status through his work with the SOE, and Andrew pledged to Pierre, "Any way that I or the United States can assist with your transition to life in America, please let me know."

The following morning, Pierre awoke to a gray dawn

and the splatter of a spring shower. Soon a blustery rainstorm pelted the windows. Desperate for coffee, Pierre rummaged around the dimly lit kitchen; a tin of canned Maxwell House coffee hissed open. He poured milk into a saucepan and prepared to froth the milk with a wire whisk when he was startled by a blood-curdling scream.

He ran to Ellie who had panicked when rattling windows woke her in a room she did not recognize. "It will be okay, ma chérie." Pierre soothed his wife. "This is our new home for now and we are safe." Pierre stroked her head.

In a stone-cold voice, Ellie murmured, "Anna is not safe." They held each other and sobbed. They were scheduled to see her psychiatrist soon and Pierre prayed the doctor could help his depressed wife. Ellie's future hung by a thread.

From their home in Scarsdale, IBM mathematician and friend, James Turner and his family drove into the city to offer their condolences.

Pierre whispered, "James, my greatest fear is that Ellie may become more overwhelmed by this move to New York and sink even deeper into despair."

"Pierre, we are here to help in any way we can. Let us know what we can do, whatever you need." Mary brought a basket of corn muffins, a crock of homemade chicken noodle soup and a chicken casserole seasoned with sautéed shallots, celery, fresh thyme and cream.

Ellie's indifference toward their friends was distressing. She stared into space, seemingly bewildered by their visit even though the couples had socialized in London; she and Mary had corresponded routinely with one another.

The Turners introduced their two teenage sons, Edward and Patrick. The boys hit it off immediately. Patrick threw his basketball to Michi who caught it on the spot. "Let's head to Central Park and get a game going," Patrick said.

Federico Verdi asked to visit Ellie. He also invited Pierre

to join him for dinner at his favorite New York restaurant, Amalfi, on Forty-Eighth Street.

The Duke rang Pierre and Ellie's doorbell. Pierre enthusiastically embraced his dear friend who looked well. He said, "Ah Federico, I can't tell you how pleased I am to see you. We all have missed you!"

Federico was a charismatic and gregarious gentleman. In Paris, he had become a welcome presence at Ellie's table; he charmed her with sincere affection. Pierre also recalled the playboy's globetrotting stories and his knack for witticism: "Aah Pierre, you know that I like good wine, good food and women with good long legs!"

But tonight, a subdued Federico embraced Ellie and presented her with a jeweled rabbit brooch which he pinned on her scarf. In Paris, Federico often called Ellie his *petite lapine* (little rabbit). The colorful brooch brought a slight smile and the only smile on Ellie's chafed lips since before Anna's death. He held her hand and tenderly placed a kiss on each cheek. The Duke remarked in perfect French, "Elsa, my pet, you look as beautiful as ever. Tonight, we boys are going out to talk business. But soon we all shall dine together. I will take you and Pierre to the best French restaurant in New York, oui? Please feel better my dear girl."

Ellie searched Federico's warm brown eyes and slowly nodded her head, an unexpected response which gave Pierre a tiny prism of hope. One thing Pierre and Ellie knew about Federico, the Duke would regale you with compliments, but you always knew he spoke truth.

Seated at Amalfi and anticipating what was surely to be an abundant Italian meal, they were greeted enthusiastically by the chef.

"It is a pleasure to welcome Freddie's friend!" The chef offered the men a delicious amuse bouche, an *orecchiette* of spiced duck to begin their meal.

With no hint of embarrassment, Federico expressed

deep sadness over Pierre's tremendous loss. "My heart is broken over sweet Anna, my friend. An angel taken too soon. Please, let me know how I can help you."

"Federico, I can't tell you how overwhelmed we are with this deep sadness. I miss my daughter terribly and my son is grief-stricken. My wife is an angry and broken woman who is gone from me. Ellie feared that our activities against the Germans might be uncovered and our children would be harmed. I didn't listen. And now this tragedy is more than she can take." Pierre threw his hands into the air.

Pierre leaned in, "Federico, I regret not leaving Paris when you sailed for America. I was arrogant and convinced that we could do more to aid the resistance and thwart the enemy. Now, I feel as though life is over, and I don't know how to move us forward or where to begin?"

Duke Verdi patted his friend's shoulder. "Pierre, listen to me. Don't ever forget that you and Ellie disrupted German efforts and gave many French citizens dignity and a little hope during this terrible war. Ellie has always been a strong woman. She will improve over time."

Federico lowered his voice. "Pierre, you know that people envy my lifestyle—the wealthy duke who leaves a trail of beautiful women and broken hearts behind. But I envy *you*, my friend. I have never found the love that you and Ellie share. I have seen the way you look at one another. Ellie is a much-admired and magnificent woman, and she *will* return to you. Meanwhile, when the time is right, you must get back to your work, to what you do so well and to ease your mind away from this tragedy. Pierre, you need to keep busy while the doctor helps Ellie."

"Listen... I only mention this now because a small, coveted space will become available only one door away from my own boutique on Fifth Avenue at Fifty-Seventh Street. I know it's far from your mind right now. But the present owner has an oriental carpet business and he plans to retire. Just give it some thought. I will help you start over and establish Bijoux

New York. Pierre, we would have our own little jewelry enclave—exclusive, exceptional, European style! *Please*, let me
help you while Ellie gets the help she needs."

Pierre was touched by his friend's generosity. "Federico,
you are most kind. Let me get Ellie settled into a routine and
we will talk. I don't know... Let me think about it. First, I have
to see how Ellie responds..."

Returning to their former lives in Paris was foremost
in Pierre's mind, if and when Ellie could handle the everyday
memories of Anna in Paris. Pierre felt lost in New York and
yearned for a more genteel life. But Pierre also understood
that Ellie needed time and therapy. The war had not ended
and Europe must rebuild. Luxury had become rare in Europe.
Trying to re-establish a successful jewelry business anywhere
on the Continent would be disastrous. Food rationing could go
on for years.

The Duke's proposed location was ideally located near
their rented brownstone on Sixty-Second Street. His renowned Italian friend would be the perfect mentor in America.

Pierre touched his friend's shoulder. "Federico, let me
think about your kind offer. I will need to support my family
and pay for Ellie's care."

The next day, Dr. James Nolan, the pioneer of the most
recent advancement in outpatient psychiatric movement,
examined Ellie. After attempting to talk with her, he agreed
with Dr. Macpherson's assessment in London.

"Mr. Ambrose, your wife has suffered a terrible one-two
punch," the doctor explained, "By that I mean, two extremely
severe emotional shocks during the same time period. Anna's
death is simply too much for your wife to bear or for her mind
to comprehend, especially following your escape and the
nightly trauma of intense bombings. Right now, as a defense
mechanism, Mrs. Ambrose has no other way to cope than to
block out the painful reality of Anna's death. Simply put, she

has retreated into another world. And, of course, she is a very angry woman. To make matters worse, she has deep feelings of despair and even worthlessness. She feels her life is no longer worth living. We now call her condition depression, and it is not easily understood."

Pierre pleaded, "Doctor, then what are Ellie's chances for a normal life again? She has always been an anxious person living under the strains of war twice and childhood poverty. Pierre explained Ellie's difficult childhood. He added, "Ellie's doctor in Paris suggested that she take up smoking cigarettes to settle her nerves? But my wife never liked the smell of smoke."

Dr. Nolan nodded, "Well, I'm certain that her doctor meant well. But I don't believe that smoking will help your wife's condition. Over time and with consistent counseling, I feel that she can recover. We are making excellent strides in learning to understand depression and its treatment. The truth is that Mrs. Ambrose may never become a carefree individual. Trauma in early childhood often manifests throughout our entire lives. She may suffer from bouts of anxiety. And, of course, she will always suffer the pain of losing Anna. However, I believe that we can help her gain control of her life. I am hopeful that she can return to her life as a fully functioning woman and enjoy many aspects of living."

The doctor reiterated that he wanted to keep Ellie out of a mental institution. "There is no certainty, of course, but I strongly feel that with regular counseling and family support in a loving and safe environment, your wife will slowly improve without hospitalization." At the very least, the doctor reassured Pierre that his treatment would not risk driving her deeper into despair. Counseling was her best chance for a normal life.

Dr. Nolan would see Ellie in their home two days a week for the first four weeks, to establish trust in a familiar setting. Eventually, as Ellie improved, they would transition to weekly visits at his office on Seventy-Second Street. Though this outpatient counseling treatment seemed unconventional, Pierre felt comfortable that it was the best approach to help his distraught wife.

Dr. Nolan advised Pierre, "Patience is not only a virtue but an important aspect when dealing with the mind. Please remember, Mrs. Ambrose will heal at her pace, not ours. She needs time."

Chapter 33

Initially, Pierre sat back and watched the counseling sessions. Ellie had little to say. Meanwhile, Michi attended his new school. Kristin befriended a Swedish nanny from the neighborhood.

Pierre and Michi explored their brash new city. Father and son walked the ethnic neighborhoods from their Upper East Side enclave to the West Side midtown Irish immigrant neighborhood known as Hell's Kitchen, to the avant-garde, artist enclave, Greenwich Village and its nearby upper-class neighborhood, Washington Square. Until recently, the glittering neon glow of Times Square had been darkened each night by a "dim-out" to protect New York's skyline from air or naval attacks. Pierre and his son avoided the heavily German neighborhood, Yorkville located above Seventy-Ninth Street.

A neighbor, friendly with Brooklyn Dodgers' manager Leo Durocher, invited Michi and Pierre to watch their first baseball game. Most of New York's premier baseball players, like Yankee Joe DiMaggio, had enlisted, were drafted or were placed on tours to entertain the troops. But Pierre and Michi did not know the difference as they watched this beloved American pastime. Sweat, tobacco and freshly cut grass filled the air. Pierre ate his first casual American meal without a plate or utensils, the Nathan's "hot dog." Pierre told Ellie about these unusual sandwiches that "are messy but quite tasty."

Over time, Michi adjusted to life in New York just like he did his nickname, Mike, as he became known to new school pals. Michel asked his father and Kristin, "Call me Michael or Mike. I found out that Michel sounds like a girl's name." Pierre thought Michael, like his cousin's, was a fine name. Pierre reminded his son, "You do know that you will always be Michel or Michi to Maman."

Teenager Michael Bessette Ambrose became hooked on America; he bought his first baseball cap at the Dodgers game. In contrast, the informal American culture was unsettling to Pierre. He was uneasy with the scruffy lower east side with its tattoo parlors, ethnic push carts and second-hand shops. On the other hand, his son found the relaxed culture and neighborhoods, filled with the foreign-born like him, exciting and brimming with life.

Federico had arranged an introduction for Pierre to meet some reputable sources in the jewelry district. Diamond prices had escalated with the sophistication and elegance of white on white diamonds and platinum jewelry. Pierre ventured down to Forty-Seventh Street between Fifth and Sixth Avenues to sell some of his gems.

Pierre smelled hot corn-on-the-cob wafting from the push carts. He yearned for the streets in Paris where delicate crêpes were sold from venders. He had decided to open a small Bijoux New York. Pierre needed money— to pay for Ellie's medical care, to rent his brownstone and for Michi's education. Pierre was grateful for the kindness his family and friends had shown him. However, he would take responsibility for his family.

Pierre missed the satisfaction he gained from designing and creating his own jewelry. Pierre imagined intense designs inspired by the colorfully dressed immigrants wearing rich green and maroon saris woven with gold as well as the strikingly beautiful African prints Ankara and Kitenge. Yes, that was it... His new designs would reflect the vibrancy of New York!

Deep in thought Pierre said aloud, "I'll begin with big and bold designs, brilliant semi-precious stones set in dramatic settings, and colorful ribbons and bows that will appeal to women from all walks of life."

Out of the blue, a booming voice broke up his thoughts. Binyamin Strassberg, a bulky Jewish diamond merchant from Antwerp bellowed, "Pierre, is that you?" Over the years, Pierre had done business with Binyamin in Belgium.

"My God, Bin, I can hardly believe it! What are you doing in New York?"

With a big smile and an affectionate bear hug, Binyamin replied, "I could ask you the same thing, my friend. What are *you* doing here? It is so good to see you, and how is the family? Well, I hope. God willing."

Pierre and Binny sat down at a kosher deli. Bin ordered a matzo ball soup and dug into a juicy pastrami on rye. Pierre ordered coffee and a warm, fragrant cinnamon rugelach fresh from the oven.

"God forbid, Bin, but American coffee is even weaker than the tea we drank in London."

"London?"

Pierre then related their work with the French Résistance and their ensuing escape. "Binny, we barely made it out; the Nazis were nipping at my heels."

Binyamin was one of more than 40,000 Jews in Antwerp prior to the war. Bin mentioned that thankfully the entire Strassberg family— he and his wife, Miriam, their son Aaron and his family had fled Antwerp before the Germans attacked Belgium. Bin's eldest son, Aaron had become a diamond cutter.

"Together, we set up our family business here in New York along with the myriad, thousands really, of other European Jews who had fled the Nazis."

Pierre told Strassberg about Anna's fate, which tore at

Bin's heart as he recalled the pride and joy Pierre expressed whenever he spoke about his family.

The Belgian ran his fingers over his gray beard, anguish written on his lined and leathery face. Bin shook his head. "Pierre, I am terribly sorry to hear of your loss."

It was getting late, and with a hand on his shoulder, Binny let Pierre know he had a lifelong friend in New York. "Miriam and I would love to have you as a dinner guest in our home just like the old days in Antwerp. Come visit, and this time we would like to meet Ellie when she is up to it and Michel and Kristin. I promise. Our coffee is stronger now that it is no longer rationed." The men embraced and said goodbye. Business would be continued fairly as always with "a blessing and a handshake."

Chapter 34

The Duke introduced Pierre to a group of European émigrés who had settled in New York. Socialite Peggy Guggenheim entertained her French friends at grand soirées. It felt comforting for Pierre to hear the pleasant, soothing flow of his native language.

Ellie remained indifferent to socializing. Pierre would come home and tell her the news of the day. "It seems that New York has become the new home for us French vagabonds. And, everyone worries about Picasso. He has stayed in Paris and even taunts the Nazis from time to time. Since he cannot show his artwork, apparently he has taken up writing poetry." For the first time since arriving in New York, Ellie chuckled over this revelation about her mother's defiant old friend, Pablo Picasso.

Kristin continued to make friends with young New Yorkers. She enjoyed the dances and social activities hosted by the Swedish American Club.

Pierre and Michael took a weekend excursion to visit Cousin Maggie and Andrew in upstate New York. The stunning Beaux-Arts Grand Central train station reminded Pierre of the historic buildings throughout Paris. He thought about the loss of Ellie's affection and likened Grand Central's elegant arches to the delicate curve of Ellie's back. Pierre hungered for his wife who had turned her back on him.

On the train ride to Dutchess County, Pierre discussed their tragedy now that his son was older. With great animus, Michi had talked openly about taking revenge for Anna's death and his mother's depression.

"Son, I regret not letting Maman take Anna's portrait with us; it would mean the world to us now. I feared that the painting would expose us as a family fleeing. Every day her anguish weighs heavily on my heart. Your mother showed tremendous courage right under Nazi noses... In the end, I failed her. Now your mother has little to remember Anna by or her own mother for that matter."

"Michi, I lied to your mother after we arrived in London, and I had learned that a German family occupied our home." Dropping his head, Pierre continued. "Your mother has lost faith in me. I can't blame her. I did not fully understand the importance of those paintings. To make matters worse, we left in such a hurry that we forgot the photographs of her own mother and of you and Anna that she had set aside. Michi, nothing was *your* fault, nothing at all."

"Papa, I remember the chaos that morning. You could never have predicted Anna's fate or Maman's depression."

Pierre told his son that upon learning that their belongings had not been stored by Maison Entreposage, "Immediately, I hired an investigator to snoop around and to track down our belongings. The investigator discreetly interviewed neighbors and friends within the police department. He learned that when the Germans took over our apartment just days after we fled, our home already had been ransacked. It became a mystery as to where Maman's paintings went and who took them."

Pierre was not aware that the day they departed London without Anna, Michi had promised himself that when he was old enough, he would find the Nazis responsible and kill them for creating the dire circumstances that took Anna and that had hurled his mother into this deep well of despair. Now, hearing his father's own anguish, he pledged to himself once again, *I will get our family's revenge.*

But to his father he said, "Papa, someday I'll return to Paris and find Maman's heirlooms."

∞∞∞

Maggie and Andrew's country home, Laurelwood, was nestled on ten wooded acres in New York's historic Hudson Valley. After lunch, Andrew took Michi kayaking on the Hudson River while Maggie and Pierre, chatted over tea, scones and clotted cream.

"Pierre, how are Londoners holding up?" Maggie leaned forward. "I'm concerned about my brother Michael, Beatrice and young Charles."

Maggie also inquired about Ellie..." It would be wonderful if all of you could join us for a weekend here at Laurelwood."

Pierre reached for his cousin's hand, "Maggie, I can never thank you and Andrew enough for your help and compassion. What can I say? Ellie is angry. She makes a little progress but then spends days without communicating. Time will tell how much she will recover."

The visit to Dutchess County led to a stronger bond between Pierre and Andrew, an attaché with Roosevelt's delegation. He had met Maggie when the president's delegation conferred with Churchill and Sir Colin Kingsford. Andrew smiled, "It was my luck to meet Maggie at a London embassy party."

Andrew and Maggie married in 1939 and bought their historic home in charming Rhinebeck, New York located near President Franklin D. Roosevelt's country estate, Springwood. FDR was born at his estate which later served as his Summer

White House in Hyde Park, New York. It was said that the president "knew every rock and stream on the place," according to his wife, Eleanor. Maggie and Andrew wintered at their brick Georgetown home in Washington, D.C. But in the summer months and Christmas holiday, they returned to their Dutch-style fieldstone home, Laurelwood.

Andrew shared important news. "Pierre, 'D Day,' known in London as "Operation Overlord" will soon be underway. I promise to update you as soon as it happens."

Over the weekend, Andrew took Pierre and Michael hiking near thunderous waterfalls, and they played their first afternoon of golf. They were encouraged to bring Ellie and Kristin up for the Christmas holidays.

Pierre hoped that Ellie would be alert and stable enough for the three-hour drive and a visit away from familiar surroundings. Pierre was hesitant to make plans too far ahead. He had learned the hard way that life never follows a script.

Chapter 35

C ome on my friend. It's Saturday night at the Copa!" Federico enticed Pierre to experience New York's "café society." He insisted that Pierre needed a little fun in his life and these social evenings were also "good for business."

So, the two debonair Europeans, a suave Italian with bronzed skin and the handsome Frenchman, attended nightclubs frequented by the privileged and the famous—the glamorous and celebrated Copacabana, the Stork Club, the elegant 21 Club (a former speakeasy), and the glitzy rooms of lavishly appointed hotels like the Waldorf Astoria's Starlight Room where the upper crust dined and danced their nights away. The fashionable crowd swayed to the Big Band music of Benny Goodman and Duke Ellington. Champagne flowed at the Plaza and gossip spilled over as easily as it would at a coffee klatch. In a "New York heartbeat," columnist and radio personality Walter Winchell kept the public informed of celebrity misbehavior and rumors. It was another world, far from war, pain and suffering.

The socialites liked to say that life was dandy or "copasetic" at the Copacabana. On this evening, the Duke had captivated Miss Sarah Moore, a lovely Irish lass with rich chestnut hair that contrasted with her creamy skin and deep blue eyes.

The nightclub scene was uncomfortable for Pierre without Ellie. He longed to take his wife out for her favorite French 75, the sparkling champagne and gin aperitif that Pierre first ordered for her at Crystal where he had proposed.

Pierre hoped that someday he and Ellie could enjoy New York's nightlife together. Meanwhile, Pierre made friends and engaged in the talk of the town while keeping a safe distance from whispers of impropriety and gossip.

However, enamored of European elegance and charm, unattached women were drawn to the Frenchman whose blue eyes crinkled at the corners when he smiled. Though he wore a wedding ring, he always showed up without a wife. One flirtatious woman in a low-cut cocktail dress tempted Pierre. She was the young widow of a banker who had suffered a massive heart attack. Mimi Van Hoomissen reminded Pierre of a slightly older version of Genevieve with her green eyes, cascading auburn hair, a ready smile and a vivacious personality. She had the habit of tossing her shiny hair back when she laughed.

Mimi cornered Pierre with two glasses of champagne and whispered in his ear, "Pierre, let's go out on the terrace for some fresh air, just the two of us." Mimi stood so close to him that he could feel her breasts against his tuxedo jacket. He glanced at the rise and fall of her soft, milky white cleavage. Mimi's desirability and availability drove Pierre as crazy as a bee hovering over sweet nectar.

Pierre felt guilty thinking about another woman. The few times when Ellie did talk with him, it was as a sister and brother would talk about daily affairs. Pierre desired his wife and struggled every day with the thought of living without the comforts of their marriage bed. Mimi waited in the wings, but Pierre vowed to give Ellie and his marriage time to heal.

Once it became apparent that he was not available, many of the same socialites who flirted with Pierre formed a cocoon to shield him from the photo journalists and gossip mongers who preyed on the rich and famous. The ladies portrayed him as "Peter, a distant cousin" or a "good family friend." The press moved away from the mysterious Frenchman to focus on their never-ending search for fresh celebrity gossip.

To family and in close friendships, he was known as Pierre. For business reasons, he maintained the British name Peter Ambrose. In the back of his mind, he feared reprisal from the Germans if it were discovered that the French resistance activist, Pierre Bessette, was alive in New York. Who knew how long the Nazi arm could reach? A strong pro-Nazi movement that included spy rings was pervasive in the city's "Little Germany." Some Americans blamed the French for capitulating to the Germans too soon thereby dragging the United States' into the European war. Best not to draw attention to his ethnicity or background through the society pages. Pierre had learned another American slogan: "Better to be safe than sorry."

Pierre grew more comfortable in Manhattan. He held tightly to the idea of returning to Paris. But for now, Peter Ambrose would take advantage of the business opportunities in America and the medical expertise available to Ellie. Pierre thought he had noticed a slight flicker of light in her eyes.

Chapter 36

On June 6, 1944, Pierre received the long-awaited call from Andrew. "Pierre, it's Normandy, Operation Overlord; the liberation of France is underway. Thousands of Allied troops have stormed the beaches. I'm afraid souls have lost their lives. But, so far, the Allies hold a foothold on French soil."

Pierre exhaled, "At long last! I hope and pray for the soldiers and that the best is yet to come."

New Yorkers awoke and crowds gathered in Times Square to watch the ticker tape. A rally for D-Day was held in Madison Square where thousands gathered; bands played patriotic music. Mayor LaGuardia addressed the crowds and asked for prayers for the soldiers in grave harm, "We, the people of the City of New York, in meeting assembled, send forth our prayers to the Almighty God for the safety and spiritual welfare of every one of you and humbly petition Him to bring total victory to your arms in the great and valiant struggle for the liberation of the world from tyranny." Overflowing churches and synagogues were kept open all day as worshipers gathered to pray. The waters off Normandy were bloody.

The Allies captured Cherbourg and Caen. On August 15 a revolt broke out in Paris. The Metro workers, along with local police, staged a strike. The following day the postal workers refused to show up to work, igniting a city-wide strike. The Battle for Paris had begun.

The military conflict took nearly a week. Some German troops retreated. On Hitler's orders, Notre Dame Cathedral and historic monuments throughout the city were to be turned into a "pile of rubble." However, General von Choltitz refused to carry out the orders. The Free French mustered the gendarmerie, platoons of police. Patriotic citizens able to shoot banded with the local resistance to drive the remaining invaders out of Paris. Greeted by ecstatic Parisians, the Free French Résistance 2nd Armored Division reached Paris on August 24.

The German garrison surrendered on August 25 and thousands of Nazis fled the city. Pierre's cousin, Michael, called from London to confirm the tremendous news. "Pierre, though things are a bit chaotic still, Paris is liberated. She is free at last!"

Sir Michael sensed Pierre's beaming smile through the telephone, "Be proud, Pierre! Your Free French, together with the Allies, triumphantly ended the German Occupation. General de Gaulle has reclaimed Le Meurice as headquarters for the Provisional Government of the free French Republic!"

Pierre felt ecstatic. Though, he was concerned for his friends in the resistance movement. Pierre remarked, "Michael, I heard from Andrew that there is fighting still?"

In a halting voice, Michael explained, "Yes, the Germans have begun their exodus of troops from Paris. But I'm afraid that skirmishes are still being fought in the streets. I am sorry. Hundreds of vigilant local fighters have lost their lives due to sniper attacks around the city."

Pierre thought of his brave compatriots from the Hotel Celtic bar. He sat down, "Alors, they are the true patriots."

German snipers shot at Charles de Gaulle, yet he marched victoriously down the Avenue des Champs-Elysées and entered the Place de la Concorde. The day the Germans surrendered; from the Hotel de Ville the general roused the joyous Paris crowd.

Pierre wished with all of his heart that he could be standing on the Champs-Elysées on August 29. In a grand celebration with flags waving, florist Madame Bonheur and her husband Bernard, tobacconist Pascal and throngs of cheering Parisians greeted the Americans as the U.S. Army's 28th Infantry Division, men and tanks, paraded in formation down the grand avenue.

Just two days before the Parisians cheered the liberating Allies, Oberleutnant Otto Heinrich had assembled his belongings. Knowing this day was coming, he had previously removed his favorite stolen artwork from their carved frames. Regrettably, he could not take it all and he tossed one painting in the trash. Bitterly, he thought about the Picasso that had been dedicated to Elsa Bessette. The discarded painting served as a reminder that a woman he wanted got away. It stung him to think about his failure to catch an enemy of the German state, Pierre Bessette.

A lifeline had been set up for officers to protect them and route them back to Germany. Some unlucky fighters were sent to Alsace and Lorraine in eastern France where the Germans continued to fight. As Otto exited Paris, his car was showered with bullets. The attack failed and he managed to get away. Otto Heinrich was en route with his stolen loot to his hometown near Stuttgart, Germany.

Chapter 37

With Federico's guidance, Pierre had set up a small shop with the jewelry pieces that Ellie and Kristin had stowed in their jewelry cases and with the gems that they had smuggled out of France. Pierre created a stunning pair of emerald earrings designed with a gold flower head dotted with yellow and white diamonds, gold brooches with swirls of diamonds and aquamarines, and a ruby ring encircled with multi-colored sapphires and emerald cut diamonds. He designed avant-garde pieces that appealed to customers living in a more eclectic city. Seven months after leaving London, Bijoux New York held the promise of a little success for the Christmas and Hanukkah seasons.

Ellie met with her therapist every week. As predicted, progress came slowly. Her psychiatrist could mention Anna's name only briefly or Ellie would experience a setback. On some days she stopped talking altogether.

By the following spring 1945, Dr. Nolan conversed with Ellie about Anna's death and discussed the events that led to her family coming to America. She blamed herself or Michi for Anna going outside on that fateful afternoon, and grew upset with Pierre for their risky roles in the resistance and not leaving Paris for America. Dr. Nolan reassured Pierre that her anger was a good sign. Ellie was reconnecting with reality. Still, at times, she spent a day or two holed up in her room. Occasionally, Pierre and Ellie talked about the liberation of Paris.

Since their arrival in New York, Michael (Michi as Ellie still called her son) would take a pot of tea to the solarium where he would read to his mother on a daily basis. Initially, he read her novels. In recent months, he read aloud from the New York Times and the New York Evening Post.

After nearly a year and a half of intense counseling, in a grueling up and down battle, Ellie accepted that Anna was gone. She sobbed, refused to eat, and Pierre worried that she would retreat again into her solitary world. But before long she talked about a single current event or the weather.

Amused by an ad, one day Ellie asked, "Michi, is it true that a person puts money into a slot in a machine and takes out food?"

"Yes, Maman, I promise to take you to the automat, Horn and Hardart. You select your sandwich from the small glass doors, put in your coins and voila! Open the door to take your food."

Eventually Ellie took an interest in eating; she and Pierre finally dined out. Ellie gained a little weight and emotional strength. As promised, the Duke invited them to an acclaimed French restaurant where Ellie critiqued the authenticity.

One morning Ellie asked Pierre to take her Hermès travel sac that she had carried from Paris to Lyon and on to England down off her high closet shelf. After rummaging around in the roomy bag, Ellie found what she was looking for. She took out her mother's small farmhouse painting that in Paris she had kept on her bedside table. She kissed the icon and lovingly propped it up next to her reading lamp. Pierre cringed when Ellie slammed him for lying about her family heirlooms stolen from their Paris apartment.

Another day, Ellie announced, "I'd like to set up my easel in the solarium." Several days a week, she painted for hours. Sometimes, her canvases displayed dark, angry swirls of paint. Pierre did not comment. At other times, she painted realistic French scenes in soft colors.

∞∞∞

By late spring, 1946, Ellie and Pierre began to take afternoon walks in Central Park. One fine day, Ellie reached for Pierre's hand. That evening she playfully tousled his hair, running her fingers through the wavy strands. Pierre pulled her close and kissed her tenderly at first and then deeply with passion. Ellie fervently returned his kiss. Two years after arriving in New York, Ellie welcomed Pierre to her bed.

They spent Sunday mornings reading the paper and drinking strong coffee as they did in Paris. Pierre introduced Ellie to the Waldorf-Astoria hotel's famous eggs benedict with hollandaise sauce. She began to tour New York's museums. Kristin took Ellie clothes shopping.

Kristin had met a man through the Turners. Paul Perrotti was an IBM executive. Pierre had once remarked to Ellie, "I hope Kristin finds a young man. I am concerned that she might become a *vielle fille*, an old maid. They liked Paul and were delighted for the love birds.

Kristin and Paul were married at St Michael's Presbyterian Church on Fifth Avenue in early September, 1946. Pierre walked Kristin down the aisle. She wore an elegant pearl and diamond necklace that Pierre had created especially for her. The Duke had designed a gold three-point Swedish crown brooch for Kristin. He placed rubies along the base; the arches were dotted with pearls and culminated in a pavé diamond cross atop the crown.

After a Bermuda honeymoon, the couple made their home in Manhattan. Paul had inherited a family home in Chappaqua, New York where they spent an occasional country weekend. Thankfully, Kristin still spent a good amount of time with Ellie, Pierre and Michi—her family. The Bessettes visited Kristin and Paul's country house, spent evenings with the young couple at the theater in Manhattan and enjoyed good-old fireside tea visits.

But the house felt lonely without Kristin's sweet presence. Pierre did not want Ellie left alone when he was working at Bijoux New York. He hired a housekeeper. Esther Laugeson came in four days during the week. Though born in America, the energetic "Miss Essie" was a perfect fit with her Scandinavian and French heritages. She was a superb cook who treated the family to traditional French dishes like coq au vin and chicken chasseur (hunter's chicken). She introduced the Ambrose family to American favorites—southern fried chicken, pot roast, mashed potatoes and apple pie.

Miss Essie was delightful company with her spell-binding tales of growing up in rural Minnesota, spying on Native Americans from a hill, and seeing the first automobile drive down their dirt road.

Pierre renewed a favorite Sunday tradition that began in Paris at the Hotel Meurice, now de Gaulle's headquarters. After Paul and Kristin attended church, they met Pierre, Ellie and Michael for a luncheon at the historic Tavern on the Green, an iconic restaurant in a rustic Central Park setting. Federico often joined the family as did Maggie and Andrew who drove into Manhattan from Rhinebeck for the weekend. James and Mary Turner and their two boys, Patrick and Edward, Michael's first American pals, would drive into the city for the Sunday gathering. The Bessettes spent Christmas in Rhinebeck with Maggie, Andrew, Kristin and Paul.

Kristin's baby girl was born in August, 1947. She was named Eve Annika. With tears in her eyes, Ellie smiled and held baby Eve at her christening and whispered to Pierre, "She is precious."

Pierre's family had established roots in New York. London was recovering from the Blitz but many places were still a landscape of rubble and rationing continued. Paris had yet to recover from years of German occupation. Europe's economies were severely compromised. Yet Pierre's New York boutique flourished. Pierre knew it would take some time before Paris and London would regain economic stability. He and Ellie donated heavily to England's restoration fund as well as donating non-perishable food and clothing for struggling citizens in Great Britain.

In 1948, Dr. Nolan took Pierre aside. "Mr. Ambrose, as you know, Ellie has suffered a series of traumatic events. And she believed that a stronger person could have "snapped out" of her feelings. She now understands that is unrealistic. She has made excellent headway. Ellie is a remarkable woman to face war, a terrifying escape, the loss of her family heirlooms and most difficult, to fight through the death of her child. She will have ups and downs, and perhaps more dark days than many of us. Certainly, we want Ellie to remember Anna and the good times. But when she feels despair, please remind Ellie that Anna would *want* Ellie to be happy."

Dr. Nolan added, "People who suffer from loss often benefit by helping others. Ellie had made people's lives better in Paris and in London. She mentioned that she had been pulled out of childhood poverty and war, and that she feels a certain 'responsibility to serve others.' That's good, and how she does that and when will be up to her. Feeling in control of her life will help to balance Ellie's darker days."

"Although I feel that Madame Ellie's life will improve to normalcy, it is too soon, and she is still too fragile to return to Paris with so many poignant memories of Anna."

Pierre expressed his utmost gratitude to Dr. Nolan and said, "Will you be available to see my wife if she begins to slip?"

"Of course. And please remember Pierre that depression must be taken day by day. Ellie struggles to comprehend why Anna was taken from her. She *will* experience difficult times."

Soon after, Ellie volunteered twice a week at the Metropolitan Museum of Art. On her first day, she changed her outfit several times. She chose a new style, a pretty light green wool crepe peplum dress. The peplum flared out just a little to highlight Ellie's small waist that she cinched with a gold toned belt. She dabbed perfume on her wrist. Pierre had given her a bottle of Miss Dior, Christian Dior's debut fragrance named in honor of Christian's sister, Catherine, a surviving member of the French Résistance.

One year later, docent Ellie Ambrose kept her eye on a boy who became engrossed with certain artwork. He sketched the paintings with a pad and pencil taken from his school satchel. At first, he walked away and pretended not to hear when Ellie tried to speak with him. But months later, she caught up with him.

"I notice you like Impressionist art, the landscapes and soft colors. I am from France and I can tell you about the artists."

Not long after, he opened up to Ellie. His name was Antonio. "My father died in the war. My mother had to move us to a cheaper apartment in Harlem. She is a waitress."

Antonio told Mrs. Ellie, "I don't want to be home alone. Italian and Puerto Rican gangs follow me sometimes. I'm afraid of them." Antonio spent rainy or cold days in the museums or sketched outdoors in the park on pleasant days until his mother's shift ended. Antonio met his mother on the corner and they walked home or took the bus together in bad weather.

He implored Ellie, "Please don't tell on me. I walk into the museum with a family and their kids, or behind a tour group."

Ellie would tell the wide-eyed boy her first-hand tales about the artists, Impressionism, Cubism and Modern art. Fascinated with the lives of the great artists and their works, soon Antonio sought Ellie out to hear her stories. Ellie bought her young friend an art book which he received with a wide grin. He sketched from the prized book, and showed Ellie his work. Antonio was talented but needed lessons.

Overtime, Ellie's ability to inspire Antonio gave her an idea. In 1951, she could barely get the words out fast enough, "Pierre, I want to start a foundation in Anna's name AMoR—Anna's Maison of the aRts. It will be an after-school program for disadvantaged children who have a strong love of the arts but no way or money to foster their interests. Pierre, I *know* it's my calling," she insisted.

Pierre knew it would become her passion. He encouraged her. "Ellie, I love your idea." She went on, "After school the students could learn to paint, draw or play a musical instrument, free of charge. Perhaps, instruction could come from some of our artist and musician friends. They may be willing to donate their time and talents."

It would be a huge undertaking but Pierre could see that Ellie was ready to throw herself into something dear to her heart and that, above all, would help children. "We will make it happen!"

By 1953, thanks to Pierre's endowment and donations from the Duke, Maggie and Andrew, the Turners, Peggy Guggenheim and philanthropic New Yorkers, an AMoR program was up and running. Mimi Van Hoomissen's new husband, an attorney, drew up the legal documents, pro bono, for "Anna's Maison"—a yellow house covered in ivy where the children were instructed—and for the AMoR foundation scholarships. Ellie became one of the after-school art instructors.

The children took field trips to Manhattan's art museums, the New York Symphony Orchestra and the Ballet Society at the New York City Center for Music and Drama. A little girl who dreamed of becoming a dancer was given the first

AMoR grant for professional ballet lessons. A young man who demonstrated brilliant musical talent was identified, and he entered Juilliard on a scholarship.

Eventually, Ellie was approached to start a second program in Harlem with financial backing from the City of New York.

Pierre invited their son Michael, Federico, Kristin and Paul, Maggie and Andrew, James and Mary Turner, their boys, and the Van Hoomissen's to lunch at the Plaza to celebrate the opening of Ellie's second "Anna's Maison."

Prior to lunch, Ellie walked into their front room beaming, and for a fleeting moment Pierre envisioned the striking young women he first met at the university. Ellie dressed in a cream-colored Chanel suit with a knee-length skirt and cardigan style jacket trimmed and decorated with black embroidery and gold-tone buttons. She wore cream pumps, pearls and white gloves. Pierre remarked, "Chérie, success becomes you. You are regal and more beautiful than ever! Coco would be immensely proud of this moment."

"Pierre, for the first time since leaving England, I feel my life has real purpose."

Ellie broadened the horizons and fostered hope in children eager to pursue their talents. Her programs were helping to keep some at-risk kids safely off the streets. Through an apprenticeship, Antonio had helped Ellie set up the after-school programs.

At their luncheon, Ellie thanked her loved ones for their unwavering support.

"In the painting studio, I truly feel my daughter's presence. A child will laugh and I hear Anna's laughter chasing Brother Bernard in the monastery library or I hear her sheer delight at sliding down a banister. I *feel* Anna beside me as if we were together back at the orphanage in London helping the little ones with their arts and crafts. A girl will take my hand, I close my eyes and it is as though Anna is walking hand in hand with me in the Tuileries." Pierre held Ellie's hand tightly as she spoke, "I know I'm walking in a bit of a dream world, but I feel happier sensing Anna is always right there at my side."

"My chérie, this *is* your calling, and Anna is helping you. Believe that she will *always* be with you darling, with us."

"Hear, hear!" Federico pronounced as champagne glasses touched in tribute to Ellie Bessette Ambrose.

∞∞∞

Weeks and months had turned into years. Although it had been only eleven years since they settled in New York, the Ambrose family had grown and their lives flourished. By 1955, America had entered a time of post-war prosperity. Thirteen years after escaping the Nazis, Pierre knew he had come to the right country for the help his family had desperately needed. During the time when much of Europe had been digging itself out from the ruins of war, the Bessettes once again had established themselves as creative artists and humanitarians. The family spoke less and less about Paris or London.

In 1947, an ad had promised, "a diamond is forever." American G.I.s returned home from war looking for love and marriage. With a supply of the sparkling jewel that symbolized enduring love, Bijoux New York stood near the forefront of American glamour and elegance. Pierre and his son Michael talked of a second boutique on Rodeo Drive in Los Angeles, California.

Pierre appreciated the opportunities available in the United States where hard work, a bit of luck, and with help from others one could have a chance at what was called the American Dream. He purchased their brownstone and expanded the solarium which became Ellie's studio. Pierre understood that his home would remain in America: Ellie would never leave Anna's Maison.

Pierre and Ellie proudly considered themselves French, and together with other émigrés they immersed themselves in their French heritage—the language, cuisine and literature. The Bessettes became American citizens eternally grateful to an unabashed, somewhat cocky country, less formal and not steeped in many centuries of tradition, but where dreams could take root.

Manhattan had become an internationally renowned center of fashion, the arts and business. Recognizing the importance of New York, the United Nations opened up their headquarters on spacious grounds overlooking the East River. Idlewild Airport flew ambassadors, dignitaries and jetsetters in and out of New York City.

In 1946, Cousin Michael, Beatrice and their son Charles had sailed to New York on the *Queen Elizabeth* for a long-awaited reunion. In 1953, the Middletons had traveled on the elegant new SS *United States*. By 1958, the Middletons began to jet "across the pond" for Christmas where the family gathered at Maggie and Andrew's Rhinebeck home with an excursion to the Ambrose home in Manhattan to enjoy the theater and arts.

Pierre and Ellie talked about returning to Europe on vacation. But Ellie knew that she could not handle the poignant memories just yet. Pierre and son Michael had both watched Ellie on occasion pick up her mother's small farmhouse painting. It was painful to witness the tears and the sadness on Ellie's face. Missing from their lives was Grandmother Annette Lindstrom's remembrance painting of their beloved Anna.

Chapter 38

Michael Ambrose

Almost from the moment he had set foot in New York, Michael Bessette Ambrose had embraced the American lifestyle. He loved the cars, music and crooners like Frank Sinatra and Perry Como. He and his friends had watched emerging rock and roll singers Elvis Presley and Buddy Holly on the American Bandstand television show.

Michael was a natural all-around athlete—an outstanding downhill racer who had learned to ski in Chamonix, France. He skied in Vermont with the Turner boys. Michael excelled in soccer, and he was a skilled high school all-American football player. Proudly, he wore his letterman jacket.

Michael's college choice had been Patrick Turner's alma mater, the University of Southern California. When Michael visited his friend, he was captivated by the glorious outdoor lifestyle of the Golden State: the orange groves, surfing, and the sunny beaches with girls in two-piece swim suits.

Michael was offered a scholarship on the University of Southern California football team as a Trojan place kicker. However, concerned that his mother could relapse if he were so far away, in the end, he chose a college close to home.

Michael Ambrose graduated magna cum laude with a business degree from Columbia University. He was a go-getter anxious to move his life forward. Michael had taken on tremendous responsibility at Bijoux overseeing its renovation and expansion. He became a partner in his father's jewelry business.

Michael met his fiancée, Celine Mercier, at Columbia University's French club. Celine worked as a buyer at Saks Fifth Avenue department store. They were to be married in December, 1958 at St. Patrick's Cathedral. But before the wedding, Michael contemplated fulfilling a youthful promise.

When he was a boy, Michael had told his stricken mother over and over, "I will return to Paris to search for our painting of Anna." It pained the family that Anna's portrait was out there *somewhere* but not at home where it belonged and where they could gaze at Anna's sweet image.

Years ago, Pierre had to divulge a difficult truth to Ellie. *Her paintings had never been secured in storage.* Pierre shook his head, "We were barely out the door when the Germans began searching for us. Paul Roux told me that our door had been damaged and the locks had been changed even before Maison Entreposage had arrived the Thursday after we fled. I hired a detective through a friend in the police department. He discovered that our home had been ransacked."

Pierre had confessed, "Chérie, I was afraid to tell you. I feared that you might become despondent, and you had adjusted pretty well in London before the bombings. I hoped that we could return home after the war, and our home would be waiting for us."

Ellie said, "Pierre, keeping the truth from me at that time probably was the best way to spare me additional sorrow and stress."

Today, when Michael looked at his mother, he glimpsed a strong, accomplished woman running her philanthropies. Michael believed that his promise to find his mother's painting of Anna may have sparked Ellie's turnaround.

Celine encouraged him. "Michael, you were just a child, but keep the promise made to Ellie. Go to Paris now. Our wedding plans are set. I don't want you to regret that you did not take this opportunity. What a wonderful gift you could give to Ellie if you discovered Anna's painting!"

Over the years, the family had searched databases without luck. But what if paintings or their furniture had been cleared out by the local police and stored away and collecting dust with other "abandoned" pieces in a warehouse? Perhaps their bureau still contained the family photographs in silver frames or the photographs lying loosely in drawers? Or a neighbor who remembered something that could be helpful?

Over the years, Michael realized that Anna's death was an accident and not his fault. Of course, he could not kill the Nazis who forced them to flee. But Michael could inquire should the police, neighbors, nearby merchants or Genevieve knew something that Pierre's investigator had missed. Now with a European commission set up to reunite Jewish owners with their stolen goods, Michael could personally search the databases. At the very least, he would make certain that their paintings had been added to the archived journals of lost or stolen art. It would be difficult to keep a promise from the past, but he was up to the task.

On November 3, 1958, Michael booked a first-class ticket on a Pan American 707 jet from Idlewild Airport to Le Bourget airport. It had been sixteen years since his family's escape. Now, Michael found himself sipping a fine champagne as he flew back to his country of birth with an American passport.

Michael had arranged for a car and driver from Le Bourget to Paris. The driver, who had pegged Michael as American, seemed surprised by his perfect French and by his detailed knowledge of the city's historic sites. The chauffeur pulled up to Notre-Dame Cathedral, an historic French Gothic jewel on the Isle de la Cité. Michael lit a candle as light streamed in through impressive stained-glass rose windows. He murmured a little prayer, "for success in finding Maman's painting and our photographs of Anna."

Pulling up to the Hotel Meurice on a plaza designed with historic statues and fountains, Michael felt a stab of tenderness. He pictured Anna running with him through the nearby Tuileries Garden after Sunday lunch.

Michael ate his breakfast in the refurbished restaurant, Le Meurice. Eager to roll up his sleeves, his first stop would be Maison Bijoux.

A blustery wind whipped up off the Seine; brilliant red and orange leaves clung to their branches. Girls, bundled in wool coats and silk scarves, walked arm in arm. Michael raised the collar of his Burberry trench coat. His ancestral city appeared radiant.

Prior to Michael's departure, Pierre had explained, "Michi, the night before we fled, I left some inventory for Genevieve—enough jewelry to sell for a month or two. Inside our cellar safe, I left cash and a list of reputable jewelry sources. However, to carry on, Genevieve would have had to purchase fresh inventory, and the Germans would have had to let her be..."

What Pierre did *not* share with Michael were the details of a private note he wrote at his desk on the night before their escape. Pierre had taken out a crisp white sheet of bond paper. With his fountain pen, he intended to write a simple farewell note to his assistant. Pierre knew that Genevieve had feelings for him that he never acknowledged. He had worked side by side with his shop girl and had been faithful to Ellie. Pierre's tender emotions welled up. Then Pierre laid down his fountain pen, tore the letter into tiny pieces and tossed the scraps into the trash basket. He loved Ellie deeply and would *"laissez le chat qui dort"* — "let the cat sleep."

Outside their former boutique, a stand of chestnut trees lined tiny rue de Castile; Michael stood for several minutes. As expected, Maison Bijoux was no longer the house of jewelry that he knew as a young boy. He watched well-dressed women, their arms laden with packages, leave a fashionable gift boutique, *Genevieve*.

Michael opened the dark mahogany door to a pleasant floral scent with a hint of citrus. He stepped inside the familiar wood-paneled salon where he and Anna had played hide-and-seek behind the display cases. Today, additional glass shelves were stocked with perfume, monogrammed soaps, bath oils and cosmetics.

A young saleswoman was helping two pretty TWA air hostesses. They were dressed in smart, light blue uniforms, crisp white blouses and wings pinned to their hats. It was no accident that Trans World Airlines, known as the "glamour airline," attracted movie stars and the wealthy. Owner Howard Hughes made certain that celebrities received VIP treatment from the moment a limousine would pick them up from their homes. The famous waited in private airport "Royal Ambassador" lounges and were personally escorted onto the airplanes. Photographers eagerly awaited to snap a photo of the jet-setters when they arrived at exotic destinations.

The TWA stewardesses were purchasing luxurious body creams and French perfume. The shop girl filled stylish travel totes with samples from Dior, Lancôme, and Chanel. *Genevieve Paris*, scrolled elegantly onto the make-up cases, advertised this chic Paris parfumerie world-wide.

Michael spotted Genevieve, now approaching middle age. Over the years, she had put on a little weight and her face was rounder, but her emerald green eyes were unmistakable. She was helping a matron purchase a Hermès scarf. Michael recalled that it would be impolite for him to approach her, or to make eye contact while she was working with her customer. Michael browsed gifts for Celine, his mother, Kristin and Aunt Maggie—scarves, French perfume, umbrellas, perhaps a scented rose geranium diptyque candle...

"May I help you, Monsieur?" asked Genevieve in English. Once again Michael appeared to be an American.

He looked up, smiled and mischievously replied in French, "Hello, Genevieve. Do you remember me?" Naturally, he placed a kiss on each cheek.

She stood back and stared. Her eyes widened and putting her hand to her mouth, Genevieve whispered, "*Mon Dieu*! "Michi, is it really you?"

"*Oui*, Genevieve, *c'est moi!*" replied Michael with a broad smile.

The front door bell jingled when two more customers entered the shop. An older woman hurried out from the back.

"Maman, do you remember Pierre's son, Michel?"

Madame Caron looked at Michael. "Michel!" she exclaimed. "You have grown into such a handsome young man like your father! You must come to dinner tonight. I hope your family is well, oui?" Madame ran off to help the newly arrived customers.

Genevieve laughed softly and touched Michael's arm. "Maman is correct. You look like Pierre when you smile! Michi, I am so happy to see you. Please, everyone come to dinner. I want to hear everything. Alors, this is our busiest time of day; customers come in before heading to their flights." She lowered her voice, "Always last minute, especially the Americans, God bless them. Maman lives with me now. Promise you will come, seven o'clock, yes?"

Michael replied, "I am in Paris alone. But I would be delighted. Of course, I would love to come for dinner. Thank you." He would return to purchase gifts.

Michael walked over to rue Margaux taking in the picturesque neighborhood. He strolled past Pascal's tabac, the bright red awning a welcoming sight from his youth. Michael walked into their apartment courtyard and rang the doorbell. He was pleased that their handsome 19th century building with its scrolled wrought iron balconies and decorative fleurs-des-lis had not changed. His heart quickened when he looked up at two turtle gargoyles that had spewed water onto Anna's and Michael's heads on a rainy day; they would laugh and skirt away from the cascading water.

Someone buzzed him inside the small luxury building. His gut wrenched when he rapped on their former apartment door. But no one answered. He knocked again when a matron across the hall opened her door and peered out cautiously.

"Madame Simone, bonjour!

Madame Simone gasped. "Michel, is it really you?" She squinted a bit and looked more closely. "It is you!" Madame Simone exclaimed, "come in, come in!"

A familiar honey and spice aroma filled the apartment. Madame Simone hugged Michael and moved slowly to make coffee. A little bird chirped from the same Black Forest cuckoo clock. Michael did not see any family paintings or furnishings.

As though time had stood still, Michael dug into a generous slice of vanilla *Bienenstich* (bee sting cake) topped with crunchy honey and almonds. He took a sip of coffee.

"Michi, what *happened* to your family? You left so quickly."

He described his parent's work with the resistance, the last-minute escape and their lives in England and America. He alluded that his mother had suffered a breakdown following the intense London bombings but did not burden her with Anna's misfortune. He explained his mission was to locate their family's lost heirlooms, especially the artwork left behind that fateful morning.

Mme. Simone nodded with a smile. "I am pleased that Pierre and Ellie fought in the resistance movement. I detested the Occupation."

Michael put his fork down and leaned closer, "Madame Simone, did you see what happened to our apartment or our belongings after we left?"

Her eyes downcast, she said, "Well, yes. I awoke that Saturday morning and from my courtyard window, I noticed a light on in your apartment very, very early. So, I called to alert your father that two soldiers had been looking for him on Friday night."

"Later that morning, two different Nazis from the night

before, one tall and blond and another pudgy one, came to your apartment not long after your family had departed."

Madame quietly said, "They broke into your apartment, Michi. The stocky one left with his arms laden with artwork. He was cursing in German, and shouting at the taller soldier who carried away a silver candelabra." Brigitte Simone hung her head. "I was peering through a sliver of an opening in my door. I was angry and also frightened."

Michael felt heartsick. But he composed himself and inquired further if she had seen the soldier's names. "No, I am sorry, Michi. Unfortunately, I could not see their name tags. It was so long ago, and I most likely would not have remembered anyway."

She added, "A few days later, men with white gloves tried to unlock your door. I believe it was a moving company. But by then, government officials had already changed the lock. The movers knocked on my door and the Charbonnier's and the Blanchet's. But we had no idea where you had gone, and so they left."

A bit hesitant, Mme. Simone continued. "Then, a German family moved into your apartment. The father was an important military officer. I can't recall his name. I thought at that point that I would not see any of you again. Michi, I was worried for all of you. The German sent his wife and two boys back home before the Allies liberated Paris. I could see from the worry on his face that he knew the end was coming."

"When the German left, your home remained unoccupied, and I hoped that your family would return. But several months after our liberation, some men, perhaps the French government, removed your contents."

Disheartened, Michael nonetheless chatted a little more about their lives in America. He sipped his remaining coffee and thanked his former neighbor. He gave Madame his business card in case she remembered anything else during that ominous time in 1942. With a hug goodbye, he promised her that the family would come to see her if they returned to Paris. When they parted, Madame told Michael, "You were such a sweet family, and I prayed for your safety."

Chapter 39

Michael kicked a stone into the street. His spirits were dampened by an afternoon drizzle but more so after learning that German soldiers had walked away with artwork. But which paintings? And what had happened to the remainder of their furnishings? He tucked his chilly hands inside his coat pockets.

At 10:30 the next morning, Michael was scheduled to meet with a Madame Beauregard who headed up the Cultural Archives Commission for Stolen Art. Michael would search their files of confiscated paintings.

Before the war, a young woman, Rose Valland, had studied fine art at several prestigious universities. After college, she had been hired as Special Staff for Pictorial Art. Once Paris fell to the Germans, Rose was forced to remain in her job and maintain museum records. But Rose spoke German. Secretly, she had listened and kept personal notes regarding the artwork that the Germans had stolen from private collectors and museums as well. Rose noted which art had been spirited away to Goring and Hitler's collections in Germany and Austria or that were hidden throughout Germany. In 1944, Rose had disclosed her notes to the "Monuments Men" who Roosevelt had tasked to return cultural artifacts to France. Thanks to La Résistance art spy, Rose Valland, thousands of hidden paintings had been returned. Michael held out hope that Anna's portrait would be discovered in the archives.

But first, at nine o'clock in the morning, Michael would

meet with Commissioner Morel to determine if any of their furniture containing their family photographs had been catalogued. Perhaps Morel could help to locate the dresser that contained their photographs? Any remembrance of Anna would be a blessing...

Michael picked up a bouquet of flowers and arrived at Genevieve's home at seven o'clock that evening. The cream-colored stucco apartment building was built in a late nineteenth century art nouveau style with decorative arched windows, lacy wrought-iron balconies and sea foam gray shutters.

Genevieve opened the door; she looked chic and classically French in a simple black dress and multiple strands of pearls. She brought Michael into an elegant living room salon with high ceilings, carved moldings, softly worn dark French oak floors and a pale blue antique Aubusson area rug knotted with a rose and celery green medallion. A faint whiff of lemon polish hung in the air.

Genevieve, who in 1942 was a young war widow, had remarried. She smiled and introduced her husband, Jean-Marc Jourdan, an attorney who Michael thought resembled a young version of his father. They had a precocious eight-year-old daughter named Caroline.

Jean-Marc opened a Veuve Clicquot champagne while Genevieve offered an appetizer of small black bread points spread with unsalted butter, smoked salmon, a sprig of dill, and sprinkled with fresh ground black pepper.

In the dining room Genevieve and her mother served braised lamb and roasted root vegetables, an arugula and asparagus salad with vinaigrette, followed by a cheese tray of creamy brie, chèvre and blue-veined Roquefort. Afterwards, an apple tart and coffee were served in the salon.

Caroline was sent to read with her father while Mme. Caron cleared the table. Genevieve poured a brandy for Michael and herself. At dinner Michael had touched on his father's Jewish ancestry, their escape to relatives in London, and their new life in America.

A fire crackled in the fireplace. Genevieve curled her legs under her on the couch and asked pointedly, "Michi, *please* tell me what had happened. You left so suddenly?"

Michael explained that his father was not only Jewish but that he and Ellie had been working with the Free French Résistance. "My father had been followed that Friday afternoon after work. We believe that the Germans were preparing to arrest him and possibly deport our family to the camps. Genevieve, he could not tell you where we were going. Our departure on that Saturday morning was imminent. Sadly, we had to leave everything and flee."

"Oui," exclaimed Genevieve. "The Germans not only robbed Bijoux but damaged the store in anger at your father's disappearance."

Genevieve let out a small sigh, "Two Nazis came into the shop early Saturday morning asking for Pierre." Genevieve looked away and took a deep breath. She looked back at Michael and told him about the rape. "The tall, blond soldier tried to help me but he could not distract the stocky one who seemed to be in charge; the one looking for Pierre and who attacked me."

Michael's hand reached out to Genevieve, "I am so very sorry."

"As soon as they left me that morning, as the blond soldier urged me to do, I called your father to warn him that Nazis were demanding to know his whereabouts, and they were heading to your apartment. But there was no answer at your home."

Genevieve leaned forward, "Michael, I gave the soldiers misleading information. Your father indicated to me that your family had planned a vacation in Nice. But I told the Germans that your destination was Cannes."

"When they left, I ran home and did not get out of bed or return to Bijoux for days."

"I was terrified to be alone in the shop. I asked my

mother to accompany me the following Wednesday. I had to keep Pierre's business open, and we needed to survive. But when I opened the shop, we found cases smashed, chairs over-turned and papers strewn around the floor."

"Clearly, it was revenge for your father's disappearance, Michi. Pierre left an exclusive necklace for Comte Montebourg in a gift-wrapped box in the office safe. I delivered the gift for the Comtesse that afternoon. I used some of the count's pay-ment to repair the glass counters."

It took Genevieve and her mother two days to sweep up the glass, file the strewn papers and tidy the store. As they completed work in the office, Genevieve discovered a gift box and envelope that had fallen underneath Pierre's desk during the assault. She teared up, "Pierre and Ellie gave me an emer-ald necklace and matching earrings. The note said that they would not return until after the war, 'God willing,' as Pierre often said," bringing a smile to Genevieve's lips.

Genevieve continued. "As instructed, I located Pierre's cellar safe, unlocked it to find other jewelry pieces I could sell, a list of resources and funds to replenish my stock. I pretended to locals that Pierre would be returning from vacation so that his established customers would continue to support Pierre's business."

"One day, a dapper older gentleman came into the bou-tique asking for Pierre. I had seen the man several times be-fore, chatting with your father in the backroom. That day, the gentleman said, 'Pierre helps me *resist* (a long pause) such beautiful jewelry.' Michi, when I was in the cellar, I had tripped over a handsome tan La Mondiale leather suitcase with brass hinges. It was very heavy. I opened it, and was confused to find a "B2" radio used for communication. I thought of the suitcase radio and put the man's words together. I surmised then that Pierre may have been associated with La Résistance and had fled the country... or God forbid would be killed."

"I invited the man into the backroom. It was now late September. I told him that Pierre may not be returning soon, but I knew what was going on around Paris. The man said that vital information that could help to turn the war may come in for Pierre. Would I just relay a simple, innocuous message until they had a new source? Michi, I wanted to do my part to destroy the Nazis so I agreed, although I was very, very frightened."

"At first, he left me only a name and telephone number on a slip of paper. He told me to give that information to whoever came in and asked for 'directions to the Hotel Celtic.' Not long after, a fidgety, thin, young man in baggy pants and a threadbare sweater came in and inquired about the hotel directions. He left quickly. Two weeks later, a well-dressed middle-aged woman did the same, and so on... I was always scared, Michi. I had not forgotten the brutality of the German that Saturday morning. I told the woman 'Nazis prowl the neighborhood and watch the shop.' I am all that my mother has left in this world and we are barely scraping by. I was stunned when the woman told me that our dear florist, Madame Bonheur, could help me if we were ever forced to hide. She told me that your mother provided financing for Mme. Bonheur so that her basement could shelter Jewish families on the run."

Michael nodded, and held her hand, "My parents will be very proud to hear of your bravery, Genevieve."

Genevieve took a sip of brandy, "Maman and I wanted to keep Bijoux open but after a while it became a struggle to sell jewelry without Pierre's influence with the customers. Business had dwindled, even from America." Genevieve smiled. "I met my husband, Jean-Marc, when I consulted with him about the legality of opening a parfumerie or a sundry shop while Pierre was away."

In November, we replaced the Bijoux sign with our new business. We left the boutique interior as it was for Pierre's return. We renamed our little business *Genevieve's*. At first we sold basic skin care and household toiletries and essentials."

"I became bolder. I collected written messages from

Madame Bonheur." Genevieve added, "I kept the notes in an empty Hermès *eau de Victoria* perfume jar which for me simply meant victory!"

Eventually, the older gentleman from La Résistance returned. He asked for the suitcase, which I gave to him, of course. He thanked me and I no longer received inquiries." Genevieve chuckled. "Our new business had made it too dangerous for men to be observed frequenting a ladies' cosmetic shop."

"Michi, I forced myself to wipe the attack on that horrible Saturday out of my mind in order to move forward. Thankfully, the Germans left our meager business alone, and we barely got by."

Taking a deep breath, Genevieve elaborated. "We added a little more perfume and eau de cologne. Maman had been trained as an aesthetician. After the war, she started a small Institut de Beauté in our back room for local girls to treat themselves to a facial."

"The Americans stationed in Paris to help with the war 'wrap-up' shopped with us. The American GI's purchased mementos for their wives and girlfriends. We discovered that French goods were quite popular in America. We added French gifts to our shelves. As Paris began to recover, we offered more luxury items: perfume, candles, silk umbrellas and leather dress gloves."

Genevieve leaned toward Michael. "Michi, when Pierre and Ellie did not return after the war, I feared the worst for your family. As more and more tourists came back to Paris, we felt that the shop would not become Bijoux again. Years after the war, although I still prayed, I no longer believed that your family had lived through it." She touched Michael's hand, "Michi, I am so happy that I was wrong."

Genevieve said, "Over time we made a good life. We added shelves and sold luxury perfumes, then silk scarves and the most exclusive makeup brands like Chanel and Dior. Maman expanded her small beauty spa for tourists to enjoy a French facial. Word spread with the traveling set and with help from the stewardesses who passed the name of our skin care boutique along to their passengers. We hired two more aestheticians. We did quite well with the increasing influx of American tourists. Michi, without your father's initial financial help, we may not have survived. Now I can repay Pierre."

Michael took her shoulders, "No, no, please do not think of repaying us, Genevieve. I know my family wanted you to have the means to sustain your livelihood. You did exactly what you needed to do. My parents will be delighted to hear of your success!"

Michael then recounted how his parents had aided the resistance movement, their dramatic escape from Paris to Lyon, that they were hidden in the monastery and on a farm, the risky flight to England, and the medal awarded by General de Gaulle.

A grin appeared on Genevieve's face. "Yes, they deserve the honor. I remember those discreet visits from men who Pierre met with in the back office, and the radio left behind. And, I understand why Ellie came to Bijoux at times trembling or with swollen, red eyes. It was a *petit espionage!*

"Genevieve, you and my parents risked your lives and duped the Nazis right here under the enemy's nose. Pierre and Ellie will be proud to hear of your courage."

Michael told Genevieve about life in England during the remainder of the war, the "Baby Blitz" and sadly Anna's death which provoked tears from Genevieve. Michael revealed Ellie's debilitating depression, her long recovery and the success of Anna's Maison in New York. Michael recounted their plans for a second Bijoux in Los Angeles and his upcoming marriage to Celine.

"My parents are content. We made new lives in America, and they hope one day to visit their beloved Paris. They are French to the core, and would like to take a trip back while they are healthy. But, of course, they are not certain how the memories of Anna will affect them. Honestly, Maman had such a rough time trying to live without Anna; she is afraid to tempt fate."

Michael added, "Genevieve, I am attempting to recover Elle's heirlooms. Do you recall the name of the soldiers who came to the boutique looking for my father that Saturday morning? Had you ever gone back to our apartment?"

"No. After reading Pierre's instructions, I understood that you had fled. Pierre never mentioned your apartment. I'm so sorry, Michi. I don't recall the Germans' names. Over the years, I've tried to put that morning out of my mind. Genevieve knew nothing.

Jean-Marc had put Caroline to bed. He and Madame joined them for a brandy nightcap. They shared stories about the good times prior to the war.

Michael promised to encourage Pierre and Ellie to visit them. He extended an invitation to Genevieve's family to visit New York. They said they may very well take him up on the offer. Genevieve remarked that their daughter adores Mickey Mouse.

"We would love to take Caroline to Disneyland some-day." She laughed aloud. "Caroline recognized your accent when you used American words and whispered to her father earlier in the evening, 'Where are Monsieur's mouse ears?'"

When Michael got up to leave, he kissed Genevieve and Madame on each cheek, thanking them for the delicious home-cooked dinner. He shook Jean-Marc's hand. Michael gave Genevieve his business card, and wrote down Pierre and Ellie's home telephone number. "Contact us anytime, Genevieve; if you think of *anything* else, even something you may feel is insignificant relating to that horrible time. Any small detail might help us locate something of Anna. And, please come visit us in the States. Bonsoir dear friends."

The following morning, Michael met with a Monsieur Etienne Morel from the Office of Cultural Affairs. He informed Michael, "During the Occupation, discarded furniture had been warehoused in Paris and then unclaimed pieces were auctioned off." Morel had checked his catalogs, files and notes regarding *any* possible furnishings retrieved from the Bessette home address in the summer of 1942 or later.

"Monsieur Ambrose, in a case like this, the French police would have been ordered to remove abandoned furniture under Germany's newly established 'Furniture Operation Act.' Stolen items were then stored in the department store Lévitan. Desirable furniture and goods often were sold cheaply to Nazi officers and then shipped to Germany. However, all paintings would have been stored at the Jeu de Paume museum to be catalogued."

Morel looked away. "Sadly, I have no record for your former residence. After the war, some pieces may have been stolen by unscrupulous employees of the state who then sold the goods on the Black Market. It is a terrible blight on our history, Monsieur. People were desperate. I am so very sorry. We just don't know what happened in your case. However, I know people who are patriots but who were forced to work for the Germans during the Occupation. I will make inquiries on your family's behalf, Monsieur. Many Parisians knew and loved your parents. Your mother helped many families during that terrible time. Please leave me your contact information. If I have any success at all learning what happened, I will be certain to contact you."

"Monsieur, I am deeply grateful for your help. Thank you. Any furnishings or family photographs that are found would mean so much to my family."

Following the blow from Monsieur Morel, Michael steeled himself for the meeting with Sophie Beauregard whose department was charged with reuniting stolen art with their owners. Sophie was dressed in a dark navy skirt, gray sweater and a silk Givenchy scarf. Michael handed her his business card and explained their family story.

"Monsieur Ambrose, yes, I knew Ellie Bessette!" Sophie

said. "She was on the board of the Louvre where I began my apprenticeship. A lovely woman. We always wondered what happened to her, here one day and then gone." Madame Beauregard's hand swished the air as if sweeping it from the room. She leaned toward Michael and whispered, "Was she Jewish?"

Michael briefly explained about his parent's work with La Résistance, and their abrupt escape. He informed her about Anna. "Mother is well, living in New York but not able to travel just yet."

"I am searching for my artist grandmother Annette Lindstrom's *Portrait of Anna as a Young Girl*. Michael also explained about *Morning on the Seine* from Claude Monet's series and the Picasso sketches all of which were gifted to his mother: "Growing up, Ellie had a unique connection with these artists, especially Claude Monet, who had been a prominent figure in her childhood." Michael showed Madame the photographs taken of the paintings with his father's Fex camera before the escape.

Madame nodded; she was aware that a painting was missing from the *Mornings on the Seine* series.

"After Anna was born, Picasso had given my mother a sketch from one of the paintings in his series, *Mother and Child*. It was simple, but lovely: a young woman with long hair cascading gently alongside the baby in her arms. Picasso signed the sketch, and on the back, he penned 'Maman Elsa.' The painting depicts my mother. Another missing Picasso was a cubist style sketch the *Palace of Arts* in Barcelona. The painting was signed and, according to my mother, was cast aside and given to her because Picasso claimed that he used the wrong burnished red color on the dome."

Abruptly, Madame Beauregard slapped the table! She nodded enthusiastically. "Oui! Picasso sold many paintings through the Galerie Paris. His agent was my friend, Louise List. Louise became quite frustrated with Pablo for giving away perfectly good drawings that she knew she could sell. It is true that if Picasso was unhappy with a color or a particular angle, then it was gone!" Once again, Madame swished away the air.

Michael replied, "Madame, these paintings are the *only* mementos of my mother's early life and most important of her daughter. Sadly, our photo album was left behind and is lost as well. My mother had set aside several photographs to take with us. But in their haste the morning we escaped; she did not pack them. This omission has caused my mother terrible personal pain."

Mme. Beauregard nodded sadly. Undeniably there were missing Picasso sketches and Impressionist paintings still being discovered lying in attics or stashed in walls of Paris apartments. Madame and Michael spent hours looking through photographs of unearthed and catalogued artwork still missing from Jewish families.

Michael broke for lunch at two o'clock. "I will return to search more, if I may?" Mme. Beauregard was able to oblige him, but feared that his chance of finding a painting was slim.

Michael walked to Le Chat Noir for lunch. He sidestepped withered brown and yellow leaves that had drifted into piles.

Michael sat down at his family's favorite table. He sipped onion soup topped with crusty country bread and gruyere cheese; he sipped a glass of red table wine. He finished his meal with a little fruit and cheese course.

When he paid the bill, a black kitten, named Minette, jumped up onto the table and drank from his water glass just as the original Minette had done. He pictured Anna's impish face smiling and entertaining them all at lunch. Tears streamed down Michael's cheek...

Michael returned to the archives and settled back to look at more photographs. Stifling a yawn, a little after six o'clock, he felt a jolt.

"Madame, Madame, Madame Beauregard!" shouted Michael. He jumped up, *"Je l'ai trouvé, je l'ai trouvé ! Le Picasso!"* He believed that he recognized a painting that had hung in their salon while he was growing up.

Mme. Beauregard came to his side. "Michel, you found a painting?" Michael said, "I may have found the Picasso, *Mother and Child*."

Immediately, Madame picked up the telephone. She gave the clerk at the museum vault the catalog number. Michael continued his search. At seven o'clock, the Picasso sketch was brought to her office by a white-gloved steward. The note card said "the painting had been retrieved from a trash can."

As they turned the painting over, Michael exhaled and breathed a huge sigh of relief and smiled. The back of the painting was faintly scribbled "Maman Elsa B." The woman in the painting resembled his mother as a young woman. Elated to reunite a stolen painting, a Picasso no less, with its owner right before her eyes, Madame clapped her hands and exclaimed, "*Voila, le voilà!*" There it is!

There would be paperwork to fill out. But, regardless, Madame would not leave until Michael could take his mother's painting. Once she gathered all the information needed, including the customs documents, the painting was secured with protective wrapping.

Michael beamed, and kissed Mme. Beauregard on each cheek. He certainly would send her regards to his mother. Madame promised to diligently keep an eye out for the other paintings, particularly Anna's portrait. She smiled and clapped her hands together, "Oui, I am honored to continue the search for Madame Elsa and her family!

Chapter 40

Despite bleak, chilly November weather in New York, it was a glorious day. After Sunday brunch, together Ellie and Michael unwrapped Mother and Child. Ellie beamed and held the painting close to her heart. The Picasso painting that hung above their piano in Paris was now hanging in their solarium in New York. Ellie would send a handwritten note to Mme. Beauregard to express her deepest gratitude. With the recovery of this painting, their family and friends shared a renewed hope that someday they might welcome home Grandmother Nettie's Portrait of Anna.

When the immediate family was alone, Michael updated them about his trip to Paris. The air was sucked out of the room when Michael gave them the news of Genevieve's rape and her attempt to warn Pierre by telephone that Saturday. However, learning that Genevieve had carried on his work with the resistance, Pierre nodded his head and proudly smiled at his shop girl's courage. They were pleased to hear of Genevieve's marriage and the success of her parfumerie.

On Saturday, December 6th, Michael Bessette Ambrose married his sweetheart, Miss Celine Mercier. Celine wore a ball gown wedding dress designed by Italian designer Maria Antonetti. American buyers from Bergdorf's had begun importing couture from Italian designers after attending the first sumptuous post-war fashion show in Florence, Italy. Italian designers were refashioning their industry after the war and

Americans loved the styling and fine workmanship. Americans were embracing fashion from the Continent. The economic storm clouds were dissipating and Europe was growing stronger.

Pierre gave his future daughter-in-law, a delicate one-of-a-kind necklace which combined colorless and yellow diamonds that sparkled in contrast to one another as she walked down the aisle. Duke Verdi, "Uncle Freddie," presented Celine with a ruby heart-shaped brooch wrapped in a swirl of diamonds to commemorate their wedding day.

Following a reception at the Plaza Hotel, the newlyweds flew to Los Angeles en route to a honeymoon in exotic Hawaii. First, they spent two days in Los Angeles at the Beverly Hills Hotel. Michael's best man, Patrick Turner, and Patrick's wife had returned to their home in L.A. following Michael and Celine's wedding. The couples then met for dinner. Michael proposed a business idea: He and his father asked Patrick to oversee the opening of Bijoux on Rodeo Drive.

In 1959, Michael and Celine Ambrose joyfully announced the birth of their daughter, Madeline Annika Ambrose. Ellie and Pierre were overjoyed. Michael had hoped for a son to carry on the family business. But when he held his tiny daughter, he felt a rush of emotion and fell in love. Their son, Mathieu Peter was born a little more than a year later. Happily, an heir to the family's growing business.

Chapter 41

Mathieu Ambrose

Just as her mother Annette had taken Michi and Anna to the Paris art museums, Ellie showed her grandchildren, Madeline and Matt, the superb collections at the Metropolitan Museum, the Guggenheim and the Museum of Modern Art.

Mathieu Peter Ambrose had inherited exceptional talent with a brush. Ellie believed that Matt exhibited the most artistic painting ability in the family. He gravitated toward the modern with broad strokes and explosions of color. His interpretations translated to a bolder, more vivid style much like Pierre's jewelry designs.

Grandmother Nettie had enthralled Matt's father, Michael, with fantastic stories of her life as an artist in the Bohemian neighborhoods of Montmartre and Montparnasse. Today, Matt implored his own Grandmother Ellie to tell him about the "olden days." He loved to hear about the Bessettes' lives in Paris—the leafy boulevards, the cafés and their Sunday family outings. Matt never tired of hearing about distinguished artists, the ominous invasion of the Nazis, and most of all his family's heroic escape to England.

"We watched with admiration as your grandfather stood tall while General Charles de Gaulle awarded him the prestigious *Croix de Guerre* medal" said Ellie. Matt had learned that his Grandmother Ellie had helped to feed starving Parisians and found safe havens for those in hiding. He heard the heartfelt stories about his deceased Aunt Anna with whom he felt an affinity. His father, Michael, had found the Picasso painting that now hung in his grandparents' home, and he learned about his father's faithful search for the still-missing *Portrait of Anna*. As a little boy, Matt had stood as erect as his toy soldier. "Grandma, when I grow up, I will be a brave Ambrose man just like papa and grandpapa!"

Ellie and Pierre relished their Sunday lunch rituals in the Crystal Room at the Tavern on the Green. Michael and his wife, Celine, grandchildren Madeline and Matt; Cousin Kristin and Paul, their daughter Eve; Maggie and Andrew; the Turner family and "Uncle Freddie" all joined in at these lively gatherings where voices would be raised to be heard over one another.

Matt loved the wooded setting in Central Park where long ago sheep grazed in the meadow. He and Madeline hankered to ride the horse-drawn carriages that lined up in front of the restaurant.

In 1982, the family focus was on Matt. His father, Michael, ceremoniously stood and poured a crystal coupe of Krug champagne. He proudly announced Matt's graduation from Columbia University. "Let's raise our glasses to toast my son, an outstanding college man and our future business partner!"

It was no secret that Michael looked forward to opening Bijoux San Francisco with Matt as a partner. Michael continued, "The free-spirited 'flower children' of the sixties, will soon be settling into their own careers and making money. We will introduce them to the chic and beautiful world of *Maison Bijoux!*"

James and Mary Turner and their sons were present to celebrate Matt's graduation. Edward Turner had become a physician at Memorial Sloan Kettering where he worked in cancer research focusing on a deadly new disease afflicting homosexual men. Patrick, Michael's closest boyhood friend, had graduated from the University of Southern California's School of Business in Los Angeles. He married a California coed and they had settled in Santa Monica.

Patrick Turner had worked alongside Pierre's son, Michael, as an apprentice at Bijoux New York. Patrick had developed a shrewd business sense, and became an essential partner in the company. Together, Michael and Patrick had opened Bijoux Beverly Hills which Patrick now managed. Michael became CEO of the family business and managed Bijoux New York. Now, like a laser, Michael Bessette Ambrose focused on his son Matt and to opening a third boutique in San Francisco.

Matt greatly admired his father and grandfather, but he had a dilemma. Matt did not share their business interests. Matt's dream was to open his own gallery. Like the others, he had worked at Bijoux growing up. Today, Matt was interested in design through art, not by designing or marketing jewelry. His artwork had been exhibited at three prestigious and well-attended gallery shows. His bold colorful paintings sold quickly. Patrons eagerly awaited more from the young artist whom New York art critics had dubbed, *"New York's Ambrosia."* Matt Ambrose knew exactly the path he intended to take. He only needed to convince his father and his grandfather. Grandmother Ellie was a willing co-conspirator.

While studying at Columbia, Matt had taken night classes in police forensic science and criminology at the City University of New York's College of Criminal Justice. Matt attended the Police Academy program. He intended to paint for a living and to reunite stolen art with their rightful owners. He planned to work one day with the FBI or to own his own private investigation firm. To fulfill that dream, Matt needed experience.

After graduating from the police academy, Matt had collaborated on two missing person cases. He waited for the right time to approach his father and grandfather; it was a difficult task he did not relish.

Meanwhile Matt's father and grandfather granted him a little time to get painting "out of his system." Pierre kept a hand in the Bijoux business while he and Ellie ran their philanthropic endeavors. Matt's older sister Madeline loved the family business. She was a smart and creative buyer and a business graduate.

Years ago, Ellie and Pierre had sent her protégé, Antonio, to graduate school to hone his business skills. Antonio had proven to be a proficient manager of Anna's Maison and their growing scholarship foundation, AMoR. Antonio and his team now managed three branches of Anna's Maison, enriching the lives of hundreds of talented but disadvantaged children. Ellie and Pierre sat on the Board as did dear friends, James Turner and "the Duke." Thanks to the Ambrose Foundation, vulnerable children were kept away from gang influence and furthered their educations. Some former students went on to achieve lifelong dreams in the arts, which would have been impossible if not for AMoR. Ellie donated her time teaching art history as well.

Chapter 42

One morning, Ellie was contemplating Matt's recent painting, an explosion of color on the canvas. If one looked carefully, buried inside the opening poppy flower were a woman's sumptuous red lips. As Ellie and Matt stood back to view the painting from different angles, the telephone rang. In her studio, Ellie answered an unexpected call from Paris. Excited and breathless, Genevieve spoke rapidly in French.

"Maman and I were cleaning out closets. We came across my clothes and the bloody handkerchief that were stored after I was attacked."

"I had given my mother the package with the torn clothes and asked her to throw them away. I could not bear to wear them again."

However, Genevieve's mother did not throw them out. Money had been excruciatingly tight. She meant to wash and repair the garments thinking that Genevieve might need them again. After the attack and in the confusion of the moment, her mother had thrown the package of soiled clothes in the back of a drawer where they remained untouched until today.

Staring at the package, the memories of that dreadful Saturday had flooded into Genevieve's mind. She pictured the tall, blond soldier who tried to divert her attacker and who pleaded with her to warn the Bessettes.

Genevieve exclaimed, "Ellie, Michi requested that I call if I remembered anything from that Saturday morning in

1942, and now I do! Seeing that package of clothes after so many years, I visualized the tall soldier's metal name tag when he leaned over to dab the bleeding cut on my lip. It read Leutnant Stefan Schafer. Ellie, I recall that when he handed me the handkerchief for the cut on my lip, all I could do was stare at his name. The one who attacked me told Schafer to hurry so they could get to your apartment quickly. Voila! It is good, oui?"

Ellie agreed and handed the phone to Matt. "Genevieve, take a deep breath. Please speak more slowly, or in English if you can." Genevieve repeated her story in English.

"This is all *very* good news, Genevieve." Matt wrote down Stefan's name and asked her for the exact date of the assault. She replied without hesitation, "Saturday, July 18, 1942."

Matt said, "Genevieve, please don't wash the garments under *any* circumstances. Leave them exactly as they have been stored." Matt described the new procedures that were being tested that *may* someday give them a chance to identify the perpetrator. The DNA could degrade if she opened or handled the clothing. If they learned her attacker's name, they might, even so many years later, be able to bring him to justice with proof from his DNA. Genevieve agreed to store the package in its original wrap.

Genevieve's call was just the impetus Matt needed to keep his own promise made to his grandmother years ago. It was time. Matt had no doubt what came next.

Matt used his connections with Interpol to check whether a German soldier, Stefan Schafer, was wanted for war crimes. He was not. After further investigation, Matt discovered that Schafer had indeed been stationed in Paris during the Occupation. Schafer now lived in Mainz, Germany. As a graduation gift, Matt had asked for a trip to Europe.

From Kennedy airport, in late May 1982, Matt boarded TWA flight 740 to Frankfurt. He cleared customs, and rode a public train to the village of Mainz. He checked into the Hilton Hotel. His room overlooked the Rhine River; the functional Danish Modern furniture was well-suited for business. Matt ordered a room service continental breakfast with a carafe of hot kaffee HAG decaffeinated coffee. Seated at the window, Matt watched a barge tediously work its way down the river. Matt planned how to approach Herr Schafer. After breakfast, he took a nap following his overnight flight.

Five hours later, Matt turned off a jarring alarm. His eyes burned and he craved more sleep, but he headed for a warm shower. A slight wind rippled the Rhine. Cherry trees were in full bloom, and the breeze tossed petals into the air. Matt slipped into comfortable Cole Haan loafers, good for walking cobbled streets, and a suede camel-colored jacket. The concierge gave Matt directions and a local street map.

Matt did not want to give Schafer's wife a chance to forewarn the WW2 soldier. After locating Schafer's home, Matt walked back through the quaint town. Waiting until the right time, he perused shops in the historic square and visited an 18th century baroque church near the war memorial on the village green.

At a lively biergarten, Matt ordered a stein of Beck's. He thought about purchasing the decorative mug, but decided that this was not a trip for souvenir shopping. Matt complimented the shop manager on her well-spoken English. The matron curtly replied, "I thought all of you would have to learn to speak German." She walked away.

Workers began to head home. Soon after, Matt walked back to a middle-class residential neighborhood of appealing German architecture. The yards were tidy, and Schafer's front windows were open to air out the home. White organza curtains billowed in a steady breeze. Schafer's home was as quaint as the fairy tale pictures that he remembered as a child—two-story white stucco siding and half-timbered beams, a mansard roof with two peaked dormers and extensive gardens.

Matt Ambrose would approach Herr Schafer as a citizen

not as an American officer of the law. He knew that Schafer had tried to stop Genevieve's assault and to warn his grandfather. But Matt still had no idea how he would be received.

The young detective opened the wrought iron entrance gate. Fragrant yellow climbing roses cascaded over a trellis. Matt took a deep breath and lightly tapped on the brass door knocker. He heard Beethoven's Symphony Nine in the background. The door was opened by a tall gentleman with a shock of white hair and piercing blue eyes. Matt smelled a pork roast in the oven.

"Good evening, *Herr* Schafer. My name is Matt, Pierre Bessette's grandson." He let his words hang in the air. Matt had eased his foot into the door opening. Schafer momentarily gazed at the young man on his front stoop. With a knowing look, he stepped aside. Stefan Schafer gestured for Matt to enter his home.

"Please wait one moment," Schafer turned and left the room.

Matt looked around the homey front room. A small table was filled with German Hummel porcelain figurines. He did not see any French paintings or furniture. When Stefan Schafer returned, he took his jacket from a wardrobe in the foyer.

Schafer walked with a limp and slowly took Matt down the street to a nearby restaurant with an outdoor patio. They ordered beer. He asked Matt directly, "What would you like to know?"

Matt explained that he was not interested in causing him trouble. "Sir, I know that you tried to warn my grandfather. I am here to locate your partner. We believe that he may have assaulted our shop girl and according to our former neighbor may have taken my grandmother's family heirlooms, her art collection, from our apartment one Saturday morning." Matt leaned forward "Can you help me?"

Stefan took a deep breath, "I can help you, but I have questions myself. If I tell you what happened back in July,

1942, will you answer some questions for me?"

"Of course," Matt replied. "If I can, I will gladly answer your questions." Matt's heart rate picked up, but he tried to remain steady and to concentrate.

Stefan took a gulp of beer and said, "First of all, young man, how did you find me?"

Matt replied, "My father's assistant remembered the name of the soldier who tried to help her and warn my father. After nearly forty years, she visualized your name on your uniform."

"Very good," answered Stefan as he nodded. "I was hoping someone would track the bastard down. I do not know where he is, but I can tell you his name. Let me give you some background."

"Oberleutnant Otto Heinrich and I were teamed up simply because we lived in the same district in Germany. He came from Mannheim, a town outside Stuttgart. Before the war, I was a police security expert here in Mainz and that expertise allowed me to look for covert resistance activity."

Matt learned that before the war, Stefan had arranged security for popular biergartens, shops, hotels and the marketplatz in Old Town. "Tourists flock here for Rhine River cruises. Oktoberfest always presents a challenge during the beer-drinking festivities. Each year, tourists visit our Christmas markets—handcrafted toys, nutcrackers, nativity scenes. You get the idea... I saw an opportunity and started my own security business. When the war started, luckily I was put into security work rather than combat."

"Otto was the youngest commander in the army. Since he was higher ranked, I was forced to follow his orders. Otto was a diligent Nazi and ruthless in his pursuits. We followed your grandfather that Friday evening from Pascal's tabac because Otto suspected Bessette of being a key member of the resistance."

Stefan took another gulp of beer and continued as though anxious to unload the information. "Otto became sus-

picious because of a vague tip, and word that a known resistance member had shopped at Bijoux" remarked Stefan with a
shrug.

"That was all. Otto was itching to detain your grandfather for questioning that Friday even though we had no
real proof. I pleaded with Otto that it would be foolish to
grab the jeweler until we knew for *certain* if he was using
his boutique to conduct resistance work. Pierre Bessette was
very well-liked and a prominent citizen. If Otto had been
wrong, it could have brought harsh push-back from locals and
embarrassment to Otto, me and the Third Reich. So, Otto reluctantly let Bessette go about his business that Friday afternoon."

"But Saturday morning, Otto wanted to question Bessette just to see if he could throw him off balance a little. We
drove to his boutique very early to talk with him before customers would arrive. But your grandfather did not come to Bijoux. Supposedly he had taken a vacation. Otto was angry, and
the bastard took it out on the young woman which I tried to
stop. After the attack, we scrambled to Bessette's home. I had
instructed the shop girl to phone your grandfather and warn
him. Based on Otto's volatility and past behavior, I feared he
would harm your grandmother. And yes, you are correct."

Barely taking a breath, Stefan continued, "We broke
into your apartment, and Otto smashed china and crystal
stemware. *He took several paintings and forced me to carry a silver candelabra from your family's home.* He had trouble carrying
everything he wanted. He tossed a small painting into a trash
bin because he realized it could identify your grandmother by
her name on the back of the canvas." Matt's heart pounded, but
he forced himself to sit still.

Stefan took two more swallows of beer and wiped his
mouth with a napkin. "After Otto attacked the young woman,
I could no longer just look the other way. I went to the high
command to report his behavior." Stefan related the injuries that the Nazi had inflicted on a girl, another woman, and

a prostitute who never gained consciousness and eventually died. "To the Oberkommando, Otto was a champion fighting for the Third Reich. But I knew the evil in that man's heart that the authorities could not see."

Stefan hung his head. "After I reported Otto's behavior to Kapitain Adler, I was reassigned."

Stefan looked up but kept rolling, "I was removed from my unit fighting resistance activity. I was put onto the front lines on the Alsace-Lorraine border. It was punishment. Otto Heinrich was successful at procuring sought-after valuables for the Third Reich. They overlooked his atrocities."

Matt learned that Stefan fought for nearly six harsh months until he was shot. The bullet went through his stomach, grazing his spine. He was lucky to have survived and to walk again. He was discharged with honor and sent back to Germany. It took many months of intense physical therapy, but he recovered. Stefan was able to rebuild his security company and worked now on a limited basis. Like Matt's grandfather, Stefan was not ready to give up total control of the business he had started so many years ago.

Stefan continued, "Otto fled after the war. I heard that he came home to Mannheim after the Allies liberated Paris. He disappeared about a year later. At first, I surmised that he was wanted for war crimes, but I was not certain. We never saw each other after Paris."

"Now," Stefan leaned in... "Tell me, please, what happened to your family? Your grandfather made it out alive? I can tell by your accent that you are American. I was relieved when we got to your home that everyone was gone."

He continued. "Mainly, I was concerned for your grandmother and even the little girl. Otto was a monster as far as females were concerned. If your family were found, Otto likely would have retaliated and Bessette's wife could easily have been the target. Otto spoke of your grandmother's beauty on several occasions. Frankly, I feared for her."

Matt could barely contain his disgust, but he remained

calm. "Thank you for your kindness, Herr Schafer. As you said, my family was able to make it out of Paris with help from the Free French and the SOE in London. They got to Lyon and then flew out on a Red Cross plane from Geneva."

"*Mein Gott!*" Stunned, Schafer slapped his knee. "Bessette *was* working with the Free French, then?"

"Yes, I am afraid so," said Matt, leaning toward Stefan who had lowered his head. Matt looked him in the eyes. "Listen, you are a good man who knew Heinrich would likely have hurt my grandmother and perhaps even my Aunt Anna. It is one thing for a man to fight for his country, but another to deliberately harm or kill civilians." Schafer would never know that Ellie also put her life on the line working for the resistance.

Stefan took a gulp of beer and shook his head. "During the war, I thought all the time about my two little daughters at home in Germany. I simply could not look the other way and allow Otto to brutalize women and girls any longer."

Matt told Stefan about the "Blitz" and Anna's death which had plunged his grandmother into a deep depression. He would not let on that his grandmother had helped the resistance, nor tell Stefan where they lived or their Ambrose name.

Stefan replied, "I am indeed sorry for your loss." Both men quietly finished drinking their beer. They talked a little longer and agreed that war had terrible consequences for all sides. Matt thanked Stefan for his bravery, his character and for seeing him. Matt paid the bill. The men shook hands.

Stefan bade Matt farewell, then he turned toward home. Abruptly, he turned back again and stopped Matt, holding his arm. "Young man, *if* you do find Otto Heinrich and can bring him to justice, I *will* testify against him. *He stole your family paintings.*"

"Thank you, Herr Schafer. I truly hope that day will come." Both men shook hands again and parted ways.

Finally, Matt had the name his family had sought for

decades, *Otto Heinrich*. Now with Stefan Schafer's revelations, the search for Genevieve's rapist, the thief, and by all accounts a vicious murderer officially began.

Chapter 43

Matt's meeting with Stefan Schafer set in motion a bona fide hunt for the war criminal, and Matt knew his name: Otto Heinrich. Matt walked back to the hotel unaware that he was smiling and nodding to passersby.

The Hilton business center consisted only of a couple of phones, pads and pencils, a Xerox machine and an adding machine. He called Interpol in Lyon, France. Using his New York police credentials, Matt ran a dBASE information link through the International Command and Coordination Center to see if war-related crimes were associated with Heinrich's name. He gave Interpol the Hilton telephone number and his room number should information turn up. The young detective reserved a car.

Still jet-lagged, Matt ate dinner in the hotel dining room. He took a seat by the window as darkness settled over the Rhine. Famished, he ordered a chilled stein of altbier and a cup of spicy goulash soup served with black bread. A hearty Wiener schnitzel with spaetzle followed. Matt finished his dinner with a warm apple strudel, and he drank another kaffee Hag.

Excited by the day's success, Matt felt good. He imagined confronting the Nazi; this thought lulled his restless mind to sleep.

Early the next morning, Matt laced up his Nike Air running shoes. After an invigorating run by the river, he returned to his room. A red telephone light blinked. A message had come from Interpol.

In 1946, one Otto Heinrich was wanted for questioning by an Allied military tribunal set up in Stuttgart. The French were anxious to talk with him about crimes committed in Paris. However, before Heinrich went in for questioning, a young woman in Mannheim had charged him with rape. Heinrich was a person of interest. With so many serious crimes that had taken place during the war, and numerous soldiers to question regarding those offenses, the French deferred questioning Heinrich until after the Germans interrogated him regarding the more recent rape charge.

But the young rape victim had gone missing. When she was found murdered and buried in a shallow grave, Heinrich had disappeared; he had become a wanted person.

Matt thanked the caller from Interpol and hung up. If he located Otto Heinrich, Matt had agreed to inform the authorities at Interpol and the German police. Matt showered and shaved.

He checked out of the Hilton and picked up his rental car. In a heavy rain, he drove on the autobahn to Mannheim, a little more than hour away. He was happy to pull off what felt like a slippery race course. Matt checked in with the local police.

Matt explained that he was trying to locate and speak to Heinrich regarding offenses in Paris in 1942. The *polizeidirektor* reported that they would be interested in talking with him regarding the unsolved murder of the woman who had worked at the Daimler-Benz factory in Mannheim.

The *polizeidirektor* told Matt, "I am sorry but we believe that Otto Heinrich is no longer in Germany." Matt would let them know if he uncovered any new details about the fugitive's whereabouts. Matt became more convinced that he was dealing with an elusive and unsavory character.

At Town Hall, Detective Ambrose then checked birth records for the Heinrich family. Curiously, there was no birth record for Otto Heinrich. However, Matt discovered the address for a Lukas Heinrich family home. Otto had been listed as a minor child.

The rain had stopped. Matt drove to the Heinrich home address and knocked on the door. No answer. He tried a few more doors. It was the time of day when children were in school and housewives might be out shopping for dinner.

Finally, a middle-aged man answered the fourth door. He told Matt that he had moved into his home a few years ago. "Only one person lived in the neighborhood during the war: an elderly gentleman down the street who still lives in his family home."

"Look, since you are an American, I don't know how much he will tell you. He spouts off about the war now and then, bitter at the way things turned out. The old man is angry at Hitler for getting the country into war and angry at the Allies for bombing Stuttgart where monuments were destroyed by Allied bombs. But, if anyone can tell you about the people who lived on the street back then, Herr Huber would know. He has lived nearly his entire life in that house—that one, at end of the street, the cream stucco house."

The neighbor pointed to a small house with a peaked red-tiled roof, a gray front door and mustard trim. The tiny yard was bordered by a colorful flower garden. "His daughter comes in most days to check on him and brings him a meal. She tends to his yard. She probably has not been over today. Good luck."

Herr Huber took a long time to answer the door, *"Ich Komme, ich komme!"* Finally, the door opened. Huber had fair skin and gray hair; he was tall but hunched over a walker. He wore a blue sweater with what appeared to be a soup stain dribbled down the front.

"Herr Huber, I am looking for someone you may know and a long-time acquaintance of my grandfather. His name is Otto Heinrich."

Herr Huber stared at Matt and replied, "You are American. What would you want with Heinrich? No... Let me guess. He's wanted for some crime, no doubt."

Matt smiled, "Sir, he knew my grandfather in Paris." Herr Huber stared at Matt a bit longer and harder.

Hesitating and unsteady on his feet, Huber's curiosity got the best of him. After a moment, Huber said, "Well... come in. I can't stand here all day."

Huber shuffled over to an armchair in the front room and pointed to a couch. "What has he done now? Here, sit down." Although it had turned into a pleasant afternoon, the shades were partially drawn, and the house appeared dark in contrast to the sunny border of spring flowers. Herr Huber did not offer refreshment.

"Sir, what makes you think Heinrich has done something wrong?" asked Matt

"Because that kid was a mean bastard and nothing but trouble!" Herr Huber coughed and raised his feeble voice. "His mother could never control him. His father, Lukas, thought he needed more structure and got him involved in the Hitler Youth Movement which the kid loved." Shaking his head, Huber continued, "He used to go around the neighborhood and shoot squirrels. He even killed a dog once for no reason, none at all."

Huber became agitated and raised his voice. "Otto was a mean one. My son went to the same school, but I would not let my Kurt associate with him. Otto was a bully, no doubt about it. He didn't have friends. Maybe one from the *Hitlerjugend*, but that's it."

"Do you know where I might be able to locate him, sir?"

"*Nein*. Otto came home after the war. At the time, his mother was quite sick with cancer, and then she passed away. I think the poor woman waited until he came home to die. After the war, Otto seemed at a loss. His father mentioned that Otto felt abandoned by his country. Otto thought he was a big shot. We all thought he was a punk." The old man caught his breath and coughed again.

"Before the war, the kid worked in the Mannheim car factory. The Americans had allowed it to begin operating again. His father's long-time friend managed the factory and got Otto his job back. Lukas told me that Otto was uncomfortable with so many Allied soldiers stationed in the area. Lukas mentioned that his wife had a relative in South America who Otto could visit. I think it was her brother. Otto's mother had grown up in Scandinavia, Norway or someplace. Otto had no other relatives around here that I can recall."

"The next thing I knew, Otto was wanted for questioning by the police, but he was gone. Never saw the kid again. Lukas sold their family house and moved to an apartment in Stuttgart. Lukas died about fourteen years ago. He had no other children which is *guten* considering how Otto turned out."

Herr Huber took another breath and Matt jumped in, "Herr Huber, do you know which country Otto may have gone to in South America?"

"I'm sorry; I do not know where he moved. At the time, I thought Otto was heading down to South America to get away from a war tribunal. Then I heard from gossip around town that he was wanted for questioning regarding the disappearance of that woman from the factory. That's all I know. I didn't like that kid. If I knew more, believe me, I would tell you. Damn war Hitler got us into...The Allies bombed the hell out of Stuttgart where I worked." Huber threw his hands up into the air... "But what's done is done."

Matt replied, "Herr Huber, thank you. I appreciate your taking the time to talk with me. Is there anyone else who might have known Otto or his family? Do you recall his mother's maiden name?"

Huber waved his finger. "Yes, you see... I thought so! You do want to find him! You know he was up to no good..."

Herr Huber took another deep breath, "Nein. I don't recall Otto's mother's name, and I didn't know much about her. We didn't socialize with that family. I saw Lukas once in a while at the bus stop. That's all...We chatted a little but mostly pleasantries. I don't believe that they had any other relatives. I'm sorry. I'm all that is left around here. Too many years have gone by..."

Matt sensed the old man was tired. He got up to shake Herr Huber's hand. "*Guten Abend*, sir. Thank you for speaking with me."

"*Auf Wiedersehen*, young man. I hope you find him, *die drecksack*" (dirty bastard). The old man's voice wavered. "Otto was no good, no good at all! It was our family dog, Fritz, that he killed." Huber shouted, "We loved Fritzi and Otto just shot him dead for no damn reason, none at all!"

Matt left Herr Huber his card with his police credentials. Huber said he would be most happy to contact Matt if Otto Heinrich ever showed up.

Matt found the local library and looked through the archived newspapers. The librarian xeroxed a copy of the article regarding a young woman's rape and eventual strangulation. Her body was found buried in an abandoned lot not far from the car factory in Mannheim in October, 1946. There were no witnesses. The woman worked with Heinrich at the factory. The paper reported that, according to a foreman, the dead woman went on one date with Heinrich, and she had accused him of rape. When the woman went missing, Otto Heinrich was wanted for questioning, but he had disappeared.

At Town Hall, Matt looked for a marriage license for one Lukas Heinrich and his bride, but found none. The young detective surmised that they were married in another city or even another country. No birth records were filed for Otto Heinrich or his father in Mannheim either.

Matt drove to a hotel on Willy-Brandt Straße in Stuttgart. He walked to City Hall, and searched for a marriage certificate for a Lukas Heinrich but found none in the correct time frame; nor did he find a birth certificate for Otto Heinrich or Lukas. Clearly the family had roots elsewhere. The administrator called Frankfurt records department with similar results.

Matt placed a call to Genevieve at her home in Paris. When Genevieve answered, he told her that he had learned her attacker's name from Stefan Schafer who had identified his partner. "Genevieve, are you ready? I believe the man who assaulted you was named Otto Heinrich."

"*Mon Dieu*! Matt, yes that's it. I have to sit down." Seconds later Genevieve said, "I recall the tall German, Schafer, calling him Otto, pleading with him to leave me alone."

Matt said, "I'd like to fly to Paris in the morning to meet you and pick up your packet of clothes." Now that Matt had a name, a forensic specialist *may* be able to prove Heinrich was the man who had attacked her, if the Nazi were still alive and he could be located. Matt did not want to raise false hope, but he wanted to take possession of and preserve any DNA evidence.

"Yes, Matt, when you arrive, we will have lunch, *oui*?"

The following morning, Matt flew the short hop on Air France. Nearly at noon, after clearing customs and immigration, Matt hired a taxi.

When he arrived at Genevieve's, Matt was greeted by a pretty woman in her mid-sixties. Genevieve had prepared lunch and invited Matt to join her and her husband. The dining room table was pleasantly set with Gien white, rose-bordered dinnerware. A vase was arranged with yellow and pink tulips and a few blue delphiniums and paperwhites. Over quiche Lorraine, salade, and a crisp Pinot Blanc white wine, Matt found Genevieve to be a treasure trove about his father and grandparents during the war. Matt told her about his background as an artist and his recent work in law enforcement.

"DNA testing is mainly used to determine paternity, and DNA is now able to tie a suspect to a crime." Genevieve listened carefully to this news. "Please remember though, it is not routinely used in court cases yet. The FBI is working diligently on a protocol to use DNA to solve crimes. So, we will keep our fingers crossed, first that we can find Heinrich and then someday convict him of his crimes."

Genevieve verified that the clothes had not been touched since that fateful Saturday in 1942.

"Matt, I am relieved that you learned the name of the man who assaulted me. I am very glad to be rid of the clothes. Yes, please take them away with you."

Matt promised to follow Heinrich's trail and do his very best to catch the tyrant. "God willing, he is still alive, and he can be brought to justice for his crimes, *all* of them."

Genevieve invited Matt to stay with them. But he had reserved a room at a small Paris hotel. Matt shook hands with Jean-Marc; Genevieve and Matt exchanged kisses on each cheek. She gave him a warm hug. Laden with notes from his family, Matt planned to tour his ancestral city for the first time.

Matt strolled through the exquisite Tuileries Garden located near the monumental 18th century Hotel Le Meurice, to the location of the original Maison Bijoux, and his family's stately townhouse. The sumptuous Hotel Le Meurice was too showy for Matt's taste. Instead, he chose a room in the Celtic Hotel located at number 6 rue Balzac, a small hotel just blocks from the Arc de Triomphe. Matt grew up hearing that during the Occupation, his grandfather met with resistance workers in the Celtic bar, a local hideaway. Now, in the intimate wood-paneled room, Matt slowly sipped a Famous Grouse malt whiskey straight up.

Matt imagined his grandfather in 1942. In the smoky neighborhood bar with the pungent smell of Gauloises cigarettes, Pierre secretly met with resistance fighters— young working types to unshaven, crusty old men in berets. They came from all walks of life, rich and poor. Pierre had told Matt with a smile, "Our waiter, Jacques, covertly tucked messages underneath my bill or underneath my glass. At times,

I would hand Jacques a clandestine note with my payment. Your grandmother bravely hand-delivered urgent messages to me at Bijoux. It was a good scheme, and we were able to thwart some strategic German plots. My neighborhood florist relayed crucial information that she received from her husband; a baker who had been forced to work for the Germans. Mme. Bonheur tucked her notes under a paper doily in a box of pastries. All in all, our crazy schemes worked."

Forty years later, Matt slept comfortably in the cozy, old-world hotel room where raindrops spattered against the metal roof.

The following morning, Matt devoured the Paris art scene. He spent hours at the Louvre and Jeu de Paume museums. In between, he ate at bistros made famous by philosophers and writers. Matt paid a poignant visit to the Musée de l'Orangerie where grandmother Ellie covertly picked up a post office key that over a month's time would unlock their escape papers.

Matt perused the outdoor art gallery along the Seine where his great-grandmother Nettie Lindstrom displayed her paintings. On Montmartre, he found the now shabby apartment into which young women lured German soldiers who were taken away by La Résistance. He sipped a cocktail at Harry's New York Bar and later at the Ritz's Bar Hemingway where his grandparents frequently had met up with Duke Verdi, Matt's "Uncle Freddie."

Matt was reminded of Hemingway's quote and thought of the men in his life. "If you are lucky enough to have lived in Paris as a young man, then wherever you go for the rest of your life, it stays with you, for Paris is a moveable feast."

On his third day, Matt immersed himself in the contemporary works of Picasso, Matisse, Pollock and Delaunay at the modern art museum, Centre Pompidou. Matt dined at Allard. He reserved a specific table by the window where he knew his grandparents had dined on their anniversary. He lifted his white napkin. Matt traced his finger over a well-worn and faint victory "V" that Pierre had crudely carved into the table the night before his family escaped. Overwhelmed with pride at his grandparents' courage, a broad smile broke out on Matt's face.

Matt Ambrose returned to New York with renewed vigor and determination, and he knew it was time to talk with the family. Matt had kept his investigative work under wraps. It was an easy ruse since he had spent much of his free time painting.

After Sunday brunch, Ellie invited the immediate family to join her back at their home for tea. Pierre, Michael, and his wife Celine, and Matt's sister Madeline sat at their walnut dining table while Ellie served her gooey *tarte tatin*.

Matt took a deep breath and focused on his grandfather and father. "I want to talk about my recent trip to Europe. But first I need to explain what I have been doing leading up to this trip, and what lies ahead in my future."

His father and grandfather looked at each other and raised their eyebrows when Matt revealed that he had attended forensic classes and studied at the police academy. His father folded his arms when Matt divulged that he had been working with a NYC detective squad.

In a resolute voice, Matt continued. "My interest is painting, and someday I intend to own my own gallery. But there is more." Clearing his throat, Matt stated that he had a passion to find art taken from families during the war as well as art stolen in recent times from museums or galleries worldwide.

"I enjoy combining my critical thinking skills with my expertise in art. I hope to recover lost cultural heritage whether the client is an individual, a museum or even a country. And, I *will* begin this career with my own family."

He recounted Genevieve's initial telephone call and their conversation. "Through my access to Interpol and the NYPD, I plan to mount an all-out effort to retrieve grandmother's painting of Anna. I want to give it a shot like father did when he found Picasso's *Mother and Child*; I hope to bring the miserable thief to justice." Matt reminded the family that his father, Michael, had started his own search nearly twenty-five years ago.

Michael appeared bewildered and stunned. He seemed unable to comprehend what Matt was saying. With out-reached arms, Michael spoke up, "But, Matt, what about Bijoux San Francisco?" He pointed a finger at Matt. "Your family in-tends for you to join the family business and open our next boutique. For over a year now, Patrick has been perusing prop-erties in San Francisco for the best location. We hoped to get going soon and are just waiting for you!"

"I know, Papa. And that is why this is so difficult. But I simply do *not* share your vision. I'm sorry; my dream is to paint, own my own gallery and work in art recovery. But first, I want a chance to find what is rightfully ours, *as you did.* Grow-ing up, I have always wanted to emulate the courage of my father and grandparents. After receiving that phone call from Genevieve, I am determined to keep my promise to Grand-mother Ellie."

"Please listen." Looking at his perplexed father, and then directly at Pierre, Matt said, "With Genevieve's informa-tion and help from Interpol, I was able to talk, *face to face,* with the German officer, Stefan Schafer, who had convinced his su-perior *not* to arrest you in front of your home the Friday before you escaped."

Pierre's mouth dropped open.

Matt raised his voice, "The following Saturday morn-ing, the same Leutnant Stefan Schafer tried to stop a brutal as-sault on Genevieve, and he instructed her to call and warn you to leave your home immediately. Schafer gave me pertinent information about his partner, one Otto Heinrich, the very man who raped Genevieve and who, *we now know for certain,* stole our paintings in Schafer's presence. Schafer is willing to testify against Otto Heinrich if I can find him."

Pierre looked as white as a sheet. He was shaken when he heard the names of the men who had followed him that frightening Friday so long ago. The same men who had stolen Ellie's paintings.

Matt related his luncheon with Genevieve and that he now is in possession of the clothing she wore during the attack that might someday actually convict Heinrich through DNA testing.

Matt turned to address his father. "Dad, nearly twenty-five years ago, you began the search for what rightly belongs to grandmother. Now, we *know* who that thief is. And I may be able to find him and bring him to justice, and perhaps return our painting of Anna. It's a long shot... But I possess the investigative tools needed to conduct a bona fide search for this thief, Heinrich."

Matt smiled and placed his arm around Ellie's thin shoulders, "I promised grandmother many years ago that I would at least try. *These paintings belong with her and are all we have left of our family heritage and quite frankly of Anna.*"

Matt gestured at his sister. "I present the perfect person to open Bijoux San Francisco with Uncle Patrick. Madeline is a Berkeley graduate, and she has worked for Bijoux since she was a teenager. Today, women are doctors, attorneys, pilots and even astronauts. Women are accomplished executives. *Bijoux San Francisco is Madeline's rightful legacy.*"

As if on cue, Madeline stood, looked at Michael and said, "Dad, I have always dreamed of a career in our business. Bijoux has been my life. Not only can I open Bijoux San Francisco, I will make it successful. I have the education and the training. I know the Bay Area, and I would be thrilled to manage our newest boutique. Matt has a passion for art, the determination and the means to find grandmother's possessions. *Please*, give us both a chance."

Michael was speechless, still not sure how to process Matt's unnerving information. He had always imagined working side by side with his son and now this... painting and detective work? Silence had filled the room with bewilderment and a touch of anger.

After an uncomfortable minute or so, the family patriarch stood up. Pierre looked at his family one by one: his wife, Ellie, a co-conspirator; his grandson who all along had hid his intentions from the family; his granddaughter who knew Matt *never* intended to take his place in the family business, and last, his son Michael who appeared overcome by Matt's revelations.

Looking at each of them, Pierre cleared his throat. "Matt has spoken to us from his heart. If he can locate the war criminal who stole grand-mère's paintings, the man who drove us from our home, and who violated Genevieve, then he *must* be found and brought to justice!" Pierre pounded his fist on the table. He lowered his voice and continued, "Madeline is an asset to our business. She will bring a woman's touch, just as Coco Chanel had revolutionized fashion."

Ellie nodded and embraced her husband. Madeline hugged her grandfather. Michael stared at the floor. He recalled that as a young man, he wanted to seek the ultimate revenge, *death*, on this Nazi, now known as Heinrich, for his mother's deep depression and his family's losses —especially the loss of his little sister, Anna...

Michael stood.

"Matt, your grandfather is right. Finish what I started years ago and bring Mémère Ellie's paintings home to us. Find this criminal who contributed to Anna's death."

Michael drew Matt and Madeline into an embrace. He said, "I'll call Patrick. The three of us can expedite our plans for Bijoux San Francisco while Matt searches for the thief— this Nazi, Otto Heinrich."

Matt and Michael sat down with Pierre and compared details from their trips to Europe decades apart. The family now knew that the soldiers who followed Pierre home from Pascal's tabac on Friday afternoon were the *same* two men who went to Bijoux Saturday morning looking for Pierre; the same two men who had ransacked their home and stole their belongings. From Stefan Schafer, Matt had learned that the stocky officer, Otto Heinrich, had attacked Genevieve. She had verified his name and description. Neighbor Mme. Simone saw the "stocky one" remove paintings from their home that Saturday morning also verified by Schafer. *Nazi Otto Heinrich was the culprit.* Two people, Stefan Schafer and Herr Huber, reported that Heinrich was in trouble in Germany. Heinrich's neighbor, Herr Huber, said Heinrich had a relative, most likely a maternal uncle, in South America. Certainly, if Heinrich had been wanted for questioning in the murder of a young woman in Stuttgart in 1946, he likely would have fled Germany.

Matt got down to work. He managed a police case. On the side, he looked into the exodus of men from Germany. After the war, thousands of Nazis had fled Germany via "rat lines," special KLM flights. Matt used the Interpol databases and resources to research men leaving Germany for South America in 1946, soon after the young German woman's murder in Mannheim. Right away, Matt's research found two such émigrés to South America named Otto Heinrich.

The first Otto Heinrich went to Bolivia but was 52 years old at the time, possibly a war criminal but too old to be the culprit. Another went to Brazil, Otto K. Heinrich. At the time, he was a 49-year-old physician who had married a Brazilian woman and returned with her to her homeland. Again, the age did not fit. Also, Otto K. had been a medic during the war. Matt was severely disappointed and realized he had been naïve to expect an easy process.

He searched for men with similar initials. Heinrich likely could have used an alias. Ultimately, Matt concluded that numerous German males, who shared the initials O. H., had been living near Stuttgart, Germany before immigrating to South America in 1946 around the time after the woman's murder.

Two males were each named Oskar Hartmann. They were father and son. The father was 44 during the war and his son was just three years old when his family moved to Chile. Oskar senior was a chemist who had worked for Bayer. Another suspect, Othello Hochberg, supposedly worked in a munitions plant prior to the war and was a member of Hitler's youth program. At the time, he was unmarried and in his late twenties. A strong possibility...

Matt retained a Spanish-speaking freelance investigator, José Alvarez, to look into Hochberg in Bolivia. José was an interpreter who worked off and on for the New York police department. He reported back to Matt that Hochberg had a distinct speech impediment. Also, Hochberg was very tall, lanky and thin with blue eyes. Genevieve and Schafer both described Heinrich as medium height, stocky with hazel eyes. Nazi Heinrich did not have a speech impediment. The other two individuals were children. "This is not going to be a cakewalk," Matt told his family at Sunday lunch. "But I won't give up..."

Chapter 44

By April 1983, Matt had uncovered numerous suspicious individuals. After researching the men, a young man named Olof Hansson had emerged as a suspect. He had left Stuttgart for South America in 1946.

The Olof Hansson in question had flown to San Carlos, Argentina. Adding to Matt's suspicion, no age-relevant information regarding an Olof Hansson had appeared in German birth or school records in Mannheim or Stuttgart. The old neighbor, Herr Huber, believed that Heinrich's mother was Scandinavian; Hansson was worth a close look.

Investigator, José Alvarez flew to Argentina to snoop around and ask questions. Matt tried not to get too hopeful. He had been disappointed before...

José dug into Hansson's background and when Hansson's description matched the culprit, Otto Heinrich, Matt met up with Alvarez in Buenos Aires. Together, they flew on an Aerolíneas Argentinas flight from the capitol to San Carlos. They drove to an *estancia;* the ranch that José had learned was Hansson's local address in 1946 after leaving Germany.

The ranch's sprawling English lodge was situated on 12,000 acres in a breathtaking landscape beneath rugged snow-capped mountains. The owner, Guenther Hansson, had sold the ranch when he retired. Guenther now lived in a nearby retirement home with late-stage cancer. The new owners were Guenther's former ranch foreman, Santiago

Lopez and his son, Alejandro. Alejandro was fourteen in 1946.

José explained, "Señor Lopez, thank you for meeting with us. We need to speak with the former ranch hand, Olof Hansson, regarding a possible inheritance. Can you tell us a little about him and his location?

The weathered rancher invited José and Matt to join him and his son in their cheerful kitchen. On the farmhouse table their housekeeper had laid out a welcome *almuerzo* of hearty beef sandwiches and pork tamales.

Over a satisfying lunch, washed down with cold Cerveza, Santiago gave Matt and José a little background information. Despite his advancing age, Santiago retained a strong recollection of Olof Hansson.

"As I recall, he arrived at the ranch out of the blue. I was instructed by the owner, Guenther Hansson, to find work for Olof, or "Ollie" as the ranchers called him. Guenther called his nephew by another name on occasion, but I cannot recall it. Perhaps it was an endearment..."

The seasoned rancher pushed back in his chair and clasped his hands behind his head. He said, "Back then, Guenther told me that Olof's father had died years earlier and his mother had recently passed away from cancer. Guenther had promised his sister that he would take the young man in and look after him. He was not a kid, but it appeared that his uncle was Ollie's only family." Santiago shrugged, "Ollie was a lazy man and soft. He did what he had to on the ranch but never a bit more."

Santiago continued. "He worked here for about four or five years and then vanished, just up and left one day. That's about all I can tell you. I would say he was unremarkable and honestly, we never missed him. His uncle now has terminal cancer. But Guenther has some lucid days. He could probably tell you where his nephew is now."

Matt asked, "Can you give us a description of Hansson?" Santiago thought for a moment, "Well, he was perhaps in his mid-thirties when he left the ranch. He was medium height with light brown hair and, what is the word I want... "*rechon-cho*?" He trimmed down a bit after he started to work on the ranch. I don't recall his eye color."

Turning to Matt, José remarked in English, "There is that description rechoncho—stocky."

Santiago's son Alejandro could not add too much more since he had spent little time around the ranch hands. Alejandro did say that "Ollie had an accent similar to German immigrants living in Argentina." Matt and José exchanged a quick look.

Alejandro then added, "You know, I recall that Ollie was friendly with one other young ranch hand named Manuel Perez. They would go into San Carlos for a beer together. Manny also left our ranch years ago."

José thanked the Lopez father and son for their hospitality. They were given directions to the nursing home where Olof's uncle was living out his final days.

José and Matt drove straight to the *Casa de Convalecencia Santa Maria*. In the car, Matt reflected, "Santiago mentioned Olof's father was dead, but Herr Huber said Otto Heinrich's father died years later. Maybe we are on a wild good chase?"

José shrugged his shoulders. "We'll have to see... We don't know if there may be some confusion on the old man's part after so many years? But a mother who passed from cancer... that similarity could be a compelling piece of the puzzle."

They were informed by reception that Señor Hansson was resting but the staff would see if he felt well enough to speak with visitors. After a few moments, they were escorted to Guenther Hansson's sparse room. Guenther was receiving hospice care. He was thin, pale and had difficulty sitting up. He stared curiously at the two foreign visitors, especially the tall, blue-eyed younger man who looked English.

After making their introductions, José explained in

Spanish, "Good afternoon, Señor Hansson, thank you for seeing us. Santiago Lopez told us we would find you here. We are actually looking for Olof Hansson, and we understand that he is your nephew."

"What do you want with him, Ollie?" asked a concerned Guenther in a shaky, almost inaudible voice.

Matt had instructed José to tell the old man, "Olof may be entitled to certain insurance benefits, compensation."

Matt could see that Hansson struggled with an answer, as if evaluating the strangers standing before him, especially the English one. In a wavering voice he finally answered.

"He's not here now."

"Sir, do you know where he can be reached," asked José?

Making every effort to remain upright, the uncle whispered in a hoarse voice, "I have not heard from him in a while. Leave me your information and when I hear from him, I will tell him about these benefits you talk about."

"Señor," replied José, "I'm sorry but we can only speak directly with Mr. Hansson."

Guenther became agitated and raised his raspy voice, "I don't know what to do, I don't know. I told you, I don't know." His hacking cough alerted the nurses. They hustled in and asked them to leave so that Señor Hansson could rest.

José replied, "Señor Hansson, here is my card. If you hear from your nephew, please have him contact me so that we can give him the necessary information. Bueno?"

The old man poked his finger into the air. "I don't believe you!" yelled Guenther, shaking a thin, blue-veined hand at José, "Ollie does not need your money; leave *Otto* alone!"

Matt and José heard it clearly. The old man's tongue had slipped. *Olof Hansson looked to be the culprit, Otto Heinrich.*

Chapter 45

Matt and José celebrated with Argentine steak dinners at Filete Marinado Grill in San Carlos.Matt toasted his investigator, "Here's to your sleuthing!"

José raised his glass, "And now to finding the son of a bitch!"

Matt ordered empanadas —savory cheese, goat meat, and beef. To start, José had requested a chilled Torrentés white wine that he remembered from his teenage years. His cousin, a Jesuit priest, had brought the crisp white wine back home to New York from visits to his native Argentina.

The men devoured the marinated steaks, accompanied by an ensalada rusa tossed with cooked peas, diced potatoes and carrots. Their waiter opened a rich, velvety red wine Rio Negro, Bodega Chacra Treinta y Dos.

Savoring the pinot noir, Matt smiled at the thought of their success today, elated to learn the alias of the Nazi who had devastated the lives of his grandparents. He leaned back and swirled his wine.

"Man, I can't believe it! Finally, we are getting somewhere. It makes sense that Heinrich would end up in Argentina—a Nazi hotbed."

Matt was eager to push forward. "Let's try to get our foot in the door once again at the nursing home. We'll see if we can coax a little more information out of the uncle. It would go a long way in helping us to find this tyrant if we knew where he is now..."

The men spent the following day in San Carlos talking with the locals and looking for bar owners who had been around at the time and who might remember Olof or his friend, Manny. Matt and José hoped to gather more insight into the life of Otto Heinrich and to interview his drinking buddy, Manuel Perez.

After striking out at the first two bars, they were directed to a third smoke-filled *bodegones* called El Gaucho, a tavern popular with ranchers. The owner knew Manuel Perez, Ollie's buddy who had bounced around from ranch to ranch. He remarked, "Manny was a good kid."

"Yes, indeed," the owner remembered both ranch hands. "The two of them were regular customers. In fact, I'll never forget Manny's pal, Ollie. I had just purchased this bar." He rapped his knuckle on the bar's Brazilian cherry top. "Ollie ran up a big tab celebrating and buying everyone drinks. Then he disappeared the very next day without paying his bar bill. I was mad as hell and asked Manny what had happened to his friend. He said Ollie got a great job offer and left town, probably for home, wherever that was; no one seemed to know exactly. It was the last time I let any of these guys run up a tab like that. Hansson was never seen around here again."

"Sir, do you know where we might find Manny these days?"

"I'm sorry, but Manny was killed in a ranch accident a year or so later."

That evening, José ordered braised lamb shanks accompanied by a spicy bean-and-sausage stew and a bottle of Malbec red wine. After running out of luck with the locals, the men strategized their next move.

Matt reiterated, "Santiago Lopez stated that Ollie worked on the ranch for four or five years and then one day abruptly left. His rancher friend, Manuel, told people that Ollie got a job offer and may have gone home. What kind of job offer made Ollie 'up and leave' so quickly in 1950 or '51?

Where would he go? Would he return to his hometown in Germany? Certainly not to Stuttgart or Mannheim where he was wanted for questioning on an outstanding rape and murder charge… Perhaps a war tribunal had located him and he was forced to flee again?"

José interrupted, "As a German, he would not return to France where he would be wanted for war crimes."

Matt replied, "Perhaps he found work on another ranch in Argentina?"

José remarked, "I don't think so… Why would he leave his uncle's ranch, where he got away with doing less work, for another ranch where more effort would be expected? Santiago surely would have known if Ollie had been fired by his uncle or went to work for a different rancher. No, I believe it had to be some kind of opportunity away from Argentina. After all, he skipped town knowing that he was leaving a huge bar bill behind."

Matt nodded his head and took another sip of the Malbec, "Heinrich may have been homesick for Germany. With the war over, and with Germany rebuilding, perhaps he thought enough time had passed and felt safe returning somewhere near his roots? Work could have opened up in Germany, not in Stuttgart or Mannheim but in some other city. He could have returned using his alias. Or, perhaps, he had some relatives in Scandinavia?"

All they knew for certain was that "Ollie" quickly left San Carlos. The following morning, Matt and José tried to visit Guenther again but the nuns said that he was too sick for visitors. The two men were asked not to return.

Matt retained José to search for Olof "Ollie" Hansson, aka Otto Heinrich, in Germany. Hansson was a popular Swedish surname. Hanson and Hansen surnames were found most often in Denmark and Norway. Either way, José would search throughout Scandinavia and expand into Europe if necessary.

Matt would look into Olof Hanssons in North America though they felt it unlikely the Nazi would reside in America. Canada could be a possibility. Matt and José parted ways agreeing to speak weekly to discuss their progress.

Chapter 46

In autumn 1946, Otto Heinrich left Germany in a hurry. After he raped the unfortunate factory girl, Otto strangled her to stop her accusations against him. He dumped her body in a grave on a desolate weed-infested lot near the car plant in Mannheim. Otto then got in touch with an army buddy who owned a printing business. The friend was a fervent nationalist who hated that Germany once again had lost a war. The printer forged high quality passports for Nazi soldiers who feared they might be arrested for war crimes. He agreed to print Otto a clean Swedish passport for a hefty fee

The Nuremberg Trials against Nazi war criminals deemed responsible for atrocities against humanity were winding down. However, talks led to the possibility of an expanded international counsel to address the crimes committed against Jewish citizens. France would be awarded a seat on the tribunal.

Otto feared reprisal for the crimes that he considered to be his valiant work hunting down members of *La Résistance*. He scrambled to leave Germany before the tribunal detained him for his questionable activities in Paris. Adding to his troubles, the local authorities wanted to talk with him about the missing factory girl.

Otto's father, Lukas, had contacted his wife's brother, Guenther Hansson, in *San Carlos de Bariloche*, Argentina. Guenther agreed to allow his nephew to live with him. Although his nephew was known to be troublesome, Uncle Guenther had no idea that Otto had committed crimes in France including rape, assault and multiple thefts. Guenther owned a large cattle ranch and could always use an extra hand as long as the kid stayed out of trouble.

Otto's buddy forged his Swedish passport in the name Olof Hansson, using Otto's mother's maiden name. Uncle Guenther agreed with the name change, as authorities tracked Nazis living in Argentina.

Many German ex-militaries lived near Guenther's ranch in the Lake Region where they found a welcoming and sympathetic home under the Peron regime. Some Argentine leaders sympathized with the idealistic Germans; many had family ties to Argentina. The Perons were suspected of receiving stolen Nazi goods in exchange for harboring war criminals.

Otto, renamed Olof or "Ollie" as the ranchers called him, hated the tedious ranch work. He disliked working outdoors with his chapped, calloused hands. The local ranch women were rough around the edges and there was nothing vulnerable about them, a disappointment to the bully. With nowhere else to go, he promised his uncle that he would stay out of trouble. Ollie performed his chores, watched his Ps and Qs, kept out of barroom fights, and was polite to the women.

By a stroke of luck, in 1951 word spread that a Mercedes-Benz plant was opening in Buenos Aires. With his previous work experience in the Mannheim factory and a good reference from Uncle Guenther, Ollie secured a position at the new automobile plant. When he left for Buenos Aires, his uncle agreed to tell anyone who looked for him that he had tired of ranch work and had returned home.

Happy to be off the ranch and living in a metropolitan city once again, Ollie was determined never to go back to hard physical labor outdoors. He enjoyed beautiful Buenos Aires—its wide boulevards, European style architecture, parks and vibrant nightlife. He stayed out of trouble.

Ollie dated the plant manager's plain, immature daughter. While they were courting, Ollie was sweet as pie. Not having traveled outside Argentina, Carmen thought Ollie was sophisticated. He was fit, and he regaled Carmen with heroic stories about his important work in France capturing spies. She was attracted to his foreign accent; Heinrich had a knack for languages. Carmen loved it when he murmured affectionate words to her in French: "Carmen, *ma bichette*" (my fawn) or when he whispered chérie in her ear. He married Carmen in 1954. Son-in-law Ollie was promoted to a management position which included some travel.

The vibrant post-war American economy helped struggling German companies, including the automobile industry, to rebuild after the war. Ollie flew to Los Angeles to help set up the west coast launch of the Mercedes 300 SL Gullwing coupe. Ollie was apprehensive about setting foot in the United States. However, Immigration and US Customs paid little attention to his Swedish passport; Olof Hansson breezed right through. He became a frequent traveler to America.

In the late 1950s, Ollie helped to set up the auto shows in New York, Los Angeles, Chicago and Miami. He developed a proficient command of English.

At first, Ollie simply wanted to perform well enough to keep his cushy job. But before long, he awakened to the richness of America. He studied the smooth-talking salesmen who demonstrated the cars. He learned to conceal his rough edges and to dress and act as a successful salesman by emulating their engaging personalities; he learned how to schmooze. Ollie loved the elegance and playful antics of Johnny Carson on the entertainer's variety show. Before long, Ollie had polished his rough veneer.

Marlon Brando's *The Wild One* had created an unruly scenario that young American men loved. The Boxer engine motorcycles became a huge success. Through dealer contacts, Ollie cheated his father-in-law. He created a small but lucrative BMW motorcycle sales business on the side. He learned everything he could about the import business.

Ollie found Los Angeles most agreeable with its sunny

climate and golden blondes. He engaged in multiple affairs on the road. Ollie purchased luxurious gifts from the United States to keep Carmen and her daddy happy. Ollie never loved Carmen, but she was convenient for getting easy work and new opportunities climbing the ladder.

Ollie took advantage of every opening that came his way; he worked hard, and he steadily advanced in the company. By the early 1960s, confident and well-spoken, Ollie decided to immigrate to California and break out on his own. But first, he would divorce his dull wife. She weighed him down and he had no intention of bringing Carmen with him. So that she would not hamper his plans, bluntly he told her, "Carmen, I will kill you and your father if you contest the divorce or get in my way." Wisely, she believed him. Over the last year and after a well-placed bruise, Carmen feared him. By the time Ollie wanted to leave, Carmen told her father she had met someone else who wanted children. They were happy to cut him loose and see him go. Ollie left B.A. for the bright lights of L.A.

For years, he had used his wife's family's influence to squirrel away and invest dollars. Ollie had witnessed a married motorcycle distributor in a compromising position. He blackmailed the California dealer into selling a small motorcycle dealership to Ollie.

In no time, under the name, *Luxury Automobiles of Beverly Hills,* Ollie opened his first car dealership. He bought a home in Beverly Hills; it was a "pinch me" moment when the Nazi dove into his own sparkling blue swimming pool.

Ollie took numerous trips to Switzerland to remove stolen paintings that had been stored in a Swiss bank vault. Ollie smuggled his Monets and his Picasso into the U.S. behind cheap street paintings and declared them along with Swiss chocolates and a cuckoo clock or two. He appeared to be a typical businessman bringing home souvenirs. Occasionally, he declared a Swiss watch to give the customs officials the opportunity to charge a little duty.

He arranged one Monet alongside two other Paris acquisitions. Elsa Bessette's Picasso, *Barcelona Palace of Fine Arts,* was placed beside a Monet, *Jardin en Fleurs,* which he had "acquired" from a Jewish family. With its blue shutters and tile roof peeking out from behind a garden, Ollie believed that *Jardin* perfectly complemented the stolen Picasso. Ollie proudly admired his paintings side by side in his living room. Unfortunately, in Paris he had to throw out a signed Picasso dedicated to "Maman Elsa" on the back of the canvas. It would have been too easy to identify the pilfered art. *"What a shame,"* he said to himself. *"I really liked that one."* Ollie sold two of his stolen Impressionist paintings.

Californians loved their cars. In a city known for two-car families, luxury and extravagance, Ollie kept their garages well stocked. Over time, he procured dealerships up and down the west coast. The booming business made him a multi-millionaire. He invested in movies. His reputation as an astute businessman grew by leaps and bounds. Little by little, he added legitimate art to his collection which included sculpture. Ollie had become a very wealthy man, an art collector, and a connoisseur of the good life.

Once he had bought his home in the United States as a prosperous businessman and resident, Ollie called himself Olof. He married one of the Pan American stewardesses he partied with in the days when he traveled back and forth from Buenos Aires. Kathy Petersen dressed him in designer clothes, moved him to a large gated mansion, and she hired a decorator to "pull the house together."

Kathy was fun, and they were a good team. Olof had become wealthy and Kathy enjoyed spending money on clothes and lavish parties laced with cocaine. Neither of them wanted children; Kathy already had a young unmarried daughter with a toddler living in the Pacific Northwest. Olof was more than happy to send them money to keep them up north and out of his hair. Kathy flew up to see her daughter and little grandson every few months. Kathy's family came to visit once or twice every winter so the little boy could swim and go to Disneyland.

Other than the infrequent intrusion of noisy family guests, Olof was content. Kathy did not tell him what to do or what not to do. One evening, early in their marriage, Olof got excited and a little too rough with her in the bedroom. Kathy hauled off and hit him in the face. She was fit, and her punch drew blood. Otto learned to save the rough sex for outside his marriage.

Chapter 47

In 1981, the Los Angeles "June gloom" had not yet arrived and another hot summer day came to a close. Olof and Kathy had been invited to a dinner party which usually promised an evening with amusing movie people. Before the parties, Olof would look forward to a swim and a little poolside siesta beneath his lemon trees.

Kathy carried two glasses of Chablis out to the pool. "Thank you, my dear, for the refreshment." Olof smiled at his pretty wife. He was truly happy.

When he awoke from his poolside nap, Olof carried the wine glasses into the kitchen. He heard Kathy's shower running; Olof stopped dead in his tracks. On the counter stood a small elegant shopping bag with "Bijoux" scrolled on the front. The address was exclusive Rodeo Drive.

Kathy's shower sounded like an ocean pounding in his ears. Dizzy and disoriented, his emotions whirled into a tailspin. It had been years since Olof had thought about Bijoux or his "escapades," as he now regarded the crimes that he had committed in Paris. Olof carefully set the wine glasses down. His heart raced, and holding his breath he slowly opened the little bag. Yes, the box contained jewelry... a diamond bracelet. Olof thought, *how could this be possible? He was nearly six thousand miles from Paris! Could Bessette be living in Los Angeles? Was it a damn coincidence?* Olof did not believe in coincidence.

Grasping the edge of the tiled counter top, Olof took a deep breath and steadied himself. He needed to think this through. For a moment he wondered, *Could Kathy be having an affair?* Her taste in jewelry was simple. She was not drawn to dressy diamond jewelry. She loved designer clothes, extravagant trips and spa treatments, but her overall style was sporty. Kathy worked out, swam and played tennis. Recently, she had taken up golf. Because of her active lifestyle, she seldom wore bangles or bracelets of any kind and certainly never diamonds during the day.

Olof had picked out a four-carat diamond cocktail ring that she wore only evenings and on special occasions. Kathy's everyday wedding ring was a Cartier Trinity entwined three-color gold band. When Olof offered to have her Rolex dressed up with a diamond bezel, her answer was a noncommittal shrug. Olof had given Kathy a sapphire and diamond necklace, stolen from Bijoux Paris, that he claimed had been his mother's. She only wore the elegant necklace to black tie affairs. Yet today her purchase was encrusted with diamonds? Olof would have to inquire about the unusual choice of a bracelet, and be prepared himself for possible disturbing news: an extra-marital affair or the proximity of Pierre Bessette.

He held himself up and walked upstairs to the master bathroom. "I took a little peek and was surprised to see diamonds, my dear?" Trying to remain aloof, he insisted that he wanted to know more about the boutique should he decide to purchase jewelry for her.

Kathy toweled off. "It's the latest thing." She dropped the fluffy white Turkish towel and smiled, "The tennis bracelet is lightweight and won't interfere with my strokes. It has a strong clasp." Olof breathed a sigh of relief when he discovered that her friends wore this bracelet and they shopped together at Bijoux.

Relieved that Kathy had bought the trendy bracelet for herself, apparently to mirror her girlfriends, Olof kissed her cheek and remarked, "It's a perfect choice, my dear. I only wish I had purchased it for you." Still, he would look into Bijoux, and more importantly, its owner.

In the morning, Olof scoured local phone books for the last name Bessette. Two Bessettes lived in Los Angeles proper. Olof pretended to look for a long-lost army buddy when a C.J. Bessette claimed to be twenty-five years old. James Hamilton Bessette was forty-two and mentioned that he did not serve in the military due to a shoulder injury. Neither man was old enough to be Pierre Bessette. One I. Bessette lived in Anaheim. He called the number and discovered that the elderly widow, Ingrid, was ninety-one.

Olof drove to Rodeo Drive and located Bijoux tucked away on a perfectly manicured little courtyard. The shop was discreet and befitting an exclusive boutique.

Since moving to Los Angeles, Olof swam nearly every day, and he played golf and tennis regularly. Olof was no longer the pudgy man in his twenties eating and lounging around in French cafés. Work on the ranch had trimmed him down, and the Los Angeles lifestyle kept him fit. His hair was salt and pepper, mostly silver. He did not believe anyone could possibly recognize him forty years later. Nonetheless, Olof wore dark glasses.

Though Olof had been watching Bessette, the Paris jeweler's only direct encounter with him had been in front of Pascal's tabac. He reminded himself that he could have arrested Bessette on the spot had his insipid partner, Stefan Schafer, not stopped him. But now, Olof thought, *"How could anyone connect me today with that ill-bred young soldier from 1942?"* He did have a slight accent but he could exaggerate and make it sound more Swedish than German. *"Ja,"* Olof practiced on himself.

In a starched white Brooks Brothers shirt and gabardine dress pants, an affluent businessman on his day off, Olof walked into the Bijoux showroom. The misty gray walls were enhanced with creamy white trim and marble pillars. An Aubusson rug in sapphire blue, cream and gold covered a Carrere marble floor. Soft music and chandelier lighting enhanced the serene, understated atmosphere. Olof took small comfort in that Bijoux in Paris, designed with dark-paneled wood, was distinctly old-world.

A pretty saleswoman approached wearing a simple black dress. Her only jewelry was a small gold insignia ring, a strand of creamy pearls and pearl stud earrings. Olof felt an erection stir as she walked toward him. With a radiant smile, the young lady greeted Olof warmly.

"Good morning, sir. May I help you?"

"Good afternoon, my dear," said Olof assuming the pleasant, grandfatherly smile he had perfected. He had his tobacco stained crooked teeth capped years ago. A chain smoker since the age of twelve, he was proud of his gleaming white American smile.

"My wife and I recently moved back to Los Angeles. I would love to purchase a little welcome home gift for her." He gestured, "And I was told *this* was the place to come."

"Of course, I am certain we can find a special gift to your liking, sir. What did you have in mind?"

Olof said, intensifying his Swedish accent, "You know, this shop reminds me so much of the boutiques in Europe. It's really quite lovely. Is your owner from overseas?"

"Thank you for the compliment, I will tell Mr. Turner. I am new here but my boss and his family are originally from New York, although he graduated from the University of Southern California back in the fifties.

"No need to disturb him, my dear. You say his name is Turner? I knew some Turners from the east coast."

"Yes, Patrick Turner... I cannot ask Mr. Turner to speak with you now. He is in San Francisco with Mrs. Turner. They are looking at property to possibly open another boutique."

"How exciting," said Olof.

Olof bought a strand of white South Sea Mikimoto pearls with a pave diamond heart dangling from the diamond-studded clasp—understated and elegant like his wife. He planned to give it to Kathy for her birthday. He thought about paying cash so as not to give the salesgirl a credit card with his name on it. However, she would require his name for the receipt. In any case, he noticed another customer also purchase a string of pearls, not to worry, a common occurrence. His receipt would not stand out. While the sales girl gift-wrapped his gift, Olof twisted his neck from side to side and felt his tense muscles relax.

Olof still wanted to make certain that the owner, Mr. Turner, was not Pierre Bessette or a close relative. Bessette had been on the run from the Germans and could have changed his name when he fled.

Olof drove over to the USC campus that was like an oasis in downtown Los Angeles. The Romanesque buildings faced with brick and cream-colored limestone were nestled among majestic palm trees. He walked past a sparkling two-tiered fountain, up a wide staircase and stepped onto the cool marble floor of the impressive Doheny library. With a stack of yearbooks dating from 1950 to 1960, he settled near one of the stained-glass windows beneath a soaring rotunda and perused the yearbooks. He discovered numerous Turners from around the country. Finally, he found Patrick Turner. He cross-referenced Turner's activities to determine his background. Turner was indeed born and raised in New York. He had been a star athlete at Scarsdale High School in Westchester County and played basketball in college. He also had been a member of the USC ski team. Patrick would be much younger than Bessette, tall and quite lanky with wavy blonde hair and blue-green eyes. An all-American, Patrick Turner was definitely not Pierre Bessette. Relieved, Olof sat back in his chair. An unlikely coincidence—Bijoux translates to jewelry. That's all it was. He stood up. He was running late.

Google did not exist at the time. But had Olof dug deeper into the history of Bijoux on Rodeo Drive, he would have learned that it was the *second* American showroom of that name to open. The first American boutique was opened in New York in 1944 by a man named Peter Ambrose. Peter is the

Anglo-Saxon version of Pierre.

Olof missed another important clue. Like Kathy's new pearls, the sapphire and diamond necklace that he stole from Maison Bijoux Paris was adorned with a small diamond heart that dangled on the clasp.

But Olof was in a hurry and distracted. He did not want to miss his lunch date with a curvaceous red-headed divorcee whom he planned to bed. She was a shy waitress, and it had taken him weeks to get her to go out with him. To get this troublesome Bijoux scare off his mind, he looked forward to forcing himself on the woman. A little pain and torment for the unsuspecting waitress would be just the excitement and release Olof needed.

Chapter 48

Olof had donated large sums of money to the J. Paul Getty and the Los Angeles County Museum of Art, the LACMA. Olof and Kathy sponsored swanky fundraisers to procure distinguished works of art for the City. He staged some of the extravagant events at his home to showcase his growing private collection. He loved being fawned over by the Los Angeles art world.

Once again, LACMA contacted the Hanssons. The museum hoped to add to its collection and asked Olof to kindly host a special gathering for its most important donors. Celebrities would be on the guest list, of course.

Photographs of the soiree and its fundraising success were splashed all over the society page of the Los Angeles Times. The photographer had snapped a wonderful picture of Olof and Kathy (looking tan and fit in a sequined green Halston dress) talking with Marlon Brando who was smiling and holding a crystal flute of sparkling Veuve-Clicquot champagne. Normally, Olof was pleased with the attention. But this time, the nice little article featured an unexpected and irksome look into Olof's background. The journalist had traced Olof's success from Mercedes-Benz in Argentina to Los Angeles.

In the following months, questions surfaced concerning Olof's hard-to-place accent and background—especially the bit about Argentina. Olof certainly was not of Latin descent? The popular musical *Evita* had increased Olof's unease. The stories of Nazis fleeing to safe havens in Argentina straight into the welcoming arms of the Peron regime had become popular cocktail chitchat.

Hollywood popularized World War Two revivals such as the *Eye of the Needle* starring Donald Sutherland who portrayed a cunning, ruthless German spy. The movie crowd talked endlessly about Nazi Gestapo chief, Klaus Barbie, the "Butcher of Lyon" who had been tracked down by a journalist. A documentary or movie would be in the works. Olof felt uncomfortable with so much Hollywood focus on the war; curiosity had surfaced about *his* background. *When did he arrive in America? Was his accent German?*

At a Hollywood party, an acclaimed director with a little too much to drink or snort had jokingly asked, "Are you a real-life Nazi in our midst, Olof?" With all eyes turned toward him, Olof performed a silly little Charlie Chaplin interpretation of "Heil Hitler" while clicking his heels together. It got him a good laugh. But inside, Olof's stomach was in knots.

He deflected the nuisance questions by recounting his fabricated story: "The rustic little fishing village in Sweden where I grew up was idyllic for a child. From time to time, my family vacationed on my uncle's magnificent ranch in South America. One summer, I met the daughter of an executive at the Mercedes car factory. Sadly, that marriage did not work out." Now here Olof was in sunny L.A., where he had met his lovely wife, Kathy.

Olof's story seemed convincing for the moment. Nonetheless, every now and then another question would surface; he grew edgy. The safe, glamorous life he had built for himself was at risk if another nosy journalist poked even deeper into his background. His stomach ached constantly. He dreaded the time when "*The Butcher of Lyon*" might be released.

After considerable thought and sleepless nights, Olof suggested to his wife, "My dear, why don't we buy a second vacation home near your daughter and grandchildren?"

Kathy's daughter had another child; a baby girl who Kathy lamented was growing up too fast. "You could spend more time with your family if we had our own place." he pointed out to her. "I could relax a bit more away from the hubbub of L.A. Traffic is becoming such a problem, not to mention the smog."

When the smog was heavy, Olof's throat irritated him and he coughed. Sometimes his breathing was labored and it slowed him down. Although the clean-air act improved air quality, it was trendy cocktail conversation to lament the smoky air.

"The air is so clean in the Northwest." After all, Olof remarked, "I'm not getting any younger."

In 1982, Olof and Kathy purchased their country estate in Dunthorpe right outside Portland near the picturesque town of Lake Oswego. The Mediterranean style home was situated on a lush piece of property, not on the lake, but on the refreshing pine-scented banks of the Willamette River. Money was not an issue. Olof had invested in the initial public offering by a company called Apple. His portfolio had increased by millions.

The Hanssons completely remodeled the 6,000 square-foot stucco home reminiscent of a European villa. Floor to ceiling windows across the back of the property captured expansive views of the river and snow-tipped Mt. Hood in the distance. Kathy hired a prominent Los Angeles decorator who filled the home with European statement pieces—plump sofas in designer fabrics, antiques and luxurious oriental rugs. Kathy and Olof transported some of their museum quality paintings to enhance the walls surrounding a replicated 17th century floor-to-ceiling limestone fireplace.

Olof built a guest cottage where Kathy's daughter and children would have their own space during visits. He purchased a powerboat and jet skis so they could spend hours on the water, far away from him. He added tennis courts and a swimming pool overlooking the river.

The abrupt change to Olof's lifestyle was a small price

to pay for a man who wanted a breather away from the scrutiny in Los Angeles. The constant Hollywood references about the war had frayed his nerves. Over the years, Olof had sold some of his pilfered art and replaced the pieces with legitimate artwork to reduce his risk. Now, their river house provided a peaceful respite away from awkward questions and innuendos about his background.

Olof spent hours reading and enjoying the spectacular views. Portland had become known for excellent restaurants that served fresh, northwest cuisine. He discovered German restaurants with home-style food that he remembered as a boy, and Willamette Valley wineries about an hour away. He joined Westridge Country Club in a lovely wooded setting overlooking the river just minutes from his home. Olof had found himself the perfect golf retreat far away from inquisitive journalists and conversations about the war and Nazis.

Kathy loved the local farmer's market and quaint shops in nearby Lake Oswego. Soon, they increased their months in the Northwest, spending less and less time in Los Angeles. Several former flight attendant friends lived in Portland and between their "clipped wings" activities and the country club, Kathy was well on her way to building a Portland social life. Olof joined the Multnomah Athletic Club so that he and Kathy could play tennis indoors on rain-swept winter days when they remained up north.

Olof settled into a tidy lifestyle free from the movie people with overzealous imaginations. He looked forward to hunting fresh, unsuspecting females in his new neck of the woods. These days, he desired them younger and younger...

Chapter 49

It was spring 1983 and Matt Ambrose arrived home from Argentina to find panic. A family friend's grandson had been snatched from his mother's wine bar, Prosecco, the previous evening in the Chelsea neighborhood. Christopher's distraught grandparents implored Pierre and Ellie to ask Matt to look into the kidnapping. The memory of Etan Patz, the first abducted child whose face appeared on a milk carton, was fresh in people's minds. There were no clues or ransom note. Matt assured his grandparents that the detectives assigned to the case were excellent. But after seeing Ellie's disappointment, he got involved.

The following day a ransom note arrived. The shopkeepers and employees near Prosecco had been interviewed. The merchants who were working the evening of the kidnapping had commented, over and over, "There was nothing unusual or suspicious. It's a friendly neighborhood with repeat customers." Yet, the boy had vanished into thin air.

Matt wondered, "What exactly is normal activity between five-thirty and seven on a typical weekday on that block?"

That evening at five o'clock, Matt and a seasoned detective assigned to the case, Oakley Rivers, sat at an outside table at a French café directly across the street from the wine bar where the kidnapping had taken place. At Pressed for Time, the detectives sipped dark French-pressed coffees, talked over the details of the kidnapping, and watched the world hustle by.

The youngster's Star Wars lunch box had been dropped near the curb in front of his mother's establishment. Next door was a small bank with an outside ATM. A few people waited in line to withdraw money for the evening. On the other side of the bank was a small grocery store with a sidewalk fruit and vegetable stand. Customers picked out seasonal farm-fresh produce transported to Manhattan from upstate.

By six-thirty customers began leaving Prosecco to walk next door for an early dinner at Jack and Jake's Kitchen. Among them was an occasional celebrity friend of Christopher's mother, a former soap opera actress.

Further down the street, a well-dressed woman hailed a taxi in front of an upscale hair salon. Next door to the salon was the chic stationery and card shop, Maison Note. A subway entrance flanked the east end of the street. Across the street from Prosecco, a florist placed her colorful bouquets in tin buckets. On the west side of the French café, a ladies clothing boutique stood next to a men's haberdashery, Stag. And at the very end of the street stood an Austrian bakery, a Jewish Deli, and a drug store.

Taking a sip of his dark roast, Oakley sat back, "I'd like to move into this neighborhood. Doubt if Mel and I could ever afford it, though." Traffic was increasing on the narrow street as more yellow cabs picked up day customers and dropped off the dressier evening crowd.

Matt said, "Look up there, do you see it?"

"See what? What do you mean?"

"Look again. There's a shine, a glint coming from across the street. Come on… Let's take a look." Matt threw five bucks on the table.

Sure enough, a small bank surveillance camera had been placed discreetly above a green and white bank sign and was not apparent to those on the sidewalk. The two detectives walked over to look at the camera meant to watch over the ATM. Matt requested the tape from the security guard. Based on the camera angle, they did not expect the surveillance to reach Prosecco's front entrance, but it was worth a look.

Back at the station they saw a partial image of the kidnapping on the video viewer.

"Phew, look at that," Oak whistled. The youngster had drifted over toward the bank.

Tuesday through Friday, young Christopher walked home from school with his mother. He ate a snack, and his mom helped him with his homework. He then watched a little TV in a quiet back room until six-twenty or so.

His father's limousine would pick Christopher up around six-thirty; father and son would eat dinner together. The schedule worked well, with both parents able to spend quality time with their son. There had been no indication that either parent was involved in Christopher's disappearance.

About six-twenty on the day of the kidnapping, Christopher's father had called from his limo to let the boy's mother know that he was running a little late due to traffic. He estimated picking up his son around six thirty-five or so.

The mother went outside and said, "Christopher, your dad will be a few minutes late."

Christopher replied, "Okay."

The camera showed a partial shot of Mom blowing him a kiss and Christopher smiling up at her. The boy moved aside to allow a group of after-work patrons to enter the wine bar.

The tape revealed a split-second kidnapping: When Christopher came outside, a woman in a brown coat approached the boy to speak with him. Suddenly she turned and placed herself in line at the ATM when the boy's mother opened her door. As soon as Christopher's mom closed her front door, the woman reappeared. She hustled the confused child toward a creeping limousine. She propelled him inside the limo and jumped in after him. The limo drove away only a few minutes before his father's black limousine had arrived.

The police were able to freeze-frame the tape and get the last three letters of the kidnapper's license plate as it drove away. The Cadillac limo had been rented that morning. The kidnappers owned a restaurant supply company that serviced Prosecco and another food and beverage establishment on the street. The kidnappers knew the father's timing and procedure for picking up his son.

The detectives traced the driver to his apartment in Queens where Christopher was rescued unharmed. A carbon copy of the ransom note was found along with billing invoices addressed to Prosecco, and Jack and Jake's restaurant. A lady's camel hair coat hung on a coat stand.

Christopher's rescue became the top news feature in Manhattan. It was picked up by the AP and became a feature story nationwide. The welcome ending played out in the press and on the nightly news programs. Set to retire, Detective Oakley Rivers gave credit to Matt for spotting the camera above the bank.

Morning talk shows dubbed it the "Prosecco Heist." Celebrity Gossip and Entertainment Tonight ran the story and interviewed other celebrities who were friends of Christopher's mom. *TIME* magazine published an article about the kidnapping. Matt was given the city's Valor Award. Detective Matt Ambrose became a household name across the country.

Eventually, the news blitz died down, and Matt settled back into his normal routine. He wished more of his work had the same good outcome. Often, detectives had to deliver bad news that a missing person had disappeared due to money problems or a secret love affair.

Matt finished a painting previously commissioned by the patron who bought his striking *"Poppy Red Lips"* from a Soho gallery. Matt's focus returned to searching into the backgrounds of numerous Olof Hanssons residing in North America. Quite a few O. Hanssons lived in the States, primarily in the upper Midwest and Minnesota, one in Colorado and New

Jersey, and two men in California. Several women (named Olivia, Odelia and Oda) were disqualified.

Matt started with those closest to New York and then fanned out his search. All along, he expected a phone call from Alvarez to say that he had located Hansson, aka Heinrich, somewhere in Germany or in Scandinavia.

Much to Matt's dismay, José Alvarez had no luck either. In Sweden alone, José uncovered multitudes of Olof Hanssons, including hundreds of variations of the name Hansson—Hanson, Hansen, Hanssen. Then he discovered numerous Olufs and Olovs. Norway, Denmark and Hamburg contained residents with variations of Olof's name. Some were investigated. Both Matt and José discovered that many of the world's Olof's simply were not the right age or description.

Matt realized that since Heinrich had changed his name once, he easily could have done so again. The disappointing reality was that even if they found Otto Heinrich, he may very well have sold the paintings without a bill of sale or the buyer's name. The paintings could be hanging in homes anywhere across the world or they could be lying in an attic. Matt searched museum catalogs and databases in Europe. He kept in touch with the French national archives. Matt knew the authorities could not convict Heinrich of Genevieve's rape unless the DNA was still viable on the clothing.

Matt feared that keeping a promise from the past was becoming a long shot. It had been relatively easy to find the culprit's partner, Stefan Schafer and Herr Huber, the neighbor. Neither of them was hiding. But the tyrant, Nazi Otto Heinrich, remained elusive.

Matt had refused to join the family business. Would he then become the Ambrose man unable to keep his promise to return Ellie's painting of her daughter? Many nights after work, Matt and a few detectives met up at O'Malley's, a cop bar located near the station. O'Malley's became a good place to put aside his fears and frustration.

Chapter 50

E ventually, it came down to the last two Hanssons on his list. Matt was stalling, exacerbated by the nagging thought of defeat.

It was time to look into O. Hansson residing in Los Angeles and the final Olof Hansson living in Colorado. Matt also would search for his own gallery to give himself a small moral victory— an airy space to fuel his passion to paint.

On a cloudy gray morning, Matt stood over his kitchen sink with his coffee and a bagel. He perused *Gallery des Artistes*, a monthly newsletter that listed art galleries for sale. A paragraph on the back page of the publication caught his eye; a small donated wing of the Portland Art Museum (PAM) would be named the Hanson Gallery, spelled with the typical single "es." Matt made a note to inquire anyway, although no O. or Olof Hansson was listed in Oregon or Washington. Recently, Matt had discovered that the ninety-year-old Hansson from The Lone Tree, Colorado was not his man.

Still early morning in Portland, Matt would wait a few hours to call the Portland Art Museum. Later today he would check out the final O. Hansson who resided in Los Angeles.

A gallery Matt had liked in Chelsea was listed for sale. He made an appointment for the following morning to meet with the broker to look at the renovated Anglican Church turned loft with wall space and enormous windows should he be left with no choice but to move on with his life...

Matt took a subway downtown. At the precinct, he checked police records and Interpol and found no criminal record for O. Hansson in Los Angeles.

Inside the public library, Matt found articles on Hansson. Not long after he started reading, he whispered, "I'll be damned." Olof Hansson was European born and an art collector. He fell within the right age range and he donated heavily to Los Angeles museums. Matt's heart rate picked up. This was the first time *any* man with the initials O.H. had a strong connection with art. He read a short business article about the man and his tremendous business success in Los Angeles.

Back at his office desk at eleven o'clock Pacific Time, Matt called both the Getty and LACMA to speak with public relations. Posing as an art reporter, Matt stated that his publication would like to run a feature article on museum philanthropist Olof Hansson. The PR directors at both museums reported that their patron, Hansson, would be left a message. His number was unlisted and the museums could not divulge any contact information. Matt was disappointed to hear that Mr. Hansson was currently away at his country home.

Matt then called the Portland Art Museum (PAM) using the same ruse regarding an article, this time about the prospective Hanson Gallery. The young man on the other end of the phone happily chatted.

"We are so delighted and pleased that Olof and his lovely wife have pledged to donate a new viewing gallery to the museum, especially since they are not even full-time residents of Portland."

Matt sat straight up and paid close attention. "I can see how you would be so thrilled with Mr. Hanson's gift. Let me make sure I have the correct spelling of this new exhibition hall. Would you mind spelling it?"

"Of course, let me spell it for you: H a n s s o n Hall."

Concealing his excitement, Matt repeated, "Hansson, spelled with a double "ess," is that correct?"

"Yes, sir, a bit unusual but that's how his name is spelled."

Matt stood up. "And of course, Mr. Hansson comes from Los Angeles, if I understand correctly?"

"Why, yes, of course! The Hanssons are a wonderful couple who came to us from L.A. They are *esteemed* patrons of the arts. We are so lucky and very grateful for their generosity and support."

Matt fell back into his chair and gripped the phone, his knuckles turned white. Could he have found Heinrich— *in Oregon?*

Matt took a deep breath and asked, "May I have your name? When we are close to publishing our story, I will get in touch with you. It will not be for months as we already have articles in queue. I will contact you directly *if* it is approved. Please do not mention the article to the Hanssons yet. You know how fickle publishers can be, and it might take months to get them to set a date. We would hate to disappoint Mr. Hansson and his wife, wouldn't we?"

"Oh, of course, I understand *totally*. My name is Shane Taylor. I will wait to hear from you. Always love to meet a fellow art lover! I do hope you can convince your publisher to run a story. We are so proud of our accomplishments here in the Rose City."

Playing along to Shane's excitement, Matt replied, "Of course, Shane. I will contact you *directly* so we can get the proper channels moving, and *you* can make my introduction to Mr. Hansson. Remember, please don't contact Hansson just yet and risk disappointing the gentleman. And of course, we will bring our own photographer."

"Thank you, so much. Oh my, I'm very excited about this!"

Before Shane Taylor could ask for Matt's name, Matt reiterated that he'd be in touch, said goodbye and quickly hung up the phone.

Detective Ambrose leaned back in his chair, and exhaled, stunned that just when he thought he might be forced to give up, he *may* have located Olof Hansson aka Otto Heinrich. Shane seemed well aware of the Hanssons and their affinity with art. By all accounts, Mr. Hansson owned a personal art collection of museum quality. Matt prayed Hansson's art included his Great-grandmother Annette Lindstrom's *Portrait of Anna.*

Now Matt needed a pretense that would allow him to look into Hansson in Portland. But what? Hansson appeared to be a respected businessman and a discerning art collector with no criminal record. Matt could not scrutinize this man's life without cause. He needed access to the Hansson homes to see his paintings without raising suspicion. If Matt had the right man, he would need his DNA.

Matt picked up the phone and called José Alvarez.

Chapter 51

M att brought his investigator up to speed. José whistled, "Well done, man. The Northwest of all places." Matt asked José, "Can you get out to Los Angeles? José replied, "Sure. I'm free right now."

"Good. Dig as deep as you can into his business background and personal life. See if you can find *any* details that could help me to make contact with Hansson. We need to know when he immigrated to the States. Why a second home in Portland? How often does he stay up in the Northwest? It sounds like Portland has become more than a second home if he is donating an entire gallery to their art museum. According to his bio, he made his money through luxury auto dealerships and investments. Was there any hint of corruption involved or political maneuverings? He does *not* have a criminal record but perhaps accusations were dropped or the authorities were paid off? See if there might be *any* suspicious angle I could use to look into his personal life or activities."

Matt drew a breath. He then cautioned, "José, if you run into a roadblock or anyone becomes suspicious, just stop. I don't want Heinrich to think about fleeing *if* he is our guy."

Matt added, "He's in Portland now. I'd like to snoop around a bit up there myself. He donated a viewing gallery so he must have put down fairly deep roots. If I need you, be ready to join me, okay?"

José agreed. "Sure, I'll fly out to Los Angeles tomorrow."

"Stay at the Hotel Bel-Air. My family has an account

there. Ask around town quietly while I wrap things up here and join you out West."

"Okay. And Matt, leave me a message and let me know where I can reach you. I'll be in touch."

Matt cancelled the Chelsea gallery appointment. He finished up paperwork at his desk. Maybe he would stop at O'Malley's on his way home…

A sudden cloudburst scattered New Yorkers looking for cover. Matt jumped a few puddles and sprinted toward the subway steps. He shook off water and slumped down onto a cold concrete bench. He stretched his legs and reached for the tattered pages of a forgotten *USA Today*. His train screeched to a stop. Matt jumped on board.

The storm raged. Heavy wind and a steady rain pelted his windows. Matt paced back and forth. In the background, Frank Sinatra crooned *One for My Baby*. By now, a Rémy VSOP cognac had turned into three. Matt was stuck. He needed to get up close to Hansson three thousand miles away. *But how?*

Matt sank onto his couch. Distracted by the rattling windows, he stood again, looked out at the storm and stretched; he glanced over at the rain-splattered newspaper that he had tossed onto his coffee table. Adrenaline surged when the headline jumped out at him: *"Missing Daughter of Portland NBA Star Feared Kidnapped."*

Matt sat back down and read the entire article twice when an idea took shape. He felt guilty capitalizing on a family's misfortune but this was an opportunity that may not come again.

He looked at his watch. Matt steeled his nerves and placed a call to the Portland police chief. With the *Prosecco* kidnapping so widely publicized, he would use it to his advantage.

After making his introduction, Matt said, "Chief, I'm visiting my sister out your way. I'd like to take a quick look at your case. I've developed an interest in kidnapping profiles. Of course, I wouldn't want to be in your way but I could offer a fresh pair of eyes."

Matt held his breath and crossed his fingers. He expected Chief Gates to end the call.

A pause, then Gates said, "This is such a damn high-profile case. We're swamped with out-of-town reporters; their satellite trucks are all over the little girl's neighborhood. We don't need the distraction and increased pressure. We want to focus on the investigation and find this child."

Matt felt a rejection coming but jumped in, "I understand what the family is going through, sir, as well as your department. We experienced similar circumstances here in New York. The press called it the *Prosecco Heist* and turned our investigation into a circus."

The kidnapped girl's father, a point guard for the Portland Trailblazers, was one of the nation's most popular players. Not surprisingly, the entire country was watching. Both men knew that every additional day the little girl was missing increased the chances that she would not be found alive.

More awkward silence, then Matt reluctantly had to give up. "Well sir, I won't keep you any longer. Good luck with the case."

Gates interrupted, "Detective, look. I am short one guy out with pneumonia. I can pay for a few days in a hotel and meals but that's about it. It might help to have you take a look at what we have, which I'll tell you is not much at this point..."

Matt booked a flight to Portland for the following morning. Then he phoned his superior and explained that he needed to take some time away; this trip was necessary.

At dinner, Matt told his parents and grandparents that he had a solid lead out west on the culprit. He begged them, "Please do not become too optimistic. I have to take careful, legal steps and it could take time. And, he could be the wrong guy. I may be gone for days, weeks or even a month or so. I promise to stay in touch, and I'll let you know if I find anything."

Ellie had developed macular degeneration and seldom painted. Her eyesight had become less sharp, not unlike Claude Monet and Mary Cassatt's impaired vision in their later years. She still read large print and enjoyed the museums. Matt desperately wanted her to see *Portrait of Anna* and *Morning on the Seine* again before she lost most of her sight.

"*Bonne chance*," said Ellie as she placed a kiss on each cheek and hugged her grandson. "I'll miss you, and *please* be careful whatever you do."

Pierre embraced Matt and wished him well.

Michael told his son, "Go get that bastard."

Chapter 52

L ast night's storm had drifted out over the Atlantic. Bright sun illuminated Manhattan's steel and glass skyline. Matt's plane took off and flew west toward the jagged, snowy peak of Mt. Hood.

At the Portland airport, Police Chief Mike Gates shifted from foot to foot. The chief's rumpled blazer appeared to have been thrown on as an afterthought. A security badge dangled around his muscular neck. Gates checked his Seiko diver's watch for the third time.

Matt Ambrose deplaned looking fit and stylish in a pale blue V-neck sweater; he wore his lucky Gucci loafers. With a strong handshake, the chief remarked, "I hope you had a pleasant flight, detective. I'll fill you in on our way downtown. Shall we go?"

The chief's car pulled away from the curb, and sun gave way to a drizzle that sprinkled across the windshield. The gray clouds intensified Matt's mood. He had made it to Portland. It was personal, and he was ready to hunt down the Nazi. But for now, Matt would focus his attention on a missing little girl.

On the short half hour drive to the police station, Gates gave Matt an overview.

"Nine-year-old Lacy is the daughter of Trailblazer point guard Larry Dennison. She disappeared three days ago. Lacy went missing from her home in Dunthorpe, a neighborhood bordering the Willamette River, and a short distance from downtown Portland." Gates handed Matt a school picture of a little girl with a sunny smile. Her skin was the color of creamy cocoa and her eyes a cornflower blue.

Lacy had walked home from a friend's house, just around the corner and a few minutes away from her parents' riverfront home. The wind off the Willamette had made it chilly enough for a jacket. Her small Nike Trailblazer jacket was found lying on a curb halfway to her parent's home.

Matt's mind churned with various scenarios. Had she tried to run from an abductor, losing her jacket? Or was the kidnapper known to the girl, perhaps a friend or neighbor?

Gates continued, "Scuba divers have dragged the river, the surrounding woods were searched and searched again. No unusual cars or persons were spotted. I won't pretend, detective. We are worried. We've seen no ransom note. We have no clues as to her whereabouts. Personally, I'm just sick over this. It could be a sexual predator."

Police Commissioner Paul Rosen came into Gates' office to introduce himself, and Matt signed a consultant contract. Rosen had complete confidence in his police force. But, with the weight of a child's kidnapping, and worse, a celebrity's kid, Rosen had thought what the hell, and he expressed his appreciation for Matt's offer to look into the case.

"Detective, my men control the investigation. But we are grateful for any insight you might have." Everything was being done to find the child. The New York detective intensified the commissioner's hope for a good outcome.

Chief Gates called in his two senior detectives. Gates introduced Steve Bolden and Jonathan Joseph Larkin, known as "JJ" by his colleagues. Over lukewarm station house coffee, they went over the details with their New York counterpart. Bolden, the lead detective, was a bear of a man with a bushy beard and warm brown eyes. Unshaven, Bolden adapted well to undercover work. Tall and blond, Detective "J.J." would follow up on backgrounds and forensics. Matt would spend the day with Bolden going through their steps. The men were open to questions and did not appear to resent Matt's involvement. If anything, the Portland police had their own questions regarding the notorious Prosecco kidnapping.

Detective Steve Bolden drove Matt to the Dennison home situated in a neighborhood made up of riverfront mansions. To keep reporters off the property, a rope and small security detail cut off access to the victim's house. Reporters had camped out across the street on a neighbor's lawn; the wife brought trays of coffee and cookies to the journalists who were hungrier for news.

Matt and Bolden entered the Dennison home through a side entrance. Bolden introduced Detective Ambrose to the girl's parents. Jade Dennison's aqua eyes were red and swollen from crying. Larry Dennison was a tall, unshaven wreck, pacing back and forth. Lacy's father was black and her mother white. In progressive Portland, Matt thought it highly unlikely that the kidnapping would be racially motivated.

They told their story once again. Following her weekly Saturday play date, Lacy walked the two blocks home. She called, as she always did before she started for home, but this time, she never arrived.

All of the staff had been with the Dennisons a long time and had been properly vetted. Larry had no debts or gambling habits. The mother was squeaky clean. Without a doubt, the family was terrified. Detectives had looked into the nearby neighbors' backgrounds and found nothing suspicious.

Matt asked Bolden to show him exactly where Lacy had been snatched. After looking over the affluent Dunthorpe neighborhood, he then asked Bolden to drive him around the central core of Portland to get the lay of the land from the Dennison's to downtown and then east of the river. Matt had researched Portland on the flight out. He wanted to see it for himself.

Steve Bolden was a veteran detective with a larger-than-life personality.

"Man, why do you want to waste time sightseeing?" Bolden thought a drive around Portland had no value. But Matt wanted a firsthand perspective of the city.

He told Bolden, "It'll give me a window into local attitudes and what people are thinking."

"Let's get this over with then. We'll drive through downtown, then east and north and back through town. Fortunately, this won't take long."

Bolden drove the Portland streets from the tree-lined downtown across the river, east toward Mt. Hood and the airport, then toward the foothills on the west side.

The broad Willamette River separated Portland's eastside neighborhoods from the West Hills and downtown. Boutiques, hotels, restaurants, a grassy waterfront park and pleasure boats dotted the river's west bank. Matt noticed a relaxed atmosphere. The city was enveloped in a leafy green canopy; around town, flower baskets hung from lamp posts.

 Old Portland neighborhoods were made up of Victorian, Tudor, Arts and Crafts style homes, and bungalows with painted front porches. Roses climbed up telephone poles. Neighborhoods were filled with shops, locally-sourced restaurants, boutique coffee roasters and trendy clubs. Numerous bridges spanned from the eastside to the west; people flowed easily from one vibrant neighborhood to another. The more affluent neighborhoods in the Rose City were larger, dressier versions—manicured lawns and mansions hidden behind stone walls. Ancient Douglas firs towered over hilltops and highways. Matt smelled pine, and he never realized that there could be so many shades of green.

Bicycles were evident around town; drivers generally shared the road. Matt did not hear honking horns. Matt thought aloud, "People appear friendly."

Bolden nodded "Yep, that's right."

As they drove, the two detectives talked basketball and football. Bolden smiled. He had been married to his wife for twenty-five years, with two "great kids." His family had visited New York. "Man, we had a great time in the Big Apple."

Matt checked into a room reserved for him at the Hilton Hotel in downtown. He picked up a message, and walked over to the iconic Heathman Hotel for dinner. Matt was famished. He ordered a rabbit confit, crisp butter lettuce salad with chive dressing and a fresh grilled wild Chinook salmon, then he sat back and relaxed over a Maker's Mark straight up. Over dinner, Matt sipped a refreshing Cristom chardonnay and dwelled on the search for Lacy Dennison. Back in his room, he called José Alvarez.

Based on what he saw today, Matt suspected someone from the outside, not a local. Anger and frustration, often linked to crime, was not apparent among laid-back residents going easily about their day in Portland. It was strictly a judgment call. He had been wrong before, but Matt's instincts were often spot on. He suspected an opportunist who had some contact with Lacy and her family, and someone who knew their schedules. Neighbors, gardeners, babysitters, deliverymen, housekeepers and *all* of their immediate family members and acquaintances became prime suspects. Matt had requested the names of any new neighbors within the last couple of years. Anyone able to watch the little girl on a daily basis.

Scouring the notes from Detectives Bolden and Larkin, he asked José to delve further into the backgrounds of all new neighbors, the household help as well as Larry Dennison and his wife. Matt told José, "I'm looking for hidden gambling debts, extra-marital affairs and blackmail, all reasons to arrange a kidnapping for ransom or revenge." Sexual assault would have much worse implication for the little girl.

The following day a grubby ransom note surfaced in the morning mail. Matt breathed a sigh of relief surmising that they probably were not dealing with a sexual predator. Most likely, Lacy was alive. Detective Larkin and forensics went to work on the note. The deadline to respond was four o'clock the following afternoon. Commissioner Rosen, Chief Gates and Detective Bolden would work with the family on the ransom. No question, the Dennisons would pay the money.

Landscapers arrived and were shooed away. Matt followed them in an unmarked car to their next job and looked into the owner of the truck and his crew.

Matt had asked for the names of all additional help the Dennisons had hired or fired the last five years. Matt followed the housekeeper to her bus stop after work and eventually to her white foursquare home in a pleasant eastside neighborhood.

The following morning, Matt was at the Dennison house before dawn. He sat in his rental car three doors away from the home. He ate a maple bar and sipped a piping hot Rivertown coffee. The reporters had not yet staked out their grassy spots on the neighbor's lawn.

A car approached, and Matt slumped down in his seat. Just before seven-thirty in the morning, Matt watched as the housekeeper, somewhere in her fifties, was dropped off by a man; it was very hard to tell from his distance but *maybe* thirteen or so years younger. He dropped her off about three doors away. She entered the Dennison home through the side gate. The housekeeper had no record or any trouble in her past. She had worked for the family for many years. However, Matt checked and rechecked Bolden's notes. He found no mention that the housekeeper had a husband or possibly a brother or a son either.

The housekeeper had a boyfriend. Martha had met a man at her neighborhood pub and local eating establishment a few months prior. She had fallen in love.

Martha took the bus to save on gas but drove her car on chilly or showery days. Sometimes the boyfriend dropped her off or picked her up from the Dennison's home. She asked him to drop her off a few doors away; Martha felt a little awkward about her new love life. Willie worked for a land-scaping company whenever they needed an extra hand. Willie was sweet to her, polite and handsome. Martha *knew* he had nothing to do with Lacy's disappearance. She had always been a good judge of character. Even her elderly mother and sister approved of her mild-mannered and handsome Willie.

The boyfriend stayed with her most nights. The past week he had complained of flu-like symptoms and slept in his own studio apartment so that Martha would not get sick. They chatted several times a day on the phone. But today Willie felt much better. He offered to drive Martha to work. Willie took her hand and told her, "Sweetheart, I want to move in with you tomorrow if you are still interested?" Martha's heart swelled.

What Willie actually wanted was a firsthand look at any activity going on at the Dennison's house on the day he planned to pick up his ransom. Willie noticed a parked car a few houses away, but it was empty so no problem.

Several Saturdays ago, on a chilly, rainy spring morning, Willie had dropped Martha off at work. That's when an idea came to him...

The housekeeper had complained to Willie that on Saturdays, usually Martha's half-day and their "date night," if the father was out of town Martha had to stay later. Usually, Larry Dennison walked over to meet his daughter, and they would walk the two blocks home together. The mother had a standing Saturday tennis lesson. Willie checked the "away" schedule for the Trailblazers. He snatched Lacy as she walked home alone while Larry Dennison was in Dallas playing the Mavericks.

Matt discretely followed the boyfriend to his apartment complex after Willie had dropped Martha off. Matt talked with the landlord and got his tenant's name, Willie Johnson. Willie was paying month-to-month rent in cash.

Matt had asked José to run an NCIC computer search (National Crime Information Center) for the names of *any* persons wanted in nearby states—California, Washington, Idaho, Montana, Nevada and Colorado. Sure enough, the boyfriend had a previous drug conviction and was wanted in Boise for burglary.

Matt drove straight back to the Dennison's home and took Bolden aside. Detective Bolden then questioned the bewildered housekeeper about the man who had dropped her off. She gave them Willie's name, and Matt told a stunned detective squad that Willie Johnson had two prior arrests and was wanted in Idaho for burglary. Matt told them where Willie could be picked up. Martha fainted.

The run-down boarding house rimmed the Willamette River in the otherwise quaint town, Oakwood, known for its slice of Americana: antique stores, bakeries, popular restaurants and brewpubs. Several hours after questioning Martha, with a search warrant in hand, the police popped the door open to Willy's shabby room.

Willie Johnson was packing a suitcase ready to skip town as soon as he picked up the ransom. Sitting in front of the TV, Lacy was scared and tired of junk food and television. She'd suffered a rope burn on her ankle. Lacy was returned to her very grateful family.

Detective Ambrose tried to stay out of the limelight. He did not want publicity or to have someone dig into *his* background. Off-camera, he graciously accepted season tickets to the Trailblazer games. But the *Oregonian* covered the story and highlighted Matt's investigative work on both the Dennison and the talked-about Prosecco case.

The Portland Police Bureau took credit for bringing Detective Ambrose to Portland. One of their detectives was retiring and Chief Gates nonchalantly offered Matt a position on their detective squad. Gates was shocked when Matt accepted his offer on a temporary "let's see how it works out" basis.

Detective Ambrose was situated where he needed to be. Ironically, the morning of Willie's arrest Matt had been given a list of residents recently living near the Dennisons. The Hanssons were on that list. With the kidnapper in custody, Matt had lost a golden opportunity to investigate Hansson or have cause to visit his home.

Matt would meet up with José in L.A. to begin the investigation into Olof Hansson. On the way to Los Angeles, Matt planned a stopover to see his sister, Madeline.

Chapter 53

A designer had tweaked the finishing touches on San Francisco's most talked about boutique, Bijoux San Francisco on Maiden Lane. Matt was impressed with the ambience and subtle elegance that included some Madeline touches like a crystal starburst chandelier. Matt stood back and whistled, "Maddie, the boutique is exquisite!"

Their father, Michael, had been impressed with her work overseeing the plans on time and under budget.

Over sushi, yellowtail drizzled in yuzu-infused oil and Scottish salmon marinated in soy sauce, Matt told his sister that he had uncovered a very strong lead on the Nazi. He believed that the German had changed his name and had been living in Los Angeles, and he had built a second home in Portland. Matt discussed the Dennison case and that he had accepted a temporary position in Portland to give him access to Hansson, aka Heinrich. Madeline was encouraged by this promising news.

Now it was Madeline's turn. She touched her brother's arm and smiled. "I've met a man. We've dated for only five months, Matt. But he's the one."

"Richard and I are flying to New York in a few weeks. Richard wants to officially ask Papa for my hand in marriage." Matt agreed that Michael and Celine would welcome this courtesy. Grandparents Pierre and Ellie also would be pleased.

Matt kissed her cheek. I'm happy for you, Maddie! Tell me about your fiancé."

"We met when Richard approached me about displaying a few exquisite jade pieces from Asia. He is an airline captain who imports jewelry from around the world. Richard is from New York but based in San Francisco. We plan to make our home together across the Golden Gate Bridge in Marin. You will like him, Matt. He's a wonderful person."

After an afternoon catching up, Matt hugged his sister goodbye and promised to fly home for the engagement party.

Matt flew Southwest Airlines for the short hop to the Los Angeles airport, and José picked him up. José had booked rooms at the Hotel Bel-Air. Matt wanted to see Hansson's home to get a feeling for the man. He wondered if they could talk themselves into the house by posing as art reporters or with some other story.

But first, they sat down in Matt's room to go over details that José had learned about Hansson. Matt ordered up a bottle of Nikka single malt whiskey, *Miyagikyo*, José's preferred scotch.

They touched glasses and José began, "Okay, here is what I know. Hansson moved to Los Angeles around 1964. Previously, in Buenos Aires he had worked for Mercedes-Benz, married and then divorced. He started his own business in L.A."

Matt interjected, "So, he did *not* move home after all as his rancher friend Manny had said!"

"Nope. He got a factory job at Mercedes similar to the one he had in Mannheim. The plant was just reopening. Eventually he would work on and off in the States. Over time, he invested in a small BMW motorcycle dealership, and then he opened his first Mercedes-Benz automobile showroom in Beverly Hills. Over the years, he opened up showrooms up and down the west coast. His fortune also comes from investing well in movies and the stock market. He is married to the former Kathy Petersen from, where else, Portland. Kathy was a stewardess... I mean flight attendant. They met when he was commuting back and forth from B.A. to L.A."

"Probably divorced the first wife for the younger woman?"

"He did divorce his first wife. She was the Argentine plant manager's daughter. Speculation is that the divorce was mutual. From what I have been told, his current wife has a daughter from a brief former marriage and two grandchildren. The scuttlebutt is that Kathy wanted to spend more time with her family so Olof bought her a second home near Lake Oswego, and they fell in love with the area."

Matt nodded. "Lake Oswego borders the Dunthorpe neighborhood where I worked on the Dennison kidnap. It's a pretty town situated on the lake; some homes border the Willamette River. Heinrich is clever; I'll give him that... I bet he purposely told Manny, his *gaucho* friend, that he was going home to Germany for a "big job." It was a smart move that would send anyone, like the war crimes tribunal or the pissed off bar owner of El Gaucho, searching in the wrong direction... including us."

José nodded. "Agreed. Yesterday I spoke to Hansson's gardener. Told him I was interested in buying the Mediterranean style estate that's listed for sale three doors down and wanted to speak with the owner of the house where he was working. I mentioned that I was an importer who travels, and that I had some questions about the neighborhood, security, etc. The gardener speaks Spanish so he opened up to me. He told me the neighborhood was safe, etc. and mentioned that his boss leaves on and off for the year and spends most of his time up in Oregon now. He and Kathy come down to L.A. for a month or two during the rainy winter months. Sometimes, he pops down to Los Angeles to attend an event or play some golf with buddies at The Riviera Club or in a tournament. But his trips now are few and sporadic. He's semi-retired so there is no way of knowing when he might show up. For what it's worth, the home is gated and he keeps a small staff with security personnel living on the premises."

Matt replied, "Great information, all good to know... anything else?"

José took a long sip of whiskey. "Yes. I asked around at the museums and in a few galleries. The docents were tight-lipped at the LACMA and the Getty. Generally, no one talked about Hansson's personal collection. But one gal in the gift shop told me he was a 'big player in the local art world.' She said he threw parties to fundraise for the museum. Hear this... He prefers Impressionist paintings."

Matt sat back and whistled. "That is unbelievable, man. Great work! It all seems to fit, doesn't it? His timing leaving South America... It makes perfect sense that he would leave his uncle's ranch to work in a car factory in Buenos Aires. Now, I recall the old German neighbor, Herr Huber, telling me that Heinrich worked in Mannheim at a Mercedes-Benz factory. Wow, this has to be it! This man has to be none other than the Nazi, Otto Heinrich."

José interrupted. "It gets even better, Matt. The Buenos Aires plant began to operate in 1951. So, five years after Heinrich immigrated to Argentina, he leaves his uncle's ranch for the Mercedes factory. Remember when rancher Santiago said Ollie 'up and left' about five years after arriving at the ranch?"

Matt grinned. He clapped his investigator on the back. "Good work, man! José, it looks like we may have found him!" Matt leaned in. "I feel good about this, really good. It all seems to fit. I just hope to God he has the paintings. It sounds like he still collects art. It does not appear that he needs to sell for financial reasons. All I really care about is my Aunt Anna's portrait for my grandparents and my father. I'm more hopeful now than ever."

Matt poured his second whiskey and thought for a minute. "I have to meet the man, get inside his home and actually see his personal art collection. I need some DNA if there is any way to prove the rape. José, look more deeply into his hobbies and pastimes and his wife's. We know he likes paintings and plays golf. There must be some way I can meet him? Where is his art collection? Is his collection here in L.A. or up in Portland? That, my friend, for me is our million-dollar question."

José agreed to continue his research into the personal side of Hansson's life and to look for a way for Matt to get closer to the man.

Finishing up for the day, the two investigators drove over to Nate n' Al's Jewish deli in Beverly Hills for hot pastrami and corned beef sandwiches.

The next day, a clear, sun-kissed morning, Matt and José drove over to Hansson's Beverly Hills home to look around. But there was no way they could get into the house. The property was gated with electric fencing hidden behind a manicured hedge. The mansion had its own security with 24-hour surveillance cameras in addition to a small staff living on the property. Fort Knox might have made an easier target. For now, Matt would have to concentrate on Hansson in Portland. José drove Matt to the airport. They stopped for a quick In-N-Out burger for lunch and parted ways for now.

Chapter 54

Olof and Kathy Hansson were delighted with their lifestyle. They had the best of both worlds playing golf in sunny Los Angeles during the rainy winter months while enjoying the great outdoors in the Northwest the rest of the year. Interest in Olof's background had simmered down with the L.A. movie crowd where Olof was mostly out of sight. He planned to keep it that way.

On occasion, the sought-after couple would host small selective dinner parties in Portland. Politicians welcomed these events to pave the way for future campaign donations, as well as museum board members who also knew better than to gossip about their patrons.

The Portland Art Museum—PAM was in the minor leagues compared to the Getty and LACMA. To enhance Olof's stature within the local community, quietly and without fanfare, he had donated funds to expand the museum with a first-rate gallery.

However, much to Olof's chagrin, Kathy offered to sponsor a nationally touring exhibit, The Impressionist Landscape, to coincide with the beautiful new gallery—Hansson Hall. Olof had learned his lesson about snoopy journalists, but he would not disappoint his wife.

To launch the world-class exhibit, Kathy would host a black-tie gala in the museum's sunken Fields Ballroom. Entertainment included a rendition of the French Bal Musette ballet suite performed by the Portland Ballet Company accompanied by the Portland Symphony Orchestra.

Overnight, the gala became the hottest ticket on the Portland social calendar since John F. Kennedy's plated fundraiser dinner. Nike, Columbia Sportswear and Intel each donated generously. Portland's high society, known as the "Scene and Heard" crowd, could not write their checks fast enough to be included in this most talked-about social event in decades.

After Lacy Dennison's rescue, Detective Matt Ambrose had become somewhat of a local celebrity. Word traveled about his role in solving the case, and his photograph *did* end up in the newspaper. Kathy Hansson realized that if the guests could meet the celebrated detective, the evening would become even more significant. Matt received an invitation to the Hansson gala and a telephone call regarding a "much-deserved" award that Mrs. Hansson would present to the young New Yorker. Matt was ecstatic by this unexpected turn of events with its opportunity to get up close to Olof Hansson

The glittering evening would be attended by state senators and representatives, the mayor, the governor, art lovers and patrons. However, Matt had not been invited to a privileged pre-gala viewing of Olof's personal art collection at Hansson's home. Matt still had no idea what paintings Olof had brought to Portland. Over the years, Hansson had acquired paintings to add to his impressive collection. Neither the paintings nor the artists were ever disclosed to the public.

At the gala, Matt was given a standing ovation when Kathy Hansson presented him with a plaque recognizing his role in the rescue of Lacy Dennison. Guests wanted to meet the detective, especially the women.

In Olof's eyes, Matt was just a cop. He was content to say "hello," shake Matt's hand, smile and quickly move on to the VIP guests so that he could receive the accolades that *he* deserved. Matt forced a smile but felt disgust when he looked into Hansson's stony eyes for the first time

After the gala's success, the Hanssons became the toast

of the town. Olof missed hobnobbing with the Hollywood elite. But he no longer faced cocktail parties where troubling questions about the war and his ethnicity could arise. Olof relaxed. A content and happy man, he had achieved the social status that he felt he deserved. He was admired and appreciated. His Portland legacy intact, Olof would be careful not to arouse any more needless curiosity; he did not want to uproot himself again.

Chapter 55

Matt attended Madeline's engagement party in New York. Her fiancé, Richard, exuded good-natured charm; he was a sophisticated world traveler who fit in well with the French clan.

During his visit home, Matt never stopped thinking about how to worm his way into Olof's inner sanctum. Matt understood that he must take it step by step by step, day by day. It was essential that Hansson remain confident and not develop a sense that he was in anyone's crosshairs. José Alvarez would dig deeper into Hansson's lifestyle.

Over dinner with his parents, Madeline and Richard, and his grandparents, the family inquired about the Dennison case, his life in Portland, and how things were going. Matt devoured Miss Essie's home cooking—bistro steaks, garlic and rosemary baby new potatoes, and a mixed green salad. Matt slowed down and took a deep breath. He filled the family in on the museum gala and his focus on Hansson.

"I've integrated myself into Hansson's world. However, so far, I've only been able to connect with the man with a brief handshake. I've tried to become better acquainted with his wife Kathy; she's an avid tennis player. But our relationship is just too casual, a brief "hello" on and off the courts. Our age difference makes it awkward for me to strike up any meaningful conversation with Kathy or her friends." Everyone nodded.

Matt took a sip of pinot. "I keep looking for that one paramount connection with Hansson. I've become a patron of the Portland Symphony. I'm friendly with the basketball player and his wife; Jade and Larry Dennison have sponsored a membership for me at the Westridge Country Club."

"I'm also taking light-plane flying lessons out of Hillsboro airport where Hansson keeps his plane." Ellie and Madeline shared a look of concern but Pierre and his father were impressed by this news. Matt laughed when Richard announced, "Hey, if you need any tips, just give me a call!"

Matt smiled and thought for a moment. Then he said, "Portland has a good urban vibe and sophistication." He talked about the gourmet restaurants sprinkled throughout Portland's Pearl district. Sometimes Matt would meet up with his friend, Steve Bolden, and a few other cops, at the global food carts that line a city block downtown.

Matt shrugged, "I miss New York's museums and our galleries. I miss painting. I've discovered some quaint towns, fishing villages, and little artist colonies long the Pacific coast. I wish I had come out west under different circumstances... But my focus is finding our painting of Anna. I hope a door will open soon. I feel confident, but it's slow-going."

Back in Portland, Matt joined the exclusive Highlands Whiskey Club in downtown. Marking time, the detective would enjoy the ritual of a fine scotch or bourbon. (He missed the camaraderie at O'Malley's bar near his NYC precinct.) One evening, Matt spotted Hansson sitting with three of his cronies who were enjoying drinks and cigars in the clubroom. Matt was taken aback when Hansson acknowledged the detective with a slight nod. Matt made his way over to their table. They shook hands, then Matt was brushed off.

Matt had connected with the Highlands' mixologist. Andrew Pierce was a bright young man who had taken leave from Google to attend Lewis and Clark Law School.

At the wood-paneled club, Andrew unwittingly provided Matt with insight other than the characteristics of a fine whiskey. The bartender had divulged another detail of

Hansson's social life. Matt then joined the Multnomah Athletic Club, known as the MAC, where the Hanssons swam and played tennis indoors during the winter.

A few weeks went by, and a journey that began with high hopes for a promising outcome had hit a stone wall. Matt took advantage of the temperate climate and easy access to the great outdoors—rafting white water and fly fishing in central Oregon, all within an easy distance from his home. He would ski Mt. Bachelor and Hood next winter. But by then, Matt had hoped to return home with success. Matt was growing tired of the waiting game, and he wanted to get on with his life.

Detective Ambrose had built a reputation as a skillful crime solver and a methodical investigator. He talked to everyone and pushed on every door to break open a case. Despite Matt's success, Chief Gates had kept an eye on the young cop who appeared to have it all—good looks, easy money and a well-bred air of confidence and success.

Both Chief Gates and Commissioner Rosen appreciated his work ethic. But something didn't fit. Ambrose avoided recognition. They discussed another disconnect—Matt drove a silver Porsche and rented an impressive contemporary home. Although Matt and Bolden were friends, to some of the other guys Matt's lifestyle had become a thorn, an irritation, like a persistent itch.

It was just after five o'clock. Officers and staff were winding down for the day. The night crew arrived and settled at their desks. Chief Gates called Ambrose over. "Matt, come into my office for a minute, will you?"

"Close the door, and please, sit down." Gates gestured toward a chair. He opened a drawer, and placed two crystal tumblers on his desk. He reached into the drawer again and brought out a bottle of Macallan single malt scotch. He poured a little whiskey into the glasses; he pushed one toward Matt.

Gates leaned his chair back and looked into Matt's eyes. "Tell me what's going on, kid. Two messages have been sent to Interpol around midnight, one o'clock in the morning about the time when the Brussels office starts its day. Right now, you guys are working on a bicycle theft ring and a series of robberies at Nordstrom involving gift cards. We have one open case regarding the assault of a taxi driver." Chief Gates leaned forward. "Not one of our cases involves Interpol."

Gates said, "Look, you're a very good detective, Ambrose. But you and I know there is something going on... You live beyond your salary range and drive a fine sports car. That's okay. But I need to know who you and what you are doing here."

Gates took a long pull on his scotch.

Matt picked up his glass. He took a deep breath and then set it down. He replied, "You are correct, sir."

Matt explained his grandparent's role in the French Résistance, Anna's tragic death and the loss of her portrait and all of their family photographs. "I came here to expose one Otto Heinrich, now called Olof Hansson, who lives in Portland. I believe that he is a hardened criminal—a Nazi who raped our shop girl, beat a French woman to death and murdered a young German woman. During the Occupation, he stalked my grandfather, forcing our family to flee to England where my aunt died following a London bombing. He stole our family heirlooms from my grandparent's Paris home. I have tracked Hansson from Germany to Argentina to Los Angeles; he now lives here." Matt's pointed finger poked the chief's desk. "Right under our noses in Portland."

Matt leaned in to meet Gates' eyes. "Sir, Hansson is not only a war criminal, but a mean son of a bitch. I conduct my personal investigation after hours and after I've done my work. He's a shrewd one, but I intend to bring the Nazi to justice for his crimes."

Chief Gates took a long look at the determined young man, "Matt, do you have any *proof* at all that this man, Hansson or Heinrich committed the crimes?"

Matt leaned forward, "A Nazi named Otto Heinrich fits Olof Hansson's profile to a T. I have traced Heinrich through records in Germany where he is wanted for murder, to his uncle in Argentina *who gave up Olof Hanssons' name*, and to his former German partner who witnessed the rape and theft of our heirlooms. I have a signed and witnessed affidavit from this former partner who is willing to testify in person against him. And, I have photographs of my family's paintings that were taken a few weeks before my grandparents fled Paris. I spoke with the partner who personally witnessed Heinrich remove those paintings from our family home."

"The most important painting is worthless really, a portrait of my deceased aunt painted by my great-grandmother. But it is a family treasure. Among the other paintings is a Monet that was a wedding gift to my grandmother. If Hansson has them, I can *prove* ownership of those paintings. But sir, first I need to get access to Hansson's home and his artwork to be certain that Hansson retained the artwork that he stole from my grandparents. Wait one moment..."

Matt retrieved the envelope with the photos from his desk. Chief Gates inspected the aged black and white photographs: The Velox paper was thin and slightly grainy. The photographs had white borders; the back was stamped with a French street address and dated June 30, 1942. Gates gazed at a painting of a little girl with long blonde hair reminiscent of his own daughter, Melissa.

Gates handed the envelope back to his detective. "Very well then, Matt. You have great instincts and do excellent work. I can help you, but I need something in return."

Matt sat upright. "What do you have in mind, sir?"

"The photographs look authentic but you'll have to have the ages verified. I'll want frequent reports as to what you are doing and your progress *before* you approach the man. You must be certain of the legality of your actions, and I must be kept informed. You have to be positive that he has your family paintings. Detective, in no way can this become a sleuth's myopia, where you focus on Hansson and then look for incidents to create your desired outcome. I need *certain proof* he is the man responsible. While you are working for me, everything you do reflects on me and my department. You can use our resources and collaborate with my staff. If I am certain that you have it right, we'll give you back up."

"Meanwhile, I can put you into contact with the best private investigator in the Northwest. In fact, he is my brother, Rob Gates. His wife is from Laguna Beach, south of Los Angeles. Her family owned two prestigious galleries in Southern California. Debra knows the local art collectors and patrons. She handles fundraising for the Portland Art Museum and certainly can get you into their private events. Especially now since everyone knows who you are. I would be very surprised if Debra does not already know this Hansson character. But and I cannot stress this strongly enough, you cannot invade Hansson's privacy in any way or make a move without solid proof that he has the stolen paintings, and I need to know what is happening ahead of time. Is that perfectly clear and understood?"

"Absolutely, yes sir" Matt was fired up. Alvarez had been the first to mention Investigator Gates' name to Matt. Rob Gates had been out of the state when Lacy Dennison was taken, and Matt never had a chance to meet him. *Damn!* All this time and Matt had never made the connection between the two brothers.

Robert Gates became well-known across the country when he brought down a racketeering scheme that used college students to set up illegal campus football betting rings. A few University of Oregon students who could not pay up were badly beaten, as were students in Texas, Ohio, Florida and Georgia. Rob Gates uncovered the Pac-10 ringleaders, which led to the arrest of other conference betting rings and their kingpins across the country. Gates had received national acclaim for his work.

Matt shook the chief's hand. "Thank you, sir. I'd very much like to meet your brother and sister-in-law as soon as possible. Can you set up a meeting?"

Chief Gates knew that for the Portland police to capture a war criminal, it would be a once-in-a lifetime achievement for his bureau.

Chapter 56

C hief Gates arranged an early meeting at Departure, a Pan-Asian restaurant and lounge atop the landmark Meier & Frank building. Early evening city lights illuminated sweeping views of the Willamette River, the surrounding green hills, and snow-topped Hood in the distance. The small-bites menu was meant to be shared.

Investigator Rob Gates looked a lot like his brother. He was just over six feet with the same unmistakable cobalt blue eyes as the chief. Mike Gates kept his full head of salt and pepper hair neatly trimmed whereas Rob's silver hair was tied back into a small ponytail. The chief wore a crisp blue blazer and Rob wore a Seahawks sweatshirt. Each brother was congenial with a good sense of humor. Rob's wife Debra was an attractive blonde with an outgoing personality. With her connections in the art world, Debra was well-suited for her career at the Portland Art Museum. (Like Kathy Hansson, she was fit and enjoyed active sports.) The chief's wife, Sue, was a pretty, petite brunette, full of life and a decorated detective on the police force.

They sat at a back table in a corner away from listening ears and ordered cocktails. Debra ordered an Indochine with grey goose la poire, crème de cassis, and lemon prosecco. Rob preferred Jack Daniels. Matt, Chief Gates and Sue requested Knob Creek bourbon neat and touched their glasses together. For the table, the chief ordered two types of sushi - big eye tuna poke and a smoked salmon roll. They added dim sum, chicken and shrimp spring rolls and Departure wings. Rounding out the meal, they asked for Ishiyaki steak, chili prawns; and Matt was curious about the Dungeness crab fried rice.

Mike Gates made the introductions and then gave a general description of what Matt needed. Gates wanted to bring this Nazi to justice. Portland was not accustomed to seeing the likes of Hansson with his level of alleged criminal activities.

Matt began with the Bessette family story and Hansson's criminal history. Debra was shocked at what she heard and disgusted with Olof's alleged crimes—assault, rape and murder. She had been skeptical about going into this meeting tonight. She told Rob earlier, "I've known Kathy Hansson a short while, and although we are not personal friends, I'm a bit reluctant to be involved. Hansson plays a significant role in the west coast art world." Debra had met Kathy Hansson when Kathy asked for help planning the French Impressionist gala and the opening of the Hansson Hall gallery. But after hearing what Matt had to say about Hansson's alleged crimes against women, Debra would keep an open mind.

Matt mentioned that he may not have to actually see the paintings inside Olof's house. If someone could get inside and take a picture of one of them, he'd know if he was on the right track. He passed around the grainy pictures that Pierre had taken before their escape.

After hearing Matt's full story, Debra mentioned a project that she had proposed to the museum's board, a project that she believed could help Matt.

The board was interested in updating and repairing part of the original neoclassical wing after water had damaged the ceiling during a freak snowfall. The fundraiser would include four memorable soirees to benefit the restoration. These by-invitation-only events would be entitled "Vignoble and Art" and would include wines from Oregon's Willamette Valley and French champagne served with heavy hors d'oeuvres. Four board members were asked to host one evening event in each of their homes to showcase a particular collection, be it art, sculpture, or music.

Portland opera singer, Natalie Berlusconi had agreed to sing at two of the events, so did the twelve-piece symphonic band, Blush Martini. Additional details were forthcoming with the hopes that each event would raise thirty thousand dollars or more.

Debra suggested: "Matt could attend the Dennison's Vignoble and then attend the wine social at the Hansson's home as a new patron of the arts. Jade Dennison could suggest Matt's name to the Hanssons after Matt attends the Dennison's event."

Olof Hansson was smitten with Debra who was very good at feeding his ego. "I'm pretty confident that Olof would not want to turn my fundraiser down." Aware that Olof was very selective as to who was invited to his home, Debra mentioned, "If necessary, Jade and Larry could include Matt as their guest to the Vignoble evening at the Hansson's home. After all, Matt had rescued Lexy."

Everyone thought the plan had merit. Debra's idea intrigued Matt who potentially would love nothing more than to arrest Hansson in view of his grandmother's paintings.

Debra would get final approval from the museum board and then proceed with the invitations. She would schedule the Dennison soiree first, followed by the Hansson's.

Matt picked up dinner for Chief Gates, his brother Rob and their wives.

Debra moved quickly. Three weeks later, Matt received an elegant, black tie invitation to the first Vignoble fundraiser just a month away at the Dennison's home.

Matt had not brought a tuxedo to Portland. He bought a new Armani tux at Mario's boutique. Matt invited a date, Carrie Sutherland, an attorney he had met before testifying in court at a recent trial. Because he was so focused on his mission, Matt had not become involved with a woman. But prior to his first appearance in Carrie's theft trial, she invited Matt for a quick coffee to go over some nuanced details of the perpetrator's arrest. In turn, Matt invited Carrie to a casual work-related lunch to ask her legal case questions, without giving away too much, regarding Oregon law should he arrest Heinrich.

Carrie was a lovely, charming woman and a witty conversationalist. She had studied French and art history in Paris during college and was well-informed about painting and sculpture. Matt discovered that Carrie had grown up in Ridgefield, Connecticut, a little over an hour from Manhattan. She had spent her early years enjoying the New York City museums and talked enthusiastically about her time spent in Paris.

Carrie agreed to accompany Matt to the Vignoble event at the Dennisons. Matt had explained that it was investigative work and he may stand out if he went alone. "Matt, I'm delighted. I've read about the fundraiser, and I love sculpture. I'd very much like to join you for the evening."

Matt was happy with this turn of events. Carrie was a head-turner, and Matt was certain that Carrie also would draw Olof's attention.

The evening arrived. Carrie looked stunning in a white, one shoulder Armani sheath dress that contrasted with her chestnut hair and brown eyes with flecks of honey and gold. She had a gorgeous smile. As Matt suspected, Olof could not take his eyes off Carrie. Her charm was evident throughout the evening which gave Matt an opportunity, at last, to join Olof and his wife Kathy in more in-depth conversation. Carrie spoke enthusiastically about the time she had spent studying in Paris, and Matt thought he saw Olof flinch just a little. However, they quickly moved onto other topics. Matt slightly nodded to Debra Gates when she walked by...

The evening was a smashing success. Seventy-six patrons enjoyed learning about the Dennison's sculptures while the international pop rock and jazz music of Blush Martini entertained the guests. It was the best money Matt had ever spent, and between art and sports, he and Carrie found a lot to talk about. Matt, too, was smitten with the charming Ms. Carrie Sutherland. Best of all, Matt felt as though he was getting closer to the culprit.

Finally, the Hansson Vignoble —an Evening of Impressionist Art had arrived, and Matt had received his own invitation. He sipped an 18 YO Glenlivet scotch neat while dressing.

As much as he wanted to spend another evening with Carrie Sutherland, Matt did not invite her. He could not afford to be distracted on what might very well be the culmination of a life-long quest. Matt had considered escorting Chief Gates' wife. Sue would make an excellent police witness if the paintings were exposed. But, if any of the guests knew the chief and his engaging wife, it certainly would cause a stir and questions. No, best to keep things simple.

Matt would love nothing more than to walk into the thief's home this evening and for the first time look at his Great-grandmother Annette's portrait of his Aunt Anna. He would invite Carrie to dinner another time, when he could be up-front with her about his time in Portland.

Matt drove away from his home. The darkening sky felt low and threatening. Anxiety and a heavy heart weighed him down: Matt knew that his family paintings could have been sold or still be hanging at Hansson's Los Angeles home. His hands gripped the steering wheel, and he thought of his beloved grandmother, Ellie. *I can't leave empty-handed.*

Matt purposely drove up to the mansion after most guests had arrived. Rooms filled with guests milling around might provide a little cover for Matt to peek around the home unnoticed.

Matt arrived in a light rain. He found it quite peculiar that the locals did not carry an umbrella except during a rare downpour. But Matt could not get used to venturing out, even in a drizzle, without one. The valet opened his car door. Matt stepped inside the mansion and handed his Burberry coat and umbrella to a uniformed housekeeper.

In the background, Beethoven's Fur-Elise wafted toward him. His heartbeat picked up, and he tried to relax his tense shoulders. Matt took a deep breath and leaned left until he felt a gentle stretch on his right side. Taking another breath, he stretched right. He moved away from the grand foyer toward an elegantly appointed old-world living room furnished with plump brocade sofas, floral drapes and matching cornices. The elaborate home contrasted with the clean lines and subtle sophistication of the Dennison's contemporary home.

Matt stepped into the sumptuous room; a fire glowed in a massive limestone fireplace at the far end of the living room that showcased several paintings. He recognized some of the guests from various clubs around town and the previous Vignoble, but he spotted eager new faces as well. A waiter appeared with a silver tray. Matt picked up a flute of champagne and surveyed the room from afar.

Right away the detective spotted two security guards. The men were unobtrusive wearing black tuxedos and clear earpieces. They blended in with the guests. However, the detective noticed the bulge of muscle and guns under their jackets. One stood by each door of the living room.

Matt moved forward and scanned the over-decorated room more closely. He recognized two of three landscapes— a French classical Carot, a more modern Rousseau and a less impressive but peaceful composition that complemented the nearby paintings.

However, halfway down the paneled room on a side wall stood four easels. Each painting was draped with a black velvet cloth, waiting to be presented to the guests. All he needed was for just one of those paintings to belong to his family.

Hansson approached Matt whose heart was beating so

hard that he did not hear his footsteps. "Good evening, detective. I see that you could make it this evening."

He shook Olof's hand, trying his best to smile warmly, "I've been looking forward to it. Thank you for the invitation. I'm an amateur artist myself, so I am delighted to be here!"

Hansson nodded and looked the younger man in the eye, "I was hoping you could afford another Vignoble fundraiser. I imagine on a detective's salary; these events could be quite expensive for you."

Aware that he was being taunted, Matt replied with a smile, "My family has a *great* deal of money, Olof. My work on the police force is not to make money. It is to bring criminals to justice." Still smiling, Matt touched Olof's arm. "Of course, this is an evening for pleasure, not work."

Hansson grunted, "Well in that case, Matt, I'm sorry you did not bring your lovely friend, Carrie."

"I certainly would have, Olof. But she is not in town this weekend. I'm sure she would have enjoyed your hospitality and lovely home. Another time perhaps..." Like a welcome breath of fresh air, Kathy swept into the room and joined the two men.

More accustomed to seeing Kathy on the courts in a ponytail and sweaty, she looked lovely in a Dior shimmering navy blue gown that brought out her blue eyes. She wore a stunning blue sapphire and diamond necklace.

"Forgive me for interrupting." Kathy remarked smiling and touching Matt's arm. "Thank you, Matt, for coming this evening. It is wonderful to see you again."

"As an artist myself, you can imagine how thrilled I am to be here." Matt bowed slightly toward Kathy and smiled, "Thank you for inviting me to your beautiful home."

She turned to her husband, "Olof, now that the guests have had a chance to mingle, do you think it would be a good time to welcome them?"

"Of course, my dear, you are so right. Let the evening begin." He looked sourly at Matt and turned away.

Taking center stage, Olof raised his champagne flute, "Welcome everyone to our home. Please enjoy the music and refreshments. Soon we will begin a small presentation of my personal art collection."

The quartet began a Mozart concerto. Matt chatted with Jade and Larry Dennison and several guests from the Multnomah Athletic Club, as well as a few couples from the Westridge Country Club. Matt felt disappointed that investigator Rob Gates and Debra were absent. Debra was always on hand to oversee the smooth running of these museum fundraisers. Matt wondered if she may have felt obliged to raise a little fuss and comfort her former client, Kathy Hansson, should Olof be arrested. Perhaps it was easier for Debra not to be personally involved. Well, she had helped to get Matt into the event and into Hansson's home. The rest was up to him.

Matt shook hands and shared in some light-hearted conversation. Matt felt confident; he had the guy and could feel it.

Matt's stomach rumbled. He looked over at the silver trays brimming with savory hors d'oeuvres: filet mignon bruchetta, foie gras, smoked salmon, caviar, smoked trout with crème fraiche, chicken vol-au-vent puffs, stuffed baby red potatoes, cheese beignets, and strawberries dipped in white and dark chocolate. He popped a beignet in his mouth and picked up a bruchetta.

Olof clinked a spoon against his champagne flute and asked for everyone's attention: He spoke of his humble roots where he was born in a remote lakeside village outside Helsinki, Finland. He remarked about his good fortune in coming to America. "Thank you all for donating to this evening's event to repair damage to the wing of our beloved museum. Please enjoy a festive evening of art and friendship." He chuckled, "You know, Picasso was fond of saying, 'Art washes away from the soul the dust of everyday life.'" Olof continued to speak about the luminance of the Impressionist period in art history.

Finally, Olof raised the first cloth to expose his Manet still life *Vase of Peonies on a Small Pedestal (1864).* An audible gasp of pleasure arose from the guests. Olof smiled and gave a little introduction to Manet's bourgeoisie life as the leading artist of the transition from Realism to Impressionism. Of course, Olof could not resist drawing a comparison to his own mother's Swedish roots and Manet's connection to the Swedish crown prince.

No wonder it had been difficult for José to locate birth records for Heinrich if this man's Swedish mother gave birth in a remote area of Finland and at some later point, the family moved to Mannheim, Germany.

Olof raised the second cloth. On the pedestal sat Cezanne's *Le Vase Bleu.* Olof spoke about Cezanne's life in Paris and his bridge from Impressionism to Cubism.

Matt became impatient; he paced a little. He shifted from side to side when Olof teased, "Well, enough of flowers, let's move on, shall we?" His guests politely laughed.

Matt held his breath, hoping to see his grandmother's *Morning on the Seine.* Olof raised the curtain on a Sisley, *The Bridge at Moret.*

Finally, as he uncovered the last painting Olof announced with pride, "A landscape by Monet, one of my personal favorites..."

Matt inhaled deeply. He felt all of the oxygen sucked out of the room. None of these paintings belonged to his family.

People were clapping and murmuring. Matt heard Olof's bellowing, something about "variation in color and light, and air and light continually changing," Matt's head fell against his chest. Crestfallen, his family's artwork remained mysteriously hidden, *somewhere* in the dark, and may never be found. *Could he possibly have the wrong man?* Matt rubbed his chin; his head moved back and forth in disbelief. He felt sick.

He forced himself to look up and join in the clapping. Hansson concluded by thanking his guests for their generosity. He invited everyone to take a personal, close-up view of his paintings.

Regaining his composure, Matt had little choice but to turn his attention to justice for Genevieve. Perhaps the DNA on her clothes, if viable, could point to Hansson as a rapist and a thief. By now most guests were drinking brandy. Matt's mouth felt dry and he asked the bartender for a Bridgeport Blue Heron Pale Ale.

Feigning interest, Matt took a first-hand look at the artwork. Both security guards moved close to the paintings as the guests leaned in for a better look at this extraordinary collection. Although Matt painted modern art, he could appreciate the lasting appeal of the paintings before him. With sadness in his heart, Matt thought of his grandmother. Ellie would never show her disappointment; but she may never again see her daughter's image. Matt wanted to ring Hansson's neck.

The steward had offered Olof a small cordial glass from a bar cart. He selected a B & B liqueur. Matt hung back as Olof regaled his friends with stories, gesturing to the paintings one by one. He could hear the laughter and doting. But then, Olof walked over to speak with other admiring guests, placing his empty cordial glass on a side table. Matt walked over and with his back to the wall, covertly picked up the glass by the edge of its small stem with his handkerchief. He stuffed the cordial glass into his pocket.

Now, Matt could only think about getting away from the Nazi's home. He walked over to Kathy and spoke with her for a few moments about their gracious home and the upcoming museum restoration.

Thankfully, Kathy was distracted by a question from a maid about serving coffee. Olof was deep in conversation with two of his cronies from the Westridge Country Club. This was Matt's opportunity to slip away and to avoid speaking with Olof again tonight.

He returned to the foyer where he asked the maid to please get his coat as he was not feeling well. "I'd like to leave quietly and not disrupt the remainder of the evening."

The maid asked the third member of the security detail to unlock the room containing the guests' personal belongings and ladies' purses. Matt thanked the maid for his coat, and turned to leave.

He opened the front door to sheets of pouring rain and stepped back. The maid then opened the study door to retrieve Matt's umbrella.

While the maid searched for apparently the only umbrella brought to the event, Matt stepped inside. Hanging on the paneled wall was *Morning on the Seine.* Immediately, the security guard ordered Matt to wait in the foyer. It happened quickly, but Matt barely glimpsed *Portrait of Anna.* "Oh, of course, certainly," Matt replied and stepped out of the study. The maid handed him a plastic bag that contained his umbrella. The security guard ushered Matt to the front door. Matt smiled and nodded, "Good evening" and opened his umbrella.

Matt's heart was beating so hard that it nearly jumped out of his chest. The valet fetched his car. Matt drove as fast as he could, in the downpour, straight to the police station. *Of course, a thief would keep stolen art in a private study locked away and out of sight.*

Matt slammed on his brakes and ran up the station steps. He called Chief Gates immediately and gave him the news.

"Are you absolutely certain, Matt that those are your paintings? There can be no room for a mistake."

Matt replied, "I am beyond *positive*, sir. I have my grandfather's original photographs on me that were taken in their Paris home. Chief, I was *inside* his library. Hansson *has* at least two stolen paintings, sir. We have to make an arrest *this* evening, before he gets suspicious about my leaving early. I have searched for this man, responsible for two murders, at least two rapes and heirloom thefts dating back forty years. Hansson has three security personnel who could easily remove and hide those paintings for him."

Chief Gates called Detective Bolden. "Steve, get over to the station as quickly as you can. Hansson has the paintings. Matt is drafting an affidavit. I woke Judge Parker and he'll sign the search warrant."

Gates corralled two other police officers who were on duty and instructed them to follow in a patrol car, no sirens. With lights blazing, Chief Gates, Matt and Bolden drove together in the chief's car for the longest twenty-minute drive of Matt's life. It was now over two hours since Matt left Hansson's home. Matt realized he should have had a plainclothes officer parked near the property all evening to make certain that paintings were not removed from the home, or if needed, to follow the security detail.

Matt and his entourage arrived at Hansson's street. Lights turned off, the police car crept around the corner and out of sight. Chief Gates parked his unmarked car on Riverside Road close to the estate. Lights were still on inside the mansion, and the rain had subsided. Matt and Bolden quietly approached the home on foot; out of sight, the detectives peeked around a tall boxwood hedge. Matt heard laughter from the front porch. Two lingering couples were saying their goodbyes.

Matt exhaled a sigh of relief. Bolden patted his friend on the back. He and Bolden hastened back to Chief Gates' Acura and waited. A few minutes later, they watched the last two couples drive away. Three tuxedoed security guards left the house empty-handed and soon after drove off in a Jeep Cherokee. A light went on upstairs.

The moment Matt had waited for an eternity had arrived. Chief Gates signaled the uniformed officers with his radio. Matt, Bolden and Chief Gates quietly walked up to the front porch steps. Matt took a deep breath.

The chief and Bolden stood off to the side in the dark while Matt took the steps two at a time. He rang Hansson's doorbell. A minute later, Olof himself opened the massive mahogany door.

"Well, hello Matt. I see you are feeling better. Did you leave something?"

Matt answered as Chief Gates and Bolden joined him on the sweeping veranda.

"As a matter of fact, I did *Otto*." Hearing his actual name for the first time in nearly forty years, the color drained from Heinrich's face.

In a loud voice, Matt said, "I am here to take possession of the paintings belonging to Pierre and Ellie Bessette, my grandparents. And by the way, I'd also like their silver candelabra sitting on your piano."

Big, burly Bolden pushed right up against Hansson. He thrust the search warrant into his face while the two uniformed police officers stood beside the Nazi. Olof protested.

Once inside the study, Chief Gates studied Matt's authenticated photographs of the paintings from the Paris apartment and compared them to the paintings in the study. He looked carefully at Annette Lindstrom's signature.

Chief Gates nodded. Heinrich, aka Hansson, was then handcuffed. Bolden slowly and precisely read him his rights while Olof continued to scream that they had the wrong man. "You are all fools. It is mistaken identity and you *will* pay!"

Matt stood inches from Otto Heinrich's ashen face. "Listen, you bastard, you are going to pay for the pain and misery you have inflicted. You are going to pay for the brutality against innocent females who crossed your miserable path, for the rapes and murders; and you *will* pay for the theft of my family heirlooms."

Kathy was numb, wringing her hands and staring in disbelief at her husband.

Heinrich, was driven to the police station, fingerprinted, photographed and placed in their smallest cell. Under Matt's observation, the police had carefully removed the Bessette paintings and placed them in a secure lock-up under twenty-four-hour guards. Dazed and alarmed, Kathy called a famous trial lawyer from Los Angeles.

Two of the paintings were easily identified as belonging to the Ambrose/Bessette family: *Portrait of Anna* signed by Annette Lindstrom, Ellie's mother, and Monet's *Morning on the Seine* which Monet had ascribed in a wedding card addressed to Ellie and Pierre as well as scrawled on the back of the painting. The next day, Matt stood and watched as the curator of the PAM photographed and cataloged each painting.

Chapter 57

Portland reeled from shock when the Oregonian ran an in-depth front-page story regarding art philanthropist, Olof Hansson, who was allegedly Nazi Otto Heinrich, his alleged brutality as a soldier in Paris during the war, and his alleged crime of murder in Germany leading up to a multitude of criminal charges filed against him.

Olof Hansson faced further humiliation when the Associated Press picked up the story and it was published worldwide. Days later, *The Los Angeles Times* ran a complete series of articles depicting his double life as an alleged Nazi criminal to art collector, philanthropist multi-millionaire in the City of Angels while he moved with ease in movie and art circles. Some of his old movie industry pals in Los Angeles stated with confidence that they knew "all along that there was something phony about Hansson."

His DNA and fingerprints identified Hansson as Otto Heinrich. Interpol was contacted. France and Germany both planned to extradite Heinrich. He faced criminal charges for the assault and murder of the young prostitute in Paris, the rape of Genevieve Jourdan and grand larceny for stealing the Bessette paintings and antique silver in addition to the artwork stolen for the Third Reich. In Mannheim, Germany, he faced charges for the rape and murder of a young female co-worker at the car factory.

The Portland Art Museum quickly replaced the plaque on the wall of Hansson Hall and changed the name to the Ambrose Gallery as suggested by board member, Jade Dennison. Kathy did not protest. Looking at the mounting evidence, and with her daughter and friends gathered in support, she filed for divorce.

Ellie's seventy-eighth birthday was celebrated in the Crystal Room at the Tavern on the Green overlooking vibrant gardens. The chandeliers sparkled but they were no match for Ellie's smile.

The entire Ambrose family attended—Matt, his sister Madeline and fiancé Richard, their parents, Michael and Celine. Ellie's cousin, Kristin and her husband Paul Perrotti with their grown, married daughter Eve and her children were present. Pierre's cousin, Sir Michael Middleton, his wife Beatrice with their son Charles flew in from London for the grand celebration.

Driving down from Rhinebeck, Cousin Maggie Alexander and her husband Andrew happily attended. James Turner (his wife Mary had passed away) attended with his son, Bijoux partner, Patrick Turner. Patrick and his wife flew in from Los Angeles with their children. New York's prominent Dr. Edward Turner was present with his partner, Eric. Sadly, Pierre and Ellie's dearest friend, Duke Federico Verdi had passed away from lung cancer in 1982. For years, Matt and Madeline had encouraged their "Uncle Freddie" to give up smoking.

Genevieve and her family arrived from Paris and with tremendous anticipation, hugs, kisses, and tears of joy; she saw Pierre and Ellie for the first time in over forty years. Matt invited Carrie Sutherland to New York as his guest, as well as his private investigator, confidant and friend, José Alvarez. Antonio and his wife were included in the celebration as well as numerous beloved students who were making their living in the Arts, thanks to Ellie's foundation, AMoR.

Following the festive dinner, the celebration continued at Pierre and Ellie's brownstone for birthday cake. Ellie knew that Matt achieved success but she had not been told which paintings he had recovered.

The room swelled with anticipation. Family and friends watched and literally cheered when Ellie unwrapped her gift from Matt—*Portrait of Anna.* She wept uncontrollably as she lovingly kissed and held her daughter's portrait for the first time since it fell out of her hands in July, 1942. The guests beamed and hugged one another.

With tears in his eyes, Pierre kissed his daughter's beloved image. Each returned painting was ceremoniously unwrapped to cheers and whistles. Antonio, now a grown man whose own life had been transformed by Ellie, stood off to the side with moist eyes as he watched his overjoyed mentor. Matt looked over at Carrie, who warmly returned his smile.

Matt and his father Michael helped Pierre hang Anna's portrait in the master bedroom where Ellie could gaze at Anna every morning when she awoke. *Parc de la Ville* painted by Anna with help from her Grandmother Nettie would be hung at "Anna's Maison" the facility where the children took after-school painting classes.

After the party died down, Matt kissed his overjoyed grandparents. He walked Carrie back to her hotel. But the evening's euphoric celebration still hung in the air. They stopped at the Carlyle Hotel lounge for a nightcap and to listen to the sweet soulful songs of cabaret singer Bobby Short.

Matt took her hand. "Carrie, I'm very glad that you attended tonight's unveiling. After all, you do know that you unwittingly played a part in recovering those paintings? I regret that I did not explain to you what I had hoped to accomplish. I was struck by how much you love art and it just seemed like a good idea."

"Matt, I am thrilled to meet your family and to have

been part of such a joyous occasion tonight." Carrie replied that her short time in Manhattan had been perfect. Her parents had driven in from Connecticut for lunch with their daughter and Carrie loved every minute of Ellie's birthday celebration.

Carrie had booked an early morning flight back to Portland to prepare for trial on Monday. At the Plaza Hotel, their conversation lingered; Matt clung to every minute.

He kissed her, barely brushing her lips, and felt electricity shoot through his body. He hated to let her go.

Matt spent the following two weeks catching up with family and friends. His parents and grandparents were delighted to have him home. Mission accomplished, they treated him like a hero.

Matt and José Alvarez met for lunch at the Plaza Oyster Bar.

"Okay, Matt, the missing paintings have dogged you since you were a kid. What's your next step now that you've brought them home?" Alvarez winked. "By the way, I saw the way you looked at Carrie and her look back at you."

Matt smiled and shrugged. "I honestly don't know. We live on opposite coasts and barely know one another. I'm eager to pick up my paintbrushes and start looking for my own studio. A prime space has become available in Chelsea. Yet, I can even imagine a life with Carrie in the Northwest. I've wondered if she would consider returning to the east coast; her family lives not far from Manhattan?"

Deep down Matt knew he had fallen in love.

All week, his mind had drifted to thoughts of Carrie Sutherland. He could not stop thinking about her. She thrilled him with her charm and intellect. She was beautiful. He enjoyed the less hectic way of life in Portland and its outdoors lifestyle. But it would be a considerable step to live permanently away from his loved ones and far from New York City.

To complicate matters, Matt had agreed to head up a

new Bessette Family Foundation. Ellie had requested that Picasso's *Palace of Arts* not be hung. The painting would be sold at Christie's to fund this new foundation. Pierre and Ellie had contacted her psychiatrist.

Though retired, Dr. Nolan agreed to lend his expertise to help Ellie and Pierre establish a foundation—DASH (Depression, Anxiety, Suicide... and Hope). Its goal would be to help people worldwide suffering from the crushing loss of a child through violence and the ensuing depression, anxiety and the risk of suicide that could follow. Their research program would work to find a lasting treatment that would normalize the brain changes associated with depression. Dr. Nolan would assemble a Board of neuroscientists, physicians and philanthropists to begin the process. Matt agreed to co-chair this new endeavor.

Soon after, Chief Gates called to ask Matt if he planned to return. By the end of the following week, Detective Ambrose agreed to return to Portland with his decision. Matt had come to a crossroads—the possibility of a new life with Carrie, or to close out his present life in Portland. Did they have a chance at a future together? He needed to find out.

Matt called Carrie. He asked how the trial in Seattle was coming along and if she was free for dinner. He would fly back to Portland next week.

"Of course, I'd love to have dinner, Matt. I've been thinking about you. I'll be in Portland that weekend and we should get together." She asked Matt if he planned to stay in Portland.

Matt smiled and replied, "That depends."

Matt had felt the attraction. They both wanted the New York evening to linger. Listening to Bobby Short sing "Let's Fall in Love," there was no mistaking the sexual tension between them. A spark ignited when he kissed her, and she kissed him back.

Matt made dinner reservations for the following Friday

evening at a bistro in Portland's Pearl district. Matt chose the restaurant for its charm, intimacy and award-winning cuisine without being overly romantic. Matt realized he had not given Carrie much time. Although he was head over heels, they had spent very little time alone together. Their dinner and lunches had been work-related—until the New York evening.

If Carrie expressed an interest in developing a relationship with Matt, he would grab it. Matt had donated his entire salary to the Portland Police Benevolent Society. He held a month-to-month lease on his Portland Heights home. If things did not work out, he would pack up and return home.

Detective Ambrose flew back to Portland with a hopeful heart. On Wednesday, he and Bolden ate dinner at the venerable Ringside Steakhouse. They ordered aged rib-eye steaks, their famous onion rings and a Caesar salad. For the two friends, Matt ordered a velvety smooth Joséph Phelps cabernet sauvignon. After dinner, Matt asked Bolden, "Steve, join me at the Highlands for a nightcap and cigar?"

Mixologist Andrew Pierce enthusiastically greeted Matt.

"Hey man, congratulations on catching that son of a bitch!" Andrew lowered his voice, "Personally, I never liked the man. It's time for a drink on the house." Andrew poured a splash of Macallan 32-year-old single malt scotch into 3 glasses. Andrew joined the two detectives in making a toast.

"Detectives, here's to you both!"

On Friday, whenever he thought of Carrie, Matt's heart skipped a beat. He took his time getting ready. He chose a Façonnable shirt, a Brunello cashmere blue blazer, gray slacks and his lucky Gucci loafers. He wore a nostalgic after-shave that his grandfather had worn in Paris—Pinaud Clubman with a light jasmine, lavender and musk scent.

They met up at Bistro Le Petit Jardin located just a few blocks from her law offices in a Queen Anne Victorian. Carrie entered the restaurant; she was running late and out of breath. Matt caught his own breath at the sight of her. He stood and greeted Carrie with a kiss on the cheek. Her silky chestnut hair, delicately scented with rose and lavender, brushed against him.

"Matt, it's so good to see you!" Taking her seat, "I still think of Ellie's joy when she opened her painting of Anna." She held Matt's hands across the table and smiled, "I will never forget that heartwarming moment as long as I live." Matt loved watching her every move.

A bottle of Roederer Cristal champagne was chilling. He poured their glasses while they exchanged pleasantries about their families and Carrie's upcoming trial. Matt wanted to bring the conversation around to a more personal note. Carrie looked happy to see him. But he felt something missing.

As they were getting ready to order, Carrie touched Matt's arm and hesitated... "Matt, about last week at the Plaza, I have a boyfriend." Matt's heart plummeted. *How did he miss it?*

"Matt, I enjoy your company; we share a love of art and a passion for justice. I was so taken by your dedication to your family and the amazing work you did to find the man who altered their lives. I was incredibly happy to help, even in a small way. My parents live close to Manhattan and my boyfriend was out of town. Later, I realize I should not have accepted your invitation to New York and..."

Though crushed, Matt took Carrie's hand.

She said, "I am sorry." And teared up.

"Carrie, I understand, really. We both were involved in work, and when I finally got a solid plan together to get Heinrich, well, my feelings for you happened so quickly. Of course, I wish our relationship could be more. I allowed my emotions to get ahead of myself. Your guy is a lucky man."

"Matt, I did not understand what was happening before that night in New York. But I want you to know that I will always treasure being part of Ellie's celebration. I wanted to speak with you as soon as possible and of course not over the phone. Let's have dinner, my treat. Sometime I'd like to introduce the two men I admire most in this world, after my father, of course. I've been at trial in Seattle all week and my boyfriend expects to see me this evening. But I needed to talk with you in person."

Matt was devastated but understood that although he dreamt of Carrie, her heart beat for another. Still a bit stunned, he swallowed hard.

"Absolutely, I'd love to meet the lucky guy. Hey, why not give him a call now and see if he can join us for dinner?" Under the circumstances, Matt knew he would be heading back to New York as soon as possible.

"Good idea! I'll go call him."

Matt gulped his glass of champagne and felt he had little choice but to wait out the evening.

Ten minutes later Andrew Pierce walked up to their table. Despite how miserable he felt, Matt couldn't help but smile. Andrew seemed confused. He had no idea that his girl-friend, who had spent so many days working out of town, and his favorite Highland's customer even knew each other let alone shared a friendship. Andrew learned about Carrie's small role in helping to bring Hansson down.

It was Matt's turn to pour champagne for the young bar-tender, and Carrie flashed Matt a brilliant smile. Their eyes locked longer than necessary. Once again, Matt's heart stirred. Carrie blushed.

Three flutes rose in a toast to friendship. With the lin-gering look Carrie gave him, the detective anticipated a new challenge. He wanted this woman. At that moment, Matt threw down the gauntlet. In the morning, Detective Ambrose would renew his contract with the Portland police.

Epilogue

Otto Heinrich was extradited to The Hague in the Netherlands where he stood trial at the International Court of Justice. Leutnant Stefan Schafer, Genevieve Jourdan and Pierre Bessette all testified.

He was convicted on all accounts and sentenced to life in a prison known for extremely harsh conditions. Inmates who loathed the pompous Nazi beat him regularly.

A well-known Hollywood producer announced his plans to make a movie depicting Heinrich's double life. Disgraced, unable to face his future any longer, Otto Heinrich hanged himself in his cell.

Fin

Afterword

The Jeweler's Wife arose from my memories of magical Paris and falling in love with Europe 30 years after D-Day, and the experience of a friend's mother who was a young woman in Germany during World War II.

The courage of the French Resistance, made up of everyday women and men, stole my heart and continue to inspire me.

Acknowledgements

I would like to acknowledge my family and friends who encouraged me throughout this journey. I am deeply appreciative of your kind words, your honesty, but most of all for your steadfast love and support.

With a heart full of gratitude, thank you to my husband Philip, daughter Carrie, and son-in-law Art for encouraging me to write a novel and for believing in me. Thanks to my early readers and dear friends who used their red pens with flourish: Lynn Haar, Madge Walls, Angie Schane, Kathy Kremer, Liz Martin, Mary Vigo, Pat Haglund, and Nancy Shebel—thank you for pushing me forward.

To Anne Kilpatrick, Jana Hopkins, Susan Ziegler, Tracy Root, Veronica Hamstreet and Beth Caswell, thank you for having faith in me, in so many ways.

Last but not least, to my brothers and sisters-in-law, Rob and Deb Gates and Mike and Sue Gates, and my cousin Steve Bolden, for inspiring some of my favorite characters. And with gratitude to members of my family, Linda Gates, Nancy Heck, Lisa Gates, Aimee and Jackie Tucker, and Sally Moore.

Made in the USA
Middletown, DE
28 November 2020